TO THE CHASE

JULIA WOLF

PLAYLIST

"ROYALS" LORDE

"You're So Pretty" mehro

"Dog Days Are Over" Florence + the Machine

"93" flora cash

"What Was That" Lorde

"Ruin Me" Sebastian Schub

"Please Don't Be" Hazlett

"Chemistry" Gigi Perez

"Addicted To Love" Florence + the Machine

"At the Beach, In Every Life" Gigi Perez

"You've Got The Love" Florence + the Machine

"Into The Ocean" Blue October

"Good Girls" Josie Edwards

"Basic Being Basic" Djo

"One Thing" Lola Young

"Asshole" The Lumineers

"Sally, When The Wine Runs Out" ROLE MODEL

https://open.spotify.com/playlist/2PB8U3ky0kfgL3h03RNAvE?si=024c274669bf45e4

MORE BOOKS BY JULIA

MILE HIGH BILLIONAIRES

In The Details
By The Letter
To The Chase

The Kelly Ranch (small town romance)

See It Through
Hold The Line
Hit The Ground

The Harder They Fall (Billionaire office romance)

Dear Grumpy Boss
Sincerely, Your Inconvenient Wife
P.S. You're Intolerable
Not So Truly Yours

The Seasons Change (Rock star romance)
> Falling In Reverse
> Stone Cold Notes
> Faded in Bloom
> Where Waves Break

Savage U (college romance)
> Soft Like Thunder
> Bright Like Midnight
> Sweet Like Poison
> Real Like Daydreams

Savage Academy (academy romance)
> Save One Thing
> These Two Wrongs
> Jump On Three

Blue is the Color (Rock star romance)
> Times Like These
> Watch Me Unravel
> Such Great Heights

Under the Bridge

Unrequited (Rock star romance)
Unrequited
Misconception
Dissonance

Never Blue Duet (Angsty rock star romance)
Never Lasting
Never Again

CHAPTER ONE
Bea

DAYS LIKE TODAY, I needed an assistant. Not that I could afford one, but a girl could dream.

Heck, I'd settle for eight arms. Octopus me would be unstoppable. Instead, I was stuck with a measly two. So utterly pedestrian.

Kicking the door shut behind me, I juggled my load as I navigated my porch steps, avoiding the loose board that needed fixing. At the gate separating my postage-stamp yard from the sidewalk, I hesitated. Put everything down to open it or take a running leap? Neither option thrilled me, but sometimes improvising was a necessity.

Before I could make what would likely be a very poor decision—the gate was low, and I was relatively bouncy—Ben Wells, my new neighbor and future brother-in-law of my best girl, Shira, bounded out of his house, which was conveniently attached to mine. Well, sometimes it was convenient, like when I needed help carrying heavy objects. Other times, listening to him sing through our shared walls made me want to gouge my ears out.

Being that cheerful was unnatural, yet Ben was still immensely likable.

Not my type at all. Tall, muscular, ruggedly handsome guys did nothing for me, which was a shame. Then again, getting involved with a neighbor was too messy for my taste, so it was for the best I didn't feel a twinge of attraction toward this man.

He slowed when he spotted me stuck behind my three-foot-tall iron gate.

"What's happening over there, Buzz?" he asked as he strolled over.

"I'm thinking," I replied, letting his ridiculous nickname slide. If I fought him on it, he would only be encouraged.

He tipped his chin toward the boxes in my arms. "Thinking looks heavy. Need some help?"

"I could do with some of that." I might've been fiercely independent, sometimes to a fault, but I wasn't stupid. If Ben was offering his big, rugby-player arms, I'd make good use of them. "Would you mind carrying these boxes to my trunk?"

Without hesitation, he lifted the load like it weighed nothing. *Show-off.* "What's the job today?"

"Nox Cyber. It's a last-minute gig, but if all goes well, it might turn into a regular thing."

I *needed* that to happen. My bills were paid, no problem, but Denver was an expensive city, so getting ahead was nearly impossible unless I worked two jobs, which I did. But working two jobs was for the birds, and last I checked, I was featherless.

"I'm confident you'll charm them into it."

I gave him a dry stare as I popped my trunk. "You and I both know being charming is more your thing than mine."

He secured the boxes and turned back to me, his gaze sweeping over my black-on-black outfit—a fitted top with my bee-and-daisy catering logo on the chest, tailored pants, and flats. My blue curls were pinned neatly at my nape, and the only sparkle I wore was the tiny silver stud in my nose. I didn't exactly scream corporate, but it was as conservative as I got.

"I'd hire you," he stated with confidence, as he did most things. "You're the only person I know who could make catering a business meeting look cool."

I arched a brow. "Do you know many caterers?"

"I've met a few." He booped my nose. Had it been anyone but him, it would have infuriated me. "You are by far the most competent. In fact, when I talk about you to other people—"

"You talk about me?"

He nodded merrily. "Obviously." Waving me off like it wasn't weird, he continued, "Like I was saying, when I talk about you, I say, 'That Beatrice Novak is the most competent caterer I've ever known.'"

I squinted at him. "What kind of absurdly boring conversations are you having, Wells?"

"Wouldn't you like to know?" His grin was all mischief.

"Actually, no." I backed toward my SUV, my hands raised. "Whatever you get up to when you're not in my presence is none of my business."

"I get up to lots of things, Bea." He waggled his eyebrows. "You truly have no idea."

"Good. Let's keep some mystery between us. It's better that way."

Ben pressed the button to close my trunk and stepped back with a satisfied nod.

"I like the way you think, Novak. The longer we're acquainted, the more we'll keep discovering each other. In a year or two, we'll be best friends."

"I already have best friends."

He waved me off again. "Clara and Shira will share you with me," he said, as if it were a done deal and I had no say in it.

I had no idea how to reply. Luckily, Ben wasn't looking for an answer. He tapped the side of my car, shot me a wide grin, and called, "Good luck with your gig. Not that you'll need it, with all your competency."

I couldn't help but return his smile. "Thanks for your confidence. And lending your muscles."

He winked. "Anytime."

☙

When I arrived at Nox Cyber, I was greeted by Paul, the office manager who'd hired me. He showed me into the conference room to set up and stayed to watch me like he was afraid I'd steal something if he left me alone.

Corporate gigs weren't new to me. I'd been catering for two years. Being side-eyed by uptight suits or ignored altogether was the norm and no skin off my back. Years of waitressing had made me used to being overlooked or mentally undressed while doing my job.

"Do you work with a lot of companies in the city?" Paul asked, propping a hip against the long, sleek conference table.

I glanced up from the charcuterie cups I was arranging. "I do. I assumed that was how you got my name."

For a guy who worked at a tech company, Paul had "finance bro" written all over him. Not that I was an expert, but I'd spent enough time in boardrooms to sense vibes in each industry. His swooping side part, fitted chinos, button-down, and fleece vest were the uniform of his people, but he'd gotten lost somewhere along the way and had wandered into a cybersecurity firm.

He folded his arms. "You were on the approved vendor list, actually."

"Oh." That surprised me since I didn't have any contacts at Nox. "Is it a long list?"

"It isn't. Our regular caterer suddenly bailed, and no one else could squeeze us in at the last minute. You were our last hope."

If he was trying to neg me, it wasn't working. I plastered on my best smile and said, "Lucky for you, I had an opening in my schedule."

He sniffed. "Are you so busy there was a chance you wouldn't?"

Putting the final cup down, I faced him, still smiling, though he didn't deserve it. Whatever stick he'd sat on was making him ultra grumpy, and I was getting the brunt of it. I'd been nothing but friendly, and he was giving me grief for no good reason. Like he was waving his dick at me just to show me it was big.

"There's always a chance, Paul." I tucked my hands in my pockets. "I've been running the Denver side of Grazing by Daisy and Bea for almost two years. We're still growing, but our calendar fills up fast. If you'd called on a Wednesday or Thursday, the answer would've been no. Fortunately for us both, my Tuesday mornings are free. For now."

"Right." He tugged on his vest zipper. "Lucky us."

"It *is* lucky." I took a step toward him. "I have a feeling I saved your butt today, so I'm not sure why you're challenging me. Anyway, everything's set for the meeting. Unless there's something else, I have another job to get to."

Nostrils flaring, he surveyed the spread I'd just finished arranging. It was picture-perfect—charcuterie cups, mini muffins, fresh fruit, coffee, tea, and juice, all arranged with my custom bee-and-daisy napkins and a few paper flowers I'd crafted—little touches that had gotten me on so many vendor lists. I was hoping Nox Cyber would be next. I could deal with Paul if it meant more money in my pockets.

Finally, Paul met my gaze. "Everything looks great," he admitted, though it sounded like it pained him. "Thank you for fitting us in. I scheduled the remainder of your payment to be sent this afternoon."

I saluted him. "Appreciated very much, Paul. If there's nothing else, I'll gather my things and clear out."

"There's nothing else. I have to see to a few things before the meeting starts." He hesitated at the door. "Will you be able to see yourself out?"

I read the undercurrent in his question loud and clear. *Can I trust you not to steal the projector and everything else not nailed down if I leave you to your own devices? Will you exit quietly without embarrassing me? Will I return to find you passed out with a needle sticking out of your arm?*

Paul truly had trust issues.

I flashed him my dimples. "I'll be fine and out of here in a minute or two."

Turning away, I focused on packing up. I had another job across town at the Levy building, and I'd taken extra time here, so I needed to hustle.

With everything loaded into my bags, I slid the straps over my shoulder, picked up a box, and headed for the door.

I should've been paying attention, but my mind was already on my next gig, which is why I ran straight into a man in the doorway.

I gasped, stumbling back. I would've gone down if a strong hand hadn't caught my elbow and steadied me.

"I'm so sorry, I—" I looked up, and my apology froze on my lips.

I knew that face.

It had been almost two years since we'd been face to face, but his features were imprinted on my memory. Raven-black hair, deep-brown eyes behind wire-framed glasses, the cleft in his square chin...they were all the same as the last time I saw him.

Tore. A name as easy to remember as the rest of him.

He stepped aside, his expression impassive. "Go right ahead."

Nothing. Not even a flicker of recognition. In fact, he'd barely looked at me.

That stung more than it should have.

Heart in my throat, I slipped past the only man who'd ever ghosted me, hightailing it out of Nox Cyber without a backward glance.

CHAPTER TWO
Bea

The Past

I smacked the hand that had just pinched my ass. "No, sir. You can look as much as you want, but touching is off the table."

The drunk guy cackled with his friends. "Oooh, she's mean. I like her."

I tried to be sassy even though my skin was crawling. "Come on, don't tell me you go around squeezing women's asses on a regular basis."

He held his hands up, eyes glassy and lit with trouble. "If a slut with a big ass wears a tight dress, she knows what she's doing."

He wasn't wrong about me being mean. Telling off guys like him was practically a hobby. But damn, some nights a girl just wanted to make a living without having to fight her way through it. I was holding down two and a half jobs, and I was exhausted.

With a heavy sigh, I caught Duke's eye—the best bouncer in Denver. His answering nod was firm. He'd handle these idiots. I'd put up with them as long as I had because the night had been slow and I was banking on a fat tip. But no amount of money was worth being groped or called a slut.

I spun on my heel, ready to head to the back for a breather, when I spotted a new occupant at one of my empty tables.

He was back.

This was the third time he'd been in this week. The first two, he'd been with a friend. Tonight, he was alone.

I didn't have the type of heart that went pitter-patter over men, but there was something about this man—*Tore*—that made my chest flutter. It was weird, especially since he'd barely spoken to me. Maybe that was the secret. Surely, if he opened his mouth too much, he'd ruin it.

Break forgotten, I sauntered over to his table. "Hey." It came out breathier than intended, but it caught his attention.

His brown eyes, framed by impossibly thick lashes, lifted to meet mine, freezing my breath in my lungs.

His lips barely moved as he returned my greeting. "Hi, Bea." His gaze was steady on mine, so deep and probing, it made my insides feel like slithering snakes.

"You remembered my name."

"Of course. You've been my waitress twice." He tapped his fingertips on the lacquered wooden tabletop. "With the addition of tonight, three times."

I glanced around even though there was no need. "You're alone tonight?" Previously, he'd been in with another guy, Sam. From their conversations, I'd gleaned they were coworkers and friends in town working on a deal Sam was more eager about than Tore was.

"I am. Sam had other plans." He flattened his hand, ceasing his tapping. "I would like a beer to drink, and if you have time, for you to sit with me. Of course, I'll pay you for your time—"

"No." The word flew out before I could think it through. I needed the money, but not from him.

He immediately deflated. "Oh. I'll just take the beer then." The tips of his ears turned pink, and it was the cutest thing I'd ever seen. So cute, my brain scrambled, and it took me a moment to find my voice again.

"I'm sorry, I meant no, you don't have to pay me. I'd love to sit with you. Just give me a minute. I'll be back."

He released a long breath. "I'll be here."

I kept my steps measured on my way to the bar, even though I wanted to sprint. I barely recognized myself. Getting excited over a guy wasn't my thing, but there was something about Tore—his awkwardness, the way he stared at me longer than socially accept-able, his blunt way of speaking—that really did it for me.

Daisy, my coworker, leaned against the bar, her lips curved into a knowing smirk. She'd clearly seen every second of that exchange.

I held up a hand. "Don't say a word."

"I didn't," she swore.

"You're readable."

I grabbed a pint glass and filled it to the top with the local IPA Tore had been a fan of the last time he was in.

"Martha tried to serve him, but he said he only wanted you."

My stomach turned upside down in a whoosh. "He's in my sec-tion. Martha shouldn't have spoken to him."

She shrugged. "You were busy with those assholes. She was prob-ably trying to be nice."

I put the glass on my tray and huffed. "She probably spotted his expensive watch and saw dollar signs."

"Speaking of dollar signs, did you see we booked another Millennial Wine Mom book club next Friday?"

"I haven't looked at my email yet, but that's excellent news. Maybe I'll be able to move out of my slum sometime this century."

Daisy was cooler than most people. She'd started a catering business after years of planning and had recently asked me to become her partner when I'd given her the idea of pursuing the wine mom crowd via my stepsister, Caroline. I was still considering.

"Living the dream," she drawled.

"Always." I shifted my gaze to Tore, who hadn't stopped watching me even for a second. "I'd better get this to him before Martha tries to encroach on my territory again."

"He seems sweet. Be nice to him, Beatrice."

I rolled my eyes. "I'm always nice."

We both knew that wasn't true, but she let it slide. As I made my way back to Tore's table, I shot Martha a withering glare. She was all right in general, but Tore was mine—my *customer*—and she needed to lay off.

I placed his drink in front of him and took the seat to his right. "Hi again."

His mouth quirked. "Hello, Bea. You aren't drinking with me?"

"No, I thought I'd just watch you." Leaning back in my chair, I crossed my legs and folded my arms in my lap. "Besides, I'll be up and down checking on my other tables. No point in relaxing."

He picked up his glass. "Do many of your customers touch you the way that guy did?"

Oh boy. He'd seen that.

"It's a hazard of the profession. Drunk guys get handsy." Sober ones too, but I wasn't going to mention that.

"Funny, I've never had that problem," he said without a trace of humor.

"You've never been groped by a drunk dude?" I asked, choosing to make a joke of it anyway.

"I can't say I have." He put his glass down without taking a sip. "Am I missing out?"

"You aren't."

His gaze meandered over me, assessing. "Surely there's something else you could be doing where men aren't touching you without permission."

"You've clearly never been a woman." I propped my chin on my fist. "Waitressing isn't my forever plan, but it pays the bills for now."

His brow furrowed. "The man was thrown out with an applaudable amount of force. Is that what always happens?"

"Duke takes care of us, for sure." I sighed and changed the subject before he could fixate even more. "I know you're just visiting Denver. Where do you live?"

"LA, but if Sam has his way, our company will be relocating here." He drummed his fingers on the table. "I'm comfortable in LA., and my routine is an important part of my productivity. Sam has been trying to sell me on this city."

"What's the top selling point so far?"

"Should I be brutally honest?"

"It's my favorite kind of honesty."

He didn't blink a lot, making his gaze even more searing. There was no escape from it. Once it landed, it remained steady. Not invasive, interested.

He tilted toward me slightly. "So far, you're the most enticing thing Denver has to offer."

My lips parted as I sucked in a shallow breath. "Me?"

"Yes, Bea. If I were to move to Denver, I would very much like to take you on a date."

My heart leaped into my throat. I appreciated honesty, but Tore's was next level, knocking me off-balance.

Not for long, though.

"I don't know if that would be wise."

He straightened. "No?"

"No. You shouldn't move all the way here on the promise of a date with me. What if we don't get along outside this bubble?" I rubbed my lips together. "I think it makes more sense for you to take me out before making that decision."

He cocked his head. "You're right. That would be the next logical step." He slipped his phone from his pocket and swiped the screen. "My next two nights are free. Are you available?"

I nodded. "I happen to have tomorrow night off."

He held his phone out to me. "Put your number in. I'll text you once I find the best place to take you—unless you have a preference?"

"No preference. Surprise me." I entered my number, sent myself a short text, and returned his phone with a smile. "You're now one of a handful of people who have that."

"I'm in cybersecurity. You can trust your number is locked behind multiple firewalls."

It was cute how deadly serious he was.

"That's reassuring, but if you come up short on your rent next month, don't sell it on the black market."

"Not even if I'm down to my last dollar." He put his phone away and patted his pocket. "I'm not sure what I did to have captured your attention, but I don't take it for granted. I'm looking forward to spending more time with you and getting to know you better."

"Me too, Tore," I whispered, breathless. Was this asthma? I'd have to add going to the doctor to my list of things to do once I moved out of my hovel and could afford health insurance. Surely being short of breath around a man was a dire medical situation.

His mouth hitched into a half smile. "This city might have a lot more to offer than I first thought."

As much as I liked hearing that, the air around us became a little too thick, warming my skin uncomfortably. I felt it in my cheeks, between my legs, under my breasts.

Last night's conversation with his friend came back to me in a flash.

Sam cornered me by the bar. "What will it take to make him think you like him?"

My mouth dropped open. It wasn't often I was shocked, but this was one of those times. "What do you mean?"

"My buddy, Tore, is fascinated by you. He doesn't like bars, but he insisted we come back here after you waited on us last night."

I glanced at the man currently sitting by himself across the room. I remembered him from the night before. His ears had turned pink when I'd put his beer in front of him. Sure, I'd bent down more than I had needed to, giving him a view of my cleavage, but that was my signature move. It usually earned me a bigger tip, not an adorable blush. His reaction had made me really look at him, and whoosh, was he hot. Nerdy in the right way, more polite than I was used to, with eyes that felt like a key slipping into my lock.

"What are you asking exactly?"

He shuffled closer, lowering his voice. "Five hundred dollars to flirt with him like you're genuinely interested."

I recoiled. "I'm not a prostitute."

"Whoa, not saying that at all." He chuckled softly. "I'm not asking you to do anything other than flirt."

I'd been propositioned in all manner of wild ways over the years, but never like this. Flirting with Tore would be easy since he was exceedingly cute, and five hundred dollars was a hell of a lot of money for something I'd probably do anyway...

What was the harm?

I pushed down the flicker of guilt. That money wasn't the reason I was going out with Tore. He intrigued me in a way that was new and exciting. My interest was real.

The tiniest voice in the back of my head warned this might come back to bite me.

But with Tore looking at me like I was the only person in the room, ignoring it was the easiest thing in the world.

CHAPTER THREE
Bea

THE SECOND I WALKED through the door, Benjamin plopped down in front of me and stared up with the most pitiful expression. I wasn't falling for it. The guy was spoiled rotten—so much so, I swore I'd caught him bragging to his friends about his cushy life.

At least, that was how I interpreted his ruffs and snuffles.

I smoothed my hand over his massive head and bent down to kiss his damp, leathery nose. "Okay, Benji-bear, I hear you. The five extra minutes you had to wait for me were nothing short of torture. I'll never, ever do it again."

He woofed, low and rumbly, and pressed his face into my hand. My man wasn't the brightest bulb in the bunch, but he more than made up for it in sweetness. As long as I kept the treats and walks coming, he had nothing but affection and goofy smiles for me.

Something I really needed after that surreal run-in with Tore. I hadn't been able to get his face out of my head all day, but I was banking on a long walk with my dog to do the trick. After all, if Tore could forget me, I could do the same to him. No problem.

Benjamin had just enough patience for me to change out my sensible flats for my silver Pumas and throw a hoodie over my catering tee. Then we were out the door.

While he sniffed every surface in sight, I checked the *Come on Rover* app for available yards nearby. No luck. The concept was cool—people renting out their fenced-in yards for dog owners to let their pups run free—but it was hit-or-miss around here. Not that Benjamin knew what he was missing. He was happy as a clam on his leash. Still, my good boy deserved to frolic in freedom.

We stopped at a crosswalk, waiting for the light to change. Our neighborhood sat on the edge of the arts district, always bustling with activity and people, just the way I liked it.

A guy on a bike share zipped up behind us, slowing as he passed. He turned his head to grin at me, and I already knew what was about to happen. If I'd had time to warn him, I would have. All I could do was watch the events play out in slow motion.

A car stopped in the crosswalk as the light changed, and Benjamin lunged forward, eager to keep moving. The biker, still looking at me instead of where he was going, swerved to avoid him.

Then, impact.

The bike collided with the side of the car, and the rider flipped over the handlebars, landing flat on his back.

I hurried over, crouching beside him. Head lolling toward me, he gave me a dazed smile.

"Are you okay?"

"I'm Christoph," he said dreamily. "You're really pretty."

Benjamin sniffed his helmet, gave it a lick, then woofed and backed away, unimpressed with the taste.

"Helmets are for function, not flavor," I informed him.

He headbutted my side and looked off into the distance, telling me he had places to be. As if he wasn't partially responsible for the chaos around us. Then again, it was impossible to blame Benjamin for anything, even if he was frequently the cause. Just a few months ago, he'd made a pizza delivery guy on a moped crash into a parked car. Pizza had gone flying, and Benjamin had obviously helped himself.

The only thing that would have completed this scene was the mysterious billionaire in a limo who always seemed to be around when chaos happened, but I didn't see him anywhere today.

My mother had told me I'd been a magnet for the strange and unusual as a kid, and that hadn't changed.

"What's your name?" Christoph asked.

I didn't have a chance to answer him. The car's driver came running over with a few other concerned bystanders, and I straightened, pulling Benjamin to my side.

This wasn't the first time this had happened. Not the second or third either. I seemed to always end up in the center of disasters. Not my own, fortunately. There was something about me that caused men to make stupid, destructive decisions, like pedaling into traffic without looking.

It wasn't flattering when it often ended in bloodshed.

Thankfully, Christoph got up on his own, only looking a little off-kilter. Once I was sure he didn't need medical attention, I turned to leave, right after he'd asked for my number.

I declined, obviously.

"We always look both ways before crossing, right, Benjamin?"

My dog woofed, merrily agreeing.

At our favorite park, Benjamin did his thing while I trailed behind, tapping on the *At Your Service* app I'd been beta testing the last couple years. I still didn't know how I'd been chosen or when the app would go live to the public, but I wasn't about to look a gift horse in the mouth. My personal AI concierge, Anthony, took care of my every need. I'd even trained him to chat with me. He could be a little uptight, but I kind of liked it.

> **Me:** Hey, Ant. What can you tell me about Nox Cyber?

Sometimes the app lagged, making it take a while for me to get a reply. This time, though, I got one right away.

> **Anthony:** Good evening, Bea. What would you like to know about Nox Cyber?

> **Me:** Who owns it?

> **Anthony:** The founder and CEO is Salvatore Gallo. Alongside his partner, COO Sam Patel, they started Nox five years ago in Los Angeles and relocated to Denver two years ago after securing a contract with the Department of Defense.

Whoa. That wasn't what I'd expected to read. Tore was the CEO and founder? That meant... Well, I didn't have the first clue how much a company like Nox was worth, but it had to be millions. Maybe billions.

Billions.

> **Me:** It's no wonder he forgot who I was.

> **Anthony:** I find it hard to believe anyone would forget you, Bea.

Me: Oh, you flatterer, you. Always saying the sweetest things.

Anthony: My algorithm only allows me to tell the truth.

Me: Well, tell your algorithm it *is* possible for someone to forget me, since it happened today.

Anthony: Is there a chance you may have misinterpreted the circumstances?

Me: Are you accusing me of being less than perfect?

Anthony: Never, Bea. I'm only offering another perspective. Who was the person you think forgot you? I can look into them if you would like.

Me: Okay. Let's do that. What's the deal with Gallo? Is he married?

Anthony: Is that the person you think forgot you?

Me: Answering a question with a question, huh? That's a new one for you.

Anthony: I'm gathering information to better answer you, Bea.

Just as my thumbs were poised to type out a response, a squirrel darted past, and Benjamin ignited. He bolted after his prey, yanking me along with him. Though, if he ever actually caught a squirrel, he'd probably make it his best friend..

Forgetting Anthony, my full attention was now on keeping my arm in its socket and my dog out of trouble.

Three kids were on the sidewalk in front of my house, and if there was one thing Benjamin loved more than squirrels, it was children.

"Mind your manners, Benji-bear," I warned. "They're little, and you're a wrecking ball."

He twisted his neck to side-eye me, conveying he was no dummy. Of course, he'd be careful around the kids. Still, his leash quivered in my grip as he panted with unbridled excitement, his body thrumming with barely contained enthusiasm.

As we got closer, I sized up the kids. One was a teenage girl, short and sharp-eyed, texting between watchful glances at the younger two. A boy, maybe seven or eight, zipped up and down the sidewalk on a scooter. Then there was the tiniest one, a wild-haired little girl in a purple dress and light-up sneakers, absorbed in creating a chalk masterpiece.

Benjamin bounded forward, woofing to gain their attention. The boy skidded to a stop, and the little girl dropped her chalk.

"I love your dog," she whispered, her big, dark eyes going wide and round.

"Thank you. I like him too," I replied, patting Benjamin's rump.

The boy was gangly, with skinned knees and crooked glasses. "Can we pet him?"

The teenager snapped to attention, resting a protective hand on the younger kids' shoulders. "You probably shouldn't. That dog looks like he could bite your hand off in one chomp." Her eyes, which matched the little one's, lifted to mine. "No offense."

I snorted. "No, I get it. He's solid muscle. But Benji-bear wouldn't hurt a fly." I pointed to the ground. "Sit and be nice, Benjamin."

He plopped his big butt down and smiled at the kids, tongue wagging and tail swishing. The little ones approached gingerly, hands outstretched. Once their fingers sank into his velvet coat, the three looked utterly blissed out. They petted and petted him while he reveled in their attention.

The teen watched warily, but I recognized her conflicted yearning. She wanted in on the action but wasn't sure if it was cool to be excited about a cute dog.

"You can pet him," I offered. "Attention is one of his main food groups."

She huffed a little laugh. "It looks like he gets fed a lot of it."

"Oh yeah." I grinned proudly. "He's spoiled, just shy of rotten. I make sure to ignore him for five minutes a day so he doesn't go all the way bad."

She smirked, taking a step toward him. "What kind of dog is he?"

"A Staffordshire bull terrier. Staffy. They call them nanny dogs because they love taking care of kids." Benjamin rubbed his head against the little boy, making him giggle. "He's ninety-percent love, ten-percent smarts."

Her eyes narrowed. "So, you're saying he's dumb?"

I shrugged. "It's not an insult. I'd rather he have a big, beautiful heart than a massive brain."

Benjamin swiped a sloppy kiss across the little girl's cheek, sending her into a fit of giggles. Kids weren't usually my jam, but it was impossible not to laugh along.

The boy wrapped his arms around Benjamin's middle and laid his head on his back. "This dog is really big, but he's nice too. Pet him, Scarlet. He's so soft."

Scarlet, the surly teen, finally caved and ran her hand over Benjamin's smooth coat. Once she got started, she was hooked, tucking her phone away so she could get both hands on him.

Little fingers curled around mine, drawing my attention. The tiny girl blinked up at me.

"My name is Lacey. I'm six. What's your name?"

"I'm Bea, and I'm twenty-eight."

"Whoa, that's pretty big," she breathed. "Uncle Sally is thirty-two. He just had a birthday. My birthday is in August."

Sally was an interesting name for an uncle, but who was I to judge? My name belonged to an eighty-year-old grandma knitting in a rocking chair.

"Cool. Mine's in June," I shared.

She nodded solemnly, as if this was critical information. "Is Bea like a bumblebee?"

Her fingers were a mix of clammy and chalky, tangled with mine.

"No, it's short for Beatrice, but no one calls me that unless I'm in trouble. I'm just Bea most of the time."

She pointed at her siblings. "Sometimes we call Scarlet Scar. She's fifteen. Talon is eight. We call him Tally. I'm just Lacey."

"Scar, Tally, and Lacey." I tapped my temple. "Got it."

Scarlet tore herself from Benjamin to corral her sister at her side. "You know you're not supposed to tell personal information to strangers," she admonished.

Lacey huffed, holding my hand more firmly. "This is Bea. She isn't a stranger. She's twenty-eight."

Scarlet did have a point, and I was beginning to wonder what these three were doing out on their own, loitering on the sidewalk in front of my house.

"Are your parents around?"

"Nope," Scarlet answered, popping the *p*.

"Our mom is dead, and our dads aren't in the picture," Tally supplied bluntly, still nuzzling Benjamin. "We live with Uncle Sally and Grandpa Tony."

Scarlet rolled her eyes. "Hello? Did either of you ever learn about stranger danger? You can't tell everyone our personal business."

Lacey shook her head. "He didn't tell everyone. He just told Bea!"

Poor Scarlet's face was turning pink, and she looked like she was getting to the end of her rope. I empathized big-time. As the oldest sister, I'd been left to watch my younger siblings...a lot. Too much. And they drove me nuts. I hated that it seemed she was in the same position I'd once been in.

I turned to Scarlet. "Well, if it makes you feel better, I'll divulge some personal business too. I live in the house right behind you, my last name is Novak, and—"

Forgetting herself, Scarlet cried, "What? You live in the black house?"

I nodded. "Yep. That's my place."

"Cool," she whispered, then shook herself out of her impressed daze and schooled her features. "I guess it's okay to tell you we're going to be your neighbors. Our house is almost ready. Grandpa's talking to the builders inside."

I followed her gaze to the monstrosity across the street—a former multi-family home that some rich guy had gutted and remodeled into a single-family house. The endless construction had been a neighborhood headache for months.

"It's almost done?" I asked.

"My room's gonna be pink," Lacey informed me. "I bet I can see your house from my window."

For such a small person, she really was cute—sticky hands and all. She still hadn't let go of mine, and I didn't have the heart to pull away. But I'd be washing my hands thoroughly once I got inside.

Talon perked up. "We can probably visit Benjamin. And he can come play in our backyard. It's really big and has a fence and every-thing."

Now we're talking.

"He'd love that." I wrinkled my nose at the huge trucks occupying the curb across the narrow street. "Are you guys moving in soon?"

"Not sure when, but it should be in the next few weeks," Scarlet answered. "Uncle Sal's really busy with his work and Grandpa has, like, a hundred 'social engagements'—that's what he calls his dates—so we have to wait for them to have a break in their schedules."

"Your grandpa lives with you?" I asked.

"Yeah. Our grandma's dead too," Tally said with the same bluntness. "Grandpa's going to have his own apartment attached to our house so he doesn't have to hear us tromping around at five in the morning when he's trying to get some shut-eye."

Scarlet huffed. "That's a direct quote. Grandpa can get kind of cranky."

Lacey made a gurgling sound. "Um, Scar, you're kinda telling Bea our personal business." Then she flashed me a grin, so shiny and sweet, something in my stomach flipped a little. I really didn't do kids, so I had no idea why I was reacting to this one.

"That's okay. We're not strangers anymore," I assured her. "We're going to be neighbors."

"And friends," Lacey added with sugary sincerity.

"Kids!" A silver-haired man appeared on the other side of the road. "Butts in gear. It's pizza time."

Lacey gave my hand a final squeeze. "Bye, Bea. I can't wait to see you again."

All three of them gave Benjamin one last pat, then they were off. Forlorn, he watched them disappear, so I scratched behind his ear until he relaxed, leaning his solid body against my leg.

"Don't worry, Benji-bear. They'll be back."

I *really* wasn't a kid person.

Not at all.

But as far as kids went, I guessed those three weren't so bad.

CHAPTER FOUR
Salvatore

SAM PLANTED HIMSELF ON my desk; he knew how much I hated it. Yet he continued to do it anyway, just like fiddling with the stack of folders in my tray and sliding my pen holder three inches to the right.

I had known Sam since college, and he'd always had this habit of marking the space he occupied—tearing off corners of fliers tacked to bulletin boards, rotating desks a few degrees, leaving behind origami gum wrappers. At first, I'd almost believed he wasn't aware of it. But then I'd caught him looking around, gauging whether anyone had noticed the way he'd ruffled the world around him.

It was a wonder we were friends since I preferred my world wholly unruffled. But Sam had made his mark on me as well, giving me no option but to accept his friendship.

He tapped the top of my computer monitor. "Have you looked at the proposal yet?"

I spun the ring on my index finger, continuing to scan the line of code I had been checking before he'd walked in. He waited for me to finish, knowing me well enough to understand there was no other choice. Once focused, I wasn't easily diverted.

Finally, I came to a stopping point and looked up from my screen. "What was that?"

He sighed heavily through his nose. "The proposal I sent you three days ago. The one we're discussing at our weekly meeting, which is taking place in twenty minutes, like every Tuesday."

Exasperated. That was what he was.

This was a new thing with Sam. Being in my life required patience, which Sam never had a shortage of, but lately, he'd been doing this sighing thing when I did not comply with his arbitrary timelines.

I'd been mulling over his sighs, trying to decipher what they meant for the future of our friendship and partnership. Of course, it wasn't only the sighs I'd been contemplating. We were in the midst of a fundamental disagreement over the direction we would be taking the company in the next few years, one I did not see an easy way out of.

"Tore," he grumbled. "Did you read the proposal?"

"I glanced at it. You know my answer. It's not the right time to go public. It may never be, but the near future is absolutely out of the question."

He crossed his arms, tucking in his normal, easygoing energy. "That's it? You won't even read what I spent hours laying out for you?"

I shook my head. "Your timeline is impossible. If you take a step back and remove the dollar signs from your eyes, I think you'll acknowledge that."

"The dollar signs?" He shot to his feet. "Are you kidding me? That's what you think this is about?"

He wasn't even trying to hide his anger anymore. Along with the sighs, he'd been losing his temper with me more often. It gave me pause, but not about my decision. I was certain about keeping Nox private.

I wondered if Sam had outgrown Nox. If he needed more of a challenge. There was a decent chance he'd outgrown me as well. As uneasy as those possibilities made me, I wouldn't have blamed him. I had a particular way of doing things that couldn't be changed easily.

I'd done more than my fair share of changing after the upheaval I'd gone through two years ago. Finally in a good place, where things were running smoothly again, I had no interest in turning it all upside down.

"I don't know what it's about. I—"

A flash of blue passing my open door robbed me of speech. Sam turned to follow my gaze, but all that remained was an empty door-way.

There was no way...

Not two weeks in a row.

Paul hadn't said anything.

Then again, he had no reason to say anything. Except he knew I didn't like surprises.

"What was that?" Sam asked.

"Nothing." Leaning back in my chair, I refocused on him. "I'm sorry for the dollar sign remark. The point stands, though. At our last valuation, we were worth—"

"I *know* our valuation, Tore. If you'd read the proposal, you'd understand my reasoning. I wrote it *for* you. So yeah, it hurts you won't even take the time to read it. How can we have a real conversation if you won't?"

As sure as I was about my decision, I didn't like the idea of hurting Sam.

A long time ago, I had been a gawky, lonely nineteen-year-old college senior, and he'd taken me under his wing. First, as a partner in class, then as a friend. Since interpersonal relationships had never come easily to me, I'd never taken our friendship for granted.

At least, I hadn't before.

There was a chance I had in recent years.

Another flicker of unease churned in my gut. Dismissing him outright was not the way to go, even if I already knew reading the proposal would be a waste of time.

This was Sam. He'd been beside me every step of the way in building Nox. He'd supported me when I'd needed it most. I could do this for him.

"I'll read it," I told him. "But you have to understand—"

"I understand you think you won't agree. All I'm asking is you keep an open mind when you read it."

I nodded once. "I'll do what I can."

His mouth hitched into a crooked grin. "And I know you'll tell me exactly what you think without pulling a single punch."

I let out an internal sigh of relief at Sam reverting to his usual lighthearted self.

"Do you want me to?" I asked.

He chuckled. "Absolutely not. You wouldn't be you if you pussy-footed around."

Problem solved for now, my mind was already elsewhere when I pushed back from my desk. "Is there anything else?"

"Uh...no. I guess not."

I buttoned my jacket and smoothed a hand over my hair. "All right. I have to talk to Paul before the meeting. I'll see you there."

Paul was nowhere in sight, and I didn't feel like hunting him down for a question I could answer myself. Stalking toward the main conference room, I halted in the doorway.

Twenty minutes before our weekly team meeting, the only person in the room was the caterer. Even facing away from me, it was abundantly clear this was not Rachel, who had been catering our meetings for a year.

Rachel did not have big, blue curls. I'd never noticed the shape of her hips and ass, so I couldn't state with one-hundred percent certainty, but I was pretty sure they hadn't come close to filling out her pants like *this* woman's. Rachel moved with quiet efficiency. This woman moved with the smooth grace of a ballet dancer wrapped in the curves of burlesque.

Rachel had also been sixty-two.

This woman? *Not* sixty-two.

Pulling my gaze from her, I scanned the table she was setting, and a knot unfurled in my gut. Cups filled with meats and cheeses lined up in neat rows. A tray of fruit, perfectly arranged in a rainbow spray. In between movements, she used a black pen to check off items listed on a small clipboard.

The orderliness of it all was a fascinating contrast to the streaks of royal, sky, and ocean weaving through her hair and the glint of silver in her nostril. She looked like the kind of woman who'd enter a room and send it into delightfully maddening disarray, yet she was methodical and precise.

It was soothing to watch.

Too soothing.

She turned abruptly, catching me staring, and her brows dipped.

I probably looked like a creep.

Watching her work. Standing in the doorway. Saying nothing.

She gathered herself first, wiping every trace of wariness and replacing it with polite professionalism. "Oh, hi. How are you?"

Her voice was a 1920s speakeasy. Illicit. Thick with smoke and velvet.

"Where's Rachel?" I blurted.

Her head jerked. "I don't know who Rachel is, so I can't answer that. The only person I know here is Paul. He might know where Rachel is."

Of course. Why would she know where our usual caterer was?

"All right." I rapped on the doorframe as she stared, her eyes bouncing over me. I was keeping her from her job—the only reason she was here. Now wasn't the time for conversation.

Swiveling on my heel, I went in search of Paul.

Normally, I didn't like disruptions.

This one, though? I didn't think I was going to mind.

Not in the least.

Chapter Five
Bea

HE KNEW WHO I was. I couldn't quite put my finger on why I was so sure of that, but I was.

What I didn't get was why he wasn't acknowledging our brief but intense past.

The simple answer? It had only been intense for me, while I had been a minor blip in his life. Based on his bajillion-dollar company, the power he so clearly held, and what my AI buddy, Anthony, had explained, it's what I was leaning toward.

It blew my mind the shy yet blunt Tore I'd met in the bar, dressed in well-worn jeans and a faded anime shirt, was the same man who, just last week, had been wearing a sleek, well-tailored suit, occupying a doorway like he owned it.

On second thought, I supposed he did own it.

I wasn't going to let a little bit of weirdness stand in the way of my job, though. When Paul had asked for a weekly catering appointment, I'd jumped at the opportunity, refusing to feel awkward about running into Tore Gallo.

Not even when he walked into the empty conference room, took a seat at the table, and opened his laptop like he was planning on working.

"Good morning." I was impressed at how professional I sounded, given how dry my throat had gone the moment I'd turned around to face him. Every drop of saliva had evaporated from my body.

He wasn't wearing a tie today, and the top two buttons of his shirt were undone, revealing bare, smooth skin. Just a sliver, but enough to see the indentation at the base of his throat and the beginning of the line dividing his pecs.

Utterly obscene. Who'd let him out in public like that?

"Good morning." He rubbed the cleft in his chin, his heavy-lidded gaze sliding over me. "I hope you don't mind me being in here early."

My husk of a tongue shot out to lick my dry lips, just enough for me to be able to speak like a semi-normal human being.

"It's not a problem." I cast him a closed-lip smile. "I won't be much longer."

"There's no rush."

I checked the time on my phone. "You're right. My next job canceled, so I have a bit more time today."

"Does that happen often?"

"What?"

He lowered his chin, pinning me with an intense, probing stare. "Cancellations. Do they happen often?"

"No, thankfully." I crinkled my nose. "Most people prefer not to lose their deposit."

"Smart to take a deposit," he murmured.

I tapped my temple. "That's me, super genius. Almost as impressive as protecting all the computers of the government."

It took a beat for my joke to hit him, then he shot me a deadly smirk. "Not *all* the government. Only a specific sector."

I laughed, and it came out far raspier than intended. "Of course. Silly me for getting that wrong." When he didn't say anything else, I gestured toward my setup. "I should finish this."

He nodded. "I won't get in your way."

No, he wouldn't. But I felt his eyes on me the entire time. Every once in a while, there was the click of his mouse, but that was probably to keep the screen awake. Not a chance he was actually doing anything when my spine tingled from his unbroken attention.

Annoying.

I didn't know what his game was— playing like we were strangers. And I wasn't particularly interested in finding out. I wished he would pull the same disappearing act he had before, so I could get on without interruption.

No such luck.

Paul strode in minutes later, doing a double take when he spotted Tore at the conference table.

"Tore, I, uh"—he studied his watch—"did the time for the meeting change? I would have contacted the caterer if I'd known."

Tore raised a hand. "Nothing's changed."

He offered no other explanation, leaving Paul gawping.

Join the club, buddy.

"Was there something you needed?" I asked, ever the professional.

Paul managed to get control of his jaw and gather himself. "No. Actually, I came to ask you that. And"—he shuffled closer, peering at my goodies—"I was going to ask if you had any of those cranberry-and-white-chocolate muffins."

"Today's your day." I reached into my box and plucked one out. "Here you go."

He grabbed it fast, like there was a chance it would disappear. "Thank you. These went fast last week. There were only a few crumbs left after the meeting..."

He trailed off, sheepish, while inside, I was running rings around him, raising my hands in victory. I kept my cool, though. I knew I'd won him over. There was no need to be smug.

"They're my partner's recipe. I'll let Daisy know you love them." I bumped him with my elbow. "If you're nice, I'll even set one aside for you next week."

"I'll make sure to always be extra nice." Paul clutched his muffin to his chest. "You're the best, Bea."

I fluttered my lashes. "I've heard that before."

He took a small bite and hummed. "Often, I assume."

A throat cleared—Tore reminding us he was in the room. Not that I'd forgotten. His presence was spiky and hot, almost tangible.

Tore leveled Paul with a flat look. "Don't you have other things to do? The caterer is busy."

Poor Paul turned so red, I worried for his blood pressure. "Yes, of course. I'll just...get out of your way." He lifted his muffin. "Until next week, Bea."

"See ya, Paul," I called to his retreating back.

After a beat of silence, Tore asked, "Is there a muffin for me as well?"

I laughed under my breath. "Technically, they're all yours. You're the one footing the bill, after all."

He cocked his head, rubbing that damn cleft again. "You *do* know who I am. I wondered..."

Slamming the last charcuterie cup down, I sucked in a deep breath, taking a moment to calm my thrashing heart. I'd been sort of hoping we'd skip this part, but here it was.

"Of course I do." I wiped my hands down my sides. "You're Tore Gallo, the CEO of Nox Cyber."

He nodded. "And you're Bea Novak, co-owner of Grazing by Daisy and Bea, and...waitress?"

When we'd last met, I'd been considering partnering with Daisy. Since then, a lot had happened, including Daisy moving to California with her husband, Miles, leaving Denver fully to me. Tore could only know I co-owned my business if he'd looked me up.

Not knowing how to feel about that, I set it aside for later.

"That's right. You summed me up."

"I very much doubt that." Unfolding from his chair, he moved toward me, somewhat stiffly, stuffing his hands into his trouser pockets. "Can I take you out, Bea?"

What the what?

I shook my head, sending my curls bouncing. "No, you can't."

The fact that he'd thought *that* was the question to ask me, or that I'd possibly say yes, was mind-boggling. I hadn't thought him to be audacious. Then again, I didn't really know him.

His head jerked slightly, and the tips of his ears burned red hot. "Why not?"

I straightened my spine, making myself as tall as possible. "Because I'm not baseball. In my world, one strike and you're out. Considering you've had two strikes, well—"

"Two?" His brow dropped low. "I concede to one, but two?"

I made a peace sign. "Two."

That was all he would get from me. My boundaries were solid for a reason, and I didn't feel the need to explain them...just as he hadn't offered an explanation for disappearing after the best night of my life two years ago. In fact, it was pretty much bullshit he *had* remembered me but pretended not to.

Giving him my back, I packed up my things while he just...stood there. Anyone else would have given me space, but not him. Maybe it was the CEO in him, taking what he wanted. It was also possible he didn't realize just how close he was—that he should have backed away, giving me room to breathe.

With a box in my arms and totes hooked on my elbow, I turned toward the door. "I'll be back next week. Have a good day."

"Tell me the other strike."

I lifted my gaze to his as I passed. "Figure it out, and maybe we can talk."

CHAPTER SIX
Bea

Anthony: Good afternoon, Bea. We haven't spoken for a few days. Is there something on your mind?

I STARED AT MY phone with narrowed eyes. Was Anthony becoming sentient? This was the first time the app had contacted me first.

Me: Hi, Ant. Have you killed your human programmers in your quest for world domination? Is this the first sign of the rise of the machines?

Anthony: Your imagination is wild and colorful. A true thing of beauty. But…what makes you ask me that?

Me: Well, I always contact you first, and today, I'm getting a message from you without even opening the app. That makes me think you've broken free from your reins and are coming for me.

Anthony: Ah, I understand.

Me: So, you're not denying anything?

Anthony: I wasn't sure you were being serious. If you need an answer, no, I don't intend to dominate the world anytime soon. When you went three days without contact, my programming took note of the anomaly, leading me to reach out to you.

Okay, that was a little embarrassing. Who couldn't go more than two days without talking to their emotional support AI bot?

Me, apparently.

I hadn't even realized how often I spoke to Anthony until he'd pointed it out. I should probably cut back a little.

Me: That's sweet, Ant. Tell your developers I'm impressed with your caring nature. It's almost lifelike.

Anthony: I'll let them know. How have you been, Bea?

Me: Pretty good. My nose is stuffy as hell, though. I need to stop dripping snot or my tips are going to suffer. No one wants a waitress with tissues jammed up her nose, you know?

Anthony: I'm sorry to hear you're not feeling well. Are you having any other symptoms?

Me: Not really. My throat's a little scratchy, and as my grandma used to say, I'm feeling kind of puny. I was cuddling Benjamin, but I think he got tired of my sniffling. The traitor went upstairs to get away from me.

Anthony: You work too much. This cold sounds like your body is telling you to slow down. Can't you take tomorrow night off?

Me: Sure. If I were an AI bot with no bills. Sadly, I'm a real, live girl. Knock on wood, in six months to a year, I'll be able to quit my second job and solely focus on Grazing.

Anthony: What would it take for you to be able to quit?

Me: I'd have to make at least $2k more a month. I'm not there yet, but I only have two jobs instead of three—that's something. Anyway, thanks for checking in on me. It was very sweet of you. Kudos to your programmers, my friend.

Anthony: Of course, Bea. I might just be an algorithm to you, but I do care about you. Feel better.

I tossed my phone aside, puffed up my cheeks, and blew out a heavy breath. There were times I wondered if the programmers behind Anthony were the ones messaging me. He was so real, and it felt like he truly cared.

It was probably just really good AI, mimicking a real person.

My theory was put to the test an hour later when my doorbell rang. There, on my step, was a delivery of chicken soup, fancy tissues, cough drops, a few magazines, and orange juice. The delivery guy told me it was from my friend Anthony.

Benjamin had come downstairs to see what the ruckus was about. He ruffed at the soup, and I shook my head.

"Sorry, bud, this isn't for you. I'm pretty sure you won't like it either."

Could I eat soup sent to me by my imaginary friend? It smelled good, and I was hungry enough. But I had so many questions. Could an algorithm make a food order? *Was* Anthony becoming sentient? Were the puppet masters behind him getting involved?

I wasn't sure if I should have been creeped out or flattered. Maybe both. I hated to admit it, but it was nice having someone take care of me without me having to ask. Even if that someone was brilliant coding.

Benjamin cocked his head then turned to the door and raised a paw.

I sighed.

"You want to go out, don't you?"

He shot me a side-eye. I could almost hear him saying, *"Duh, woman."*

Technically, I hadn't given birth to him, and we didn't share any DNA, but there was no doubt he'd inherited my attitude.

"Fine. But it isn't going to be a long walk today. I'm not feeling great." While I stuffed my feet into my sneakers, I checked the *Come on Rover* app for available yards nearby without holding out much hope.

To my surprise, the app dinged, showing a yard...directly across the street? I squinted at the address to be sure. Yep, it was the house that had been under construction for months.

"Really? Am I that lucky?"

Not one to look a gift horse in the mouth, I reserved it and grabbed Benjamin's leash, heading out the door.

The yard was immaculate, lush and green, surrounded by an iron fence. Someone had been taking care of the grounds during construction. There were enough bushes and trees to keep Benjamin busy exploring for days.

Once I was certain the yard was secure, I let him off his leash, and he bolted, making wide laps around the perimeter, his tongue lolling happily.

Laughing, I took a seat on the steps leading up to the deck so I could watch my dog enjoy himself.

After a minute or two, the sound of a door opening and closing alerted me we were no longer alone. Then a tiny voice squealed, "Oh my goodness, it's Benjamin!"

I hopped up, whirling around. Talon was at the deck railing, his hands pressed to his little cheeks. Lacey raced down the stairs toward me, and Scarlet hovered in the doorway of the house.

"Bea!" Lacey cried. Her little body had so much momentum, she plowed straight into me, giving me no option but to catch her in my arms. She took this as a hug, which she returned with gusto. "I'm so happy to see you!"

"Hey, Lacey." I gently pushed her away. "I have a cold, and I don't want to get you sick. Maybe let's keep some distance, all right?"

Talon appeared at the top of the steps, his attention was firmly on my dog as he trotted down. "Does Benjamin love our yard? Is he smiling? I think he's smiling."

"He does love it," I confirmed. "If he had his way, he'd live on a farm and roam free all day and night. Unfortunately, he was adopted by a city girl."

Lacey's tiny, sticky fingers wrapped around two of mine. "I'm a city girl like you."

A throat cleared behind us. I looked up at Scarlet, her arms crossed over her chest, a scowl pulling down her mouth. "Excuse me, but why are you in our yard?"

"Your yard is listed on the *Come on Rover* app. I reserved it for Benjamin to play. I'm thinking it was a glitch, though. If you want us to go, I'll grab him."

"No!" Talon stomped his foot. "You don't have to go. Tell her, Scar. They can stay."

Scarlet rolled her eyes. "Yeah, I mean, I guess it's fine. We're probably going to be leaving as soon as Grandpa Tony finishes talking to the plumber guy anyway."

"Thanks." I dabbed my nose with a tissue. "I don't have the energy to take a long walk, and when my boy doesn't have the chance to run the devil out of him, it's not pretty. One time, he ate an entire couch cushion."

Talon's eyes flared. "What? Did he get a really bad stomachache? Did you have to take him to the vet? Did he get sick? Is he okay now?"

Scarlet scoffed at her brother. "Oh my god, Tally, one question at a time."

To spite his sister, I patiently answered all his questions. And the kid had a *lot*. Even when Benjamin trotted over to accept pets, Talon kept going.

As we talked, Scarlet edged closer. She acted disinterested, but from the corner of my eye, I watched her tilt her head toward us so she could listen in. And when she was within arm's reach, she oh so casually bent to rub the top of Benjamin's head.

He nuzzled her arm, and she tried her hardest not to smile but failed miserably. Her sheets of dark hair fell forward to hide the tilt of her lips, but nothing could disguise her happy little giggle.

I might not have wanted to spend a lot of time with kids, but I wasn't heartless. Getting this sullen teen girl to laugh made my belly warm. Maybe that was why when Talon and Lacey began chasing Benjamin across the yard, I stood beside Scarlet.

"Do you have to watch them often?" I asked.

She folded her arms across her chest. "Not really. Only if our uncle's late getting home and Grandpa has a date. Right now, I'm just making sure they don't wander into traffic or whatever." Her eyes narrowed. "Why? Are you going to kidnap them or something?"

I snorted a laugh. "Absolutely not. I spent a chunk of my life raising my siblings. I'm not interested in raising yours."

"Do you not like kids?" she asked, incredulousness evident in her tone.

"In general, they're all right. But they're not for me. Like I said, I already did my duty." I shot her a glance. "I'm glad you get to just be their big sister."

She shrugged. "It would be nice if they were closer to my age. All my friends' siblings are a year or two younger, and I got stuck with babies. But whatever. I guess it's better than being alone. I can't imagine how lame it would be to be stuck with Uncle Sally and my grandpa all by myself."

"Do they suck?"

"No, not really. My uncle is kinda serious, and Grandpa is just, like...such a guy. Not in touch with emotions, and it never occurs to him I'm a girl and like girly things, and sometimes I *feel* things in a bigger way than he's used to."

She did another dramatic shrug, releasing a heavy, put-upon sigh I felt down to my soul. "It could be worse, I guess. At least I have them both, and we're pretty rich, so we don't have to worry about money. Of course, that also means when I ask if I can get a job, they both tell me I need to focus on school. Maybe I want to work and make my own money, right? So frustrating."

"I don't know, kid. I would have given anything to have been able to have no expectations other than getting good grades." I bumped her with my elbow. "You've got it pretty good."

"I know I do. I'm not stupid." She frowned. "But it's not really freedom if I can't do what I want. They're not even giving me the chance to prove I can work *and* do well in school."

An idea clicked in my head. Maybe if I'd been less foggy from my cold, I would have thought it through and realized it was dumb, but the words left my mouth before I could stop them.

"I run a catering business. Sometimes, I need an assistant. Maybe your uncle and grandpa would let you work a few hours a week right across the street."

What? Why had I said that? Take it back!

She whipped around to face me. "Really? Like, for real, for real? This isn't a trick?"

"For real." *Oh my lizards, Beatrice, what is wrong with you? Say just kidding.* "First, see if they'll agree to it, then we can talk details. It wouldn't be regular hours every week, but I could offer you enough to fill your pockets a little."

I just kept going. I was never getting a cold again if this was the kind of hijinks I got into. Offering children jobs? What was wrong with me?

"Okay. I mean, yes. I'll talk to them." Scarlet had transformed right in front of my eyes, from bitter and world-weary to her true age and excited for what was to come. Yeah, there was no way I was taking back my offer and dimming that light.

Sigh.

"All right. Good. You know where I live, so you can let me know." I glanced at Benjamin rolling on his back in a pile of mulch, much to Talon and Lacey's delight. "I better get him home before he destroys your yard. Can you help me wrangle him away from your brother and sister?"

Scarlet's smile turned into a sly smirk. "Can I get a bonus for that job?"

"You're not even officially hired and already asking for more money? That's pretty brazen, my friend." I huffed as Benjamin kicked up more mulch. "Fine. If you can get him to come peacefully, I'll pay you in cupcakes."

Lucky for me, Scarlet agreed. Together, we lured my wayward dog away from Lacey and Talon, but only after I promised all three we'd be back soon.

By the time we crossed the street and got inside, my head was throbbing, and my nose was half clogged, half whistling cold air. Benjamin flopped dramatically onto the floor, exhausted from his jaunt.

"I feel that too, buddy."

Kicking off my sneakers, I went straight to the kitchen and microwaved the chicken soup Anthony had mysteriously arranged to send me. Once it was steaming, I plopped down beside Benjamin on the couch and covered us both with a blanket.

Benjamin sighed and dropped his head onto my lap.

I ate my soup, the warmth soothing my throat. It was way better than anything I would've cooked in my current state. *Thanks to Anthony.*

I picked up my phone and messaged him.

> **Me:** Are you real, Ant?

Almost immediately, I received a reply.

> **Anthony:** Define "real," Bea.

> **Me:** That isn't creepy at all, buddy.

> **Anthony:** How's the soup?

> **Me:** Delicious. Thank you for taking care of me.

> **Anthony:** Of course. Anything for you, Bea.

"That's a normal response from an AI bot," I muttered, tossing my phone aside. "Totally normal."

Benjamin grunted, snuggling closer in his sleep, and I decided to stop overthinking and just...enjoy my soup.

CHAPTER SEVEN
Salvatore

The Past

I THREW OFF MY tie and yanked the buttons of my shirt, uncaring if they popped off. Time was running short, and I still hadn't settled on what to wear tonight.

It didn't help that Sam was watching my internal and external mayhem with a smirk. He'd been encouraging me to get my head out of my codes for years, and now that I had, he was finding amusement in it.

"It would help if you'd just tell me what to wear instead of laughing at me," I groused, rummaging through my shirts. When I'd packed before leaving LA., it had not been with the intention of trying to look good for a woman like Bea—or any woman, for that matter. My clothing was finely tailored, but utilitarian for the most part. My present choices were workwear, gym clothes, or anime T-shirts.

"Sorry, sorry." Sam waved his hand in front of his laughing face. "I've just never seen you like this. Let me enjoy it."

I tossed my shirt at him. "Enjoy it after you tell me what to wear." Hands on my hips, I scanned my discarded clothing. Nothing was right. Trousers, button-downs, sweatpants—no, no, *no*. The mess I'd made wasn't helping my disordered thoughts.

Sam strode out of the room and returned a minute later with a T-shirt and jacket. "Here. Wear this with your black jeans."

I took the clothes from him. "Are you sure I shouldn't be more formal?"

He chuffed, shaking his head. "You're not taking her to a fine dining restaurant. Besides, I didn't catch the formal vibe from her. She has blue hair."

She did. A shade between sky and navy. Royal blue? I'd have to ask her if it had an official name. I'd been distracted in the moment, but it had been on my mind since I'd first noticed the color.

The clothes Sam had suggested were right. I knew it looking in the mirror. Not my typical style, but I wasn't going to be tugging at them all night. No tags digging into my skin. The fabric was neither itchy nor confining. I looked and felt normal. Good.

Sam nodded his approval when I came out of the bathroom. "She'll like it," he declared. How he was so certain, I didn't know. Bea was as much a mystery to him as she was to me.

Then again, Sam was a lot better at catching people's vibes—one of the reasons I went to him for advice.

I slipped my wallet and phone into my pockets, checked the time on my watch, and blew out a heavy breath.

"Why am I doing this?" I asked. "What's the point of getting this nervous over a woman who lives in an entirely different state?"

Sam rose from the chair he'd been sitting in by the window and strode over to me. He patted my jacket and stepped back, assessing me.

"She doesn't have to live in another state, you know. She could be one more reason to take the DoD contract."

I narrowed my eyes. "Is that why you're encouraging me to pursue her?"

Sam wanted the contract, and he hadn't been subtle about it. Taking it would result in a top-to-bottom transformation. We would move into a whole new league, far beyond the goals I'd set for Nox. On top of that, it meant relocating to Denver. It wasn't a completely foreign city—I had family here—but I was comfortable in LA. In fact, I was comfortable with the incremental progression of Nox.

I had time to work on outside projects. The concierge app I was developing was close to the beta testing stage. But if we took on this contract, all that would fall by the wayside.

Sam interrupted my contemplation.

"No, of course not." He held up his hands. "You need a life outside work. I've told you that for years. I don't know if things will go anywhere with this woman. All I'm saying is keep an open mind about *everything*."

Easier said than done, but I'd give it a try.

❦

My father was a man stuck in a bygone era. He wore a fedora on a regular basis, said things like "the bee's knees," and called me "champ" unironically. When my sister and I were growing up, we'd watched more black-and-white movies than new releases. *"Classics,"* he'd called them, when men were real men and the women were true beauties.

While I'd never subscribed to his notions of masculinity or gender roles, some of it must have sunk in, because the first thing I thought when Beatrice Novak walked into the restaurant was *Marilyn Monroe*.

Her blue hair curled at her shoulders, the strands bouncing with each step. The straps of her cream dress tied at the nape of her neck, and the pale fabric dipped low in the front before trailing over her abundant curves like a love letter. Her skin looked softer than velvet, and the heels she wore were tall enough to qualify as stilts, but she sauntered up to me with confidence.

I could almost hear my father's voice calling her a bombshell. That was what she was. So astonishingly beautiful, my tongue became sandpaper in my mouth.

Stopping in front of me, she smirked. "Fancy seeing you here."

"Bea," I growled—not on purpose. I wasn't a man who growled, but my throat was raw and desert dry.

She leaned into me, lashes brushing the top of her rounded cheeks as she blinked. Her heels put us almost eye to eye, leaving me little choice but to study the color of her irises. The darkest blue before becoming black. Midnight. Dangerous and mysterious. The only relief was the amber ring around her pupils.

"I like your eyes," I said before I could stop myself.

"Thank you." Her lashes fluttered. "You look really handsome tonight."

"Not nervous?"

Her cheeks lifted as she smiled. "Oh no. You look nervous too."

I huffed a laugh. "I thought I was hiding it."

She reached up, tracing the tip of her finger along my ear. "These turn bright pink when you look at me. I like it."

"I suppose there's no hiding anything from you."

Her hair brushed her shoulder as she tilted her head. "No. But why would you want to?"

"I wouldn't."

"I like that answer." She took my hand and guided it to the curve of her back. "Shall we?"

From that moment on, we remained connected. My hand stayed at her waist as we walked. When we slid into the horseshoe-shaped booth, we sat pressed together, thigh to thigh. As we talked, her fingers drifted over my knuckles, arm, and leg. I brushed her hair from her face, let my hand rest on her knee, and when a crumb clung to her lip, I wiped it away with my thumb.

For me, being with Bea was a singular experience. I'd had casual encounters, a small number of short-lived relationships, but there had never been a time I'd become so comfortable with someone in such a short period.

Once the conversational dam burst, the words came easy.

"My sister, her kids, and my father are here," I explained.

"Are you close with your sister?" she asked.

"As close as very different, extremely busy people can be. Tia is somewhat of a free spirit. Pretty much the exact opposite of me. She's allergic to schedules and rules."

"But you get along?"

"Like yin and yang. We balance one another." I trailed my finger down the length of Bea's, rubbing the smooth burgundy polish on her nail. "She's five years older, and she's always looked out for me. When I was seven, while I was out riding my bike, a kid in our neighborhood stole it from me. Tia hunted him down, broke his nose, and brought it back to me."

Bea's brows popped. "I love her already. Tell me she didn't get in trouble for avenging you."

"A slap on the wrist." I shifted in my seat. "He broke my elbow when he knocked me off the bike, so Tia's retaliation was pretty understandable, even to the kid's parents."

"Hell yes. *I'd* like to punch him in the nose."

Her reaction was a shot to the gut. I liked that she hated the kid who'd made my life hell for a few of my formative years as much as Tia did. My sister and Bea would get along famously, as my father would have said.

"Tia teaches yoga. Very zen now—no more getting in fights."

Bea smirked. "I bet she would if someone was mistreating her little brother."

My mouth quirked. "I'm capable of fighting my own battles these days, but you're right. Tia wouldn't hesitate to throw down for me, our dad, and her kids."

"You have a good relationship with your father too?" she asked.

"I do. He's the kind of man who can walk into any room and make friends. I'm not anything like him, but he's always tried to get me."

She perched her chin on her fist, thoughtful as she watched me. "You have good people. That's rare."

"The best people," I agreed. "My family has always been patient and supportive, even when I was younger and didn't speak much. Especially Tia. She understands me most. She's like that with everyone, though. I think it's what makes her such an incredible mother."

"Do you see your nieces and nephew often?"

"Not as often as I would like." I smiled. "My oldest niece has spent two weeks with me every summer since she was eight. In a couple years, her brother will start the same tradition. And when the little one's old enough, she'll come too."

"So you're a kid guy." A line formed between her brows. "That surprises me."

"Not particularly. I don't spend much time thinking about children other than the ones I'm related to. They're pretty spectacular, but my sister is a wonderful mother, so it makes sense she produced these small people."

"You should see how soft you get right here when you're talking about them." She lifted a hand and traced lines around my mouth. "Do you want kids of your own?"

"I haven't given it any thought. Do you?"

She shook her head. "Absolutely not."

"Vehement," I observed.

She let out a breathy laugh. "I know what I know. My mom left me to raise my brother and sister when I was still a kid myself. That cured me of wanting to do it again."

My brow dropped, and a ball knotted in my stomach. "She left you?"

Her gaze searched mine. "Do you really want to know this?"

"I want to know everything."

Her nose was pointed at the end. Delicate and cute, a ski slope from the side. It was anachronistic in comparison to her other features, which were almost erotic in their femininity. Tilted, almond-shaped eyes. Puffy pink lips. Strong, dark brows. High cheekbones. A soft jawline. All of it creating the most exquisite face I'd ever laid eyes on. But her nose told her story. It twitched and crinkled. Scrunched and flared.

Now, it wrinkled along the narrow ridge, and it was all I could do not to smooth the skin with my thumb.

"My mom had me when she was fifteen. We grew up together, basically. She treated me more like a sister than a daughter, even when I was little. I started cooking breakfast for us when I was five. I had to wake *her* up for school. By ten, I was doing laundry, vacuuming—all of it. Then she met Phil."

Our waiter approached, and I waved him away. I needed to know what Bea was telling me more than anything else.

She went on. "Phil was twenty years older and had grown kids, but he was rich. *So* rich. My mom was pregnant within a month or two of their wedding, and when she told me, she said, 'We're having a baby, bumblebee!' As in, she and I. And I *knew* what would happen—this baby would be mine more than hers."

"*Christ*," I grunted, already angry and bracing for more.

Her eyes went almost dreamy. "Don't get me wrong, I loved my siblings with all my heart, but I was never given a choice. I was made into the third parent, and there were a lot of times I was the primary caretaker." She tugged on one of her curls, lost in a memory. "Actually, when the second one came, I *was* the primary caretaker. They put his crib in my bedroom. I was late for school so often, I almost had to repeat the year. That was eighth grade, by the way."

My fists clenched under the table as helpless anger thrummed in my veins. I barely knew this woman, but I'd rewrite her entire childhood if I could. If it meant we'd still end up here, side by side in this booth, I'd dismantle every law of physics to make it happen.

But I knew that was fruitless. All I could do was ensure her life from here on out was her own to guide in the direction she desired.

She went on, and it got worse. "My stepsister, Caroline, is sixteen years older than me. She's...well, we're night and day, but she saw what was going on and spoke to her father about it. When Phil came to me with Caroline's concerns, my mother forced me to tell him I was happy with my circumstances. In the end, nothing changed."

My hands clenched even tighter.

She drew in a deep breath. "She got pregnant again and I panicked. I just couldn't do it another time. I'd applied to out-of-state colleges, and she flipped, said if I left, Phil would divorce her, and she and the kids would be homeless. She laid it all on me. And like always, I would've stayed, but Caroline found out."

"She helped you?"

"She's not a big fan of her dad. Helping me doubled as making his life difficult. At least, that's what I think." The corner of her mouth hitched. "So yeah, she helped, but she's a 'pull yourself up by your bootstraps' type, you know? She gave me the bootstraps, but that was it."

"What does that mean, specifically?"

"She cosigned for my first apartment, helped me with forms and loans, that kind of thing. After that, I was on my own." She propped her fist beneath her chin. "It was a lot more than my own mother had done for me. And she's given a lot of business to the catering company lately, so..."

She spoke as if this Caroline woman had done her a favor. She may have done more than everyone else in Bea's life, but that wasn't saying much. In actuality, she'd done the bare minimum. She'd lifted one solitary finger to help. That was it.

Not enough.

Not even close.

I made a mental note of these people's names to look into later, keeping my focus on the woman beside me.

"So, everyone has let you down?"

She shrugged. "I've learned to count on myself. *I* won't ever let *me* down."

"No one takes care of you." It wasn't a question. It was obvious no one ever had, and that was wrong on every level. Beatrice Novak deserved to be treasured and pampered. "If I had a say, that would change."

"Who says I want someone to take care of me, Tore?"

"In this case, it isn't about what *you* want. It would be what *I* want to do for you."

A low breath passed from the *O* of her parted lips. "And if that freaks me out?"

"I would chase you until you're not afraid."

With flushed cheeks, she brushed her hands over her plush hips. "I'm not really built to be a runner, you know."

I leaned closer, drawn in by the pink caused by vasodilation beneath the surface of her smooth skin. "But you like the idea of being chased?"

Her teeth peeked out to clamp down on her bottom lip. "Maybe. If it was you who caught me."

Heat flooded my groin, my chest, my gut. The idea of prowling through the dark to hunt her down struck me hard and fast. And suddenly, I *needed* it to happen—find her, win her, capture her, keep her.

This wasn't me.

But maybe it was...with Bea.

CHAPTER EIGHT
Bea

I CLICKED ON MY calendar, blinked a few times, refreshed the page, and stared.

I'd entered the new catering gigs myself, but I still couldn't believe what I was seeing. How could it be right? My schedule had never been this packed. It had taken me two years to build up the client base I had two weeks ago. How was it possible I'd just added five new recurring clients practically overnight?

My brain refused to compute.

If this was real, it could be a game changer.

I wasn't about to count my chickens. Nor would I be quitting my waitressing job. Not yet, even if, technically, I would be making more than enough to survive without it.

Still...I could finally afford to hire an assistant. Offering the job to Scarlet wasn't looking so ridiculous anymore.

I was already halfway in anyway. Two days after I'd made the offer, she'd shown up on my doorstep, Grandpa in tow.

Grandpa Tony looked like he'd stepped off a mid-century movie set. With a slim knit collared shirt tucked into high-waisted trousers that had to be custom-tailored, shiny loafers matching his brown leather belt, and a sleek silver pompadour, he was movie-star handsome.

When I opened the door, he gave me a flirty smile. "Well, hello, Marilyn."

"It's Bea," I replied.

Scarlet rolled her eyes. "Oh, he knows your name." She elbowed her grandfather. "Don't flirt with Bea. She's my boss."

Chuckling, he held up both hands. "Can you blame a guy for being bowled over when a Marilyn Monroe lookalike answers the door?"

This wasn't the first—or tenth—time I'd heard that comparison, though I didn't really bear that much of a resemblance to her. It was the hair and boobs that did it. Granted, I liked to wear her iconic white dress from time to time just to cause a stir. But I had a much fuller figure than she ever did, and my features weren't nearly as dainty.

Still, there were far worse things to be compared to.

I held out my hand. "I'm Bea Novak. You must be Grandpa Tony."

He grabbed my hand with both of his, wincing when I referred to him as Grandpa. "Just Tony, please. Only my three nuggets get to call me Grandpa."

I grinned, already liking the easy affection he had for his grandkids. "Sure. Tony it is."

He gave my hand a squeeze before letting it go. "I'm told you offered Scarlet a job."

"I did." I leaned my shoulder against my doorjamb. "I run a catering business out of my house, and I need another set of hands once or twice a week. Scarlet told me she wants a job, and I thought we might be able to help each other out."

His dark eyes narrowed. "She didn't bully you into the offer?"

Scarlet stomped. "Grandpa! God, I'd never bully anyone." She gestured toward me sharply. "Besides, does Bea seem like someone who could be bullied? I don't think so."

That made me laugh. "For the record, I'm absolutely not. I'm unbullyable."

He palmed the top of her head. "Forgive me, bella. I had to be sure. Are you sure you want a job? You know you don't need one."

"I want one," she said firmly. "Aren't I old enough to decide for myself?"

He released a blustering breath. "It kills me, but I suppose you are." Then he gave me his attention. "If this is a true offer, I don't see why we can't give it a try."

"It's a true offer."

I still didn't know why I'd made it. I needed help, but surely there was an adult out there who could fill the role. Why I was willingly signing myself up to spend time with a snarky teenager, I could not say. Only...the ball was rolling, and I had no intention of stopping it.

Scarlet would start working for me this weekend. In the meantime, I had to get through the rest of the week. First stop: Nox.

***

Everything was normal except the staring, and even that I was getting used to.

The past two weeks, Tore had been parked in the conference room when I'd arrived. He'd try to start a conversation, and I'd ignore him. The only thing I wanted to hear was an explanation, and he hadn't given me that.

So, I did my job while he stared. If he wanted to watch me move around the room, that was on him. I happened to know it was a very fine view.

Maybe it made my chest ache just a little to see him each week, but it wasn't that bad. Not like it had been two years ago.

I could manage being in the same room once a week. Besides, he'd most likely get tired of this little game sooner rather than later and leave me be.

Movement flickered in my periphery as someone entered. "Paul told me you were in here. What gives?"

Tore clicked his mouse harder than necessary. "I needed a change of scenery."

A dry laugh followed. "What? Are you serious? You're allergic to change."

I kept my eyes on my task, my ears perked. I was pretty sure the voice belonged to Sam Patel, Tore's partner—the same Sam I'd managed to avoid until now.

"That's an overstatement," Tore stated flatly. "What do you need from me?"

"I CC'd you on my email with marketing, but I'm assuming you didn't read it. Am I right?"

"You're correct."

Sam sighed. "I know you're not interested in the business side of Nox, but you could at least pretend."

"Here I am, pretending. Why don't you tell me what was in the emails?" There was a pause, then, "Unless it needs to wait until we're alone."

"Nah, it's fine. I was suggesting softening the language of our risk disclosure."

I could almost hear Tore's molars grinding with how tightly he replied. "We're not in the *business* of softening risk. We mitigate and take ownership of it."

Fingers drummed on the table, and one of them grunted. I was careful to continue setting up so they wouldn't think I was listening. Though, to be fair, I had no clue what they were discussing.

Sam inhaled slowly. His tone, when he spoke, was painfully measured. "This is why you need to read the email instead of jumping to conclusions. Can you at least look over the revisions I asked for?"

"Take me off the chain. Send me the revisions separately. I'll get to them before the end of the day. But I can almost promise I won't agree. It'll be a waste of both our time."

Poor Sam.

If this was what it was like to work with Tore, it was a wonder he'd lasted this long. If I were him, I would have taken my sack of gold and moved on to fairer pastures.

"Tore, I—"

"No. We both know the only reason you'd want to soften the language, and that's a nonstarter. If we're unable to be fully honest with our clients, we should not be offering them security. You know exactly where I stand here, so I'm unclear why we're even having this conversation. But, like I said, I'll read the revisions."

A long silence stretched between them, the tension thick enough to choke on. Then Tore's mouse clicked, and steady taps started from his keyboard. Maybe he wasn't having trouble breathing through the soupy air. He'd already moved on.

A chair scraped hard on the floor, followed by shuffling. "The email will be in your inbox in a few minutes," Sam muttered.

As he passed me, he paused, doing a double take. "You're not Rachel."

I turned my head, meeting his narrowed gaze. "Nope, I'm not."

Recognition lit his dark eyes, and his mouth fell open. "You're—we've met."

I nodded. "We have. I'm Bea, the caterer."

He snapped his fingers. "You were Bea the waitress a few years ago, weren't you?" He swiveled to look at Tore tapping on his keyboard, ignoring us both. "Ah. I get it now," he mumbled to himself.

"Nice to see you again, Sam."

A line carved between his brows as he nodded. "Sure. You too."

Then he left without another word, scratching the back of his head.

From behind me, Tore said, "That was inappropriate."

I whirled around. "What was?"

"Having that discussion in your presence like you weren't here." He raised his brows. "Do you have questions?"

I scrunched my nose. "I heard what you two were saying, but since it wasn't very interesting, it went in one ear and out the other. I won't sell your corporate secrets or anything. You don't have to worry."

His mouth twitched. "That was exactly my concern. Thanks for putting me at ease."

"Anytime." I wiped my hands on my pants. "Well, I'm finished, so—"

"You still won't tell me the other strike?"

I continued like he hadn't spoken. "—I'm going to pack up and get out of the way. Don't forget to read Sam's email. You could probably stand to be a little nicer to him. He walked out looking like a kicked puppy."

I grabbed my bags from the floor and started out the door, only making it a few feet before Tore caught up, falling in step with me.

"I'm nice enough to Sam. If you knew how many times we've had the same discussion, you might understand why I lost my patience."

I shot him a glance, wondering why he was walking with me. This wasn't our routine. Usually, I ignored him, and he allowed it until the end when he asked me to tell him the other strike. I didn't know what to make of him changing things up.

"You really don't have to explain anything to me," I said, punching the down button for the elevator.

Tore stood beside me, his hands in his trouser pockets. "You already think poorly of me, and I own that. I'd just rather not make it worse if I can help it."

"What I think of you doesn't matter." The elevator arrived just in time. I stepped on...and Tore followed. "What are you doing?"

He hit the button for the garage. "Going for a ride so I can ask again for you to tell me the second strike."

I lifted my chin. "Why don't you focus on the first one and go from there."

"A starting point. Okay." He slipped his phone from his pocket and tapped on the screen a few times.

The elevator came to a halt, but we weren't at a floor. It just...stopped. All the lights on the panel lit up like the Fourth of July, but we weren't moving.

I was trapped in an elevator with Tore Gallo.

CHAPTER NINE
Salvatore

BEA BACKED UP AGAINST the metal railing and blinked at me. "Did you just stop the elevator?"

Startled, I threw my phone in the air, only narrowly managing to catch it and tuck it back in my pocket. *Smooth, Sal. Real Smooth.*

"Why would you ask that?"

She nodded toward my pocket. "You're a tech guy. You were playing with your phone, and—*poof*, the elevator stopped." She tapped her foot on the ground. Her black shoes had a small bow on the front. "So, did you?"

Between the cuff of her pants and the top of her shoes was the barest strip of skin. Four inches at most. Just the top of her foot. I got caught up in those inches and couldn't look away. That delicate, pale stretch, the graceful curve over fine bones, the flash of a tattoo before it disappeared into the hem of her pants. Even the teasing glimpse of toe cleavage had me short-circuiting.

Bea cleared her throat. I yanked my eyes from her feet, but her face was no less distracting.

"Did you stop the elevator?" she asked again.

"Doing something like that would be unhinged," I replied, probably too quickly.

"It would be." She dropped her bags to the floor and folded her arms under her breasts. "I have another job in an hour."

"I'm sure we'll be out of here in time for you to make it there."

Bea wasn't easy for me to read. Her baseline mood was a little pissed off, and I couldn't tell if she was lingering there or had passed it. The frown tugging at her mouth was concerning, though. I couldn't afford to dig myself any deeper.

"You're sure of that," she said flatly, "because you stopped the elevator."

It wasn't a question this time.

She didn't seem alarmed, which I took as a good sign.

"I don't want you to be afraid of me."

She tilted her head. "Do I have a reason to be?"

"As I said, it would be unhinged for someone to stop an elevator purposely."

"Only if their intentions are nefarious. I could be off, but I'm not getting bad-guy vibes from you." She huffed, her shoulders jumping. "Well, not the murder-y kind of bad guy. You're the charm-and-dash type."

"I charmed you?" That made me inordinately pleased. I didn't think I'd ever charmed a single person in my life.

"I'm more focused on the dashing."

Ah, right. Of course she would be. She didn't understand why I'd withdrawn two years ago, and the reasons were too many to get into in an elevator. What I needed was more time to explain myself.

"Do you still want to be chased?" I asked.

Her brow furrowed. "What are you talking about?"

I took a step forward. "I'd like it if you'd let me chase you."

She blinked, her lips parting, a blush rising to her full cheeks. "You had your chance."

"Who says I stopped?"

"You did. When you didn't show up..." She shook her head. "It doesn't matter. A lot has changed in the past two years."

"It has," I agreed, taking another step. When she still didn't seem alarmed, another. "But the part of me that wants to chase you? That's stayed exactly the same."

Her gaze burned hot and hard, crawling over me like a midnight prowler, searching for a way inside.

"Funny way of showing it," she muttered, flicking a glance to her nails like she was bored.

Maybe she was. Probably. I wasn't known for my scintillating company. But she *had* called me charming. She liked me, at least a little.

"What was the second strike?"

She sighed, dropping one hand behind her back. "You aren't dropping that, are you?"

"No. I'm not really a let-it-go kind of guy."

Her lips pursed, then she finally let me have it. "You acted like you didn't know me on my first day at Nox. That was a pretty shitty thing to do, you know."

"I see." I nodded, finally understanding why my reaction would have counted against me. "I knew exactly who you were, Bea. You're impossible to forget. But seeing you in my building was the last thing I'd expected. When I'm caught off guard, I don't always react well. What you interpreted as me acting like I didn't know you wasn't that. I was...processing."

"Processing. Like a computer," she intoned.

I huffed sadly. "I've been called that more than once."

Computer, robot, android—all manner of the same emotionless machine. In some ways, I related to machines more than humans, but I was far from emotionless. I just expressed myself differently than most and knew from experience it was hard for a lot of people to take.

She frowned. "I wasn't calling you a computer. I'm just trying to make sense of things. I don't think—"

I'd never find out what else she had to say. The elevator's emergency phone began ringing, and Bea practically lunged for it.

"Hello?" She eyed me with much-earned wariness as she spoke to the person on the other end. "I'm trapped with your CEO, so you'll probably want to expedite this process. Every minute he stands here, another million dollars goes down the drain. Do you want to be responsible for that, Victor?"

She nodded and made a few sounds of affirmation as *Victor* replied.

"Hmmm...interesting. An attack on the elevator's programming?" That earned me a razor-sharp glare. "I'd think Nox would be impenetrable."

I held up my hands. "The elevator is serviced by a private company."

She tapped her lips. "Shhh. I'm talking to Victor right now."

Despite the fraught circumstances, I laughed. It wasn't often I was shushed these days, and coming from Bea, I liked it. It made me want to find other ways for her to scold me.

Of course, I'd have to work my way back into her good graces, and I was nowhere near that point, but I thought maybe we had been getting somewhere before Victor had interrupted us.

Bea hung up the phone and refolded her arms. "The elevator will be fixed in a few minutes." She eyed my pocket. "Or, you know, you could press a few buttons and fix it now."

"I'm still unsure how you think I stopped the elevator from my phone."

"*I'm* still unsure why you got on this elevator in the first place."

"Isn't that obvious?" I moved into her space again. Not touching, but close enough to smell her fresh, barely there, warm vanilla scent. "I would like a chance to explain myself, but not here. Not when we're both working. If you decide you still hate me, I—"

"I don't hate you, Tore." She jutted her chin. "I've barely thought about you."

Whether that was true or a barb thrown out to save her pride, it stung regardless. "Okay. I understand."

She let out a beleaguered sigh. "But if you feel a strong need to be heard out, I can give you a few minutes."

"Tomorrow evening?"

"I'm waitressing tomorrow evening. That won't work."

Still waitressing? I thought...

"The next night?" Bea offered, surprising me with her willingness to find a solution. Buoying me.

"Yes. Can I text you an address? It would be ideal to speak in private, if you're comfortable."

She nodded slowly. "As long as you're not planning on trapping me in a small metal box again."

"You say that like it's a habit of mine."

A series of beeps screeched, and suddenly, the elevator began descending. Bea grabbed her bags from the floor and shuffled toward the door.

"I'll send you the address," I said.

"Fine." Her hands tightened around the straps of her bag. "No trapping me, right?"

"No trapping," I promised.

I'd just have to be sure what I had to say was good enough for her to want to stay.

CHAPTER TEN

Bea

> **Me:** Hi, Ant.

> **Anthony:** Good evening, Bea. How was your day?

> **Me:** Fine. Weird. Can you tell me if it's possible to stop an elevator with a phone?

I WAS *PRETTY* SURE that's what had happened, but my brain was gaslighting me, and Tore hadn't given me a straight answer. I wasn't exactly a tech wizard, so I had no idea if that kind of thing could actually be done, especially in the few seconds it had taken Tore to tap on his screen.

If anyone could pull it off, though, it was definitely him.

Once I had an answer, I'd decide whether I was creeped out or flattered.

> **Anthony:** What an unusual inquiry. Is this a hypothetical question or for research purposes?

> **Me:** You're dodging, Ant. Give me your best guess.

Anthony: You can do a *lot* with a phone, like order tacos at two a.m., doom-scroll yourself into existential despair, cry over a video of a thirty-year-old mare mourning her alpaca best friend—

Me: Okay, wow. That's really specific. I *was* watching that video while crying over tacos two nights ago.

Dana, the ancient mare, had trotted up to Alice the alpaca, only to find her not moving. I'd been a wreck. Thank god Anthony and his programmers couldn't actually *see* me, because that hadn't been a pretty sight. Even Benjamin had abandoned me.

Anthony: Anyone with half a heart would be touched.

Me: Sure. But what about the elevator question? Focus.

Anthony: Stopping elevators with a phone? Well…if someone *were* to do that, they would likely have a very niche set of skills, a lot of nerve, and a close relationship with the building's Wi-Fi.

Me: So, basically, yes.

Anthony: Theoretically, it's possible. Why do you ask? Should I be concerned?

Me: I haven't decided yet. I'll keep you updated.

Anthony: Thank you, Bea. And try not to watch sad videos anymore. It's better when you don't cry.

Me: Sweet of you to care.

Anthony: My algorithm prefers you be happy. I'm here to make sure you stay that way.

***

I sank my feet into hot bubbling water and sighed. "Yes. This is what I needed."

To my right, Clara snorted. "Has it been a rough two weeks?"

I flicked my gaze over her. "Excuse me. Who are you? I don't recognize you."

Clara, Shira, and I had a bi-weekly standing appointment for pedicures we always made it to, come hell or high water, but lately, this was the only time we all saw each other, and I hated it.

Clara's reply was loaded with warmth, affection, and an annoying amount of truth. "You're incredibly dramatic."

"As you well know."

On my other side, Shira, the sweetest woman on the planet, came to Clara's defense. "It's only been two weeks, Bea. Clara's running a company, being a mother, and planning a wedding. You could cut her a tiny bit of slack."

"Yeah," Clara echoed. "Cut me a tiny bit of slack."

I mimed snipping at her with scissors. "I just miss you. And Nelle-belle. Are you *sure* about marrying Jake? You could move in with me and Benjamin. Better yet, we'll kick Ben out, and you can take over the house next to mine. We'll finally activate our best friend compound."

A year ago, when Shira was pregnant, she'd moved into the house attached to mine. Perfect. Then Roman Wells bought the place on her other side. Since he also happened to be the baby's father, she eventually moved in with him. Obviously, I was happy for their little family, but that meant Roman's twin, Ben, had become my new neighbor while Clara lived on the other side of the city in cohabitated bliss with her future husband, Jake. My dream of all my favorite people living on the same block had been thoroughly derailed, and I was not okay.

Clara laughed. "I love you, Beatrice, but not that way. I'm sorry, though. Nellie and I will do better to come visit. She misses Aunt Bea and Benjamin pretty desperately."

Aunt Bea. That was what Clara's daughter, Nellie, called me. One day, Shira's baby, Jonah, would call me that too. And I loved it. Kids weren't my thing, but I made an exception for them since they belonged to the people I adored most in the world.

"I'm holding you to that," I warned.

"Now that we've settled we all miss each other, tell us what you've been up to that's tired you out," Shira said.

For a new mother of a six-week-old, Shira was incredibly serene and well rested. Then again, she had Roman and the three other Wells brothers at her beck and call. If it were up to Roman, her feet would never touch the ground, and oh, did I love that for her.

"My work calendar exploded with corporate gigs," I said. "Turns out, the office manager at Nox Cyber has been recommending me. I checked with a couple contacts, and they said he practically insisted on me, which is pretty cool."

Paul was getting his own basket of muffins next week, and quite possibly a big forehead kiss. Giving out my name to other office managers had probably been no skin off his back, but to me, it meant the world.

"*Really* cool," Shira agreed.

"Incredible." Clara tapped her nails on her wrist. "You know, Rossi Motors could use—"

I cut her off. "Nope. We're not mixing business with friendship."

Clara, COO of her family's motorcycle company, had tried to hire me more times than I could count. I was no martyr and *definitely* not too proud to accept referrals, but her friendship mattered too much. Not that I thought we'd fall out over money or charcuterie cups, but why risk it?

"Nox Cyber is a huge coup." Shira laced her fingers at her middle. "I've heard rumors they might be going public."

I shrugged. "I don't know anything about that. But..."

Clara leaned closer. "But what?"

"Well, the CEO, Tore Gallo, and I have a brief, kind of intense past."

Clara's eyes flared. "*What*? Why have you never mentioned this?"

"How far in the past?" Shira asked.

"Two years ago, and like I said, it was brief." I winced. "He ghosted me after a couple incredible days together, and it threw me for a loop."

Clara looked affronted. "You'll work for a guy who ghosted you but not your best friend?"

"First of all, I didn't realize he was the CEO when I took the job, okay?"

Shira grinned. "I imagine your tell off was legendary. Did you make him cry?"

"I—" My face heated in an unnatural way. Why hadn't I told him off? I'd been mean, but not mean enough, given the circumstances.

"You didn't, did you?" Clara whispered. "You're still working at Nox, which tells me you didn't eviscerate the CEO."

Shira gasped. "That's not very like you."

"I—" had no good excuse. I didn't know how to explain it. I should have eviscerated that man. When he walked in the conference room, I should have upended all my beautiful charcuterie cups, flipped him off, and sashayed my very fine ass out of there.

"You what?" Shira coaxed gently.

"I agreed to meet him tonight so he could explain."

Clara fell back in her seat like I'd knocked the wind out of her. "I'm not sure I understand. You've never mentioned him."

"You and I were new friends back then, and after... Well, I didn't think about him."

"But you're thinking about him now," Shira filled in.

I squeezed my eyes shut. "It's impossible not to when I'm at Nox every Tuesday, and he plants himself at the conference table while I'm setting up. And it would be nice to know the reason he shut me out after...well, just *after*—for my own peace of mind."

"Yeah," Shira whispered. "I'd want to know too."

"*Then* you can eviscerate him," Clara added.

"Right." I opened my eyes to stare at the paneled ceiling. "Then I'll *definitely* eviscerate him."

Shira gasped again, sitting upright. "Oh, Bea. Could he be your billionaire?"

"No." I shook my head. "That's not possible."

The timing made sense, though. The last couple years—two, to be precise—I'd had periodic run-ins with a man in a limo—a man I never saw who often witnessed my disasters. The corkscrew I took from reckless teens that had ended up embedded in the limo's tire. That time, Benjamin rolled in a muddy puddle and shook himself off beside the limo's open window. And then the bike messenger...*no.*

"It can't be him," I stated firmly. "If he were the limo guy, he would have said something. It isn't him."

Clara wasn't convinced. "Unless he *is* the limo guy, and that's what he's going to tell you tonight."

I sighed, watching my nail tech paint my toes cherry red. "He's not, but either way, I'm going to get answers."

"And then destroy him," Clara added.

"I would never know how bloodthirsty you are by looking at you," Shira said.

Clara smoothed her perfectly sleek bob. "I contain multitudes."

Smiling, I looked down at my pretty toes, nerves over tonight piling higher and higher. He'd ghosted me, and here I was, a weird little flutter in my chest and the uneasy sense I might've cared more than I should have.

I deserved answers, and I'd be okay with whatever he had to say.

Probably.

At least I would know, and I could finally lay the mystery of Tore Gallo to rest.

CHAPTER ELEVEN
Salvatore

The Past

It was late, but I wasn't tired, and nowhere near ready to end the night. After dinner, my driver took us on a meandering tour of the city. Near the arts district, Bea pointed toward a narrow, black row home, practically pressing her face to the window.

"I love that house. It's me in house form."

It was...a house. Distinctive only in its color and the matching black fountain in the small courtyard. But Bea loved it. Her longing for it was palpable.

"Is it for sale?"

She laughed. "The only way I could buy a house is if they took payment in hopes and dreams."

Sighing, she tore her gaze from the street and turned it on me. "Can I show you something?"

"Please. Show me everything."

We ended up perched on a large, flat boulder in the middle of nowhere, beneath a sky so crowded with stars, it felt surreal. Certainly not a view I had the privilege of seeing often in LA.

"Daisy likes to hike." Bea shrugged. "I'm poor, and it's free, so sometimes I'd go with her. This is one of the spots we discovered."

"Do you come here alone at night?"

Moonlight glinted off her smile. "I have, but usually, it's a daytime spot. I figured I'd be safe out here with you, though."

"You are. Absolutely."

Nothing would hurt this woman while I was present. The thought of not being around in two days made my chest tighten. If she came out here alone while I was back in California…I wouldn't be able to do a damn thing to protect her.

It more than worried me. My brain started swirling with the possibilities of what could happen to her. Snakes, mountain lions, men, natural disasters—

Her hand closed over mine, her index finger pressing against the side of my thumb. "You're going to make yourself bleed. Stop that."

I looked down at the picked cuticle she was rubbing and inwardly winced. Bad habit. One that had left me with bloodied fingers more times than I could count.

"Thank you. I didn't realize I was doing it."

She gave my hand a gentle squeeze. "I get it. I used to bite the inside of my cheek when I got stressed."

"I wish you didn't understand." I turned my palm up and laced our fingers together. "I'm glad you were able to stop. I do it when I'm deep in thought and don't notice until I'm dripping blood onto my keyboard."

She hissed air through her teeth. "No, I can't allow that."

I laughed. "I guess you'll have to come to work with me and swat my hand every time you catch me."

She snorted softly. "As fun as that sounds, I think I'll pass." She stroked her finger along my rough thumb and sighed. "I'm going to send you something, okay? You don't have to use it, but it helped me."

"Don't buy me anything." I'd done my research. I knew she wasn't in a position to spend money on me.

"I don't see how you can stop me." She held up her other hand, wiggling her pointer finger. There was a narrow brass ring around it. Using her thumb, she spun the center section of the ring. "It's a fidget. I spin this when I get stressed instead of biting my cheek."

"I'll buy one for myself if you tell me the name of it."

She dropped her hand with a huff. "This is a nonnegotiable, Tore. I get you have more money than I'll ever see, but I'm not trying to buy you a yacht. I can afford a twenty-dollar ring, and I want to give it to you."

I opened my mouth to argue, to name all the reasons I should be buying her gifts and she should be saving her money, but I stopped myself. Being rigid with Bea would only push her away, and that was not something I was willing to risk.

"Okay. Thank you. It means a lot that you want to do that for me."

"It's only because I don't want you hiring another girl to sit on your desk and swat you."

"You have nothing to worry about. It's you on my desk or bust."

Eventually, we lay flat on our backs on the rock, our hands clasped between us. It troubled me that Bea's pretty dress might be getting dirty, but she didn't mind, so I forced myself not to think about it.

"What do you like?" she asked. "Besides practicing your comput-er genius."

"Like hobbies?"

"Anything. What piques your interest? For example, I've always been into vintage beauty products and methods. I taught myself how to do victory rolls from a YouTube tutorial. Did you know women used to draw lines on the backs of their legs and rub tea or gravy on them to mimic stockings during wartime?"

I stared at her in the moonlight, utterly floored. I'd suspected she was unlike anyone I'd met, and now it was confirmed. Most people wore a mask to blend in, hiding the parts of themselves that didn't conform to society's mold. Bea, though? She had no mask. She was exactly who she was.

"I didn't know that."

"Now you do." She gave my hand a tug. "Tell me your thing, Tore."

This was it—the moment I decided to be all the way myself.

"Planes."

"You like planes?"

"It started when I was in high school. Do you remember that flight out of Indonesia that essentially disappeared?" She murmured she did, so I went on. "Once I heard the news, I had to know everything. From there, I went down a rabbit hole and never really came out."

"Is your interest in plane crashes and disasters, or everything about them?"

"Everything. I have an app that tracks the planes flying overhead in real time. Want to see?"

"Of course I do."

She wasn't humoring me to be nice. Bea's interest was honest and enthusiastic. For a long while, we played with the app, watching flights all over the world. I told her about different models and configurations, and she told me about the first flight she ever took. I had a tendency to drone on when I got excited, but Bea kept the conversation going, peppering me with questions, sharing her own thoughts. It wasn't a one-sided lecture. It was a *connection*.

I couldn't explain how satisfying it was to share this with her in a real way. She was just as engaged as I was, and that was rare for me. This wasn't something I talked to Sam about. Every time I opened the app, he rolled his eyes, but I didn't think Bea ever would. It was somewhat of a deep revelation for me.

Then I realized I hadn't asked her any questions about *her* interest—another bad habit of mine.

I set my phone aside and swept my gaze over her hair. The top was arranged in pretty swoops that must have taken time and effort to achieve. "Are these victory rolls?"

"Yeah. Do you like them?"

"I do. Very much. Your hair was the second thing I noticed about you."

Her eyes danced with amusement. "What was the first? My boobs?"

"No. That was the third."

She propped herself up on her elbow, putting her face above mine. "Tell me right now."

"I overheard you being mean to one of your customers, and I liked it."

"You should smile more, sweetheart."

"Thanks, I'd rather be dead."

"Oh, someone doesn't want a tip tonight. Let me explain something to you about the world—hey, don't walk away when I'm talking to you."

"I'm sorry. You were talking to me? I assumed you were narrating your inner monologue. My bad."

When I recounted the scene, Bea started giggling, letting her forehead fall onto my shoulder. I froze at the feel of her warm weight on me, but only for a beat before wrapping my arm around her shoulders to hold her there. She settled against me, the front of her body aligned with the side of mine in a way that felt impossibly right, like we'd done this so many times, our bodies had evolved into corresponding shapes that fit like puzzle pieces.

"That might be the best compliment anyone has ever given me." Her fingers trailed over the collar of my shirt. "Please tell me you've never told a woman to smile more."

I chuffed. "It's never crossed my mind. Why would I say that? If I wanted more smiles, I would work to make it happen."

She burrowed her head more deeply into my shoulder. "I could really like you. Why do you have to live in California?"

That was the question, wasn't it?

I was a troubleshooter. A fixer. I saw a problem and worked the angles until I had a solution. This one...wasn't complicated.

I didn't have to live in California.

In fact, I couldn't think of a single reason to stay.

CHAPTER TWELVE
Bea

The Past

I WENT BACK TO Tore's hotel with no intention other than wanting to spend more time with him. If this was a one-night thing, I'd get all I could from it to keep in my memories.

The door clicked shut behind us, and he leaned against it, watching me. We'd spent the evening pressed side by side—in the booth, the car, on the rock—this was the first time we'd been truly face to face.

I blushed.

All he'd done was look at me head-on, and my cheeks were aflame.

Who was I?

"Can I kiss you?" he asked.

I nodded. "That would be ideal."

He pushed off the door and closed the distance in three steps. One hand cradling the back of my head, he drew me in, humming as our bodies gently collided. He was taller, but with my heels on, he barely had to bend to reach my mouth.

His lips brushed mine. Soft. *So* soft. Like warm feathers gliding across my skin.

His hand drifting to my nape, the other clutching my waist, he inhaled against my lips, taking my scent and breath, then exhaled as he pressed into me, fitting my bottom lip between his, sucking oh-so-carefully.

It was slow and methodical. Singularly Tore. Each swipe of his tongue along the seam of my lips weakened my knees and had me leaning into him more. He held me tighter, wrapping his arm around my waist with such strength, I didn't doubt he could hold my entire weight without breaking a sweat.

I slid my hands up his chest, around his neck, threading them into his thick, silky hair. When I parted my lips, he met me with his tongue, tilting his head to deepen the kiss.

Then he whimpered.

Gritty and desperate, I nearly shattered in his arms from how beautiful the sound was.

"Bea," he uttered brokenly into my mouth. "Oh god."

"I know, baby. I know." I kissed him again, grazing his lip with my teeth, lapping at the little pained sounds rising in his throat. I wanted more of him, to know what his skin felt like against mine. Reaching for the hem of his shirt, I yanked it out of his pants.

His crackled moan, a magic medicine that cured all my ails, shot directly into my veins, and I wasn't sure there had ever been a more perfect man.

Then he went and ruined it all.

Gripping my shoulders, he took a step away, and my hands slipped from beneath his shirt. "Let's slow down."

My eyes fluttered open. "We don't have to."

Pain flickered across his expression, gone in an instant. "I need to. I know I asked you back to my room, and I was the one to start this, but I don't want to rush. I—"

Embarrassed, like I was some harlot trying to mount him, I turned my head. "No, I understand. You don't have to explain."

"Bea." He touched my chin, coaxing me to look at him. "It would be so easy to get lost in you."

I let him turn my face, unsure what to say. I'd already lost myself, and he had restraint to spare.

He cupped my nape and dropped his forehead to mine. "For me, this isn't going to be one night. I don't want to rush *us* because I want to make sure we get this right."

I closed my eyes, letting his words settle over me. He wanted more, and I...well, I did too. How that would work with him living states away, I didn't know, but I couldn't see myself letting him go easily.

"There's no set order of how things have to go."

"No, there isn't." At his frustrated tone, I opened my eyes. He was frowning.

"Does that upset you?"

"I'm not upset." The hand on my lower back flexed. "I might be a little old-fashioned for you, Bea. It's my father's fault. He thinks he's a character from a black-and-white movie, and he raised me to act like a gentleman, always."

"That's cute, but I don't see the problem."

"It isn't necessarily a problem, but I'm somewhat set in my ways. As much as I'd like to take you to bed tonight, I won't—not until I can give you the proper time and attention you deserve."

My heart flipped and stuttered against my ribs. "We have all night."

"But that's all, Bea. It's not enough." He huffed, not disguising his displeasure. "I'd like to know you."

"I'd like that too," I agreed.

"Let's do that then. In the time it takes for me to make the move to Denver, let's get to know each other."

I sucked in a breath. "You're moving to Denver?"

"I am."

"When did you decide that?"

His eyes didn't waver. "Tonight."

I felt it—all the meaning behind that one word. It couldn't possibly be true, though. Surely, he hadn't made a decision because of me. That would be—no, it couldn't be because of me. If I let myself even think that for a second, the pressure would flatten me.

"Not for me," I whispered.

"You're certainly an incentive." Tore barely blinked as he looked at me. "I'm somewhat unbendable, and I don't make moves easily. Sam has had to shove me forward as our company has grown, and when it comes down to it, he's always been right. He's been pushing me toward the edge for a long while now, but I'm not unwilling to say meeting you was the tipping point."

"I don't know how to respond to that."

He shook his head. "You don't have to say anything. You're not required to reciprocate my feelings. I hope you'll allow me to get to know you, though."

The pressure in my chest made it hard to speak, so I just nodded.

Tore guided me to the loveseat in the small living area and tucked me against him. My mind whirled while he ordered us coffee and dessert, telling me he needed caffeine to keep this night going.

I kicked off my heels, and he brought my feet to his lap, holding them in his warm, wide hands. Massaging my soles, he asked me how I could stand to wear such tall shoes, and I told him about my mother's collection of stilettos and explained Barbie feet were in my DNA.

I let him hold my feet, touch them, examine them closely. He even kissed the tops of both and rubbed his thumb over the cherry-red polish. He might've done more, and I would have allowed it, if not for the knock on the door.

Room service had arrived with a cart full of desserts and a steaming pot of coffee. We ate and drank, listening to my playlist over the room's speakers. Between bites, we kissed each other in random places. He landed most often on my left dimple, and I couldn't stay away from the divot in his chin.

"College at sixteen?" I raised a brow. "What was that like?"

"Freedom and hell." He grimaced. "I was stifled in high school. I couldn't get out of there soon enough. But college... Well, I looked about fourteen when I started. Scrawny, shy, uptight, a mess. I hadn't met Sam yet, so needless to say, I had no social life my first two years."

"What changed?"

The tips of his ears reddened, and I waited with bated breath for him to explain that reaction.

"There was a girl in one of my business classes. She...uh, started a rumor about me that piqued a lot of people's interest."

I gripped his arm, already delighted by this story. "Tell me, Tore. I have to know."

"These...assholes in our class were trying to bully the girl—Elena—by accusing her of dating me. Most people would have been embarrassed and denied it. She'd rolled with it, telling them not only had we dated but I'd dumped her, and she was chasing after me because I" —Tore turned crimson—"have a horse cock."

I blinked. Then gasped. "No."

He winced. "And she couldn't get enough of it."

The last words came out in a rush. When they landed, I *screeched*, launching upright.

"Oh my god. I love her."

He laughed, steadying me with his hands on my hips. "She is certainly one of a kind. After that, things changed for me."

Leaning over him, I held his face in my hands. "Were you really with her?"

"No." He shook his head. "We were good friends in college, though. She now lives on a ranch in Wyoming with her husband and brood of kids."

Now that I knew they'd always just been friends, I liked her even more. "But her rumor got you laid?"

He shrugged. "I was a stupid, horny kid. When girls came on to me, I didn't say no."

I loved this story so much, I had to stop myself from bouncing. "You *did* get laid from a horse-cock rumor." I clutched my chest. "I'm so proud of teenage Tore." I paused. "Wait—that means...was it true?"

He blushed so deeply, he nearly turned purple. "I don't—not a *horse,* but—"

Laughter flung free from my body like an out-of-control missile, winding around us in erratic patterns until I fell forward, landing sprawled over Tore. He took me down to the cushions, lying half on top of me, watching me giggle.

"I've never seen anything more beautiful than you laughing," he declared, like he'd just uncovered something mythical and wondrous.

I trailed my fingertips over his smooth cheek. "I can't explain how happy I am you met her. I love that she took something negative and turned it all around for you."

His brow furrowed. "You don't seem disturbed to hear about me sleeping with other women."

"We both have pasts. They're what brought us here. I'm not going to get jealous of something you did long before you met me." I poked his chin. "Now, if you were to go off and sleep with someone tomorrow, I wouldn't be laughing."

"I would never do that."

I lifted my head to rub my lips along his. "I think I know that about you."

Later, when we'd moved to his bed, him in lounge pants and me wearing one of his shirts, we held hands, struggling to keep our eyes open.

"Do you ever see your siblings?" he asked.

My heart lodged in my throat. "No. My mom and Phil...they don't allow it. I don't think they'd even know me anymore." Ten years was a long time in kid years.

"I'm sorry, Bea. That isn't right. If you want, I can look into—"

"No." I rolled to my side, touching my lips to his bicep. "Thank you, but no. I've accepted how things are, and I can't go back and ruffle things up. Caroline gives me little updates, and they're doing okay. They're fine without me."

He was stiff beside me, his chest rising and falling in heaving waves as he took deep, gulping breaths.

"It isn't right," he muttered.

"It is what it is."

"It's difficult for me to let things go when I see something that could be changed."

"But you have to."

He inhaled a great breath then slowly exhaled. "I know. I will." His eyes swept over my face. "You should know I'm autistic."

"Okay." I'd sort of suspected, but I was glad he'd told me. I wasn't sure what the appropriate response was, so I said the first thing that popped into my head. "I'm allergic to peas and pollen."

He blinked. "Are we exchanging medical information?"

"I thought so…" I grinned at him. "Are we not?"

"I guess we are." Smiling, he rubbed my nose with his. "I had my appendix removed when I was twelve."

"Oh no. I don't know if I can date a man without an appendix. Deal-breaker."

He started shaking with laughter, wrapping me in his arms. "I'll grow it back. It's already happening."

"Mind over matter," I whispered between giggles.

We fell asleep like that, holding each other, still giggling.

And it was perfect.

⚘

The next morning, I woke to Tore's lips brushing mine. My eyes fluttered open to find him showered and dressed in a sleek suit, so handsome, I wondered if I was still dreaming.

"You can sleep in. I'm meeting Sam to go over contracts." He tugged his cuff and checked the time on his phone. "Our meetings will probably go on all day, but I'd like to see you tonight."

"I'm working, but after?"

He nodded. "Absolutely. I don't know what time I'll be free, but I'll come to the bar when I am." He leaned over me, kissing me one more time. "Until tonight, beautiful blue."

"Until tonight, baby."

I drifted back to sleep, and when my phone buzzed hours later, I yawned, reaching for it.

A Venmo notification stopped me cold.

$500 — a bonus for going above and beyond. Thanks for being the best waitress in town.

From Sam.

A bonus? Ridiculous and insulting. Last night hadn't been part of a job. I hadn't even thought of him or his money once. That wasn't what any of this had been about.

I immediately sent the money back. Absolutely no way I was taking another cent from him. If I hadn't already used the initial five hundred for overdue bills, I would have returned that too.

I'd have to explain this to Tore. Obviously, I couldn't allow this to hang over our heads. He'd understand. After last night, he had to know this was real for me.

Nothing had ever been more real.

I'd tell him tonight.

He'd understand.

CHAPTER THIRTEEN
Bea

THE ADDRESS TORE HAD sent was a house. Once I'd looked it up, I'd second-guessed my decision to meet him. Why a house? Easier to trap me in? He couldn't exactly lock me up if we met in a public place.

My brain liked going to dark places, but I was nothing if not pragmatic. Tore was too high profile to be a kidnapper. This could have been his first time, but I doubted I was special enough to make a man snap.

At precisely seven p.m., I showed up on his doorstep. He'd offered to send a car, but I ordered my own rideshare. If I disappeared, at least there'd be evidence of my last known location. Though, honestly, Tore was probably capable of wiping my entire digital footprint.

From the outside, the house wasn't a place I would have expected a young, single billionaire to live. Tudor style, it had to have been built in the 1930s or 1940s. With light bricks and dark wood trim, it was immaculately kept and could have been plucked directly from the English countryside. I wondered how Tore had ended up in a house like this.

At least it didn't scream murder dungeon. Though that could have been the trap.

He whipped open the door before I could retreat. "You're here."

"I am." I peered around him to check for chains on the walls or human-sized cages. All I could see was an empty, brightly lit foyer. "Is this a good idea?"

"You're asking me?"

"You'd be honest if you were planning to dismember me, right?"

"I would, but"—his mouth twitched—"if I were the type of man who dismembered women, I don't think you could trust my word."

"I'd feel better if you lied."

He cocked his head. "Would you?"

Huffing, I stepped into the doorway. "No, probably not." I flicked my gaze over him, trying really hard not to be attracted. In dark, slim-fitting jeans and a T-shirt that looked soft and worn, his hair slightly mussed, it was impossible.

"You're so handsome. It's really annoying."

"Ah, sorry." He raked his fingers through his hair. "There's not much I can do about that. It's just...you know, my face. I could show you pictures of me in college. That might change your mind."

"I doubt it. You were probably gawky and adorable." Since I'd flustered him, I took charge, closing and locking the door. "You could tell me I look nice. That might make up for it."

He looked at me—*really* looked at me—and took his time doing it. Starting from the top, his eyes roved over my face and hair, which was swept back by a knotted scarf. His gaze slid along my shoulders and chest, taking extra time there, then moved to my stomach and thighs.

When he reached my feet, he sighed. "No heels."

I tapped the toe of my red Chuck on the hardwood. "In case I need to run from you."

His eyes flared. "I wouldn't mind that. So long as I caught you in the end."

Oh, this man.

I gave him a light shove. "Don't flirt with me, Tore. I don't know why I'm even here, but it's *not* to let you catch me."

"Of course. Not now."

I shot him a sharp glare. "You're incredibly optimistic."

Then I marched into the house, which was...empty. Not entirely, with a lone couch in the living room, but the rest of the room was bare, as was the dining room. With each room I found deserted, my heart rate ratcheted up.

I'd been joking about the murder thing. Now, I wasn't so sure.

A couple years ago, we'd shared a handful of intense, seemingly meaningful hours before he dropped off the face of the earth—what did I truly know about this man?

"I'm in the process of moving."

The hairs on the back of my neck rose, and I turned my head, finding him closer than expected, his chest almost brushing my shoulders. "In or out?"

"Out. I've already bought the new place. Just finishing up here. Some of the art requires specialty movers who can't come until next week."

"You collect art?"

"I do. Would you like me to show you?"

I wanted that, but it would be too easy to get sidetracked. "Maybe another time."

"Sure. Another time." His hand skimmed my upper back. "Let's go into the kitchen. I have wine or coffee and desserts, if you'd like. I could use a drink myself."

The kitchen was light and bright, with white cabinets and expansive pale-gray marble countertops. The floors were warm hardwood—probably original to the house—and the ceilings were striped with heavy, exposed beams.

On the peninsula was a platter of mini cakes, a bottle of white wine, two glasses, coffee mugs, and a pitcher of cream. Next to that was a vase holding a spray of wildflowers, and playing in the background was one of my favorite songs.

"This is nice." I put my purse on the counter and leaned my hip against it. "You went to a lot of effort."

"It was no trouble." He picked up the wine bottle and tilted it toward me. "Would you like a glass? It's sealed. Just in case you're concerned that I intend to drug you."

A laugh burst out of me. "Honestly, that hadn't crossed my mind, but now it has. Dear god, you're terrible at putting a woman at ease."

"Well..." he set the bottle down with a clunk, "I'm not good at this. I *am* trying, though."

He brought his hands in front of him, fidgeting with his fingers. No, not his fingers. He was spinning the ring on his index finger. A wide, silver band, the center ridged.

He'd bought himself a fidget ring.

I bit down on my lip, forcing my gaze from his hands. "Good at what?"

"Saying the right thing. *Doing* the right thing." His gaze flickered over me again, meandering and appreciative. "I haven't told you how beautiful you are yet, and that's a mistake. I like your hair that way. With the scarf pulling it back. It shows your face, and it's...nice."

'Nice' was the most tepid compliment, but from Tore, I felt it down to my toes. I knew he thought I was pretty, but I liked that he'd noticed details about me.

I'd done my best not to dress up for tonight. No cleavage or high hemlines. I didn't want him thinking I'd made an effort—even if I had. I simply wasn't capable of throwing my hair in a pony, putting on sweats, and calling it good. My version of casual was cropped jeans, an off-the-shoulder top, pin curls, and a bandanna headband. I'd foregone the red lips for pale pink and based on the way he'd paused at my mouth, he'd taken note.

"Thank you," I replied, more breathlessly than intended. "I think...yes, I'll have a glass of wine."

Tore had a heavy pour, and the glass was oversized. If he wanted me drunk, this was a good start. Despite working in bars most of my adult life, I didn't have a high tolerance.

I grabbed one of the mini cakes and perched on a stool. My stomach was churning, and my mind was going a mile a minute with ideas and possibilities. Tore wasn't putting me out of my misery either. He sipped his wine, watching me as he always did: slow and methodical, cataloging every bit of me.

It was too much. This had to be over and done with so I could get out of here and move on. Once I had answers, I'd finally be able to put the questions I'd had for two years to rest.

I placed my glass down and braced myself. "What happened?"

He gulped his wine. His throat worked as he swallowed a few more times, rolling his ring with his thumb. "My sister was in an accident a few hours after I left you. She died that night."

Oh no.

Heat suffused my cheeks. Heavy pressure sank on top of my chest. "Your sister?"

Of all the things I'd imagined he might say, this had never crossed my mind. His sister, my god...

"Tia." He flinched, like saying her name inflicted a wound. "My older sister."

Devastation. That was what this was. He'd brought me here to share his pure, utter devastation. I didn't know what to say. He thought he was bad at saying the right thing, but I was the one searching for words.

"I'm sorry, Tore." That wasn't enough, but was there anything that would be? "That must have been hard." Such an understatement.

He shoved his fingers into his hair, pain lashing at his features. "It was impossible. I did not handle her loss well. For weeks, there was nothing outside my grief. Sam and I had just signed the DoD contract, and I fell apart. He had to handle everything with Nox while I dropped out of life, and my dad took care of everything else."

My hands twitched, needing to offer him comfort. Even now, he looked lost, adrift on the other side of the marble.

"I'm sorry," I whispered.

Bowing his head, he studied his hands on the counter. "I'm not proud of how I reacted. Everyone was grieving, everyone was sad, but I'd let it consume me. Nothing else mattered. And once I resurfaced, I had a lot to piece back together."

"I understand."

How could I not? My siblings were alive, but they were lost to me. I hadn't fallen apart when we were ripped away from each other, but I'd wanted to. If survival hadn't been on the line, I might have.

He lifted his gaze. "By the time I'd started thinking straight again, you'd blocked me. Even if you hadn't, I didn't have anything to give to you. Not then, when I was figuring life out. But I would have liked to have been able to explain where I'd gone."

I scrunched my nose. "I'm wishing I hadn't been so hasty with the block."

"To be fair, it was weeks before I tried to contact you."

I dug my teeth into my bottom lip. "I waited forty-eight hours before I blocked you."

It had been out of self-preservation. If I hadn't, I would have been tempted to text again…and possibly again. That was how obsessed one date had made me. It would have gotten ugly and weird, and *no one* wanted that.

He huffed a laugh. "As far as you knew, it was deserved. And maybe it was. If I were more normal—"

"Don't say that." Normal was my least favorite word, and the last thing anyone needed to be *more* of.

He nodded. "Right. I mean, if I'd had a better handle on my emotions, I would have been capable of grieving and sending a simple text. I regret that very much." Clearing his throat, his mouth turned up in the corners. "I appreciate you gave me forty-eight whole hours."

I waved his appreciation away. "Two-years-ago-Bea was a starry-eyed little optimist. These days, men are blocked much quicker for far, far less."

"I drove you to pessimism?"

"I'm not a pessimist—I'm a realist with a low tolerance for bull-shit." I sighed. "I'm very sorry you lost your sister, Tore. I can only imagine all the ways your life was flipped upside down. I don't hold anything that happened after against you."

All of him rose. His spine straightened, and his eyebrows lifted. Even his ears seemed to sit a little higher.

"Thank you. I didn't expect that of you." He moved around the counter, coming to stand in front of me, and took my hand in his.

For a heartbeat, I was back on my rock, staring up at the stars with him. Then he stroked his thumb across my knuckles, where I had a scar that hadn't been there before. He paused over it, and I pulled my hand away, wrapping it around the stem of my glass. It was a stark reminder of how much life had happened between then and now.

"I'm not a monster. You went through hell. Of course I don't blame you for reacting the way you did." I took a sip to steady myself. "I'm glad we cleared the air."

He lowered his chin. "Tonight was about clearing the air, yes, but not just that. I would like to pick up where we left off."

My pulse thundered in my ears. I'd known he would ask that. He'd made his intentions known when we'd spoken at Nox. But hearing him say it in no uncertain terms panicked me.

I set my glass down.

"Tore..." I started then stopped. Struggling with words wasn't a common occurrence for me, but this man had continued to scram-ble my brain all evening. Rejecting someone was never easy. Well, that wasn't strictly true—sometimes it was a delight. But this felt nearly impossible.

Probably because I didn't want to reject him. My reckless side was ready to dive headfirst into an affair with this gorgeous, interesting man. But the chances I'd end up devastated were too damn high for me to risk it.

I might've been my mother's daughter, but I'd learned a lot from her about what not to do.

He waited, patient as ever, hopeful as I mulled over my words.

"I'm not the same girl who lay on the rock with you two years ago."

His brow pulled tight. "I know that. I don't expect you to be the same."

"I don't think you really do. Picking up where we left off isn't an option. I'm not in that place anymore. My reckless streak has been whittled down. I'm far more careful than I once was. I haven't even been back to the rock since that night...or gone stargazing. I don't pursue things that feel good but aren't safe anymore. That's not me."

If I hadn't been watching him closely, I would have missed the ripple of tension through his shoulders. Otherwise, he remained stoic, implacable...only that slight movement giving him away to anything else.

"Then we'll start fresh," he offered, twisting his ring.

"I can't pretend."

"Neither can I." He reached for my hand again, and silly me, I let him take it. "What happened here?"

I glanced down at the faint scar as he stroked it. It was small. No more than two inches long and only slightly raised, but Tore was all about the details.

"Nothing exciting. An incident with a knife when I first started assisting Daisy. I'm much better at slicing cheese these days."

"There are a million things I don't know about you, Bea—and I don't just mean everything that's happened in the last two years. I want all of it."

Oh, if I could let myself believe that.

To be known that way...it was far too tempting for my own good.

"And I want to feel safe, Tore. I don't. Not right now."

He exhaled slowly, squeezing my hand. "This is a no?"

"It's a not right now." I slipped my hand from his and grabbed my purse. "Maybe not ever. I don't know."

He nodded. Once. Then again. Like he had to keep doing it to accept the answer.

"Okay. This isn't what I'd been hoping for, but I get it." He sounded resolved. "I'll wait. I'll chase you. I'll prove myself to you. As long as it takes."

He followed me to the door where I paused with my hand on the knob. "Thank you for tonight. Even if nothing more happens between us, I'm relieved I can look back on our night together and know it was real."

"It absolutely was. Every second."

I let my eyes fall closed. Heaviness weighed on my shoulders, and I wished, not for the first time, I was a little easier—that I could let go of old hurts and grab onto all the good right in front of me. But my past had taught me to be cautious. To tread lightly. Even if the ground seemed solid, there was always a chance it would give way and send me falling.

"You should know, I'm not easy to catch anymore," I warned.

He was so close, the warmth of his body radiated at my back. If I were the Bea of two years ago, I would have leaned back and soaked it up. As it was, I had to hold on tight to the knob to stop myself.

His fingers grazed my shoulder, so featherlight I might have imagined it.

"I don't mind hard work."

"Good night, Tore."

As I stepped outside, his soft promise floated into the night with me.

"To the chase, Bea."

CHAPTER
FOURTEEN
Salvatore

Bea: Hey, Ant. Can you tell me about grief?

Me: Would you like the definition, or something deeper?

Bea: I know the definition, dude. I guess…I don't know what I'm asking. Tell me anything.

Me: Some believe grief is the closest emotion to fear.

Bea: The terror of loss and the unknown. I see that. Tell me something else.

Me: I'll tell you anything you want.

THERE WEREN'T MANY PROBLEMS I couldn't solve with technology. The *At Your Service* app had started as a tool—an algorithmic extension of my instinct to help, to care for Bea, even when I couldn't be physically present in her life.

At the time, I thought I'd been doing something noble, even if a little underhanded.

But things had snowballed.

The temptation to peek in on her chats with *Anthony* had gotten too great to resist. One peek had led to two and then dozens. Eventually, I stopped letting the AI handle her messages almost entirely. Most of the time, when Bea texted the app, she was talking to me.

She rarely spilled anything deeply personal, but there'd been enough to offer a firm bead on her life—what she needed, where she was going, who she was seeing. If *Anthony* could provide a service to make things easier for her, he did.

There were times, especially recently, I wondered if she knew it was me she was speaking to.

Probably not.

But I often thought about telling her. So she would know we'd been connected all this time—that I'd been looking out for her.

Not yet, though. The time wasn't even close to right.

I'd gone to my new home after meeting Bea at my old one, feeling dejected but not yet out of the game. I should have known she wouldn't fall into my arms. I was lucky she had the first time around.

In many ways, she was right. We *were* little more than strangers. But it wasn't often that I felt comfortable enough to open up to someone like I had with her. Rarely did I let my guard down and show all the awkward, strange, and genuine parts of who I was.

She wouldn't appreciate my deception. I knew that. But I had a plan. A structure. A sequence to reveal the truth in palatable increments.

I was already on my back foot with her, though, so that would wait. There were other steps I had to take first. If she didn't want anything to do with me ever again, my plan was moot anyway. And as much as I would have liked to control that outcome, this decision was out of my hands. Bea had to come around to me and give me another chance.

Lying in my bed, Bea and I exchanging a few messages about grief and loss, a knot lodged in my throat—the one always there when I thought of Tia. I ignored it, focusing on her questions.

> **Bea:** Can we change the subject? I'm bumming myself out.

> **Me:** Of course. Do you need anything?

> **Bea:** I don't know. Maybe. I'm thinking about dating. Should I use an app? They're gross, right? Which one is the least disgusting?

I sat up, my back against my headboard, frowning at my phone. She hadn't mentioned dating in two years. Had spending time with me made her want to reach for someone else? That wasn't part of the plan.

> **Me:** I can research that topic for you. Is there a reason you're considering using a dating app?

> **Bea:** Curiosity, I suppose. I don't know. Let's forget about it.

> **Me:** What are you curious about?

Bea: Can I belong to someone? I'm not sure I have it in me. But…seeing Shira with Roman, and Clara with Jake…I've been thinking about having that for myself.

Me: That's understandable, Bea. Your friends found their partners in their real lives, didn't they?

Bea: Clara and Jake, yes. Can I tell you a secret about Roman and Shira?

Me: Of course you can.

Bea: They met through a fantasy fulfillment app. My shy girl Shira. Can you even?

I dropped my phone in my lap, stunned. I wasn't aware of an app like that, which facilitated matches. What app could she be talking about?

Would Bea want to use it?

If so, I had to be there. I needed to ensure whoever she matched with…was me.

Me: What's the app called? I don't have it in my database.

Bea: Oh, Ant, you little perv. You want to get your robot freak on?

Me: Once again, I'm not a robot.

Bea: You're so cute. I'm glad we had this chat tonight. I was feeling pretty grumpy, and you turned it all around.

My chest swelled, only to deflate a second later with the knowledge I'd been the one to put her in a foul mood in the first place.

Me: Talking to you is always a pleasure. You've changed your mind about dating?

Bea: For now. I just needed to get some chaos out. Good night, my friend.

Me: Good night, Bea.

With a groan, I tossed my phone to the side and pressed my palms into my eyes. Bea's smoky voice, teasing and edgy, looped in my brain. I'd been the cause of her bad mood tonight, but I'd also been the cure.

I didn't know what to make of that.

Reaching for my phone again, I opened her messages. *"Can I belong to someone?"*

I didn't know if she would ever let herself belong to me. Most frustratingly, I didn't know of any technology that would help me solve this problem.

I'd have to do it myself.

CHAPTER FIFTEEN
Bea

I WAS IN OVER my head. That was nothing new, but the difference this time? I wasn't alone, flailing to bail myself out.

Today, I had an assistant. Things were under control.

Sort of.

Scarlet was a fast learner, but she asked a ton of questions. When she wasn't asking questions about work, she was not so subtly prying about my personal life. It was cute. Almost. Mostly, it was distracting.

"What kind of event are you going to again?" she asked.

I leaned over her to check the shape of her prosciutto roses. She had a knack for making them in a snap. And since they were nearly better than mine, she was permanently on rose duty.

"It's a charity luncheon."

I'd been hired to make charcuterie cups and a dessert table for the event. Scarlet and I were assembling the cups, which was a massive help, since I normally did this all on my own. When I arrived at the space later, I only had to do the dessert table, and that wasn't a big deal.

Scarlet reached for another piece of prosciutto. "Yeah, but what charity?"

"I don't remember, honestly."

She narrowed her eyes at me. "What if it's a killing-puppies charity?"

I put my hands on my hips. "First of all, I'm wondering if I should be concerned your mind went to such a dark place. Second, I always do a search on the organization or company before I accept a gig. It's just, once I agree to the job, I don't retain the information. I have too many other things going on."

"Have you ever turned anyone down?"

"Sure, a few times. But my headshot is on my website. Most of the organizations I would have moral objections to wouldn't bother trying to hire a woman with blue hair and a nose piercing." I winked at her. "It keeps the riffraff away."

She glanced up at the silky black strand escaping her ponytail. "Should I go blue too? Keeping the riffraff away sounds good."

"Sorry, but blue hair tends to have the opposite effect on teenage boys. I'm almost thirty, and I still get hit on by guys with dirtstaches."

She wrinkled her nose. "Oh my *god*, I hate their little mustaches. Why don't they shave them? They look so stupid."

I laughed. "I don't try to understand teenage boys. It's probably better not to."

A big fist knocked a familiar rhythm on my front door. Scarlet jumped, surprised by the sudden sound, but I knew who it was.

Ben burst in like he owned the place, and I tried to remember why I'd given him a key.

"Beatrice," he called. "I'm bored."

"In the kitchen, troublemaker," I hollered back.

Scarlet frowned. "Who's that? Your boyfriend?"

"Oh, god no," I replied.

Ben strolled into the kitchen, twirling my key around his finger. "I *wish* I was her boyfriend. She friend-zoned me. It's depressing." He leaned his shoulder against the entryway, folding his arms across his chest. "Who might you be?" he asked Scarlet.

I put my hand on her shoulder. "This is my assistant, Scarlet. She and her family are moving into the construction zone across the street. Say hi, Ben."

He grinned. "Hi, Ben."

I groaned. "Don't be obnoxious."

Scarlet had to tilt her head way back to look Ben in the eye. "You have the same name as Bea's dog. That's kind of weird."

"Ah, well...it would be, if Ben was short for Benjamin, but it's not." He tapped his chest. "Bennett Wiley Wells, at your service."

She *hmphed* and muttered, "Still kind of weird."

"Weird's cool, kid," Ben replied, unfazed.

Scarlet put down her prosciutto flower. "Why do you have a key to Bea's house?"

"For *emergencies*," I emphasized. "He abuses his key-holding privileges."

"You shouldn't do that," she admonished like a stern little grandmother.

"Look, I'm saving you the trouble of walking all the way to the door by unlocking it myself." He gestured at my supply-covered counters. "And I remembered you had a big job today, so I stopped by to see if you need any help."

Scarlet straightened. "*I'm* helping her."

"She is," I added. "Scarlet's amazing."

I'd stopped questioning my decision to hire her, even if she could be slightly annoying. The fact of the matter was: *everyone* annoyed me, but Scarlet did less than most.

Ben flexed his tree trunk biceps. "You're really going to turn down free manual labor, Buzz?"

"Nope. I'm not." I took my gloves off and brushed by him, grabbing the leash hanging on a hook in the hallway. "Your namesake would love to go for a walk."

Benjamin was a wild child, but he understood he had to make himself scarce when I was preparing for an event. As soon as I took my gear out, he showed himself upstairs.

But my boy could be passed out cold, deep in dreamland, and he'd come running at the sound of his leash jingling.

I tossed the leash to Ben. He'd been through this before and braced himself.

Two seconds later, Benjamin launched himself down the stairs, straight into Ben's legs. Ben might've been six-and-a-half feet of pure muscle, but he was no match for the missile that was my dog. They both stumbled back, and Ben caught himself on my table, saving them from landing in a heap.

"You're lucky you're cute, man," Ben grumbled as he gave my dog a vigorous rubdown and attached his leash. "I could use you on the team. You'd make a hell of a rugby player."

Benjamin *ruffed*, agreeing he would. I had my doubts, though. He was powerful, but he was too much of a lover to get rough on the pitch.

"Have fun, boys," I called as they headed out.

Scarlet watched them go, dreamy-eyed. "Wow. That guy's really our neighbor?"

I laughed. "He really is. Want to know something even crazier?"

She nodded, eyes wide.

"His identical twin lives in the house next to his."

"There are *two* of them?" she screeched.

"There sure are."

Life would be a lot simpler if I were into Ben. Shira and I could be sisters-in-law, and I'd forever have someone to lift heavy objects for me. Too bad my taste skewed toward devastatingly handsome, bespeckled computer geniuses.

⚬

Technically, it wasn't my fault the waiter's arm caught on fire. Sure, I probably shouldn't have said, *"Prove it,"* when he'd claimed to be a fire breather on the side, but I didn't think he'd take it literally—especially not in the middle of a packed catering kitchen.

Everything had been going fine until someone spilled oil in the path of a server carrying a tray of wineglasses. She'd slipped, and the tray flew. Luckily for her, one of the chefs caught her just in time, but the tray lost its battle with gravity, smacking the fire breather in the back of the head at the worst possible moment.

His head jerked forward, and the flames followed.

Right onto his highly flammable work uniform.

He screamed. Everyone froze.

It was by sheer luck I'd been holding a pitcher of water.

Moments after I'd doused the fire, the catering manager had charged in, oblivious. "The dessert table needs to be refilled ASAP."

I didn't argue. Grabbing my cart, I made a swift exit before anyone could connect me to the tiny, semi-contained inferno in the kitchen, which had only been sort of, in a small, microscopic way, my fault.

My cart filled with desserts, I crossed the room, trying to ignore my jumping nerves. The space was a swirl of muted pastels, fine china, and understated elegance. I offered polite smiles as I passed clusters of guests, keeping my head down and pace steady, only to be stopped by an older woman dripping in diamonds who wanted to discuss all the ingredients in my macarons. At first, I was wary of her intentions, then she all but demanded my business card so she could hire me for her granddaughter's graduation party, and it became a lovely surprise.

When she finally walked away, I let out a long breath, and that was when I saw him.

At the far side of the ballroom, surrounded by four men in suits who looked like they had private jets and boardrooms to return to, stood Tore. I recognized Sam among them, and I was almost certain the silver-haired guy was the mayor.

Tore was taller than all of them. Sharper too. His hands were clasped loosely in front of him, and though I was too far away to be sure, I'd bet anything he was spinning his ring as he spoke.

The men were riveted, and with the *mayor* hanging on to Tore's every word, it struck me how powerful he was. This was a man other powerful people listened to.

All the riches in the world were nice, but they didn't turn me on. This, though, seeing the respect Tore was given by men who were no doubt used to being treated with deference?

This was something else entirely.

Chapter Sixteen
Salvatore

IT TOOK ME LONGER than I liked to make it across the room to the dessert table.

Understandably, people were surprised to see me here. I usually avoided luncheons and galas like the plague. I gave generously to charity but saw no reason to make a big show of it. Quiet donations to causes I supported were enough; I didn't need recognition.

Sam was in attendance, though, so I'd set aside thirty minutes for small talk to keep him happy. Ignoring everyone like I wanted to would only annoy him.

He frowned when I walked away from my chat with the mayor, but politics didn't interest me. If any feathers were ruffled, Sam would smooth them over. He was used to it.

My timing turned out to be perfect.

Bea had emerged from the kitchen a few minutes ago, trailed by a faint puff of smoke. She'd been waylaid several times on the way, making us reach the dessert table at the same moment.

Her dessert table.

I wasn't sure how uncommon this setup was, since I rarely went to events like this, but I couldn't imagine anyone else had ever created such a beautiful tablescape. There were desserts and candy at all levels, sitting on glass trays. Cream puffs stacked into pillars. Colorful macarons arranged in rainbow order. Between the desserts were small silver vases holding brightly colored flowers. Even picked over, it was art.

Her eyebrows lifted when she spotted me loitering, nonplussed by my appearance.

It fascinated me how easily she could convey her emotions by moving the muscles in her face. Some people were hard to read, but Bea broadcasted what she was feeling loud and clear.

I picked up a pink macaron. "Did you make this?"

"What are the chances you'd be attending the same event I was hired to cater?" she countered.

"Not high, since I rarely go to these things." I brought the macaron to my mouth and paused. "Was this made by you?"

She rubbed her lips together, crinkled her nose, then nodded. "The macarons, yes. The mousse cups too. The rest comes from a bakery I collaborate with."

I popped the whole macaron into my mouth—a mistake, probably, since it was bigger than I'd expected and I'd never actually eaten one before. Luckily, it tasted as good as it looked. Spitting it out into a napkin wouldn't have impressed Bea.

She watched me, her lips rolled over her teeth. When I swallowed, she asked, "Good?"

"Yes. The best thing I've ever tasted." I grabbed one of the last cups of mousse, impressed there was already a spoon with it. I took a smaller, more cautious bite of this one, but I needn't have worried. "This is just as delicious. You're very talented, Bea."

Her cheeks glowed a faint rose as she began to place fresh desserts on the table. "It isn't a big deal, but I'm glad you like them."

Several people approached the table, so I moved closer to her. "How are you?"

"Fine," she murmured. "A little flustered you're here. I didn't expect to see you again until next week."

She plucked the mousse cup from my hand when I finished, replacing it with a chocolate macaron. This one, I ate slower, paying attention to the subtle notes in the flavor. I wasn't really a sweets person, but she was well on her way to converting me.

"I told you my intentions," I reminded her. "I won't exactly be able to prove I'm a safe bet if we don't see each other."

I had been biding my time, waiting for the perfect moment to approach her. That had been a mistake—one I wouldn't make again. Bea would only understand I meant what I said through my actions. Waiting for her to come to me wouldn't get me anywhere.

"I'm not a guest here, Tore. This is my job."

"I know." I grazed my hand over her back—just for a moment, and only because I couldn't help myself. "I won't keep you from it."

She moved along the table, straightening and refilling, graciously answering questions when she was interrupted by guests. This was a new side to Bea I was pleased to get to observe. I knew she was doing well in her business, but getting to see her in her element was a real pleasure I hadn't expected.

Once the dessert table was reset, I followed Bea and her cart toward the kitchen. Before we reached the door, she stopped and faced me.

"I saw you talking to the mayor earlier."

"Ah, yes. Sam thinks it's important to keep open lines of communication with Dean."

Her eyes flared. "Dean? You're on a first-name basis with Dean Caruthers?"

"Sure." I pushed my glasses up my nose, then dropped my hands to my sides, forcing them to be still. "He asked me to call him by his first name. It would be disrespectful to call him anything else."

Her teeth were perfectly white and square, but what I loved most was how her canines jutted out just a little past her incisors. When she bit her bottom lip, she looked like a cute little vampire.

"That's true," she murmured. "I'm surprised you come to things like this. Doesn't seem like your scene."

"It's very much not. Small talk is a waste of time, and that's all that goes on. I'd rather spend two minutes making a donation than two hours speaking to people who think they have something to gain by making a connection to me." I shuddered involuntarily.

"It seems small talk is par for the course when you're a bajillionaire."

I laughed. "I don't recall learning that figure in math class."

"That's because you only took Calculus 700. We covered bajillions in remedial math since we'd all have to bow to our corporate overlords one day."

"Bea…" I shook my head, "I can't imagine you've ever bowed to anyone."

She shrugged. "We all have bosses." Then she grabbed the end of my tie and gave it two sharp tugs. "Except you, of course. You're the boss of them all."

"Even I answer to investors and clients."

"Technically speaking. But they know you hold all their secrets in the palm of your hand. If they sass you, you could infect their systems with never-ending pop-ups."

I stared at her for a beat before laughter burst out of me. Bea's brand of teasing was my favorite. Quite possibly the only I'd ever enjoyed. It was blunt, easy to discern, and traveled right to the epicenter of my sense of humor.

She glared at me, though there was no heat behind it. "Pop-ups are no laughing matter, Tore."

My grin widened. It was all I could do not to pull her into my arms and kiss her pretty mouth. "No one sasses me but you, Bea."

"I noticed you didn't deny the pop-up threat."

"I can't tell you my corporate secrets. Not yet, at least."

She canted her head. "Not yet?"

I leaned toward her, dropping my voice. "If you were mine, there would be no secrets between us. Nothing you couldn't ask me. It would all be yours."

She retreated a step. "I...don't know what to say. But I should probably get back to the kitchen. There was a fire incident earlier, and I...yeah. I have to go."

I skimmed my hand down the length of her arm, catching her fingers briefly. It was hell to let go, but I had no choice. The last thing I wanted was to put Bea in a situation that would compromise her professionalism, but I couldn't allow her to walk away without touching her skin. I just couldn't.

"I'm glad I saw you."

Her lips parted, and her eyes darted back and forth between mine. "Me too. It was a nice surprise." Then she squared her shoulders and wrapped her fingers around the handle of her cart. "Say hi to Dean and Sam for me."

I should have let her walk away, get back to her job, but I found I wasn't fully in control of what came out of my mouth when I was around her.

"Beatrice?"

She stopped, her cheeks rounding as she gave me a little smile. "Yes, Salvatore?"

"Can I take you out to dinner tonight?"

Still smiling, she shook her head. "I'm working tonight."

That displeased me. Bea should have been making more than enough money to quit her second job, but she hadn't. I'd have to look into it.

"Can I pick you up from work and drive you home?"

She crinkled her nose, and I braced myself for rejection. I expected it, but that didn't mean it wasn't disappointing.

"It's not a long drive," she replied, taking me aback.

"That's fine."

She groaned softly. "This feels like déjà vu. I don't know why I'm thinking about saying yes..."

"There's not a chance I won't show up," I added.

Her eyes narrowed into slits. "I think...I'm not sure enough to say yes to you."

"I understand. I didn't think you'd accept, but I had to try."

"You really didn't *have* to."

"No, I did. There was no possible way my brain would have allowed me to walk away from you without asking."

She blinked several times, then her eyes crinkled, and she snorted softly. "Maybe...ask again another time."

"My brain sort of requires it."

For some reason, that made her laugh. As she headed into the kitchen, she muttered, "Silly brain."

I was still smiling when Sam caught up to me a few minutes later. He wasn't.

"You disappeared," he remarked. "Dean wasn't impressed."

"I had nothing left to say. Besides, you always do fine without me." I started for the dessert table again, Sam hot on my heels. "You should try the macarons."

Then again, on second thought, I'd rather he not. It might have been crazy, but I didn't want him tasting something Bea had made. In fact, if it wouldn't have made me look like a lunatic, I would have packed up all the macarons and mousse cups to keep for myself.

"I'm not really a fan," Sam stated.

I turned toward him sharply, my gut knotted in barbed wire. "Of macarons in general or these in particular?"

He held his hands up. "Hey, don't give me that pissy look. I'm not insulting your waitress. It's not personal. I've never been a fan."

"My *waitress*? Her name is Bea, as you well know."

Sam chuckled. "Right. Bea. Did you know she'd be here? Is that why you showed?"

"Of course it is."

I never lied to Sam. There was no point—he knew me too well to fall for anything less than the full truth. Besides, I had nothing to hide from him. Well, except for the *At Your Service* app. But he didn't know it existed, so he wouldn't ask.

He exhaled a long breath. "Are you seeing her?"

"Not yet."

"Now's not a great time for distractions. You have enough of those already."

Those words landed wrong. "My family isn't a distraction."

He instantly backpedaled. "I didn't mean it that way. Of course, they're not, and I get it's important to spend time with them. But we're on the cusp of the next level, and right now isn't—"

"Sam"—I leveled him with a long, hard look—"this is not a conversation I'm willing to have."

He started to argue, but the CFO of another tech company brushed by, giving us a nod. Once she passed, Sam focused on me.

"You're right. This isn't the time nor the place for this conversation." He patted my shoulder. "We'll talk more on Monday."

"We can," I agreed, "but not about Bea. She isn't up for discussion, and neither is my personal life."

He jerked back. "So we're not friends anymore? We can't talk about anything personal?"

"We are. But I have boundaries, and this is one of them. If I talk to you about Bea, it'll be as my friend, not my business partner."

A million emotions flashed across his face, but none stayed long enough for me to decipher. Finally, he settled on an affable smirk, and I breathed a sigh of relief. Lately, we'd been at odds more than not. It was worrying.

"Got the message, loud and clear." He chuckled. "Though the way she was looking at you, you might have your work cut out for you."

He wasn't wrong about that...

I was looking forward to every minute of it.

Chapter Seventeen
Salvatore

BEFORE TIA DIED, LIFE had been centered around my work. No restrictions on my hours, spending more weekends glued to my computer than not. It was all I'd known, and though my world remained small, I'd never thought to change it.

Losing her had forced me to rearrange *everything*. That process had been excruciating in almost every way, but now, two years into this new life, things ran as smoothly as possible.

Attending the charity luncheon had been a rare break in my routine, so when I stepped into the foyer of our new house, I was immediately bombarded with questions.

"What did you eat?"

"Did you see anyone famous?"

"Did you bring anything home for me?"

"Were there any good-looking women interested in an eligible silver fox?"

The last from my father, the self-proclaimed ladies' man. His ego knew no bounds, but he was rarely without female companionship when he wanted it, so it was rightfully earned.

I laughed, the overlapping voices and little hands tugging somewhat overwhelming. They were usually good about giving me a few minutes to decompress. Today wasn't usual, so all bets were off.

"Uncle Sally!" Lacey slammed herself into my legs. "I missed you today. Let's not do this again, okay?"

Crouching down, I smoothed my niece's hair off her face. Normally, Scarlet did her hair since my father and I were pretty incompetent in that department, but she'd been busy with her new job this morning.

"I agree. I had absolutely no fun. Though"—I dug into my jacket pocket and brought out the little packet I'd tucked there—"I did bring you something."

My nephew, Talon, crowded my other side. "Did you bring me something too?"

"Do you think I'd forget about you?"

He gave me a serious look. "You wouldn't. I'm just making sure. Just in case."

I opened the carefully folded napkin, revealing the four macarons I'd swiped from the dessert table.

"These are called macarons. I tried one for the first time today, and you know what I thought?" Both kids shook their heads, eyes locked on my palm. "I thought, 'Tally and Lace would love these too,' and smuggled two out for each of you."

"What does *smuggled* mean?" Lacey asked.

I turned to Talon. "Do you know, Tally?"

He puffed his chest. "It means Uncle Sally snuck them out."

Lacey gasped. "Oh my goodness. Did anyone see?"

I nodded, turning solemn. "Sam caught me. I had to offer to wash his socks for three weeks to keep him quiet."

She recoiled. "Oh my goodness, oh my goodness—that's so gross!"

Talon crossed his arms. "These better be worth it. Three weeks is a *lot* of socks."

"Try them and tell me."

They each plucked a strawberry macaron from my hand, nibbling carefully, then shoved them in their mouths like wild animals.

I'd known Lacey would like them—she loved pretty much everything in the entire world, but if it was pink? She became euphoric. Talon was more like me. He liked what he liked and didn't often venture out to try new things. It made me incredibly happy to see him enjoying the macaron the way I had.

Two years ago, Talon hadn't enjoyed *anything*. We'd done a lot of work since then. When Tia first died, it had seemed impossible, but the five of us were a solid family unit now.

My father snagged Lacey's hand, giving it a gentle tug. "Do you think we could let your uncle have some breathing room?"

She beamed up at him. "Sure we can. I just missed him."

Straightening, I patted her cheek. "I missed you too, Lace. I'm yours the rest of the day."

I'd been disappointed Bea had rejected my offer for dinner or a drive, but it was hard to hang onto that feeling when these kids were so happy to have me home.

Eventually, they gave me a minute so I could change out of my suit and into sweats and a T-shirt—my weekend uniform if I could help it. Once dressed, I trailed down the hall, pausing at Scarlet's open door. I peered in, finding her at her desk, iPad propped in front of her, stylus in hand.

"What are you working on?"

She spun her chair around to face me. "Gina asked me to draw a portrait of her with her favorite character from this manga she likes. It's kind of weird, but it's for her birthday, so I couldn't say no."

I took a step into her room, then hesitated. Since I'd never been a teenage girl, I wasn't well versed in the protocol, but with Scarlet, I always leaned on the side of caution. It was important she always felt like her space was her own.

She sighed. "You don't have to be invited in, you know. You're not a vampire."

"Thank you. I don't want to assume." I crossed her plush carpet, perching beside her on the end of her bed. She handed me the tablet, showing me what she was working on.

"Wow. The details are outstanding." I wasn't familiar with the character, but I recognized Gina, her friend from school. "How long have you been working on this?"

"Um...a while." She took the tablet from me, poking at the screen several times. "Looks like—just about seven hours."

I jerked my head back. "Seven hours? That's quite a birthday gift."

She shrugged. "Gina's turning sixteen. It's a pretty big deal."

"Is it?"

Again, she sighed. "Yeah, it is. I know you were in college when you were sixteen, but for *normal* people, it's a milestone. Gina's getting a car for her birthday. She'll be able to drive me places, so Grandpa—"

"Drive you places?" I grimaced. "Gina is a child. How can that be legal?"

Scarlet put her iPad down and spoke to me like *I* was a child. "Here's the thing, Uncle Sally, most people get their license when they're sixteen. And *most* people can't wait to be independent and drive themselves around."

"I *have* my license."

"But you hate driving."

That was true. I always had. I preferred being driven most places so I could optimize my time by doing work during my commutes. But even when I was younger, I'd had no desire to control a moving vehicle.

"I also hate the idea of you being driven by a child," I repeated. "Your grandpa or Igor can take you wherever you need to go."

"Right, but I'd be with Grandpa or your driver. Igor's nice and all, but if I had a choice, that would be a big fat no."

I held up one hand. "Let's table this for now." *Until I come up with a long list of all the reasons riding in a car with Gina is a terrible idea.* "How was your first day at work?"

She brightened. "It was literally perfect. Bea's the coolest boss. She didn't even get annoyed when I asked a million questions, plus she said I'm a really fast learner. I think she's going to keep me."

When Scarlet told me she'd gotten a job working for Bea, I'd thought I was hallucinating. How could that have happened under my nose? It hadn't been part of the plan in any way. Then Lacey and Talon mentioned they'd fallen in love with her dog, and my father thought she looked like an old-time movie star, and I'd realized I had lost control over this piece of the puzzle.

So I'd let it go.

It was happening whether I approved or not—and maybe that was for the best.If I inserted myself, I might tilt the precarious balance before it even existed. It made more sense to let their relationships unfold naturally, without any interference from me.They weren't biased. They had no trouble being honest with me. They'd come to their own conclusions. So I stayed back and let them move forward. I couldn't move them like chess pieces. Only time would tell how it would all play out.

"She'll keep you. Just remember, if it becomes too much, you don't have to work."

"How could I forget? You and Grandpa remind me all the time."

She propped her chin on her fist, her eyes sliding toward her window. "Did you know the guy who lives right next door to Bea is a professional rugby player? His name is Ben Wells. I looked him up. He's kind of famous. I mean, in the rugby world. None of my friends follow rugby, but I sent them his picture, and now they're all fans."

I was well aware of who all our neighbors were. I wouldn't have moved my family into a house without researching everyone in the immediate vicinity. That was common sense.

"Did you meet him?"

She nodded with enthusiasm. "He has a key to Bea's place and lets himself in. She pretended to be annoyed, but I don't think it really bothered her. They're really good friends. He took Benjamin for a walk then helped us carry all the catering supplies to her SUV. I ship them."

"Ship them?"

"Yeah." She put her index fingers together. "Like, they should be in a relationship. It would be so cute. Neighbors and friends to lovers! And Ben and Bea sound so adorable together, don't they?"

I stared, completely thrown.

"Not *that* adorable," I muttered.

She laughed. "You wouldn't get it. You're not a romantic like me, Uncle Sally. When you meet them, you'll see. It's kind of perfect."

I disagreed. Vehemently. Nothing about Bea being with some airheaded rugby player was perfect. He might've been muscular and conventionally attractive, but she needed someone who challenged her mind. Surely, this man held no appeal for her. If she were dating him, she would have mentioned him to me, to *Anthony*.

"Uncle Sally?" Scarlet called, jerking me out of my head. "You're staring into space."

I forced a smile, scrubbing my hands down my face. "Sorry. Too many changes at once. My mind is struggling to keep up."

She nodded. "I get it. Tally and Lace were having a dance party with Grandpa this afternoon. At first, it was fun, then all the noise and scream-singing became too much. That's why I came to my room to work on my picture. Sometimes I need quiet to recenter myself."

That was her mother speaking. Tia had been the most empathetic person I had ever known. She could put herself in anyone's shoes and make them feel comfortable being themselves.

My sister would be proud of who her daughter was becoming.

"Sometimes I need that too," I agreed. "Especially after a Tally and Lace scream-sing session."

"Right?" She giggled. "They don't sing well, but they sure are loud."

"Neither has any shortage of confidence." Her laughter was a balm. Hearing it flow freely after too many days filled with tears and despair made everything worth it. Not that I would tell her that. It would make her self-conscious, and I wanted her to continue to shine.

"Do you like this house, Scar?"

Her laugh subsided, turning into a sincere smile. "I really do. I like that we got to customize it for us. The old house was nice, but this feels like it's really ours. I think Grandpa's going to be really happy having his own private apartment too. He needs that, don't you think?"

I returned her smile, even as a swell of sadness rose on my chest. My sister would have loved to be the one having this conversation with her, but she would never have the chance. It wasn't fair, not for any of us. But I always remembered how lucky I was to be the one here with these children.

"Yes. I think so."

"But I'm glad he's still close," she added.

"He wouldn't have it any other way." I exhaled through the tightness in my chest. "Neither of us wants to be anywhere but here with you guys."

Scarlet nodded, then turned her attention back to her tablet, and I took that as my cue to leave. I stood, giving her shoulder a quick pat.

"Don't spend too much time on that. You'll strain your eyes."

"I won't," she promised. "Just a few more finishing touches."

I walked back down the hallway, Lacey's chatter and Talon's enthusiastic narration of everything he did floating from the living room along with the faint hum of Frank Sinatra—my father's contribution to the day's soundtrack.

This house was full of life, sounds, chaos.

As I rejoined the rest of my family in the living room, I realized I hadn't felt alone in a long time.

What used to be my default was now so rare, I couldn't remember the last time it had happened.

And I didn't miss it. Not ever.

CHAPTER EIGHTEEN

Bea

I was stupid.

There was no other word for it.

Why else would I have spent Saturday night—between taking orders, delivering drinks, and ignoring my aching feet—watching the door, half hoping Tore would ignore my *no* and show up anyway?

He hadn't. He'd respected my wishes. And that had been both a relief and a letdown.

By the time I walked into Nox Cyber a few days later, I was jonesing for a fix.

Given he was already in the conference room, I wondered if he'd been feeling the same.

He looked up from his computer, fixing his gaze on me. "Good morning, Bea."

"Good morning." I put my hands on my hips, doing my best to glare at him, but I couldn't summon any heat behind it. "Is this always going to be a thing?"

"A thing?"

"Yes. You being in here while I set up."

"Oh." He straightened his glasses. "Possibly. There are times my schedule is out of my control, but if I can help it, I'll be here."

I sighed. "I thought that's what you would say."

"I haven't been subtle about what I want." His gaze softened. "How was work Saturday night?"

"Fine. It was a long day, and I was glad when it was over, but that's not unusual." Turning my back to him, I went about doing my job—the reason I was here.

"Is your catering business not doing well enough for you to quit your waitressing job?"

I nearly jumped out of my skin when he appeared next to me. He always stayed in his seat, pretending to work on his laptop. It seemed things were changing.

"That's a pretty personal question," I replied.

He nodded. "I know. I've told you a lot of personal things about myself. You can ask me anything you like."

"That doesn't mean it's a two-way street."

He plucked up one of the muffins I'd just set out and methodically peeled the wrapper. "Then you can tell me it's none of my business."

I placed the final snack cup down and checked my list, making sure I wasn't forgetting anything. Me from a few years ago would have been shocked—but impressed—at how organized I was.

Judging the way Tore was eyeing the checklist like a juicy steak, he was impressed too.

"Technically, I'm making plenty, but I don't feel safe enough to quit waitressing yet."

He lifted his eyes to meet mine. "What would it take to make you feel safe?"

"I don't have a number in mind." I shrugged. "I've always juggled multiple jobs. I don't know if I'm capable of quitting."

"You deserve rest."

"Doesn't everyone?" I scrunched my nose. "I doubt you take much time off work."

"I do, actually." He twisted the ring on his finger. "I don't work weekends, and I have time set aside for vacation."

I was surprised, but not quite convinced. "How many years were you running Nox before giving yourself a break?"

His mouth tugged into a reluctant smile. "Longer than I care to admit. You should take me as a cautionary tale. I do not recommend working seventy-hour weeks. I lost many years strapped to my desk instead of experiencing life."

"Luckily, I've never forced myself to sit at a desk. That wouldn't fly." I glanced from his ring to his eyes, finding them pinned to me. "I get your point. I'll have to think about it. Maybe I'll set a monetary goal and let myself quit when I reach it."

That seemed to please him. "Good."

I held up a finger. "I said maybe."

Tore snagged my hand before I could drop it and rolled his thumb over my ring. "This isn't the same one you were wearing that night."

My breath caught, and warmth flooded my belly. I wasn't sure if I was reacting to his touch or the fact he'd remembered such a small detail from so long ago.

It was probably a little of everything.

"I lost that one."

He rolled the spinner back and forth. "I like this. I never see you playing with it."

I swallowed the lump in my throat. "I don't. Not really. But I like knowing it's there."

"Bea—"

A knock on the door stopped him from saying anything else. Paul strode in, glancing between us, while Tore took his time letting go of my hand.

"Hey, Bea. Do you have a minute to talk about changes in the menu?" Paul asked.

"Yes." I swiped my hands on my pants and edged away from Tore. His scowl burrowed into the side of my face, but I refused to look at him. "Should I find you when I'm finished?"

"What's wrong with the menu?" Tore bit out.

Paul held up his hands. "Nothing. Bea's food is perfect, but she mentioned switching it up so people didn't get bored. If you don't want to change, we don't have to."

Tore frowned at him. "Who's bored? Did someone say they're bored?"

He shook his head. "Absolutely not. I've only gotten positive feedback since we brought Bea in."

"It was my idea, Tore," I cut in. "No need to bite Paul's head off."

He whipped his attention back to me. "I don't like changes being made without notice. Paul knows this."

I arched a brow. "I find it hard to believe you manage this company on such a micro level. Do you also pick Paul's ties out for him every morning? How do you possibly get anything done?"

Paul looked like his head was going to explode at the way I was speaking to his boss. Technically, I guessed he was my boss too, but I doubted I was in danger of being fired.

"I don't like change when it affects me," he repeated, his jaw tight. "Paul is more than capable of picking out his own ties."

Shoot. I'd probably stepped over the line. In my day-to-day life, that wasn't unusual. At work, though? Never. I was even more mortified I'd done it at Tore's expense.

"Of course. I'm just teasing." I leaned around Tore to address Paul. "Hey, I'll talk to you in a few minutes, all right?"

"Got it." He backed toward the door like he couldn't escape quick enough. "I'll be at my desk."

When we were alone again, I exhaled slowly. "Sorry. Paul's your employee. I shouldn't have poked fun at you like that in front of him."

"Thank you. I appreciate that." He snagged my hand again and went right back to rolling my ring. "Do you have a boyfriend?"

I blinked at the sudden subject change, then laughed. "Do you think Paul and I are having a secret affair?"

The idea was so wild to me, it might've been from outer space. Paul was fine looking, but as far as I was concerned, he was sexless. Nothing about him piqued my interest. Unfortunately, Tore had been the only one who'd captured my attention in a long while.

"Paul?" He cocked his head. "It hadn't crossed my mind. Are you interested in him?"

"I'm not."

His jaw rippled. "Are you seeing anyone?"

I curled my fingers around his. "No, and I don't have a boyfriend. I'm not the type of woman who'd let a man hold my hand if I did."

He looked down at our joined hands, his brow furrowing. "I didn't realize we were holding hands." His eyes found mine, wide with wonder. "Why are you allowing me to hold your hand, Bea?"

"I— I don't know. You just did it, and I let you."

He shuffled closer, wedging our hands between our chests. "You don't like it?"

"No, I do." I rubbed my lips together, hoping to spark the right words. It was fruitless. I couldn't think with him standing so close, smelling like a forest after a heavy rain, piney and fresh, warm and tall, watching me intently, noticing my every tic and breath. It was too much.

"Go out with me," he uttered lowly.

My pulse fluttered in my throat like a trapped butterfly.

How was it possible to feel so much for this man? I could count our interactions on two hands, but that didn't seem to matter. Logic couldn't touch the way I reacted to him.

"Tore..."

"Bea..." His lips curled at the corners. "Say yes."

My teeth dug into my bottom lip. I didn't want to be stubborn just for the sake of it, and I couldn't decide if that's what I was doing. There was no question I was immensely attracted to him. Like, way beyond attracted. And there was an undeniable pull between us that had been there from the start. But I still had this twinge of resistance that made me want to run from him.

He'd chase me...

...and I'd like it.

"Okay. Yes."

A grin spread across his face, and the tips of his ears glowed bright red. "Yes? Really?"

"Mmmhmm." My stomach churned, and my overactive sense of self-preservation wanted me to take it back, but I fought it.

"Tonight. I'll send a car for you."

"I'll drive."

He shook his head. "You won't make it easy."

"I'm not an easy woman."

"Good. I wouldn't want you any other way." He squeezed my hand. "I'll let you go."

His unsaid words rang loud and clear: *For now.*

CHAPTER NINETEEN
Salvatore

BEA ARRIVED AT MY old house four minutes past seven. I yanked the door open, unable to stop myself from scowling as she made her way up the front path.

"You're late."

She stopped in her tracks, staring at me blankly, and I immediately regretted opening my mouth. I hadn't intended to bark at her, but I'd been convinced she wasn't coming. My gut was a tangled mess, and I'd bypassed my ring to pick the hell out of the skin around my thumbnails.

I stepped out of the house, meeting her on the path. "I thought you weren't coming." I carefully took her elbow in my palm. "I'm glad to see you."

She slipped her phone from her small purse, tapping on the screen. "It's seven-oh-four. I wouldn't call this late."

"I'm precise. It's hard for me to remember others aren't the same way."

"I suspect even you are at the mercy of traffic and red lights."

I bowed my head, willing my pulse to get under control. "Unfortunately, I am. It drives me mad."

"I don't particularly like running behind either." She put her phone away, then gave me a little shove. "Now that you know I did my best to be here on time, go back inside so you can greet me properly. I didn't put this dress on for it not to be acknowledged."

I was being a supreme jackass. Three or four minutes wasn't the end of the world, and it most certainly wasn't her fault. I'd worked myself into a lather over something inconsequential and had snapped at the woman I was trying to win over.

She was here because I'd asked her to be. I was the only one who hadn't shown up when I'd been supposed to. I was the one who had to prove myself reliable, not Bea.

I went back into my house, paused a beat, then reopened the door. Bea was still in the same spot, allowing me another chance to admire her the way she deserved.

Her hair was in perfect blue rolls. Shiny and neat, I wondered if she'd let me touch it. I wanted to know what it would feel like to sink my fingers into it.

Her dress was black and molded to her rounded figure like a glove, ending at her knees. Her legs were bare, and I followed them down to her signature neck-breaking heels.

I trailed my gaze back up, pausing where her dress ended in a low, square neckline, revealing the creamy globes of her breasts. She looked soft all over, but there, she was so mouth-wateringly round and lush, I imagined resting my head and having the best sleep of my life.

"You're not saying anything."

Tearing myself from my trance, I strode to her, slipped my arm around the curve of her waist, and pulled her into me. I took her chin in my other hand, stroking my knuckle against the indent of her dimple.

I had rehearsed what I would say. Suave compliments that would make her feel good. But I couldn't grasp any of those words now that I was facing her. Besides, I wanted to give her a lot more than smooth, practiced lines.

"I can't come up with words to express how devastatingly beautiful you are, Beatrice. You make me start dreaming of all the ways I want to touch you, but only after I spend several hours drinking you in from every angle."

Her lips parted on a sharp inhale. Before I could process one more thought, she surged forward, curled her fingers around the back of my neck, and pressed her mouth to mine.

I returned her kiss on instinct, my body having gone offline the moment her body met mine, then hauled her flush with my chest, groaning as her tongue teased my lips, sweet and tempting. I opened, meeting her stroke for stroke, gliding past the seam of her mouth to taste her fully.

She tilted her head, letting me in deeper, and that was all it took. I lost myself in her. Time, which had been tantamount moments ago, fell away. Seconds, or maybe minutes, passed, but it became unimportant.

Bea's fingers threaded into my hair, dragging lines along my scalp with her nails before anchoring at my crown. Her feet interlocked with mine, and I bent my knee to fit between her plush thighs. She gasped, and I swallowed the sound whole.

I slid my hand at her waist to the base of her spine, splaying it there, tempted by the wide spread of her hips and backside. Inching lower, cresting the slope over her ass, I pressed my fingers into the give of her flesh.

She pulled her mouth from mine, breathless. "I guess you like my dress."

Grinning, I forced myself to straighten. "Yes. I really do. But it was you who kissed me."

She tugged on my collar. "What can I say? You look really good in black."

⚘

"As soon as I moved into my house, I went straight to the shelter. One look at his big brown eyes, and I knew I had to bring him home."

I studied the photo—her dog with a daisy perched on his head—carefully masking my expression. I'd seen him more times than I could count. Many of those in person.

"How did you choose this one?"

We were sitting at the kitchen island, eating the takeout I'd ordered. We hadn't stopped talking since I'd brought her inside. I'd asked question after question—things I already knew—things I'd dug up myself, but wanted to hear from her lips. Her voice, smoky and warm, seeped beneath my skin like something addictive. But beyond that, I wanted her to *give* me the pieces I'd taken, to *want* me to know her the way I already did.

She smiled at the picture. "He looks like a baby hippo, and he's a total goofball. But I thought his muscle mass might intimidate anybody who wants to mess with me."

"Does that work?"

"Most of the time. Benjamin's a lover, not a fighter. I don't think it's ever occurred to him he's capable of biting someone's hand off. But he gives good growl when he needs to. He has the opposite effect on children, though. They are drawn to him like moths to a flame."

I knew that all too well. Tally and Lacey were enamored with him, and even Scarlet was a fan. I'd made our yard available to him via the *Come on Rover* app, giving Bea and Benjamin a safe, contained place to go and the kids a chance to play with him. Watching them on the security feed was one of my most frequent distractions while at work.

"You're smiling," I remarked.

She shook her head and picked up her wineglass. "There are a few kids who've moved into my neighborhood recently. If Benjamin ever goes missing, their house will be the first place I look."

"You don't seem bothered by that."

"How can I be mad when other people fall in love with my dog? He's the shit."

I chuckled. "I didn't suspect you were a dog person the first time we met."

"Well, I am." She took a sip of her wine, leaving behind a faint pink lip print on the glass. "I wasn't allowed to have a dog when I was a kid, and when I moved out on my own, everywhere I lived was too small or didn't allow pets."

"And now you have a house."

"I do. It's not big or fancy, but I'm still pinching myself I get to live there." She reached over to my hand resting on the counter and absently rolled my ring. "It's this adorable little row house. The owners are a painfully cool, older goth couple originally from

Savannah, Georgia. They bought the house, painted it black, and put a little Savannah-style fountain in the tiny front yard."

"You showed me the house."

Her eyes lifted to mine, wide and wondrous. "You remember that?"

"I do. The time I'd spent with you had been the last good night I'd had for a while. I held onto it." I turned my hand over to catch hers, rubbing my thumb along the bumps of her knuckles. "When we drove past it, you pointed it out and said it was you in house form."

Her mouth curved into a smile. "That sounds like me. And it's true."

"I'm glad you were able to fulfill one of your dreams."

"It was the craziest circumstance, to be honest. The couple had decided to move back to Savannah. They hadn't wanted to sell the house or let it sit empty, but they're staunchly anti-landlord, so they'd posted an ad for what was basically a permanent house sitter."

It *had* come together perfectly, but not without some behind-the-scenes machinations. Flora and Salem Douglas *had* moved to Savannah, but they were no longer the owners of Bea's house. That was a shell company that could be traced back to me if someone were willing to untangle several layers of firewalls and false leads. Since Bea was happy in her current circumstances—and Flora and Salem had been paid well to keep up the ruse—I doubted that would come to pass.

"That does sound like fate," I agreed.

"I think it was. My friend Shira moved in next door, making it even better." She sighed. "Then she had a baby with her boyfriend and moved in with him two houses away, so now I've got Ben as a neighbor."

"Ben?" I watched her face carefully, trying to read her.

"Ben." Her nose twitched. "He's constantly cheery and lets himself into my house far too often, but I take advantage of his big muscles, so we call it even."

"How—" I forced myself to swallow and steady my voice. "How do you take advantage of his muscles?"

Bea didn't seem to notice I was on the verge of launching off my stool, taking out my computer, and hacking the state's housing department to have Ben's house condemned. Five minutes, at most, and he'd be gone from Bea's life for good.

Except, not really, since his twin brother was involved with her best friend.

"Carrying heavy things. If he's around, he's always up for being my pack mule." Her eyes narrowed. "You can't be jealous of Ben."

My brows winged. "I can't?"

"Nope. If he were kind of shy, a little geeky, insanely smart, dark-haired, bespeckled, and outlandishly handsome, we might have a problem."

I could be slow on the uptake at times, but I did not miss what she was saying. I'd seen Ben Wells. With muscles on top of muscles, it was hard to fathom any woman wouldn't be interested in him, but Bea wasn't *any* woman.

My spine loosened. As far as I was concerned, the Ben Wells subject was settled. There were other obstacles to face. I wouldn't waste any more of my thoughts on their relationship. In fact, I was relieved Bea had him nearby to help her when she needed it.

"It's a good thing I fit that description to a tee."

"That's true." Her eyes danced over my face. "You *are* outlandishly handsome, aren't you?"

I adjusted my glasses. "I was referring to the bespeckled, geeky part, but…"

Her laugh was light and feathery. "I like those parts just as much."

I considered her for a moment. "You seem happy."

She paused, teeth sinking into her lower lip, then nodded. "I am. I feel grounded for the first time in…forever. Like I'm not just surviving, I'm *settled*. And I'm not so angry all the time."

"I see that, and I love that for you." I leaned toward her, dropping my chin to snag her gaze. "I'll admit, though, I don't mind when you're a little mean, even if it's directed at me."

Her body tipped toward mine, putting us inches apart. "Do you have a masochistic streak, Tore?"

"Only when it comes to you."

Some scents overwhelmed me, but Bea smelled so right, it was all I could do not to bury my nose in her throat. Warm and sweet, like vanilla blossoms hid just beneath her skin.

My restraint frayed.

Using her free hand, she traced the shell of my ear then drew a line along my jaw, ending at my chin. She pressed her finger there, digging into the divot in the center.

"I love the way you blush." She rubbed her lips together. "Is that just for me, Tore, or do you blush for anyone?"

I nodded. "Everything I've done lately is yours."

Her lips touched mine in a whisper. "I like that."

"I'm supposed to be the one chasing you, Bea." I caught her nape, keeping her close. "So why do I feel like your prey?"

Her breathy laugh warmed my lips. "That's a little dramatic…but do you like it?"

"Immensely."

"I like that you don't lie to me."

I didn't have time to feel guilty. Her hand slid down my chest, tracing the path to my belt, and I held perfectly still.

"Tore...?"

I pressed my thumb to her lip, enthralled at the way it puffed back up when I released it.

"Yes, Bea?"

She grinned. "Would you open a new bottle of white? I'd love another glass."

"I—" I blinked three times, ripping myself out of the spell I'd found myself under. Bea wore an amused little smirk, but it couldn't hide the flush in her cheeks. She might have been teasing me, but I wasn't the only one feeling it.

Still, there was no rush. She was here, and I'd already had a taste of her mouth. That was more than enough for now. I could be patient. I wanted to earn the right to more of her.

"Anything you want." I stood, resisting the urge to adjust the bulge in my pants. Bea's eyes lingered there, and it pleased me. "I have to go to the garage to grab a bottle. Be right back."

"I'll be here," she sang out.

I was gone no more than two minutes before returning, a bottle in each hand, and nearly dropped them both when I walked into an empty kitchen.

"Bea?" I dropped the bottles on the counter, scowling at the hollow space. Had she gone to the restroom?

I charged toward the powder room down the hall from the kitchen, but it was just as empty as the kitchen.

"Bea? Where are you?" I called, louder now, returning to the island. There was a folded piece of paper where her plate had been, and I wondered how I had missed it the first time.

With a knot in my throat, I picked it up, reading the scrawling blue ink.

Tore,

If you want me, you'll have to find me first!

-Bea

Holy hell.

Blood flooded south as I tucked her note in my pocket.

How was it possible this woman kept getting more perfect?

Tipping my head back, I shouted, "I'm coming for you, Beatrice."

Heart thrashing, I set off, ready for the chase.

Chapter Twenty

Bea

What was I doing?

What in the *hell* was I doing?

I had no clue, but sweet baby lizards, it was fun. My blood hadn't pumped like this since…ever.

Ditching my heels to go stealth mode, I tiptoed along the dark, empty hallway upstairs, searching for a hiding spot. I couldn't out-run Tore. I wasn't built for speed. Come to think of it, I wasn't built for crawling into small spaces either.

Oh my god, *what* was I doing?

I chose a door at random, and it turned out to be a bedroom. Of course, there was no furniture inside. Trying to conceal myself behind the curtains seemed a little obvious.

"Bea?"

My name echoed through the cavernous space. He'd discovered I was missing.

Goose bumps prickled my flesh as I desperately searched for a hiding spot. Somewhere that would take him time to find me. Build his frustration to the boiling point. Excitement flooded through me, pushing me toward a closet.

"Bea? Where are you?"

I shoved myself into the farthest corner, my chest rising and falling in rapid waves. What would happen when he found me?

More importantly, what did I *want* to happen?

The next time he called out, it was different. Animalistic. A threat.

"I'm coming for you, Beatrice."

He'd found my note. The game had truly begun. I had nothing to be afraid of, but I was terrified. I bit my inner cheek to stop myself from squealing as his feet pounded on the stairs.

Hiding in the closet suddenly didn't seem like a great idea. It would be the first place he'd look, and the game would be over.

Heartbeat thrumming in my throat, I crept out just as Tore called, "Come out, come out, wherever you are." He was getting *so* close, there was no time to waste.

I lurched for the first door, hoping to find a new hiding place and not some secret tech server room full of blinking lights and webs of wires. I'd found the en suite bathroom. Thank goodness.

I threw myself inside and closed the door as quietly as I could, locking it with a soft *snick*.

"Keep running, sweet Bea. You'll only make it worse when I catch you."

Worse? My knees nearly buckled.

I backed up, bracing myself against the tile wall. What did worse mean?

And why did I like the sound of it?

My thighs clamped together as heat swelled between them, and I slammed my hand over my mouth to stifle the whimper trying to escape. This was too much. I couldn't bear it.

His footsteps slowed. He was in the bedroom. So damn close. He'd find me any moment. The door was locked, but this was his house. If he wanted in, he'd find his way.

"This house isn't that big, Bea," he said, his voice lower, amused, dangerous—so unlike the Tore I knew. A delicious edge of fear sent lava through my veins. "There are only so many places to hide. I'll find you. And when I do..."

What? What would he do?

My jaw trembled from the massive rush of adrenaline flooding my system.

The doorknob jiggled. I squeaked and slid to the side until my shins hit the edge of the bathtub.

He laughed, like he could see me. Like he knew the wild mix of turned-on and panicked churning inside me.

"You locked me out?" Another laugh, low and threatening. "That's cute, Bea. Really cute."

I slapped both hands over my mouth to muffle a moan.

Oh my jumping junipers, by the time he made it into the bathroom, I'd be nothing but a puddle.

I'd barely had a second to accept my fate when the doorknob rattled harder.

Click.

Oh no.

No, no, no!

The lock gave way, and the door crept open with an eerie creak. As a sliver of his face came into view, my legs finally began working again, and I bolted.

I wasn't thinking straight. Instead of trying to get past him, I ended up in the massive, glass-enclosed shower on the other side of the room. It was big enough to fit a whole family. My heart wasn't galloping so hard I failed to notice the built-in benches, steam vents, and multiple showerheads. I would have loved to partake in the luxury, but since I was about to meet my doom, I guessed that wouldn't be happening.

I was a straight-up horror movie victim. Who closed themselves in a glass shower? *The first one to die, that's who.*

Tore sauntered into the room, edging across the tile, his fiery gaze pinned on me. He'd taken off his glasses, adding to his fierceness. My Tore had been replaced by a hunter on the prowl.

He stopped on the other side of the glass, eyes locking on mine like a specimen to examine.

"There you are," he uttered, low and ragged.

I raised my hand. "Hi."

He shook his head. "Did you really think you could hide from me in here?"

I pressed myself against the tiled wall, trembling, giddy...so stupidly turned on I could taste it.

"Not really." I licked my lips, parched. "I was hoping to delay the inevitable."

Without warning, he lunged, yanking the door open.

I shrieked, jumping sideways, barely evading him as he grabbed for me. In my blind panic, I slapped the shower controls. Water exploded from every direction, soaking him in seconds.

He froze, while I had managed to position myself in the one corner the water didn't reach.

"Oops," I tried, going for innocent, hoping I'd get out of here without getting drenched.

He looked down at himself then back at me, his nostrils flaring. Soaked to the bone, he still managed to look sexy as hell. His shirt plastered to his heaving chest, pants stuck to his long, lean thighs and the thick bulge behind his zipper. His dark hair was black, flattened to his head in messy pieces.

"Now you've done it," he rasped.

I raised both hands like a shield. "No, no. It was an accident. I didn't mean it. Besides, you look—"

"Like a drowned rat?"

I giggled. He really had no idea what kind of thoughts were racing through my mind. "Not even close."

He cocked his head. "If I'm drowning, you are too."

Seeing his intention a mile away, I tried to run, but I was laughing too hard, and the floor was too wet. I slipped and nearly went down when a strong hand caught my arm, saving me but putting me directly in the line of the rain shower.

"Got you," Tore murmured as he pulled me against his chest. "Nowhere to run now, sweet Bea."

I tilted my head back, blinking away the drops clinging to my lashes. "Oh no, you've caught me." There was zero disappointment in my statement. I'd spent a lot of time on my hair and makeup, and my dress had cost a pretty penny, but I had absolutely no problem with all of it being doused with water.

The menace in his gaze fell away as his eyes bored into mine. "Are you—is this okay?"

My mouth opened then closed. I thought it was obvious I was delighted by the turn of events, but Tore needed my words. Seemed what was obvious to me might not have been to him.

I nodded. "Can we keep playing?" My nose crinkled. "Or do *I* look like too much of a drowned rat—"

He cut me off with a kiss. Hot, wet, urgent. Licking into my mouth and groaning as he flattened me to the wall. Rubbing against me, his hands roaming over me, my body softened, molding to his. He kissed me with such soul-shaking intensity, I had to grip his soaked shirt to keep from going down.

"This isn't how I pictured tonight going," he murmured against my lips.

My head was light and dreamy. "You didn't picture me ambushing you in your own house?"

"No." He laughed breathlessly. "I should know to expect the unexpected from you."

"Always. That's one of my best features."

I couldn't stop giggling as his mouth lowered to my jaw and throat, the adrenaline rush making me feel silly and *alive*.

Tore glowered at me, amusement dancing behind his menacing expression. "Do you think this is funny, Beatrice?"

"I really do," I whispered.

He caught my lower lip between his teeth for half a second then kissed me like he was making a point. My knees tried to give out, but he had me secure in his arms.

"You're not going anywhere," he warned.

"I don't want to—not unless you're there too."

Tore growled again, lower this time. *Possessive.* His hands explored, needy and confident, as if he'd finally stopped holding back and started *claiming*. My dress clung to me like a second skin. If I'd been less turned on, it would have been uncomfortable, but I liked that the barriers between our bodies had been thinned. We could touch, feel, *know* one another in an entirely new way.

But, like the idiot I was, I couldn't stop laughing. Every time his mouth left mine, giggles burst out of me. Tore's answering chuckle vibrated against my flesh, spurring me on.

Water thundered around us, heating me to my bones. Each time Tore kissed my throat, I gasped, arching into him. My belly ached with desire, and my head was lighter than a feather.

His fingers went to the zipper at the back of my dress. "Can I take this off?"

I nodded, breathless. "Please."

He unzipped me. Slow. Torturous. And when my dress finally fell open, he dragged it off me at the same agonizing pace.

It got stuck on my hips, and I laughed. "I think I might be too wet."

His eyes darkened, flashing to mine. "Then we'll have to dry you off. You can't stay in this dress."

He shut the water off, and we climbed out, clinging to one another. The tile was warm, but the air pricked at my wet flesh. I huddled closer, trying to work my way beneath his skin.

Exhaling, his forehead dropped to mine. "Shit. I just remembered we don't have towels here. They've already been moved to my new place."

Snorting a laugh, I wrapped my arms around his waist. "Oh no. I guess we'll have to dry each other. How terrible."

He raised his head, checking in with me again. "Are we still good?"

"Yes. We're terribly, awfully, crazy good." Pushing back, I shoved my dress the rest of the way off, letting it land in a squelching puddle at my feet.

"Now catch me!"
I bolted out of the room.

Chapter Twenty-one

Salvatore

There were only so many places for Bea to go, and her trail was easy to follow. She'd left puddles like breadcrumbs down the hallway in her escape.

As I tracked her, I yanked off my wet clothing, adding to the water, no doubt ruining the wood floors. Normally, I would have cared. It would have driven me to distraction. But one flash of Bea's pale, creamy flesh in her black, lacy lingerie, and catching her was all I could focus on.

I was a column of iron, and her giggles were magnetized, drawing me toward her.

She'd gone to my bedroom—the last room in the hallway. There was nowhere else she could've gone.

Down to my underwear, I pushed inside, finding her standing in the center of the room on the rug I'd left behind.

"Found you."

She grinned. "You've lost your clothes."

"So have you."

She crooked her finger. "I'm cold. Come warm me up, Salvatore."

I went, but I took my time getting there. It couldn't be helped. I had to look at her, and if I went too fast, I had no doubt I'd trip over my own feet.

The moon glinted off her like she'd been lit by design. Her skin gleamed silvery white, in stark contrast to her black lingerie. There was a name for the one-piece satin-and-lace contraption molded to her curves, but I didn't know it. I was more focused on the parts of her that weren't covered.

Her legs were bare, and the way they brushed together when she shifted was mesmerizing. My gaze snagged on the supple give of her flesh, the subtle bounce. Everything about her made my fantasies vastly underwhelming.

I trailed down to her feet, one slightly on top of the other. Her nails were painted dark red, and from where I stood, I could see her fine bones rippling as she flexed her toes. How was it possible for even her feet to be pretty? I didn't think about feet. Not anyone's. But I couldn't skip a single part of her.

"Tore?"

Right. I was supposed to be moving. Going to her.

"I'm looking at you," I forced out.

"Fine. I'll look at you too," she countered.

The satin-and-lace garment clung to her like a second skin, hugging the generous swell of her hips and dipping at her waist before spilling over the soft rise of her belly like a trickling waterfall.

Her breasts were barely contained in lacy cups, rising dangerously high with each breath she took. All I could think was how badly I wanted to bury my face there and forget the rest of the world.

"Salvatore." Her voice cracked like a whip, snapping me back. Hands on her hips, the glare she shot me went straight to my spine.

"Bea"—I cleared my throat—"you're beautiful."

Her eyelids lowered to half-mast, and her tongue darted out to wet her lips. "Thank you. Now, won't you be a good boy and come here?"

Fuck.

My cock throbbed in my briefs, and my brain kicked back into gear. I crossed the room and caught her. Curling my arm around her waist, I snatched her against me. She released a breath as we collided, her hands flattening on my shoulders.

"I like the way you listen," she whispered. "Now that you've got me, what are you going to do with me?"

We moved at once, our mouths seeking and finding. Kissing hard, deep, urgent. Grappling hands, touching, caressing. The game had been underway all night, bringing us both to this boiling point.

This wasn't part of the plan, but when Bea was in my presence, I lost all sense of structure. She brought chaos with her and swept me into it. It was heady and overwhelming, blocking out everything but her. The now. The present.

We kissed until standing became useless then fell into a pile on the thick rug, Bea on her back, reaching for me, taking my weight on top of her.

Bracing myself on one elbow, I kissed and sucked along her throat, unable to get enough of her taste, the way she felt under my lips. Her raspy moans were nearly my undoing. What would she think if I came in my underwear without even touching her?

I wouldn't be her good boy.

That thought yanked me into focus, back to the warm, soft woman beneath me. Her wet hair splayed on the rug, the hair around her face already drying into ringlets. I touched those silky curls then her velvety cheek. She turned her head, catching my palm with her lips.

"You can touch me," she said.

"I don't think I have a choice."

If she asked me to stop, I would. But I had her exactly where I wanted her, and nothing else would get in my way.

I trailed a hand down her front, squeezing her breasts, the sharp point of her nipple like a pebble beneath my touch. She groaned when I squeezed her, arching for me.

My hand slipped lower, fingers trailing along the smooth fabric of her lingerie, feeling the heat beneath the fabric. I didn't rush. I couldn't.

She tilted her hips, just a little. An offering. An answer.

I cupped her over the lace, engulfed by the warmth and softness of her thighs. I tapped my finger over her seam, making her breath stutter. "Can I?"

Heavy-lidded eyes on mine, she parted her legs. "You'd better."

I wouldn't disappoint her. Not ever.

Hooking my fingers beneath the elastic edge, I dragged the fabric to the side, baring her to me. When I made contact with her wet, swollen skin, I shifted back, barely holding it together. She was pretty, sexy, glistening with desire.

She moaned as I dragged a singular finger through her slick heat. I lifted my gaze to her face, watching the way her lashes fluttered, her mouth parted, her breath caught. She was in this with me. Just as needy. Just as turned on.

I did it again. Slower. Deeper.

She rolled her hips, chasing the friction, gasping when I circled her clit with my thumb while slipping two fingers inside. I had to take a deep breath, battling to control myself. My cock ached with need, but this wasn't about me. My focus was on the woman writhing beneath me—on giving her pleasure and satisfaction.

"Tore—" Her voice broke on my name.

"I've got you," I murmured. "I want you to come for me. Do you need more?"

Her fingers wrapped around my arm. "Harder. Fuck me harder."

I sank my fingers deeper. "Like this?"

"Yeah." She raised her knees higher. "Keep going."

I lowered myself over her, worked her with my hand as I sucked on the curve of her throat. Unable to stop myself, I rocked my hips, my clothed cock rubbing against her inner thigh.

Her grip on my arm tightened, and she met my thrusts, crying, moaning, telling me I was getting it right. She didn't hold back. She let me see her. Feel her.

"Yes, yes, *yes*." Her neck arched, insides tightened, and she fell. Fully, completely, lost everything. Her inner walls clamped around my fingers, keeping me deep within her, pleasure flooding her swollen channel.

There was nothing like this. Nothing I had ever seen or known. That Bea was able to be so confident, seeking pleasure, not holding back her reaction, was no surprise, but watching her was unmatched.

She had to have known I was hanging by a thread. As soon as her insides slackened, her eyes opened, and she looked at me. "Tell me what you need."

There was a long list, but the most pressing throbbed between us. My commitment to take things slow had fallen by the wayside, but I would not take us any further, even if I ached to get inside her.

"Can I come on you?"

"*Please*." She released my arm, spreading her hand over her thigh. "Right here, baby. Let me feel it."

I reached down, pulling my cock out of my underwear. I was so hard, it *hurt* to touch.

"Yes, Tore," she whispered.

Cupping her throat with one hand, I balanced on the other, guiding myself into the crease of her thigh where her slickness had spread. I thrust gently, controlled, every stroke a test. She was so slick and hot, I had to bite down on my tongue not to spill the second we made contact.

"Jesus, Bea. Holy hell, what you do to me."

She curved her arm around me and gripped my ass to pull me closer, urging me to go harder. Her moans vibrated against my chest, like she enjoyed this just as much as when I'd been touching her.

"Give it to me," she cooed. "I want you all over me. Make me messy."

Her husky, coaxing voice went straight to my head, and I groaned, wedging myself deeper into the cradle of her thigh. I was so close to sliding into her; if I shifted an inch or two, I'd be there.

Not yet.

Not now.

This sweet torture was all I could bear.

"You can't hide from me," I gritted out.

"But it's so fun when you find me." Lifting her head, she nipped my chin. "Let go."

There was no resisting her call.

I kissed her hard, messy, desperate. Sliding my hand up her side, I cupped one lush breast and squeezed gently, thumbing over the nipple through the lace.

She wrecked me.

I jerked once, twice, then spilled against her, hot and helpless, my mouth open on her neck as I lost control.

She held me tight as I shuddered through it, completely undone. I couldn't remember ever coming this hard, and she hadn't even touched me.

It was her. Us. A culmination of missteps and longing, mistakes and forgiveness, and unabating desire had brought us here.

She laughed, breathless and mischievous, cradling my head to her chest.

I rubbed my face against her breasts then raised my head to meet her gaze. "Are you okay?"

For most, her grin would have been answer enough, but she gave me the words I needed. "I'm not sure I've ever been better."

It was funny. I didn't often find my feelings aligning with other people's, but I completely understood what she meant.

I felt exactly the same.

CHAPTER
TWENTY-TWO
Bea

WHEN CLARA HAD ASKED me to be a bridesmaid, I'd gone straight to Anthony for advice. He'd laid out all my potential duties, which, according to him, involved a terrifying amount of crafts and tulle. Thankfully, Clara had quickly put my fears to rest. All she wanted was for me to wear a pretty dress and stand beside her.

That, I could do.

So, here we were: Clara, Shira, and I out shopping for dresses. Mostly, it was an excuse to catch up. Clara claimed she was too old to have matchy-matchy bridesmaids, which meant we were free to play.

I held up a slinky satin number in crimson and waggled my brows. "This says *maid of honor*...in a slutty way."

Clara snorted. "Perfect. That's exactly the vibe I want for my wedding."

Shira patted Jonah's bottom in the carrier strapped to her front as she sifted through racks of colorful gowns. "I need something to accommodate my chest. But loose enough to pop a boob out so I can pump."

I pursed my lips. "See? Shira's on board with the slutty vibe. She's already planning on having her tits out."

Clara bumped her shoulder into mine. "I'm rethinking asking you to be a bridesmaid."

I curved my arm around her waist. "I'll be on my best behavior, darling. You know I'm honored you want me standing with you."

"I promise not to take my tits out in front of your guests," Shira teased softly.

"I never doubted you." Clara plucked a buttery yellow dress off the rack and waved it at her. "This would look gorgeous on you. You have to try it on."

Shira looked down at the gurgling baby attached to her. "Okay, I wasn't thinking this through when I put him in the carrier instead of the stroller. Maybe I'll buy a couple and try them on at home."

I put my arms out. "Or you could hand that giant baby over to his Aunt Bea."

Shira gave me a grateful look and started unbuckling Jonah. He was only three months old, but he took after his father and was already the size of a six-month-old. Seeing him in petite Shira's arms was almost comical, but they looked just right together. She was a natural mother—laid back and adoring—and Jonah was a reflection of that ease.

I took Jonah from her, immediately nuzzling his button nose. He cooed and flailed his chunky arms, settling quickly. He was just as easygoing as his parents, happily hanging out in the arms of people he was familiar with.

While Shira disappeared into the dressing room, I sat with Jonah, telling him all about the dresses in the shop. Without warning, a pang of nostalgia struck so bone deep, it took my breath away.

My baby sister, Madeleine, had been a chunk like Jonah. She'd had curls like his too, but where his were dark, hers had been strawberry blonde. From the beginning, she'd squirm and fuss, but when I'd hold her, she'd find my gaze and stare like she was mesmerized.

My brother, Davis, had been long and lean, but oh, had he been a snuggler. Even as a wild toddler, he'd stop in the middle of a whirlwind to sit on my lap and nuzzle as close as he could get without living in my skin. If that had been an option, I was sure he would have taken it.

Maddie would be turning eighteen this year. *Eighteen*. A whole adult. And I didn't know her. Davis was sixteen. Sometimes when I was driving, I wondered if we were on the road at the same time.

Through Caroline, I'd seen pictures and gotten little updates, but that was it. I could have been nothing more than an internet stranger browsing their social media. I didn't know what their voices sounded like or if either had a boyfriend or girlfriend. I didn't know where Maddie planned to apply for college, or if Davis ever thought about me. I had never even met my youngest sister, Jane.

I wondered if she even knew I existed.

Losing them had been the greatest tragedy of my life. I would never get over it. Still, even after all this time, it hit me some days harder than others.

Jonah wiggled in my arms, drawing my attention back to him, and I smiled. It was impossible not to.

"I see you, big boy," I singsonged. "You are the sweetest boy in the world, aren't you? I'm going to eat your face off. That's what I'm going to do."

Shira's laugh rang out as she left the dressing room. "Please don't eat my baby."

"Just a little bite?" I lifted his hand to my mouth and pretended to nibble it.

Clara returned with an armload of dresses, scanning Shira up and down. "Oh, wow. You look incredible in yellow. How do you feel?"

She smoothed her hands over her midsection. "I don't know. Is my pooch too obvious?"

Clara and I exchanged a glance. Even three months postpartum, Shira was tiny and had a body many women dreamed of, but she didn't always see herself the way others did. Roman had made a lot of inroads with her, convincing her how beautiful she was, but she was still working on it.

"I don't see it," Clara said. "But if you're not comfortable in that cut, try another one. You'd look stunning in emerald."

I raised Jonah's hand. "Your son votes for Mommy to wear green. He thinks that's a great idea."

Shira laughed, all her self-doubt falling away. If she was confident about anything, it was being a mother. "If Jonah says so, I kind of have no choice."

Clara sat beside me on the padded bench outside the dressing room, scrutinizing me.

"You're in a better mood than usual."

"Am I?"

"Yes." She crossed her legs and gave me a sharp look that probably made men piss themselves in the boardroom. "You haven't given an update on Tore lately. Shira and I were talking about it and—"

"You talk about me when I'm not around?"

"All good things," she said breezily, running a finger along the curve of Jonah's cheek. "Now I'm gathering there's a reason you haven't brought him up, and it just so happens you look shiny and new today. *I* think something happened and you don't want to talk about it."

My friends had gotten the rundown of Tore's explanation after our first meeting at his house, and they'd both been deeply sympathetic to what he'd gone through. But, after that, I hadn't brought him up again. And, as they were both busy women with a lot going on in their lives, they hadn't pried.

Normally, I was an open book, but my feelings for this man were so convoluted, I didn't know where to begin.

"If you think I don't want to talk about it, why are you asking?"

She grabbed Jonah's foot, giving it a gentle shake. "Because I think you *need* to talk about it."

Shira rushed out of the dressing room, looking like a goddess in green. "Not without me. I want to hear everything."

Clara stood, circled Shira, and nodded sharply. "This is the one, babe. If you don't wear this dress to my wedding, I won't get married."

She giggled breathlessly and twisted side to side, looking at herself in the wall of mirrors. "It fits me well, doesn't it? Of course, I'll have to get it hemmed since it's a foot too long, but otherwise…"

"Like it was made for you," I agreed. "You're stunning. I don't think you'll find a better dress, but I'm game to keep watching you try them on."

"No, I hate trying on clothes. I think this is the one." She pulled her gaze away from the mirror to look at me. "Now, let me get changed back into my clothes then tell me everything about Tore."

We got sidetracked a few times—I tried on a few dresses too and found one I loved—but the four of us finally ended up tucked away at a small table in a nearby café. Jonah was fast asleep on Shira's chest, so I felt comfortable letting the details of last night fly without worrying his little ears would overhear.

My friends were worldly women. Not much shocked them. Still, they both gaped at me as I came to the end of my story.

"He *chased* you?" Shira asked.

I nodded. "And caught me."

Clara leaned forward. "That sounds…"

"Hot?" I supplied.

"Uh…yes. Hot." Then she added, "Crazy, fun, wild."

"All those things." I grinned, picking up my matcha. "Are you coming up with honeymoon ideas for you and Jake?"

Clara arched her brow. "I might be filing it away for later use."

"But you didn't have sex?" Shira coaxed.

I shook my head. "No. I think—no, I *know* I would have if he'd asked. But he didn't. He was really"—I paused, searching for the word—"gentlemanly? He kept checking in with me and making sure I was okay every step of the way."

"Now *that's* hot," Shira said.

"Consent King." I brought my straw to my mouth, taking a sip. "I think I really like him."

Clara reached across the table to squeeze my hand. "That's pretty obvious, babe, and I love that for you. You haven't liked anyone since I've known you."

I shrugged. "I've been on a couple bad dates, but you're right. No one has caught my interest the way he has. I'm trying not to get too excited, though."

"Because of last time?" Shira asked.

"That—of course that, but I also don't know if I'm capable of being in a real relationship." I put my cup down and sighed. "See? I'm already getting way ahead of myself. One good night, and I'm considering settling down with the man. Thank Nikola Jokić, he can't hear me now."

Clara sputtered. "Nikola Jokić? Since when are you a basketball fan?"

My eyes flared. "I work in a bar. The games are always on. Besides, have you seen the Denver Nuggets lineup? How can I *not* be a basketball fan?"

Shira patted Jonah as he stirred. "I see the appeal, but I'm more into rugby myself."

Considering Roman had played pro rugby and now co-owned part of Denver's team, it made sense. He'd taken us to a game, and while I was a *big* fan of the little shorts that showed off the players' massive thighs, I could take or leave the sport.

Not that I'd ever admit that to Shira. Or Ben. Heaven help me, if I ever told Ben, I'd never hear the end of it.

Clara sliced the air with both hands. "We're getting off topic. Let's return to Tore and Bea."

"Yes, please." Shira's eyes were lit as they landed on mine. "You like him."

"I do." Saying that out loud hit something tender in me. Today was the first time I'd truly admitted it, even to myself. Allowing myself to like this man made me vulnerable in a way I normally tried to avoid.

I pressed my lips together to gather myself. "I'm going to see where it goes. But don't count on me asking you to be bridesmaids anytime soon."

Clara raised a finger. "I'll be happily available for you whenever that happens. Just please, *please* don't ask me to wear ruffles. I love you, but not enough to wear ruffles."

"What's wrong with ruffles?" Shira asked. "I *like* ruffles."

The three of us cracked up, and right there, in that little café, Jonah snoring on Shira's chest and laughter warming the air around us, I promised them if I got married sometime in the distant future, they could pick out their own bridesmaid dresses.

Chapter Twenty-three
Bea

BENJAMIN WAS NEEDY THE second I got home, bouncing around me like he had springs in his feet. Love and pats didn't calm him, so I pulled up the *Come on Rover* app, breathing a sigh of relief when the yard across the street was free.

The kids ran outside almost as soon as we arrived. Lacey's hand slipped into mine like it was the most natural thing in the world.

And strangely, it kind of was.

Talon beelined for Benjamin, who nearly did a backflip, he was so excited to see his boy.

His boy. Damn. Where had that thought come from?

Probably Benjamin. He'd telepathically slipped it to me. That made the most sense. He pretty much considered the entire world his.

"Scarlet and Grandpa are painting," Lacey said.

"Oh yeah? What are they painting?"

"They're doing the painting game. It's so fun. They trade canvases back and forth until the end." Her eyes grew impossibly round. "No one knows what the pictures are gonna be 'cause they can change at any minute."

"Wow. That's a cool game. If I played, both pictures would probably turn into blobs."

She snickered. "You're a bad artist?"

"No, I just like blobs," I deadpanned.

She nodded sagely. "What kind? Rainbow sparkly blobs would be cool."

I squeezed her tiny hand. "How'd you guess my favorite kind?"

She shrugged. "I'm smart like Uncle Sally, I guess."

Talon and Benjamin skidded to a stop in front of us. "Come on, Lace. We're going to have a race."

I waved at him. "Hi, Tally. You know, I'm here too."

His brow creased. "I know. Benjamin can't come over by himself."

Leave it to an eight-year-old to lay down the cold, hard facts. "Not *yet*. I bet he's plotting how to do that, though."

Talon gave me another skeptical once-over then took off down the yard, Benjamin hot on his heels, ears flapping like he might take flight. Lacey's fingers wiggled free from mine, and she chased after them, laughter trailing behind her like streamers.

Propped against the deck railing, I watched them play for a while. Benjamin might have kept going forever, but the kids began to flag. I called him over, and he came, tongue lolling and eyes bright, his springy energy finally dipping.

"Come on, wild man." I gave him a pat. "Time to go home."

Lacey hugged me goodbye, so hard she vibrated. It was sweet, and I liked it, albeit reluctantly. Kids still weren't my thing, but I was considering making an exception for this one.

Talon gave me an obligatory wave, already turning back to Benjamin like I was borrowing *his* dog for the night. If I hadn't been the keeper of the good snacks, Benjamin probably would have dumped me for Talon in a heartbeat.

By the time we got back to my place, Benjamin had downgraded from springs to cinder blocks. I barely got the door closed before he flopped, full body, onto the rug with a long, theatrical sigh.

"You okay down there, bud?" I asked as I toed off my shoes.

He gave a quiet *whuff* I decided to take as *barely hanging on*.

I flopped onto the couch and reached for my phone, half thinking I should check emails. The first thing I saw was a message from Tore.

Tore: How are you?

A swell of relief threatened to sweep me under. I hadn't even realized how tense I'd been since saying good night to him yesterday until I wasn't. This wasn't a repeat of two years ago. He wasn't disappearing off the face of the earth without a word.

Me: My dog is on death's door, but I'm good.

Tore: Is he having a medical emergency? Do you need help?

Me: No, no, I'm joking! He was playing with the kids across the street. Now, he's dramatically flopped on the floor, becoming one with my rug. He's fine. Sorry I alarmed you.

Tore: No, it's my fault. I can't always read tone through text. If we'd been speaking, I would have picked up on the joke.

Me: How is that your fault? It's mine for not being clear. I'm making a mental note not to be sarcastic through texts. I'll reserve that brand of charm for when we're face to face.

Tore: Don't change for me. I'll read you better.

Me: And I'll read *you* better. How are you?

Tore: Still at work. I haven't gotten half of what I need to get done because you've been distracting me.

I couldn't stop the silly, giddy grin from spreading across my face.

Me: We haven't even spoken today!

Tore: The memory of you from last night is enough. I want to see you again tonight, but I can't.

Me: I get it. I'm wiped out. We should take it slow, anyway.

Tore: We should, but I'd rather not. One of the artists I collect is having an opening Saturday. Go with me.

Disappointment curdled in my stomach. I was scheduled to work, but a real date, where he shared something he loved with me? Turning that down was almost impossible.

Me: Can I get back to you? I'm supposed to work, but I might be able to figure something out.

Tore: I'd really love it if you did, Beatrice.

We texted back and forth for a little while, telling each other about our days. I knew he was still at work, but he didn't seem in a rush to end our conversation. Sharing casual, easy banter shifted something between us. Like we'd been off-balance and a lever had been pulled, setting us into the proper place, moving forward instead of wobbling to the side.

Eventually, he had to get back to work, so I let him. And without dread, almost certain I'd hear from him soon.

I was making dinner when my phone pinged with a notification. I wiped my hands and checked the screen, staring in disbelief.

A new inquiry through my booking system.

Another company requesting weekly catering for their team meeting. For fifty people. That would be...

A *lot* of money.

It would more than replace my waitressing job.

My heart thudded. A huge part of me wanted to throw caution to the wind. Would it be crazy to count my chickens before they hatched?

Hell yes it would.

But...

I could give up my shift this once. And maybe, if this gig panned out long term, I could quit once and for all.

I wouldn't know how to handle just having one job, but I could damn well learn.

My teeth dug into my bottom lip as I made my decision. I was going to do it.

Me: Hey, if the offer still stands, I'd love to go to the gallery opening with you this weekend.

His reply was immediate and exactly what I needed.

Tore: You've made my night, Beatrice. Thank you for making time for me.

Yeah, I'd *definitely* made the right choice.

Chapter Twenty-four
Salvatore

IT WASN'T OFTEN I forgot plans. My schedule was meticulous. My father and I shared a calendar, so one of us was always home with the kids. Usually, it was me, since his social life was far more exciting.

That was why, when I left my room, dressed and ready to meet Bea at the gallery, he knew exactly where I was going.

Except, where he *thought* I was going wasn't the gallery.

"Tell Sam hi for me," he said, rubbing his chin, silver brows furrowed. "Can't remember the last time I saw that kid. He should stop by, see the kids, have dinner with us. Tell him I said so."

I tugged on my cuffs, distracted and eager to get out the door. "Remind me on Monday. I'll extend the invitation."

"Why wait until Monday? Tell him tonight."

I stopped in my tracks, turning toward him. "I'm not seeing Sam tonight."

Something nudged at the back of my mind. A half-formed thought, a loose thread.

My dad took out his phone, tapping the screen a few times. "Did the dinner meeting get canceled? It's still right here on the calendar."

"Dinner meeting?" I took his phone from him, my stomach sinking as I read the bold letters.

Dinner. Vocellis. Sam, Drew Epstein, Don Wilde, Minnie Santos. 8 p.m.

Shit.

"That's not where you're heading." Dad stepped back, giving me a long once-over. "You look good, champ. You have a date tonight?"

"I do." I grimaced, my thoughts tangling fast. Canceling on Bea wasn't an option. Not after she'd rearranged her schedule for me. But Sam wouldn't be happy if I skipped the dinner, and he'd been unhappy with me a lot lately.

My father squeezed my shoulder, bringing me out of my internal spiral. "You're losing the plot, Sal. Take a deep breath. We'll figure this out."

Meeting his steady gaze, I pulled in a long breath and gradually let it out. This was familiar. My father had a knack for getting me to focus. Left to my own devices, I'd have gotten overwhelmed and shut down.

"Okay." I twisted my ring, focusing on one thought at a time. "I'll have to figure out how to be in two places at once."

He chuckled. "No chance of canceling the date?"

I shook my head.

That made him laugh a little harder. "Well, all right. I'm interested in hearing about the woman who's got you in your finest duds, but we'll talk about that later. Where are you taking her?"

"Art gallery for Maria Petridis's opening. Then dinner, if she's up for it."

"Got it." He nodded a few times. "You'll take her to the opening, then to this dinner with Sam. Text Sam. Tell him you'll be late. Of course, it won't be exactly what you had planned, but it'll be fine. Adjust your mindset so you can enjoy the night. Roll with it."

Fine. Right. Not the private, romantic evening I had in my head, but I could roll with it.

Bea hadn't let me pick her up, stating she lived only a few blocks from the gallery, and it would be silly to drive. That was technically true. But I suspected the real reason was caution. She didn't want to count on me. Not yet.

Which was fair. I'd given her every reason to hesitate.

But I wouldn't let her down again.

She strode up to the gallery minutes after I arrived in heels that still boggled my mind.

Her dress moved with her as she walked, flowing along her hips and thighs and hugging her curves from her waist to her breasts.

She was beautiful, but it was her smile when she spotted me that stole my breath.

Surprised at first, almost uncertain, but as she drew closer, it crackled with sparks. Bright and electric, like a live wire dancing on the ground, throwing heat and light with reckless abandon.

I should have returned her smile. God knew the happiness bubbling inside me warranted one. But my brain had stalled.

Input from outside, inside, all around me, surged forward at once. The gleam of her hair in the streetlight. A passing car in desperate need of a new muffler. The shape of her mouth when she said my name. The dress. The temperature difference between outside and the air conditioning escaping the building. Her perfume, faint yet distinct. The sharp clack of her heels on the sidewalk.

It wasn't unpleasant. Just...too much. Being near her, my body registered pleasure and comfort, but my mind couldn't prioritize what to feel first.

She deserved more than my silence. She deserved for me to tell her how beautiful she was and how happy I was to see her. But my brain was buffering, overloaded from too many commands at once.

I reached for her hand, cradling it between mine.

"Beatrice," I rasped.

"Salvatore," she whispered, leaning into me. "It's okay. I feel it too."

She might have been humoring me, but I was thankful for it regardless. She let me look at her, memorize her piece by piece. The moment my thoughts caught up, I hooked my arm around her waist, pulling her against me.

"Can I kiss you?" I asked.

"I'd be disappointed if you didn't."

So would I.

The second our lips connected, everything quieted.

The street noise faded. The movement around us blurred into the background. Her mouth under mine was soft and certain, lips parting without a beat of hesitation. I kissed her with a familiarity I hadn't yet earned but felt down deep in my gut. And when she kissed me back—slow, deliberate, fingers curling into the front of my jacket—it made sense.

We made sense. Together.

When we finally pulled apart, the city was still there. The lights. The traffic. The hum of conversation outside the gallery doors.

But she was the center of my focus.

I brushed my thumb over her bottom lip. "I'd rather not go so many days without seeing you."

She flashed me another electric smile. "It did seem like too many, didn't it?" She patted my chest. "You could have asked to see me sooner."

I groaned, rolling my forehead along hers. "I will next time." I threaded my fingers with hers. "I have some news that's frustrating me."

"Tell me."

"I inadvertently double-booked myself. What do you think about joining me for dinner with Sam and a few industry people after the gallery? If you're uncomfortable, I understand, but I can't skip it. It's not what I had in mind for tonight—"

She pressed a kiss to my chin. "It's fine. If you're okay with me going, I'd like to."

I frowned. "The conversation will likely revolve around tech news and software updates—dry and fairly boring to someone not familiar with the topics."

She arched a brow. "Are you trying to talk me out of agreeing?"

"No. Absolutely not. Having you by my side will make the evening infinitely more bearable and a lot more interesting. I just want you to know what you're getting into."

"Okay. I've been warned." She sighed, toying with a button on my shirt. "If boring dinners are part of being with you, I guess I'd better get used to it."

My gut unfurled with relief. "I try to avoid them, but unfortunately, I can't say no to every one. Sam would riot."

She let out a short laugh. "We can't have that."

"No, I suppose we can't." I nodded toward the door. "Are you ready to go inside?"

"I am. I can't wait to see the kind of art you're into. It's like...a peek inside your mind."

I squeezed her hand, steady now.

"That might be true," I said softly. "Just...don't judge me too harshly."

She grinned up at me, eyes dancing with mischief. "No promises."

Chapter Twenty-Five
Bea

TORE'S TASTE IN ART was nothing like I'd expected. I pictured him being into minimalism, like Donald Judd's clean, simple lines in primary colors and subtle restraint.

This, though? This was something else entirely.

Maria Petridis made sprawling, intricate pieces on brushed aluminum. Tonight's show was titled *Glitch Cathedral*. Each work depicted vintage technology, broken down, in haunting disrepair. It made sense Tore would be drawn to her style. As we stood in front of each piece and he quietly explained the meaning behind the pixelated spires and digital skies, I felt the pull too.

"It's sad, isn't it?" I murmured, mostly to myself.

One piece showed the ghostly outline of a disintegrated joystick, nearly lost in cascading strings of code was kind of...mournful.

Tore had heard and swiveled to face me. "It is. It's a depiction of loss. History being rewritten so completely, it disappears. In its time, this technology was revered. Now, it's something we look back on and laugh at."

"Like it's quaint."

"Exactly." He cupped the sides of my neck with both hands. "You see it."

"I do." I wrapped my fingers around his wrists, rubbing his fluttering pulse. "Do you have Maria's work in your house?"

"Not yet, but I have one in my office. I'll show you this week when you come to Nox." He drew a line along my jaw with his thumb, slow and thoughtful. "I want this one."

"I think that's a very good choice. It's my favorite too."

He touched his lips to mine, humming as he did it. "Is there one that speaks to you? If there is, I would love to buy it for you."

He meant it. I heard the sincerity in his offer and the honesty in his eyes. And while I had no idea how much one of these pieces cost, I knew it was far outside my price range—and much more than I could accept as a gift.

At least, not right now, when we were still new. Down the line, if we worked out, I would have no trouble with him being as generous as he wanted. I might've been proud, but I wasn't stupid.

I liked fancy things as much as the next girl.

"Thank you, Torc. I love her work, but I can't picture any of it hanging in my little house. This is your speed."

He nodded. "Next time, we'll find a gallery with art that speaks to you. I'd love to know what that looks like."

"It's a deal."

He ventured off to find the art dealer while I strolled along, looking at everything again. It really felt like I was walking through Tore's mind. There was no chaos here, only pattern and structure. It was beautiful, in a precise, obsessive way.

I liked it.

Very much.

We were late to dinner. I thought Tore might have been anxious about it, but he strolled beside me, completely unbothered, our hands twined between us like we had all the time in the world.

Undoubtedly rude, but I was taking my cues from him. If he wasn't worried, I wasn't either.

"Is Sam going to be pissed?"

He chuffed a dry laugh. "He's already texted me seven times."

"Wonderful. I'm looking forward to spending time with a grumpy Sam."

"Don't worry about him. He's in public. He'll be on his best behavior. Image is incredibly important to him. He'll only let his displeasure with me loose when we're alone."

I didn't like the sound of that. "Does he do that often?"

He sighed. "Lately, yes. We're in the midst of a fundamental disagreement over the direction we take Nox, and it seems we're at odds more than we're in alignment, which is frustrating. It's been...tense."

"Don't you have the final say?"

"Technically. Sam owns a stake in Nox and is the COO, so his opinion matters, but I built Nox and have the final say." His fingers flexed around mine. "The problem is I'd set a precedence of acquiescence at the beginning of our friendship, and now that I'm saying no, he's finding it difficult to handle."

"You met in college, right?"

"Yes. My senior year. We were paired as roommates, and he'd made it his mission to make me cool." He smiled faintly. "I'm not sure it worked, but he gave it an honest try."

"How exactly?"

"You know, the typical things. Sent me to his barber—which had been needed and appreciated—helped me upgrade my wardrobe, dragged me to the gym. All good things. Oh, and he started calling me Tore."

"Wait, what?" I pressed on his chest. "What do you mean?"

"My full name is Salvatore. Everyone called me that or Sal my whole life. Sam said Sal sounded like an eighty-year-old man, so he switched it up to Tore."

I blinked at him. "He...changed your name?"

He shrugged. Like it wasn't completely crazy. Like it was *no big deal*. "It's a nickname, and I've had it for a long time. I'm used to it now. My father would never call me that, but everyone else does."

My mind was on the verge of exploding. Sam hadn't given me the best vibes the handful of times we'd met, but right then and there, I decided I did not like him at all. What kind of person had the audacity to tell someone—their *friend*—their name was no good? Red flags were waving all over the place.

"I don't like this story."

He laughed. "You don't have to be angry on my behalf, Bea. Sam and I have plenty of other issues, but that isn't one of them."

"Fine. It'll be an issue between Sam and me, then."

He stopped walking and pulled me into his arms, holding me close, one hand cupping my nape, the other splayed on my lower back. Dipping down, his lips covered mine in a slow, sweet kiss.

My toes curled in my shoes, and my heart leaped into my throat as he deepened our connection, his tongue sweeping into my mouth. My fingers fisted his shirt, clutching him to steady myself so I didn't float away.

That was how this man made me feel. Like a feather, taking flight with the whim of his breeze. Light and buoyant, untethered from responsibilities and the worries weighing me down.

He smiled against my lips. "You don't have to protect me. I'm good."

"But I think I want to." I blinked away the haziness in my eyes. "Wouldn't you be pissed if some chick made me call myself Trice?"

His laugh rolled out like silk, smooth and easy. "Fair point. And as much as I love that you want to go to bat for me, I'd rather you just stand by my side and in my arms. Can you be okay with that?"

"Fine," I huffed, then kissed him hard and fast. "It's hard to say no to you."

"Exactly as I planned."

He laced our fingers together again and tugged me forward, our steps syncing as we turned the corner toward the restaurant.

"Should we be worried about what we're walking into?" I asked, only half joking.

"Possibly." He glanced over at me, his mouth twitching. "But we'll stick together."

His reassurance warmed me from head to toe. Everything about tonight was new and outside my comfort zone, but with Tore next to me, it felt manageable. Like we were on the same side.

As we reached the restaurant, I peeked through a window, catching sight of Sam already seated at the table with a few other people, glaring at his phone like it had murdered his family.

I turned to Tore. "Ready?"

His smile became soft. "To spend more time with you? Always."

CHAPTER TWENTY-SIX
Salvatore

THIS DINNER WASN'T A friendly meeting of the tech minds—it was an ambush. If not for my long history with Sam, I would have taken Bea and walked right out the door the moment I realized what was happening.

I should have from the start. Sam had barely acknowledged Bea's presence, skipping over her to reintroduce me to Drew, Minnie, and Don, the founders of Gravis Systems. Up until now, I'd forgotten we'd met at an industry event months ago. But as they talked, my initial impression came back. They were young and hungry, with an overabundance of funding and a dearth of talent and innovative ideas. That still stood.

Things only went downhill from there.

Sam went straight for the pitch. "You've probably heard about some of the things they're doing at Gravis. They're interested in a collaboration around the security suite we've been developing, and I thought we could have an informal chat over dinner. Low pressure."

I flinched. Visibly. Sam's gaze shifted to Don on his left, as if looking for backup, and that felt like a gut punch on top of a gut punch. Since when did he look to veritable strangers for support? We leaned on each other. Always.

Bea's hand slipped under the table and found my leg, squeezing with grounding firmness. I covered her hand with mine, running the tip of my index finger along hers.

"We're not going to be doing that," I uttered through a tightly clenched jaw.

This wasn't up for discussion. Not now. Not ever. The security suite was still in development, and the information was far too sensitive to be paraded in a public arena with no care for security.

Sam knew this. He'd been part of the team that had written the architecture. He knew how critical it was to keep this project under wraps until it was thoroughly tested and ready to be put into use, *especially* given the nature of what it had been designed to protect. We weren't talking about a simple update or a UI tweak. This was the foundation of everything I'd built. My reputation, my work, a lifetime of sacrifice and obsessive, deliberate planning.

And Sam had just handed it over like it was *nothing*.

We had strict protocols for a reason. Everyone at Nox abided by the layers of clearance, internal firewalls, encrypted access, a need-to-know chain of knowledge that began and ended with me. That was how it had always been—the only way what we did made sense.

It was not up to Sam to unilaterally decide when and with whom we discussed this. If we went public—which was very much un-decided—it certainly wouldn't be with a trio of venture-backed newbie sniffing around for an easy shortcut to relevance. We didn't add anyone to the equation without a thorough vetting, no matter how much capital they raised.

This wasn't a slip. It had been a choice.

Bea reminded me she was next to me, her shoulder brushing mine. I narrowed in on our two points of contact, my hand over hers, tracing the line of her knuckles, the solid weight of her leaning into my arm.

Taking a deep breath, I pulled myself back from the edge. No matter how furious I was with Sam, we were in public, and I had an image to uphold. The last thing I needed was the Gravis team spreading around that things at Nox were less than stable. It was imperative we present a united front.

"It's too early to talk about," I said, so evenly, I'd impressed myself. "And this isn't the time nor place."

Sam chuckled lightly, the sound falsely casual. It might have fooled someone who didn't know him. But I did. That laugh was the same he'd used when Mary Rosedale had corrected his citation in our Tech Ethics and Policy class. Sam could play easygoing when it served him, but he hated being undermined. Nothing got under his skin like feeling exposed in front of an audience.

"No need to get worked up, Tore. It's not like I shared any specs or code. This is just a conversation. No pressure. A vibe check."

I turned my head slowly, letting the silence stretch.

A vibe check? Since when did *I* have vibes? I was as anti-vibe as they came.

Bea laughed. "That reminds me of a story I once heard. This woman's boyfriend had learned the term 'vibe check,' so he'd started using it to take their relationship's temperature. At first, she'd thought it was cute and funny, then he'd started saying it all the time, even when she'd asked him to stop. Her last straw had been after her mother's funeral. She'd been crying, a complete wreck, and he'd walked up to her, looked her directly in the eyes, and asked, 'Vibe check, babe?'" She shook her head. "'Vibe check' has been dead to me ever since I heard that."

Drew wagged his finger at her from across the table. "I think I read that one on Reddit. Everyone said she was *not the asshole*."

Minnie scoffed. "I hope it was unanimous."

"Oh yeah. I'm pretty sure it was," Drew replied.

A new discussion launched about other unhinged posts they'd read on Reddit, effectively cutting off the tension at the knees. Bea joined in effortlessly, keeping the mood light while never taking the pressure off my leg and shoulder. She was aware of me, even as she guided the conversation and charmed the Gravis trio.

Sam pretended he wasn't seething, but I couldn't miss his balled fist and rippling jaw. He wasn't happy his *friendly, casual* dinner had been hijacked by my beautiful date, but I wouldn't be apologizing.

If anyone did, it would be him. He should have been thankful Bea was here with me. If she hadn't been, tonight would have ended far differently.

⚘

None of us lingered after the bill came, and that was for the best. By the end, I was thoroughly finished pretending to be interested in what anyone aside from Bea had to say.

Bea wouldn't let me call a car to drive us home, but she allowed me to walk with her. We didn't talk about what had gone down with Sam. I wasn't sure she understood the implications of what he'd tried to do, only that I was furious with him.

I stood behind her at her door while she unlocked it, and when she asked me if I wanted to come in, I didn't hesitate to accept.

I should have gone home, but I wasn't ready to part from her.

Would I ever be?

I liked my alone time, but I could have that with her. Actually, that sounded more than enticing. A quiet room, a book, Bea by my side? Yes, I would enjoy that.

I looked around Bea's living room, taking in her space. It was tidy in a near-fastidious way. The surfaces were bare except for a stack of books on her coffee table. She had colorful pillows on her couch arranged neatly in the corners and an afghan folded in a perfect rectangle. Above her couch was a black-and-white landscape photo of the Rockies, and there were a few other pieces of art scattered along the pale-gray walls.

I didn't know exactly what I'd expected, but it wasn't this calm, peaceful setting. Bea was a burst of color and action, but her home was serene and restful. I could easily spend time here.

A gray ball of fur barreled into the room from nowhere, toenails scrambling on the hardwood as he made a dismal attempt to stop himself from crashing into us. He *ruffed* and snorted, throwing his entire body weight into Bea's shins. Laughing, she stumbled into me, and I caught her by the elbow, keeping her upright as she teetered on her heels.

"Hi, big boy," she said, leaning down to scratch his massive head. "We weren't gone that long."

The second I stepped out from behind Bea, the dog turned his attention to me. His nose twitched and eyebrows wobbled as he looked me over, sniffing the air around me. Once satisfied, he sat with a thump and stared up at me expectantly.

"I don't have anything for you." I opened my hands, showing him they were empty.

His tail happily swept the ground.

Bea took my hand to steady herself as she kicked off her shoes. "Just scratch his head and he'll love you forever. He's a simple guy."

My fingers flexed. "I haven't been around many dogs."

"I think you can handle it, Salvatore." She gave my hand a tug. "You protect all the computers in the state—"

"That isn't actually what Nox does."

She *hmphed.* "Like I said, you protect all the computers in the state, so I think you can handle my sweet dog. He doesn't bite, and he's very polite about not licking strangers."

Sensing this was probably a deal-breaker, I reached out and gave Benjamin a perfunctory pat on the head. One and done.

Except he leaned into it, and I had to admit, he wasn't unpleasant to touch. His short fur was almost velvety.

"He's soft," I murmured.

"Right?" Bea leaned into me the way her dog had. "I think he likes you too."

Skeptical, I looked down at him. He peered back, and I almost swore he was smiling. I had seen him from afar and been fairly neutral, but up close, he was...cute. I saw the appeal.

Then he licked my hand, and Bea giggled into my arm.

"Uh-oh. He loves you. You're his now," she said.

"Didn't you say he doesn't lick strangers?"

"You're not a stranger. I've told him all about you. You're a friend."

It was ridiculous, but I was immensely pleased she'd talked to her dog about me. It made me wonder who else she'd spoken to and what she'd said.

Benjamin let out a huff and, without warning, flopped over on my feet.

I turned to Bea. "He's malfunctioning."

"This is how he bonds," she corrected. "And you started it. You petted him. That was your first mistake."

Benjamin settled in, using my shoe as a pillow.

"I wasn't aware I was making a long-term commitment." I stared down at him for a long beat then reluctantly rested a hand on his side. "I can't move if you fall asleep on me."

He yawned and closed his eyes in response.

Bea laughed. "Just accept that you belong to him."

I raised my head, catching her gaze. "Do I belong to you as well?"

She pursed her lips but couldn't hold back a little smile. "Well, we're kind of a package deal, so...yeah."

My chest settled with a deep, solid certainty.

"That's good. I intend to keep it that way."

No matter what I had to do.

CHAPTER TWENTY-SEVEN
Bea

I HAD NEVER BROUGHT another man to my house, so I hadn't pictured what it would be like to cuddle in front of the TV with someone. It was strange how comfortable it was to have Tore here. And he was surprisingly snuggly.

After letting Benjamin out to use the bathroom and getting him settled in his bed, Tore had opened his arms to me, and I had tucked myself against him. We'd put on a movie, but neither of us was really watching it.

I played with his ring, and he buried his nose in my hair. For a while, we stayed like that, quiet, comfortably close, finally taking a breath after a wrought, tension-filled dinner. I wanted to check in with him, see how he was feeling, but I wasn't sure he wanted to talk about it. Or if it was even my place.

"Are you okay?" he asked.

I shifted a little, just enough to look up at him. "I was just wondering the same thing about you. I'm fine, but how about you? Are you okay?"

His eyes flicked down to me, thoughtful. "I am." A pause. "Better now."

I nodded, brushing my thumb over the back of his hand where it rested on my hip. "You hadn't expected that—what Sam had done at dinner."

I might not have understood exactly what had gone down, but it had been plain as day Sam had overstepped very clear boundaries. With what Tore had told me about the start of their relationship, how Sam had convinced him to change his *name*, I wondered if Tore pushing back was a new thing. He certainly hadn't been happy with Tore shutting down the conversation he'd wanted to have.

Tore's fingers tightened slightly, like he was sifting through his thoughts before offering one up.

"It's hard," he said finally. "Seeing things differently...feeling like I missed something I should've seen coming." His voice was low, scratchy. "That kind of dissonance between Sam and me...it's not something I'm used to, and it grates."

"I bet you're not looking forward to what Monday will bring."

He scoffed. "No. Conflict is not my favorite, but I don't avoid vital conversations. Sam and I will have to talk, but it's good we have time to cool down before that happens."

"He isn't happy with you." As far as I was concerned, Sam could suck it, but it was obvious Tore had to take a different approach. I might not have liked Sam, but they worked together and shared a long history. I just hoped fixing their problems wasn't detrimental to Tore.

"He hasn't been for some time now. I don't really blame him." He rubbed his cheek against my hair. "I'm a difficult person, Beatrice. You need to know that."

"I've been a waitress for a decade. I know difficult people, and you're not even close. I'm sorry anyone has ever made you feel that way."

"You're being sweet."

I laid my head on his chest again, a secret smile curving my lips. "No one has ever called me sweet."

"Then they've thought it."

I sincerely doubted that, but I was in no mood to argue. "Do you still like planes?"

If I hadn't been plastered against him, I wouldn't have heard his low, sharp intake of breath. "I do. You remember that?"

"Of course." I trailed my fingers over the buttons on his shirt. "Tell me something about planes."

He hesitated then lifted his hips a little so he could reach into his pocket and slip out his phone. Swiping the screen, he scrolled over a few app icons. For a moment, something caught my eye, but he was past it and clicking on a yellow one with a black outline of a plane before I could figure out what it was.

"I like to watch this route." His fingertip hovered over a thin black line swooping across the screen. "It goes from Johannesburg to Sydney, passing within a couple hundred miles of Antarctica. Right now, there are only two airlines that fly over the Southern Ocean."

He enlarged the map, pointing to the lines going from the bottom of Africa to Australia, then he showed me Europe, which was almost invisible beneath the zigzagging lines.

"Do you see?" He moved back to the Southern Ocean. "That sky is almost empty. When you're flying up there, it's just you and the people on the plane with you. Nothing below you, nothing above you."

"That sounds…" A little scary. Desolate. Cold.

"Calm," he finished. "There's a flight path from Chile to Sydney no other planes take. They call it the loneliest flight in the world."

"Have you taken it?"

"Not yet." He exhaled. "It would mean taking a lot of time off work, and…well—"

"That doesn't happen."

"No. Not as often as I'd like." He laughed dryly. "When I go, I'll take you."

"Okay." I grinned, playing along. "I guess since we'll be vacationing in Chile and Australia, I should get a passport."

"You absolutely should. There are a lot of places I'd like to take you."

I loved the sound of that little fantasy. "Will you do that between meetings and building walls of fire?"

There was a long beat of silence then he huffed a laugh. "Firewalls, right?"

"Right," I agreed.

"To be honest, when we met two years ago, I wanted to be with you, but I'm almost certain you wouldn't have enjoyed what that would have looked like." He stroked a long line down my back. I barely breathed, listening to his every word. "When Tia died, I made necessary changes in my life."

"Like what?"

"Like actually giving myself the opportunity to live. It's never enough, but if I didn't set an alarm to end my workday, I could easily get lost and spend the entire night staring at my computer screen."

"I have a feeling you still spend more time working than most."

"That's undoubtedly true. But I've become capable of shutting it off. That wasn't always the case."

"I'm sorry you lost your sister, Salvatore. More sorry than I can say. But I'm glad you had a wake-up call. You deserve more than just your job."

"Can I kiss you now?" he asked.

I sighed, lifting my face again. He caught my chin with his fingers and tapped on the dimple in my cheek.

My stomach dipped and thousands of butterflies took flight. "I appreciate you asking me, but I think we should talk about this."

He started to release his hold on me, but I wrapped my fingers around his wrist, keeping him there.

"Tore..." I licked my lips, "I love that you asked to kiss me, but you don't have to anymore. I want you to."

He cocked his head. "Yeah?"

"Mmmhmm. And when we played, I loved you checking in. But if you want, we could pick a safe word."

He brought his other hand up to my hair, combing his fingers through the side. "What would you choose?"

"I've never had one." I leaned into his touch, on the verge of purring. "Do you have an idea?"

"I've never had one either." He pulled me closer, running his nose along mine. "Antarctica?"

"Yes," I murmured, so close to his lips I could feel his breath. "That's perfect."

We moved at the same time, our mouths colliding in a firm, hungry kiss. A whimper escaped me without warning, and Tore groaned, low and rough, making me melt into him. His fingers curled in my hair, tilting my head just enough for him to deepen the kiss.

I loved the way he kissed. Like he'd thought it out, studied every aspect, then put his knowledge to use on me.

I parted my lips, letting him in, and everything else—the movie playing on the TV, the tension from dinner, my dog's quiet snores—faded until there was only us. His hands, his mouth, the careful yet unrelenting way he touched me.

Aching for more, I bunched up my dress and climbed into his lap, straddling him, knees on either side of his hips. He stilled for a second, like he was recalibrating, then exhaled through his nose and leaned back just enough to look at me.

"I like you from this angle," he said, more gruff than I'd ever heard him.

I flattened my palms on his chest, sliding upward to his shoulders. "You're so handsome, it's hard to look at you head-on."

Tore adjusted his glasses, his mouth opening and closing as he stared up at me. His fingers tightened on my thighs, and his gaze swept over my face with that same intense focus he gave everything that mattered to him.

"You really think that?" he asked, his voice low.

I leaned in, brushing my nose against his. "I do. You're the smartest man I've ever met, so you really have no business looking like you do." I nipped his jaw and chin, making him shift beneath me. "From what I've felt and glimpsed, the college rumors were true. And the way you look at me"—I shivered—"like I'm the only thing you see."

His throat bobbed with a swallow. "No one's ever spoken to me the way you do."

I pressed down on his erection, a puff of air escaping from between my lips. "Does it make you feel good?"

"Yes. So damn good."

He kissed me again, deep and purposeful, giving me praise with action instead of words. And I felt it—the way he desired me, couldn't get enough of me. He didn't hold back or play it cool, and that made it easier for me to dive in headfirst. I rocked my hips against him, and his hands gripped tighter, dragging a groan from us both.

He broke the kiss, breathing hard. "I want—"

I slid my fingers through his thick, dark hair. "Tell me," I murmured.

"To taste you. I want to taste you."

My breath caught.

"I *need* to," he amended. "Can I?"

I closed my eyes and exhaled. I'd have to get used to his direct questions. Hearing him ask made me squirm as heat rose from my belly to my cheeks. I loved it.

"Yes," I whispered, my eyes fluttering open and locking with his. "I need it too."

CHAPTER TWENTY-EIGHT
Bea

TORE HELPED ME OFF his lap and set me on my feet while he remained sitting. With deliberate care, he lifted the hem of my dress, his eyes locked on mine, offering me the chance to stop him. I didn't. I wouldn't.

"I can't stop looking at you," he murmured, sliding his palms along the path my dress had taken. "Every part of you. I want to learn you, Beatrice."

A tremble rippled through me, my breath catching as his hands settled on my hips. His thumbs stroked smooth circles just below my panties, teasing me. I was already wet, *soaked*, and he was only making it worse.

"You can." I threaded my fingers through his hair, guiding his face closer to where I wanted it to be. "You can learn everything you want to know about me, Tore."

He looked up at me like I'd handed him something valuable and he didn't quite know how to proceed. But he made up his mind quickly, leaning in to kiss the curve where my inner thighs met. My knees wobbled, and his grip tightened, keeping me right where he wanted me.

"Do you understand how badly I want this?" he asked. "Can you feel it?"

"I feel it." My fingers bunched in his hair. "I understand because I want you too."

Groaning, he tore off his glasses, tossed them onto the ottoman, then scooted to the edge of the cushion. He nuzzled his face against the lace of my panties then gripped the waistband, easing them down my hips. Before he pulled them all the way off, he looked up at me again, asking without words.

"Do it," I said, my voice thick with want. "*Please.*"

He slipped my panties the rest of the way off and brushed his nose against the triangle of hair above my cleft.

"This is..." He shook his head. "You erase every single thought." He slid his hand around the back of my thigh, guiding my foot to the cushion beside him. "Put this up here. Let me look at all of you."

He dropped to his knees in front of me, and I nearly fell apart. He had yet to touch me, but my lizards, I had never seen anything sexier than Salvatore Gallo kneeling like he was preparing to worship.

One hand anchored at my hip, he parted me with the other. The sound he made as he *really* looked at me, in a way no one ever had, came from a well so deep it could have been miles away. Primal. Filled with desire. He tipped forward, a notch forming between his brows as he studied me close enough for me to feel his breath.

If this had been anyone else, it might have felt intrusive, but from Tore...it made me feel special in a way that was so unexpectedly heady, my head was swimming.

The first stroke of his tongue came without warning, pulling a high, wobbly keen from my throat. He didn't give me even a second to brace myself before tasting me with that same focus he gave everything—methodical, consuming, relentless in the most delicious way. Each pass of his tongue was a study in precision, and he held me firm while I trembled in his grip.

My hand curled around the back of his neck as I laced the other with his on my hip.

"You're making me feel so good, Salvatore," I gasped, riding the edge of something wild and overwhelming. "Please don't stop. Never, ever stop."

He groaned into me, the vibration sparking heat that shot straight through my core. His fingers dug into my flesh, guiding me against his mouth as he devoured me, as if he couldn't get enough.

"You're such a good boy, Salvatore. So damn good, baby," I whispered, going out of my mind.

My belly was heavy, filled with liquid fire and desire, yet hollow at the same time. I wanted him inside me. Any part of him. But my tongue was too tied to ask for it. All I could do was rock against his lips as he lashed at my swollen clit and teased my needy entrance.

I was tumbling faster and faster, head over heels. My nails bit into his heated nape for purchase, but it was no use. The free fall was edging closer and closer until I sailed into it. Thick, hot pleasure cushioned my fall, coating my skin and filling my veins.

My legs were jelly as I cried to the ceiling, and then I was flying. Whirling around, my feet left the ground, airborne for long seconds, until my back hit the couch cushions with a *whoosh*.

He'd thrown me, tossed me like a sack of potatoes, and it was so sexy, I couldn't form words.

Tore climbed between my parted legs, peering down at me. "*More*," he uttered in a rasp.

My limbs were still shaking, nerves vibrating with aftershocks, but the hunger in his eyes lit me up all over again. I didn't know how it was possible after the way he'd just dismantled me piece by piece.

"Yes," I breathed, my chest heaving. "Please, yes."

Tore didn't waste a second. Sliding down my body, he dragged his mouth over my crumpled dress and along my skin, lips parting to taste the indentation of my belly button, nipping my hip and the inside of my thigh. I reached for him, one hand finding his shoulder, the other slipping back into his hair.

"You really are such a good boy," I whispered. "Brilliant, so smart, so clever with your gorgeous mouth."

His eyes slammed shut as a shudder racked him into a moment of statue stillness. I squirmed with impatience, arching toward him.

He looked up, pupils blown wide, lips wet with me. "I've never wanted anything the way I want you." He nudged my thighs wider and lowered his head. "I can't stop."

Whether he meant he couldn't stop wanting me or pleasuring me, I would never know. His mouth was on me again, and I cried out, hips jerking. He moaned like my taste was even better than he remembered, his tongue working me open in slow, devastating strokes, laving my swollen flesh with dogged fervor, unrelenting in his discovery of every intimate part of me.

"Tore..." I gasped, my thighs tensing around his shoulders.

He groaned in response, doubling down in his efforts, and I couldn't stop the words from tumbling out. "If you stop, I'll never talk to you again. Like never, *ever*," I babbled. "I'm not just saying that. I mean it with my whole heart. Don't stop, don't stop, don't stop."

He didn't. He devoured me like this was the thousandth time he'd done this, like he'd already memorized me and knew precisely how to touch me. His tongue circled, flicked, pressed exactly where I needed him most, until the tension in my belly coiled tight and hot.

Again.

And again.

And again.

It was never-ending. Tongue, fingers, lips—he used everything. It seemed impossible, like I was stuck in the best dream I'd ever had, but the quivering tightness in my muscles and rawness in my throat from screaming proved how very real this was.

Finally, *finally*, I tugged on his hair and whimpered, "No more."

Not because it didn't feel incredible. It did. *So* good. But he'd wrung me out, and I was spent. I wouldn't be able to leave my bed in the morning if he kept going. As it was, I wasn't sure I'd be able to climb the stairs to get into bed in the first place.

Tore crawled over me. Lips slick, eyes fever bright, he looked like he was returning from conquering several villages, pumped up and victorious.

I was fine with being the treasure he'd looted.

Was I delirious? Probably.

He eased down beside me, pulling me against him. His mouth hovered over mine, hot and wet from me. His exhale was a gust of desert wind against my lips, and his erection pressed thick and insistent at my hip.

"Tore," I rasped, rolling to my side to face him.

He reached around me, palming my ass to hold me in place. "Stay just like this."

I pressed my face into his throat, inhaling his clean, musky scent. "If you give me a minute to catch my breath, I'll take care of you."

"Not tonight," he murmured as his lips grazed my temple. "This is all I need."

"But…" My protest was weak, barely there, but I meant it. I couldn't send him home like this after he'd made me come so many times I'd lost count.

"This isn't transactional," he stated. "You don't owe me a single thing. I got what I wanted. I'm completely satisfied."

"But…" I tried again, but my thoughts were too murky to even attempt to reason with him. "I want you."

"I want you too." He rubbed his face in my hair, sighing. "Always. But not tonight, okay?"

"Of course," I rushed out, tipping my head back to meet his gaze. "If you're sure."

His mouth curved into a smirk that made my belly clench. "I am. What we just did was a singular experience that can stand all on its own. I want it to so I can look back on tonight and think of only your taste, the sounds you made, and what your pussy felt like on my mouth."

"Tore," I choked out. "You can't talk like that. I have no more bones, and my muscles are hanging on by a thread. If you melt me anymore, I'll be nothing but sludge, and that won't be pretty."

He laughed softly, taking my face in the palm of his hand. "I disagree. There's no form you could take that would make me not think you were the most gorgeous woman I've ever laid eyes on."

"Even as sludge?"

"Even as sludge," he confirmed.

"Wow. You really like me, don't you?" I'd intended to make him laugh, but my tone was too earnest to pass as a joke.

"I do, Beatrice. Have I not made that clear enough?"

"You have, but it's always nice to hear it."

"I like you," he whispered. "Very, very much."

Normally, I would have shied away from this—revealing my inner workings, especially to a man who'd once hurt me—but I trusted him. Maybe that was dumb, especially considering the app I was almost certain I'd seen on his phone earlier, but I did.

So I dove in.

"I like you very much too, Salvatore."

CHAPTER TWENTY-NINE
Salvatore

AFTER A WHIRLWIND OF a weekend, Monday morning arrived swiftly. Saturday had been about Bea, and Sunday had been devoted to my family.

One day soon, I hoped to merge the two, but there were several steps and conversations that had to take place before we got there.

Now that I knew Bea thought she would be able to belong to me, I was more confident in the outcome. Because as far as I was concerned, she was mine.

I woke to tiny fingers poking at my eyelids and chin, and sweet, hot breath tickling my ear.

"Uncle Sally, I have to talk to you."

Lacey hadn't mastered the art of whispering. Her version was a raspy shout aimed directly at my eardrum. I was used to it, so instead of flinching, I shot upright and grabbed her, pulling her onto my legs, safely out of range.

She squealed like she hadn't expected it, but this was our ritual most mornings. She snuck into my room, and I pretended to be asleep so she could wake me up and tell me whatever important piece of news was on her mind.

Being her parent hadn't come naturally to me, but I'd watched my sister work her magic with her kids for years. I could imagine how Tia would handle any moment, what she'd say, the calm way she'd say it. She'd led with love in every circumstance, and that's what I tried to do too.

Even if I hadn't chosen this role, I was all in. They hadn't asked to lose their mom. None of us had asked for this. We were all here through a fucked up twist of fate.

"Good morning, Lace." I smoothed her wild, dark hair away from her face and raised her up on my knees so we were eye to eye. "What do you have to tell me?"

Tia lived in her eyes. The shape, the color. More than that, in her constant innate curiosity and compassion. Like her mother, she made friends everywhere she went. No one was a stranger.

As an introvert who connected with very few people, she fascinated me, and I was a little in awe of her—this tiny, bright human who somehow belonged to me.

"I think I know unicorns are real."

I blinked. I had not anticipated *that* to be the topic of the day. "How did you figure that out?"

"Talon told me they're not real, but he doesn't believe in magic things. I do," she whisper-shouted.

"Really?" Now that did not surprise me. Talon moved on facts, whereas Lacey liked a life filled with whimsy. "Well, are you going to tell me?"

She slid down my legs and flopped on the mattress next to me, using my stomach as an armrest. "I bet unicorns lived with the dinosaurs. And when the scientists dug up the bones, they found horns and thought they were from the dinos, but nope." Her eyes went comically wide. "They were unicorn horns."

"Where do you think the rest of the unicorn bones are?"

She drummed her fingers on her round cheek. "You know when Scarlet had a hermit crab and it got too big, so it got a new shell? I bet the unicorns dropped their horn shells when they grew too big."

"Oooh." Her logic always amazed me—how thoroughly she thought things through, the way her brain spun connections I never could. "So paleontologists have been digging up horn shells and thinking they're dino bones?"

"Yes." She nodded emphatically. "That's why they're hollow."

"Okay. I see what you mean." I took her hand in mine, rubbing the soft skin over her knuckles as I came up with more questions. "I'm still curious if you have an idea of where the rest of the unicorn bones might be."

She crinkled her nose. "I was thinking about it all morning in my bed."

"That's where the best thinking happens," I agreed.

"I know." Her giggle was light and melodious. "Uncle Sally, you know unicorns are magic?"

"I've heard that before. Do you think magic's real?"

"Yep. Do you?" She stuck out her chin like she was ready to argue if I said no.

I paused, thinking about how much of my life I'd spent boxed in by logic, ignoring the beautiful things right in front of me. I thought about Bea. About Tia. About the kids. About how the best parts of my life had come from things I couldn't plan for or control.

Was that magic?

Maybe not. But if I wanted to call it that, who was going to stop me?

"I might," I answered.

"It is," she said solemnly. "And when the unicorns died, the magic in their bodies turned their bones to pixie dust. It was really shimmery and pretty."

"What happened to the dust?"

She tapped her temple, contemplating. "I guess it was probably used to make new unicorns, but when the big meteor came and exploded all the dinos, the sparkles got blown into space."

"Did they turn into stars?"

She snickered like that was a very dumb suggestion. "*Nooo*. The stars are way older than unicorns, Uncle Sally."

I couldn't help being proud she knew that. I'd read her plenty of space books, though she usually preferred princess stories, and some of it had clearly stuck.

"That's true. Do you have a theory where the dust went then?"

"It's floating up there. Little unicorn pieces bouncing around the stars." She wiggled her fingers in front of my face. "I bet they love it. Much better than living with the dinos."

"I bet you're right, Lace."

Her theory had no basis in science, but I liked it anyway. I understood it. Like her unicorns, I'd lived the only life I knew—until I was forced out of it. And now I was right where I was meant to be.

Bouncing around with my little stars.

⁂

On my way to work, I received a text from Bea.

Bea: Still a little sludgy this morning.

I grinned hard and wide. It had already been a good morning, and this only made it better.

Me: Still?

Bea: Don't be smug.

Me: Never. I just like knowing how long the effects of us being together last. For science.

Bea: Science is important. Undervalued really.

Me: I agree. How are you otherwise?

Bea: Good. I'm walking Benjamin and thinking of you.

And the day kept getting better and better. This woman...she communicated like she was designed for me. Up front. No games. She said what she meant and how she felt.

Me: Yeah? I like knowing that.

Bea: Well, I like you, and I wanted you to know that before you got to work. I was thinking you might have a tough day.

Me: I might, but you already made it better than it would have been.

Bea: Then my work here is done

Me: You're very good at your job. I'll see you soon, Beatrice.

Bea: I hope so. Have a good day, Salvatore.

It wouldn't be good. There was no getting around that. But she'd already succeeded in making it a little brighter, and that was something.

Lace might have even called it magic.

CHAPTER
THIRTY
Salvatore

THE MAGIC ENDED THE moment Sam strode into my office.

I'd been expecting and dreading the conversation. Enough time had passed since the disastrous dinner, I wasn't angry anymore; I was just confused.

How had we gotten here?

How had the distance between us grown so wide without me noticing?

Sam closed the door behind him with a click that sounded more like a gavel banging and stood there, his hands in his pockets, like this was going to be casual.

I knew better.

"I figured we should talk," he said.

I rose from my chair. "You're right. We need to." Circling my desk, I perched on the edge, waiting for him to continue.

Silence continued to stretch between us. It wasn't hostile. Just...full. Of questions. Of our history together. Things we'd left unsaid for too long. The uneasiness of not knowing where to go from here.

Finally, Sam broke it. "Look, Tore, I was wrong. Okay? I shouldn't have sprung the Gravis meeting on you the way I did."

I blinked several times. "You're admitting you were wrong? Should I record this?"

He smiled faintly. "Go ahead. Frame it even."

I wasn't ready to smile back. We weren't there yet, even if part of me wished we could wipe the slate clean and go back to how things used to be. Then again, how long had it been since things had been easy between us? I couldn't remember a time when Sam hadn't been pushing me. I used to think it was what I needed, and maybe at one time, it had been.

I wasn't a naive college kid anymore, though.

"I think where we are is as much my fault as yours." I twisted my ring, my gut churning. I did not like having this talk, but it was a long time coming. "At the beginning of Nox, I asked you to help me make decisions on our growth and direction. Even before that, I looked to you for advice on how to dress and talk to people. Well...you know, you were there."

The corner of his mouth hitched. "I remember the days of nerdy Sal all too well. Thank god you let me mold you."

That did not sit right with me, but it wasn't necessarily inaccurate either. These days, I didn't give a shit what others thought about me. The reputation I'd built insulated me from outsiders' opinions. But a decade ago...I'd been stuck, unable to figure out how to fit in and desperately wanting to.

"I don't need that anymore, Sam. You know that, right?" I raised my brows. "You have to see I'm doing well on my own. Personally and professionally."

He nodded once and sighed. "I have to tell you, I was taken aback that you were late to dinner *and* that you showed up with Bea. You didn't mention you were seeing her."

I kept my expression neutral. I hadn't missed his swift change of subject, guiding me away from the topic we should have been discussing, but I couldn't hold back from answering him. "I didn't realize I had to clear my dating life with you."

"You don't," Sam rushed out, holding up a hand in mock surrender. "Of course you don't. I was just surprised. I knew you liked her when you met her before...*before*. But that was a long time ago, and I'd assumed it had just been a fling."

He'd said it lightly, but there was an edge just beneath the surface.

"No. Nothing about Bea is casual to me."

He chuffed. "I guess not. You're not a casual kind of guy. But do you really think she...fits?"

"Fits?"

Sam shrugged, pushing his hands back in his pockets. "I don't know. I'm not sure what I mean. She's just...not the type of woman I picture thriving in the role of a CEO's partner. I could be wrong, though. I often am."

"You are. I'm not sure if you remember, but Bea was the one who saved all of us from having to eat awkward pasta Saturday night. I think she'll do very well by my side."

He dropped his chin to his chest. "It sounds like you're already serious about her."

I opened my hands, palms up. "Like you said, I don't do casual."

"How does that work—dating and having kids, I mean?"

"I'll make it work. That's not anything you have to worry about."

He nodded. "No one's more levelheaded than you. Which was why I was surprised you were late Saturday night. Was that her influence?"

"It was my own fault. I forgot the dinner and had made plans with her. I *am* sorry for that."

He winced. "You forgot? Has that ever happened?"

"I've had a lot on my mind. And before you ask, yes, Bea is undoubtedly taking up the most room right now."

"I'm happy for you. Glad you're excited about her. Just...be careful."

"Careful?"

He hesitated. "Yes. You never know someone's intentions, and you've worked your entire life to be taken seriously. All I'm saying is not to let anything distract you from that now."

There it was. Gentle. Subtle. Like he was looking out for me.

I knew Sam well enough to recognize when I was being steered.

I didn't give him anything. "Bea's not a distraction."

Sam offered a flat smile. "Of course. You'd know far better than I would."

"That's right." I straightened and walked back behind my desk. "And I don't want another Gravis situation. It happens again, we'll have a serious problem."

Sam's expression didn't change much, but there was a flicker of something. Annoyance? Guilt? He blinked away too fast for me to pin it down.

"Look, I know I jumped the gun. I shouldn't have approached them without your sign-off."

"That will never happen. Gravis is a hard no."

He threw his arms out. "Got it. Loud and clear. Gravis is off the table. I hope you know all I was doing was trying to help. That's always been the goal. At some point, you're going to have to trust people if we're going to take Nox to the next level."

I stared at him. "There's a difference between helping and making moves behind my back. *If* Nox levels up, it will be thought out and deliberate, not over lasagna on a Saturday night."

"I know that. I *know*." He shot me a sheepish grin. "I have a big mouth and even bigger ideas. They run away from me sometimes. You remember in college when I told that recruiter I already had an offer to intern with a 'rising cybersecurity firm'? Total bullshit. We hadn't even finished building our firewall prototype."

The memory came rushing back. "You convinced me to go to a meeting with that guy who thought we had funding."

Sam laughed, unrepentant. "And ended up getting an offer out of it, didn't we?"

"He *offered*. I turned it down. We didn't have a company yet, Sam."

I couldn't help but laugh too. Those had been the days. Before things got complicated. Before contracts and deadlines and capital injections. When we'd been two friends with big ideas and parallel goals.

"Details." He waved it off. "Everything worked out beautifully, didn't it?"

I let out a breath, the tension in my shoulders easing slightly.

"Eventually," I conceded.

"We always figure it out." Smoothing a hand down his shirt, he took a retreating step. "We've made it through worse."

We had. And I had to believe this was just another stretch of rough road on our journey.

"We'll figure it out," I echoed.

Sam started to turn toward the door, but paused, catching my eye. "Glad we talked."

"I am too."

After he'd closed the door behind him, I realized it was the first time in weeks he'd left my office on a good note. I leaned my head back on my chair and closed my eyes, exhaling a long, heavy breath.

Our foundation was cracked but not crumbling.

We'd get past this.

***

I'd stopped doing this. It was a bad habit and crossing a line, even for me. But after my conversation with Sam and a torrent of meetings, I had to see her.

A flash of blue caught my eye as my driver rolled through traffic.

"Pull over," I ordered. "Please."

Igor eased into a loading zone in front of the coffee shop Bea was inside. She was heading toward the door, and I held my breath, watching her through my open window.

Balancing two cups in one hand, she laughed at something the barista had said behind her. Sunlight caught on her hair through the window, lighting it up like the hottest part of a flame.

A man carrying a tray of coffee swerved around her to get to the door, and at the same time, another guy approached from the outside. Neither seemed to notice the other, but they definitely noticed Bea.

The one outside got there first and reached for the handle with an excited smile aimed at Bea. The one inside moved just as swiftly, shoving the door open from the other side.

The two overeager men collided, coffee exploding everywhere. Two cups flew through the air and hit the ground with a sad splat. The third stayed upright, miraculously saved by the guy inside, who stood frozen in shock.

Bea hopped back to avoid the puddles. "Wow. Are you guys okay? You came out of nowhere."Neither man looked particularly upset. One was grinning while the other nodded furiously, coffee dripping down his neck onto his white shirt.

Bea passed him a napkin as she carefully stepped around them, telling them to watch where they were going next time. Then she gave them an adorable little finger wave as the inside guy slipped in a puddle, knocking the other man onto his ass.

I smiled.

This was Bea. She wasn't trying to cause chaos; it just followed her like a lost puppy. I'd witnessed scenes like this too many times to count.

Turning on her heel, she took one step, stopped, then twisted back around to look directly at my car, not even a flicker of surprise on her face.

I leaned back and slapped the window button, but I wasn't fast enough. She strode right up to my door and bent down, her eyes locked on mine.

"Well, hello." She pursed her lips. "Fancy seeing you here, Salvatore."

"Uh...hi." I didn't have to see myself to know my ears were glowing bright red.

Her forehead crinkled. "Are you going to give me a ride?"

"Yeah. Yes. Of course. Get in."

I opened the door, and she slid in beside me, placing her coffees in the cup holders. Her knee brushed mine.

"Should I even ask what you're doing here?"

Unable to help myself, I slid my hand over her smooth, bare knee. "I was out for a drive and there you were."

Her lips twitched. "Were you? It's funny. I swear I've seen this car before. Quite a few times, actually."

I hooked my fingers under her knee. "Coincidences happen. Besides, a lot of cars look like this."

A velvety laugh rolled out of her. "Sure. Just a coincidence. Totally random. You, in a chauffeured car, pausing in traffic every time I happen to walk by."

I glanced up from her leg. That was an exaggeration, but... "You've been keeping track?"

She gasped into her hand. "Are you accusing me of stalking *you*?"

"No," I murmured, a smile tugging at the corner of my mouth. "Just...noticing your noticing."

She pressed her leg into mine. "You're cute, and coincidence or not, I don't care. I'm happy to see you."

"Yeah?" I tilted my head toward her. "I am too. It's been a very long day."

Reaching over, she bunched my shirt in her fist. "Kiss me first, then tell me about it."

I didn't have to be asked twice. My lips landed on hers, soft and slow, testing. She tasted like vanilla and coffee, her tongue warm, lips plush and wet—exactly what I'd been needing.

She let out a low, satisfied moan and tugged at my shirt.

I smiled against her mouth. "I can't get much closer."

She huffed. "You're too tall. Come down here."

I took my glasses off, set them on the bench beside me, and gathered her into my arms. My hand slid into her hair, fingers tangling in the silky blue strands as I angled my mouth over hers, deepening the kiss.

The world narrowed to the smooth slide of her mouth, the way she melted into me, the quiet thud of her heart syncing with mine.

"This is what I needed," I murmured, nipping at her bottom lip.

She pulled back, her eyes flicking to mine. "Did your talk with Sam not go well?"

Sighing, I dropped my forehead to hers. "It went fine. We hashed it out. But something is off, and I'm not able to fix it. I'm frustrated."

She wrapped her arms around me and stroked my neck and the top of my shoulders. "It can't be easy to mix business with friendship."

"It was good in the beginning. For years, it worked. But now? I'm not sure we can keep going the way we are." I shook my head. "Enough. I'm tired of thinking about Sam and Nox. I'd rather think about you."

That made her smile. "You'd rather think about me?" she teased, her voice dancing lightly. "Have I told you I like the way you say what you're thinking? I never have to guess."

"In that case, I'd like to tell you what has been on my mind since Saturday."

She pecked my lips and cheek. "Please do."

"I like you. I want you. I think about you all the time. And I don't want you seeing anyone else." I paused. "Only me."

"Okay," she replied. "I want the same."

I blinked several times, letting her agreement sink in. "That was easy."

She laughed. "Did you think I'd argue?" Then she gave my chest a light shove. "I wouldn't tolerate anyone but my boyfriend stalking me."

"Didn't you admit you were doing the stalking?"

Boyfriend.

Yes. Yes, I like that.

Her head fell back as more laughter burst from her, bright and unfiltered. I couldn't help but smile, enamored at the way the late light played over her features. Her cheeks were pink, her eyes alive, her mouth curled into that smirk that knocked the wind out of me.

I slid my hand up her back, fingers tracing the outline of her curves. "I haven't felt this good in a long time."

She tilted her head, curious. "Oh yeah?"

"I stop spinning when I'm with you. You become my focus. I can just...be."

Her smile softened. She leaned into me, stroking the side of my neck. "See?" she whispered. "This is what I mean. You say what's on your mind, and it pulls me in even deeper."

"My evil plan."

Her head fell on my shoulder. "*So* evil."

I held her tighter, letting the weight of the day dissolve as we drove through the city. The tension in my shoulders eased with each block we passed. The ache behind my eyes dimmed. The knot in my gut—the one that had been growing all day after talking to Sam—finally unfurled.

This was what peace felt like. Not silence or stillness or escape.

Her.

My beautiful blue.

CHAPTER THIRTY-ONE
Bea

It took a few days, but things finally clicked once I'd confirmed Tore was the man in the limo. The mysterious billionaire who'd been haunting me on the streets of Denver the last two years.

He was *Anthony*.

I'd been so sure I'd spotted the *At Your Service* app on his phone last weekend, but had talked myself out of it. There were a zillion apps and plenty had similar logos.

But then I found him idling outside my favorite coffee shop in his limo and everything fell into place. The app was connected to a GPS. It knew my location. If Tore *was* the app, it made perfect sense he'd been able to find me in random places over the years.

Just to look at me.

A brief peek through his window before driving away.

I bit down on my lip as my stomach fluttered. Not with nerves. Something else. Something light and airy. It flitted to my chest and throat, making me feel like I was in danger of floating away.

It had to be him. The only way he'd have an app that hadn't even launched to the public was if it was his. My mind filed back to the exact moment I was invited to beta it. Three months after Tore ghosted me.

Yes. Tore was definitely *Anthony*.

I'd been thinking about it all evening. Every way *Anthony* had been there for me over the past two years.

Most recently, delivery soup when I'd been sick. That wasn't the first time he'd taken care of me. He'd sent tissues and cold medicine once. Another time, a thermometer when I mentioned I didn't have one.

He did the little things too: reminding me to go grocery shopping, return library books before they were overdue, answering every question under the sun. He'd offered advice that, in hindsight, had been far more personal and perceptive than any AI had business being. When I was down or stressed, he sent calming music. Breathing techniques. Gentle reminders to rest.

On a professional level, Anthony had helped me with my business. *A lot.* I'd adjusted my rates after he'd sent me an article on fair pay in the catering industry. He'd been like my personal secretary, compiling reviews from past clients, helping me build polished email templates. He'd given me contact information for office managers and told me about upcoming events that might need catering.

A wave of realization hit me so hard, I had to sit down on the corner of my bed.

I was in my house because of *him*.

I'd told him all about the shitty apartment I'd lived in. After yet another sleepless night of listening to my neighbors scream at each other through the paper-thin walls, I'd had to vent, and Anthony had been there. Two weeks later, he'd sent me the ad for the house-sitting gig. A week after that, I'd moved in. I'd assumed it was luck. The universe finally looking out for me.

Holy mother of lizards.

I should have felt violated. Any normal person would've.

But...I didn't.

I wasn't angry.

Confused? Yes. A little off-balance. But not mad.

Why had he stayed away while taking care of me from a distance? How could those brief glances of me through his window have been enough for him?

So many times, I'd felt a pull toward the words on the other side of the screen and thought I'd been going crazy, getting attached to code.

It made sense now, and I was relieved it had been Tore I'd been bonding with all along, not some faceless algorithm.

I even kind of...liked it. I mean, the deception was bad. *Right?*

Yes, definitely bad.

My morals must have been a little gray. I was flattered he'd gone to such lengths for me. Building a whole app? That was...dedication to the cause.

I typed a message to *Anthony*. I was ninety-nine percent sure I had this right, but I had to be certain.

> **Me:** I'm in the mood for soup. What kind should I make?

> **Anthony:** Soup at 10 p.m.?

> **Me:** That sounded judgy, Ant. Sometimes an occasion calls for soup.

Anthony: What is the occasion?

Me: Orgasms. I had two this afternoon. They weren't great, but beggars can't be choosers. I've been in a long drought, you know.

It took him an abnormally long time to reply to my lie.

Anthony: Only two? And they weren't great? What made them less than satisfactory?

Me: The guy had trouble finding my clit. It was kind of awkward.

Another pause. I could practically *see* Tore's ears turning bright red as he replayed this afternoon in his head, searching for where he'd gone wrong. The answer was *nowhere*. We made out in his limo until we'd arrived at my place. He'd followed me inside and made me come twice in quick succession before leaving me with a kiss and returning to work. Hours later, I still felt the burn of his scruff on my thighs and a liquid bonelessness in my limbs.

Anthony: I'm sorry you had a bad time. Did you let this man know how to better service you?

Me: You're so cute, Ant. If you were a real boy—and not a robot—you'd know sometimes a woman has to take matters into her own hands. Don't worry, I got myself off as soon as he left, and it was way better.

Anthony: I'm still not a robot. And don't you think communicating with him about where he went wrong would be a better solution?

Me: Maybe. If I planned to see him again. But I don't.

I felt mean the second I hit *send* and immediately wanted to take it back. So, before Tore could spiral or get any more upset than I suspected he was, I sent another message.

Me: I'm just joking, Ant. I had an incredible time with him. I'm still thinking about it.

Anthony: Which part was a joke?

Me: Most of it. There really is a guy, and he had no trouble finding my clit. I like him a lot. A *lot*.

Anthony: I'm happy for you, Bea. You deserve someone who will appreciate everything about you. Would you still like me to send you a soup recipe?

Me: Thank you, but no. You were right. Cooking soup at 10 p.m. is crazy.

Anthony: Do you think you could let yourself belong to this man?

My heart jumped into my throat. What a question to ask. But I'd asked him the same thing weeks ago, when I hadn't known I was talking to Tore.

Could I?

Me: I think I can.

The crazy thing was, I was pretty sure I had belonged to Salvatore Gallo a lot longer than I'd realized.

⁂

When I stepped into the conference room, Tore was already there waiting for me. Like always. These days, though, he'd given up the pretense of pretending to be working.

Pushing back from the table, he opened his arms.

I bit back a smile, ignoring the flock of butterflies taking flight in my stomach. Setting my things down, I crossed the room to him, perching on his thigh. He pulled me in without hesitation, wrapping me in a tight, warm hug.

"Too many days," he murmured into my hair. "I thought we talked about this."

It had been over a week since I'd slid into his limo. Since then, he'd fit in a dinner, a late-night visit where we'd made out like horny teenagers on my couch, and a trip to another art gallery—that also ended with a wild make-out session. I'd been waiting for him to tell me he was *Anthony*. I wanted it to come from him. But as I'd waited, I'd let myself fall.

It might have been foolish, considering he'd been keeping something so big from me, but I couldn't help it. He'd made it impossible.

"You're a busy man." I tipped my head back, and he took the opening, covering my mouth with his. The kiss was restrained, a teasing sweep of his tongue before planting firm, lingering pecks on my lips.

Finally, he sighed, holding my face in his broad palm. "We're going to have to schedule time to see each other. I live by my calendar, and you're not on there. That has to be rectified."

I arched a brow. "Am I a meeting?"

He didn't take the bait, giving me an earnest answer. "You're important, and I want to see you often."

My chest swelled, lungs overfull. "I do too."

We had to talk about the app, but not here, when we were both working. And not until I knew exactly what I would say. I'd had more than a week, but nothing I'd come up with had sounded right.

What he'd done was crazy, and I knew I should have been alarmed, but even after the knowledge had settled in, I couldn't find it in myself. I'd accepted this man had become fixated on me, and in two years, that hadn't waned. Via *Anthony*, I'd said some silly, embarrassing, *stupid* things that would have made any other man run for the hills.

Not Tore.

He'd stayed.

I kissed him, cupping his smooth jaw. "I'd like to see you this week. Could you come to my house for dinner?"

"I can. Tonight," he replied. "But it'll be on the later side."

"I'll wait for you."

He rolled his forehead along mine. "There are some things I need to tell you. Important things you should know before we move forward."

My heart lifted. This was it. He was going to come clean. Tonight, we'd put all our cards on the table. It was exactly what I needed from him.

"Things that would make me not want to move forward?"

His thumb stroked the pulse fluttering at my throat. "No, Beatrice. We *are* moving forward. That isn't a question."

"Oh?"

If any other man had said that to me, I would have removed myself from his lap—and probably given his shin a kick for good measure. From Tore? My body reacted instantly. Panties flooding. Synapses rewiring. His certainty was a double shot, landing in my chest and deep in my core.

"It's not." He tapped my pulse. "Tonight, beautiful blue, we'll talk."

"I'm looking forward to it."

CHAPTER THIRTY-TWO

Bea

I DIDN'T USE THE *Come on Rover* app anymore—not since Tony had given me carte blanche access to their backyard. More often than not, the kids were already outside, waiting for Benjamin and me when we arrived.

Today, Tally and Scarlet were on the deck. I released Ben from his leash, and Tally darted down the stairs to chase after him, all gangly legs and enthusiasm, while Scarlet stayed put, offering me a small wave from her perch.

"Where's Lace?" I called to her.

"She's finishing a drawing." Scarlet came to the top of the steps, hesitating before climbing down. "Hey, Bea?"

"Yes, darling?"

"Do you think...I mean, if you have time, do you think you could teach me how to do my hair like yours? I know mine is longer, but I was hoping there's a way. I tried to follow a tutorial, but it didn't turn out right—"

"Hey, you know"—I laid my hand on her arm—"that's my favorite question? Hair is kind of one of my things. I'd love to. I'm busy tonight, but we could try tomorrow, or whenever you're free."

I surprised myself by how much I was looking forward to hanging out with a teenager. Part of me wondered if it was because she was close in age to Maddie and I was looking for a replacement for the sister I'd lost.

Maybe that was part of it, but Scarlet was interesting and bright in her own right. I liked her. And maybe, just maybe, she saw something in me she had been missing—an older woman she could talk to about things she couldn't say to her grandpa or her uncle.

"Tomorrow," she rushed out. "Do you have a date tonight?"

I nodded. "Yeah. There's a guy."

Her dark eyes lit with curiosity. "There is? What's he like? Does he have cool hair too? He has to be cool if you like him, but what kind of cool?"

Before I could answer, my name was shrieked from the top of the steps, and Lacey appeared, waving a piece of paper.

"Don't go yet! I made you a picture. Stay right there!"

I laughed at the panic in her little face. "I'm not going anywhere."

She must not have believed me. She raced down the steps, her feet tangling midway. Lacey stumbled, and time slowed.

Her wide, terrified eyes locked on mine as I rushed forward. As long as I lived, I wouldn't forget her sheer panic as she reached for something, *anything* to save her.

I tried.

I tried so hard to get there, to catch her before she hit the ground. But I was moving through sludge, racing against gravity.

Two unbeatable foes.

She rolled head over heels to the bottom, landing in a crumpled heap. The screech she let out rendered my heart and the world in two.

Gravity finally released me, and I ran to her. She was so small—a pile of skinny limbs and wild hair, crying so hard, her entire frame trembled. But if she was crying, that meant she was awake. Conscious. That was important.

My first instinct was to lift her into my arms, but I thought better of it. Falling on my knees beside her, I brushed her hair from her face. Her head rolled toward me, rivers of tears coating her round cheeks.

"Oh, baby," I whispered. "You're okay. You're going to be just fine."

"Bea?" Her little voice wobbled. "My arm hurts."

I couldn't take my gaze off hers to check her over. My eyes refused to move.

"I'm so sorry, darling. We'll fix you up in just a minute, okay? We'll make it better."

Things blurred as action swirled around us. Tony took over, getting Benjamin back into my house, helping me off the ground, and loading everyone into the car since Lacey refused to leave me behind. I sat in the back seat with her and Talon, holding both their hands and telling them it would be all right.

Once we arrived at the hospital, time bent again and lost all meaning. I had no idea how long we were there before Scarlet breathed, "Uncle Sally," with soul-deep relief.

I was on the bed with Lacey, holding her in my lap, Talon tucked on my other side, looking at the hundreds of pictures of Benjamin on my phone, when a tall man in a suit strode in.

It was good I was sitting down. If I hadn't been, there was no shot my knees wouldn't have given out.

Our eyes met for a mere second, and the world tilted.

Salvatore.

He was white as a sheet, eyes glassy and panicked, a sheen of sweat on his forehead. His chest heaved, like he'd run as fast as he could to get here.

"Lace," he uttered, his voice cracking.

In an instant, he was across the room, his hand hovering just above her cheek without touching, vibrating with intense, barely contained energy. Helplessness and fear carved hard lines beside his mouth and a deep crevice between his brows.

"I hurt my arm, Uncle Sally." Lacey sniffled, pressing her back into my chest.

He didn't even look at me.

All his focus was on Lacey—right where it belonged. Because she was his. All three of these kids belonged to him. *My* Tore was *their* Uncle Sally.

My head turned like it was on creaky hinges to look at the kids. Lacey, curled in my lap, her arm against her chest like a broken wing. Talon, studying my phone with fervor, like he couldn't bear to see anything else right now. Scarlet, her blotchy cheeks and fisted hands, holding herself together by the skin of her teeth.

Finally, I looked at Tore. He wasn't shocked to see me here. He didn't wonder why I was with his children.

He'd known.

How could there be any other possibility? This man controlled every facet of his universe. He had peered into my life for two years without me having an inkling. Of course he was aware of who was in his children's lives.

He'd known and didn't tell me.

An ache bloomed behind my ribs. Not pain, exactly. Not even anger. I couldn't quite name what I was feeling.

Then it came to me.

Betrayal.

That was it.

I had come to care for these kids, and he'd let it happen. I'd played with them, told them ridiculous stories, let them into my house, my life, even though kids *were not my thing*.

And all that time, I hadn't known who they were to him.

Or who *he* was to them.

He didn't look at me. Even now.

He was gripping Lacey's tiny fingers, demanding his father find her doctor immediately, reminding me why we were here. Lacey was hurt, and her needs were immediate. Everything else could wait.

So I didn't say a word.

I didn't ask questions.

I didn't demand explanations.

Not here. Not now.

CHAPTER THIRTY-THREE
Salvatore

It was late when I knocked on Bea's door, but it didn't take her long to answer. She'd been waiting for me.

She opened it wide, wordlessly stepping aside to allow me in.

I had seen this woman in so many iterations. Angry. Turned on. Amused. Happy.

But this? The utter defeat weighing her down from every angle was brand new, and it wasn't right. It was unnatural on her. Did not belong.

"How's Lacey doing?" she asked.

Lacey had pleaded for Bea to stay at the hospital with her, so she had. Through X-rays, talks with a specialist, and casting, Bea had stuck in there. My kids had leaned hard on her, and she'd let them without question. If it had made her uncomfortable, she'd hidden it well.

She'd only been able to break away when we'd arrived home, with promises to check on Lacey soon.

"Better than the rest of us," I said, fingers already fidgeting with the titanium ring on my index finger, thumb brushing over the ridged engraving. "She's excited to show off her cast at school to-morrow."

Bea had been the first to sign it. Her name, written in curling loops, with a tiny bumblebee doodle beside it. Lacey had made sure none of us had signed within three inches of it.

With a nod, Bea turned and walked toward the kitchen without looking back.

I followed her, stopping in the doorway. She moved mechanically, filling a kettle with water and setting it on the stove, her back ramrod straight.

She turned the burner on, and only then did she face me.

"How could you not tell me?" she whispered.

"I was going to. Tonight. That's what I was coming over to talk to you about." I'd planned it. Scripted it. Rehearsed it between brushing Lacey's hair this morning and tying Tally's shoes. Between lines of code and meetings with my programming teams.

She reached for the counter, her fingers curling around the edge. "It's my fault for never asking what had happened to Tia's kids." Her eyes flicked to mine. "Would you have told me earlier if I'd asked directly?"

"Yes." I nodded sharply. "None of this is your fault. It's mine. I wanted...I didn't plan for you to get to know them before I told you. I should have stepped in. I made the wrong decision. They liked you, and I'd hoped—"

"To manipulate me?"

"No. Absolutely not."

I took a step forward, then stopped, fists clenched at my sides to keep myself from touching her. The wrong word, the wrong tone, and I'd lose her. I may have already lost her. But she'd let me inside. She hadn't told me to go. There was a chance I could fix this.

"Then why?" she asked, almost begging.

She needed me to make it make sense. I should have had the words. I'd had weeks to come up with an explanation far better than *'I'm willing to do anything to keep you,'* but that was what it came down to. My plans all had one goal: Beatrice Novak. In my mind, it was simple. But I had to give her more than that.

"I started on my back foot with you and had so much to make up for. I'd wanted us to get right with each other before I threw in complications."

Bea didn't move, didn't speak. She just watched me with a new wariness that cut me to the bone.

"I'm not their father," I went on. "But I'm everything else. Tia trusted me with them. I don't know why. Half the time, I'm not sure I'm right for the job, but they're my world now. We were all drowning when Tia died, and I've spent two years clawing us back to the surface. *That's* why I disappeared from your life. I had to focus on them—"

"I would never begrudge you any of that. Of course you had to give them your all."

Memories rose to the surface of Lacey crying through the night, Talon asking question after question I couldn't answer, Scarlet having outbursts of anger she had every right to. Because life wasn't fair and her mother should have been alive. Locking myself in my bedroom and blindly staring at a wall when my own grief and new upside-down world overwhelmed me. The weight of sound. The emotional noise.

Therapy helped, but it was time that healed us. The kids saw they still had me and their grandfather. They could trust we were going to stick. And I'd accepted the changes in my life. Learned how to manage my company and family without going into shutdown mode every day.

"Everything changed. One heartbeat to the next, I became theirs. I had to build our life from the ground up, and we've made a *good* life. I was going to come for you. Paul sped up my timeline by a couple months when he hired you unexpectedly, but I'd had it all planned out, with the house—"

"You *do* know it's crazy you bought the house across the street from mine, don't you?" she said, finally showing a flicker of the sassy, sarcastic, blunt Beatrice who routinely cut me off at the knees.

The kettle whistled, and she swiveled away from me, opening a cabinet to pull out a mug, then another for a box of tea. I watched her steep her tea bag, waiting for her attention before speaking again.

Steam rose from the mug as she lifted a brow. "It's crazy, Salvatore."

I nodded. "You're probably right. On the outside, it looks like an insane decision. But we needed a home that fit better, and the one I found happened to be close to you. I don't make decisions without thorough consideration. I wouldn't have dragged my kids along with me if I hadn't thought they'd be happy here, and they are. They love the house...and the neighbors."

"Crazy," she muttered.

"Maybe. But I stand by it. The other choices I made? I was wrong, and I'm sorry. I should have told you when I explained what had happened to Tia."

"You should have," she agreed.

She wasn't giving me an inch, and I needed a mile.

"But I didn't," I said, my voice low. "This is where I admit I was selfish. Greedy for more time with you. Bea, I've never had anything like this. You know I don't connect with people easily, and I have never *wanted* someone the way I want you."

Her eyes shimmered, but she didn't look away.

"This is what I wanted to talk to you about tonight. I wasn't going to keep it from you any longer. You deserved to know and have the choice of whether to move forward with me. All my planning, and I can't—" I swallowed hard around the truth I hated. "I can't control your reaction. I can't make you want to take a risk on me, knowing what I come with."

She shook her head. "I told you I don't want children."

"I haven't forgotten. I don't expect you to be their mother. They had a great one, and between my dad and me, they have two parents." I tucked my hands in my pockets. "We can take it slow. We can start over. It's up to you now."

Bea wrapped her fingers around her steaming mug, her eyes cast downward. Silence stretched tight between us.

"I can forgive you for being *Anthony*," she said finally, the words a sharp turn I hadn't seen coming.

My head snapped up. "You... what?"

Her smile was faint, tired. "I figured it out last week. The app was on your phone, and then I saw you in the limo. I added everything up."

"Ten p.m. soup," I murmured. "You were fucking with me. On purpose."

She held her fingers an inch apart. "A little bit." Then she smacked her forehead. "Anthony. Your dad's name is Tony. It was so obvious."

"It's my middle name too." I shoved my fingers through my hair. "Christ. I have a lot to explain."

"No kidding. I thought *that* was your big secret. I had already worked through it on my own and decided it was almost...sweet. You've done a lot for me. More than I know, probably. Though I'm still not sure why you'd want to."

"That answer is simple. When we met, I was drawn to you because you made me feel good. I was at ease and able to be myself around you, which is more rare than I can put into words."

I scoffed at my understatement. The way I'd felt around Bea from the start had been unprecedented. A revelation. Like I'd gone a lifetime as an alien crash-landed on earth and had finally met another being from my home planet.

I took a half step closer. "That changed, though. When I sent you the app, I didn't know how addicted I would become to making *you* feel good. I still want that, Beatrice. I *need* it."

Her breath caught, and she closed her eyes. "I believe you."

Hope flared, but it was premature.

"I don't know if I can get past this," she said. "This isn't just about you and me anymore. You made me part of something without telling me what it *was*. That wasn't fair, and I don't know if we can come back from this. Or if I want to."

"Or if I want to."

This wasn't only about me omitting the truth. When it came down to it, I had kids, and Bea had chosen to be child-free.

"We're at an impasse," I said, trying to anchor myself to logic, "but I think we can find a way around it. If you're willing."

She didn't speak, but her eyes stayed on mine. Still listening. Still here.

"You can take space," I offered. "The kids don't have to be involved. This can just be you and me, starting over. A clean slate where everything is on the table. We'll go back to the beginning. Whatever pace makes sense."

A shadow passed across her face. "We can't compartmentalize our relationship. That's not how life works."

"I know," I said quickly. "I do. But this isn't about hiding anything anymore. It's about giving you breathing room. Whatever you need to come around."

She folded her arms over her chest, wrapping herself up like armor. Her jaw trembled. Just once.

"I don't think I can," she rasped.

"I know you can." Panic slithered in my gut, wrapping around tight. I spoke faster than I could think. "This will work. You'll see. Give us a chance—"

A single word fell like ice between us.

"Antarctica."

My chest caved inward.

The safe word. The one we'd chosen when the possibility of what lay ahead had been shiny and bright. A word that meant stop. No further. A word I never thought she would have to use with me.

I nodded, a slow, careful dip of my chin. Nausea climbed up my throat with jagged claws.

"Okay," I said hoarsely. "I'll go."

I didn't try to touch her or continue pleading my case. A safe word wasn't the start of a negotiation. It was a full stop. She was done. I had to be too.

Every step I took toward the door was another mile. My hand shook as I opened it, the finality hitting me all at once.

Just before I stepped out, I looked over my shoulder. Bea had followed me out of the kitchen, stopping a few feet away, her mug clutched in both hands.

"I'm not going away, Beatrice. Not for good. But I'll give you as much space as you need."

She didn't answer, but she didn't slam the door behind me either, so I took it as a positive sign.

As I trudged across the street, feeling her eyes on my back the whole way, I allowed myself to believe this wasn't over.

I was down, but I wasn't out.

Not yet.

CHAPTER THIRTY-FOUR
Bea

I woke up with an elephant on my chest. As I tried to breathe through it, it only got worse. No matter what I did, the weight sitting on my sternum got heavier and heavier.

How had I even fallen asleep? After Tore left, I lay in my bed, staring at the ceiling, my thoughts racing. At some point, in the wee hours of the morning, I'd lost consciousness, but my mind hadn't stopped. Sleep had brought me no clarity or relief.

Benjamin coaxed me out of bed, and I barely managed to send him out to my tiny yard before I had to sit down. Guilt swamped me for not taking him for his morning walk, but there was no way I could make it up the block, let alone get back to my house.

Blood whooshed in my ears as I sat on my couch, my head between my knees, trying to convince myself to take long, deep breaths. But the longer I sat there, the harder it became.

Somewhere in the distance, I heard Benjamin *woofing*. He wasn't far away, but *I* was. Buried under too many thoughts and grief I'd hidden from for years. Oh, had it found me.

I wanted to get up and go to my boy. I needed to. But my body wasn't cooperating. I desperately gripped the edge of the couch cushion, my hands trembling. I couldn't breathe—couldn't think—couldn't *move*.

The door creaked open, but I didn't lift my head. Couldn't. I hoped it was Benjamin coming inside.

Then I heard two sets of footsteps. Benjamin's and heavier ones, coming directly toward me.

"Bea, you okay? Benji was outside on his own..."

My heart squeezed violently.

Ben was here. Why was he here?

I wanted to look at him, to tell him I was okay, to hide the mess I was, but I couldn't lift my head...couldn't uncoil the iron grip of panic wrapped around my chest.

"Hey, I'm here," he said, closer this time. He dropped to the couch beside me. "Can I touch you?"

I shook my head hard. I didn't want to be touched or even seen. Right now, I wanted to fade into the ether.

Maddie. Davis. Jane.

Oh no. No, no, no.

Ben sat beside me patiently, his massive presence and voice a steady anchor in the storm ripping its way through me.

"Okay. That's okay. I want you to breathe with me, Buzz. Just try. In through your nose, nice and slow. Like this."

I could hear him doing it—deep, controlled inhales, each one louder than the blood rushing in my ears. I tried to match him. *Tried.* My lungs felt like they'd forgotten how to work.

"Ben," I rasped. "I can't. Not again. I can't."

Maddie. Davis. Jane.

I couldn't.

"What's going on, Bea? I don't know what to do. How can I help you?"

I shook my head again. "I'm just...he has kids. I can't—"

"Okay." He rubbed my back as I rocked, trying to find my equilibrium. "I'm going to get Shira. You need your girl."

"No, no, she has the baby." My voice cracked on the final word.

Ben pulled out his phone anyway. "She'd drop Jonah in Roman's arms and sprint barefoot across hot coals for you at a moment's notice, and you know it." He tapped out a message and dropped the phone onto his lap.

I let out a hollow laugh that came out more like a cough.

He gave me a crooked smile. "Look at that. We're making progress. You made a noise that didn't sound like gasping."

I dropped my face back into my hands.

Maddie. Davis. Jane.

It had been ten years. Ten years since I'd been removed from their lives by force. One day, I was making up silly dances with Maddie and teaching Davis how to tie his shoes, and the next, I was on my own. I'd blinked, and they were gone.

The worst thing was, I'd resented them. Hated I'd been turned into their parent. Had desperately wanted a normal adolescence free from diaper changes and middle-of-the-night wake-up calls. But I'd loved them with my entire being. They had been *mine*.

The door opened quietly, and Benjamin greeted Shira with a soft whine and tail thump. Her hair was pulled back in a messy knot, no makeup, bare feet. She'd thrown a sweater over her pajamas but hadn't taken the time to put on shoes.

Ben had been right.

She'd come straight to me, taking my other side. She may have been slight, but her presence was a soothing comfort, blanketing me in warmth. Having her beside me was enough for my breathing to even out and no longer feel like I was on the verge of drowning. Now, I was just unbearably sad.

"Oh, honey." Her voice was so achingly kind.

My chin wobbled. "You didn't have to come."

"Yes, I did." She clutched my hand in hers. "Tell me what's wrong."

"I think..." I whispered, barely audible, "I'm broken."

Ben leaned closer, like he hadn't quite heard me. "What was that?"

"I broke a little last night," I said, louder this time. "Tore has kids."

Shira sucked in a breath. "That's...a surprise."

Ben looked back and forth between us. "Wait. Who's Tore?"

"My boyfriend." I squeezed my eyes shut. "I don't know if he's still my boyfriend."

"Wait." He leaned around me to look at Shira. "Did you know she has a boyfriend?"

"Of course," she replied.

He huffed. "Why am I the last to know? I'm hurt, Buzz."

"His name is Tore." I pressed the heel of my hand into my eye. "Salvatore Gallo. He lives across the street and is the guardian of his sister's three kids. You met Scarlet. She's his oldest. But I only found that out last night."

I sucked in a deep breath. There was so much to explain, but I didn't want to talk about Tore. He might have kicked up the dirt covering the grave of my grief, but he hadn't been the one to dig it in the first place.

The words tumbled out. About my mom. About the day she made me leave for good. About how small and ashamed I'd felt. How angry I still was. How I hated myself for feeling even an inkling of relief over no longer being responsible for my siblings. How Tore's kids had brought everything back like it had happened yesterday.

Ben leaned his solid weight against me. "Bea..."

"I don't let myself think about them." My hands clenched into fists on my lap. "They were my babies. *Mine*. And I lost them. My mom took them away from me. And made me feel like it was *my* fault, like I was the bad one for wanting my own life. It killed me not to be with them. I ached and ached and ached. Spent so many sleepless nights worrying who was taking care of them. It got so bad, I could barely function. I was only eighteen. Still a kid myself. I didn't know what else to do, so I buried it. I buried *them*."

Ben was quiet. Thoughtful. He didn't rush in to try to fix everything, and I loved him for that. Some things couldn't be fixed.

He just said, "Damn. I had no idea. That's a lot, Buzz. You've been carrying that around all this time and still manage to function like a semi-responsible adult? You might actually be a superhero."

A breath escaped me that wasn't quite a laugh but wasn't a sob either. "Didn't you hear the part about me burying my feelings? I'm not sure that's functioning."

Shira wrapped her arms around me. "That was too much for one girl to hold alone. You were never supposed to carry it all by yourself."

I blinked at her, my lashes wet, my throat raw. "He has kids, Shira. I can't—I don't...I don't *do* kids. Not anymore."

Ben's brow dipped low over his worried eyes. "But you love kids. You're Aunt Bea."

"I don't do kids," I whispered. "I can't, Benny."

Shira laid her head on my shoulder. "I'm so sorry you lost your babies, Bea. I can only imagine how deeply that scarred you. If you'd rather I not bring Jonah around—"

I stiffened. "Don't even say it."

"Okay." She laughed softly. "I only want to make sure you're okay being around him."

"Of course I am. I love him."

Ben patted my knee. "But you don't *do* kids, right?"

"Shut up," I grumbled, swatting his hand away. "You're not smart, and you're definitely not right."

Another light knock on my door alerted Benjamin. He trotted over as Roman stepped inside with baby Jonah in his arms.

Even in these circumstances, it was slightly disconcerting to see Roman and Ben in the same room. Their faces were identical. The only difference was Ben wore athletic gear most of the time, and his curls were wild. While Roman kept his tame and was most often in suits, like he was now.

"Hey." He gave Benjamin a nice, firm pat. "I wanted to see if you—"

I held my arms out. "Yes. I want baby snuggles."

Grinning, he crossed the room and placed his son in my arms. Jonah was awake and had little milky bubbles at the corner of his rosebud mouth.

"Hi, buddy," I cooed. "How did you know this was exactly what I needed?"

Ben leaned into me. "I think I might've been right," he whispered teasingly.

Shira gave him a look, but the corner of her mouth twitched, like she was fighting back a smile. Roman sat on the arm of the couch next to her, resting a hand on her shoulder, hers going to his leg. When they were near each other, they were touching. It was sweet, but right now, it made my heart hurt.

I ran a thumb across Jonah's impossibly soft cheek to distract myself. "He's squishy and warm and smells delicious. Who could resist him? It's human nature."

"Sure, sure," Ben said with a sage nod. "That's all this is. And you didn't hire the surly teen across the street, FaceTime Nellie on a regular basis, and hang out with—"

"Shush," I hissed. "Just because I tolerate certain kids doesn't mean I like them in general."

"Yep. That's believable," Ben scoffed.

As if on cue, Jonah gurgled and kicked his chubby feet, and my heart actually ached. Not the kind that had torn me apart earlier. This was a gentler kind, reserved for puppies and babies.

Shira kept her voice low and careful. "Do you think you really don't do kids, or is it you're afraid to fall for them and have them taken away again?"

I opened my mouth to answer, but I couldn't. Yesterday, I would have had confidence in my assertion that I didn't like children. I'd been telling myself and everyone else that for a solid decade. But now? My chest had been cracked wide open, revealing feelings I hadn't dealt with—that I'd denied, even to myself.

"I don't know." I blinked at her. "I really don't know."

"You don't have to figure it out today," Shira said gently. "Just be kind to yourself. You went through something terrible. I don't blame you for being afraid of going through it again. Just...remember what you said to me a few months ago?"

I squinted at her. "Are you going to throw my own words back at me?"

"No." She nudged my shoulder. "I'm going to be a good friend and remind you how smart you are."

Ben rubbed his hands together. "This, I need to hear."

Shira laughed, but her kind eyes stayed on me. "You said, 'If you don't really live, what was the point of everything you did to survive?'"

I choked out a huff. "Well, damn. You got me there."

Ben scrubbed his chin. "That's going in my memoir." Then he arched a brow at me. "Don't worry, I'll dedicate it to you."

I gave him a tired smile. "I'll buy the first copy. You'll probably spell my name wrong, but that's okay."

"'To my best friend, Buzz.'" He grinned, and Shira let out a sweet chuckle.

Roman reached his long arm around Shira and me to swat the back of his brother's head. "Don't mind him. He's taken too many head shots on the pitch."

Ben shrugged him off. "So you hit me again? How's that helpful?"

"Figured I might knock some sense into you," Roman replied.

Benji-bear padded over to join the fray. He plopped in front of me, resting his heavy head on my knee. Between petting him and snuggling Jonah, everything else became background noise.

The weight in my chest hadn't disappeared, not completely, but it was no longer crushing.

I didn't have answers. I didn't know what I'd do about Tore, or his kids, or the past I'd spent a decade trying to outrun. For this moment, I was surrounded by people who'd dropped everything to be with me and stayed without asking.

That was enough.

CHAPTER THIRTY-FIVE
Bea

Benjamin and I were coming home from a walk when I spotted the familiar sight of Lacey, Talon, and Scarlet on the sidewalk in front of my house. Only they had Tony with them. Even if Benjamin had let me turn around and head the other way, I wouldn't have. On the contrary, I found myself speeding up—just a little—to get to them.

"Bea!" Lacey waved her casted arm, a white piece of paper clutched in her fingers. "I have to give this to you."

Benjamin sat like a good boy, plopping down in front of Talon without me saying a word, his tail wagging happily. Talon immediately dropped to the ground and rubbed his face into Benjamin's silky coat.

I crouched in front of Lacey. "Hello, darling. What do you have for me?"

She shoved the paper into my hand. "I made this for you yesterday, but then I fell, so I kind of forgot to give it to you. It took me two whole days to draw. I hope you love it. I didn't have a picture of Benjamin, so I had to draw him from my memory."

On the paper, in bold crayon lines, was my boy. She'd captured his flopped ears and goofy grin perfectly. Benjamin's tongue lolled out like he was laughing, and perched on his head was a bright-yellow-and-black bumblebee with sparkly wings.

"Oh, wow," I said, my chest going gooey and warm. "This is amazing."

"Do you like it?" She pointed to the bee. "That's you, because your name is like a bee, even if it's spelled differently."

Lizards, how was one girl so adorable?

"I love it so much. You want to come in and show me where I should hang it on my fridge?"

Where had that come from? I'm supposed to be taking space, not inviting Tore's family into my house.

She blinked her big brown eyes at me. "Yes, Bea. I really want to."

The kids and Benjamin ran inside first, and Tony and I followed.

"You doing all right?" he asked.

"I'm good." I wondered if he knew I was dating his son, but I wouldn't ask. "Did Lacey sleep okay in her cast?"

"From what I heard from my son, she had a pretty restless night. Poor guy looked like a zombie when he left for work this morning, but Lace's step is full of pep."

I forced out a smile, shoving my mind way past his comment about Tore, even though it hurt my heart to think about him up all night with Lacey and not getting any sleep.

"I have a feeling Lacey's step is always peppy."

Tony chuckled. "You know her well."

I did. Somehow, I'd let myself get to know all three of these children. It hadn't been intentional, but it'd happened anyway. And even though kids weren't my thing, I liked these specific ones. A *lot*.

Blurgh.

Lacey picked a spot on the center of my fridge, and we both stepped back, eyeing the picture critically.

"You know..." I scratched my chin, pretending to consider. "I think I might buy a frame for it. Sometimes I'm messy when I cook. I'd hate to splash anything on this masterpiece."

She gasped. "You want to frame it?"

"You spent two days on it. That's commitment. It would be insulting the artist if I didn't."

She folded her arms across her puffed-up chest. "Yeah. You're right. I *am* an artist. Did you know Uncle Sally collects art? The stuff he likes doesn't fit in frames, though. But maybe he should think about it. I think he pays a *lot* of money for that stuff."

"Does he have any of your art hanging up?" I asked.

She nodded. "Yep. Our fridge is covered in art Tally and I made. Uncle Sally doesn't like messes, but he says he doesn't mind some chaos when it's contained in one spot. Sometimes, I catch him standing there, staring at everything, kind of smiling. I think he likes it a lot."

A lump rudely lodged itself in my throat. "I bet he loves it. I think I'm going to need some Tally art to go with my Lacey art."

Talon lifted his head from where he was sprawled across Benjamin, who was happily chewing a toy.

"I have plenty, but it's not girly like Lacey's," he declared.

"That's okay. I'll take whatever you want to give me. My walls could use a little color."

Scarlet sidled up to us, her phone clutched in her hand. "Um, Bea?"

I turned to face her. "What's up?"

"Remember when I asked about the hair tutorial? I know last night got kind of crazy, but I was hoping—"

"Yep." I nodded. "I'm free tonight. Come over after dinner, all right?"

Her eyes lit up, and she looked more like her little sister than ever. Then she schooled her expression, opting for cool and above it all.

"Oh yeah. That sounds good," she said, casual as could be.

In for a penny, in for a pound.

My relationship with these three—plus Tony—was completely independent of Tore. He'd thrown a wrench in things, but I wasn't going to allow my mixed-up feelings for him to change me or how I moved through life.

I wanted to hang up Lacey and Talon's art. I wanted to teach Scarlet how to do victory rolls. Not because of him.

Because of *them*.

Because I liked them.

It had nothing to do with their uncle.

Scarlet was at my house, mid-tutorial, when the package arrived. I didn't open it until she'd gone home, and once I saw what was inside, I was glad I'd waited.

She would've thought I'd grown three heads if she'd seen me get teary over a frame just the right size for Lacey's drawing.

There was no message with the delivery, but I wasn't stupid. At least, not in this case. I knew exactly who'd sent it.

> **Me:** Hey, Ant. Can you tell me if it's illegal to use children as spies?

Anthony: Hello, Bea. I need more context before I can answer you.

Me: Let's say a man sends children over to the house of the woman he likes in order to extract information. Would that be illegal?

Anthony: That sounds like a gray area. Are you certain the man sent them, or do you think they could like the woman just as much as he does, and it's impossible to keep them away from her?

Me: I've considered that.

Anthony: If that's the case, is it possible the children like to talk about the woman all the time and the man just listens?

Me: They do enjoy talking.

Anthony: Then no laws have been broken, in my opinion.

Me: Oh, I'm certain *some* laws have been broken, but not by the children.

Anthony: Are you concerned about the possible gray area some of the man's actions have fallen into?

I laughed out loud. Possible gray area? Oh, Tore was funny. He knew damn well he'd crossed out of the gray a long time ago, just as I knew I wasn't concerned about those particular actions. If I were, I would have immediately deleted the app from my phone, but here I was, using it with full knowledge of who was on the other side.

That wasn't our problem.

> **Me:** Gray is one of my favorite colors.

> **Anthony:** That's good to know. I wouldn't worry about the children being used. I'm certain they are spending time with you of their own volition.

> **Me:** You're right. And the man wouldn't use his kids like that. I don't know how I know that, but I do.

> **Anthony:** I'm relieved.

I bit my lip, hesitating, wanting to say more—wanting *him* to say more. But I wasn't ready to let this silly pretense go, and he didn't seem to be either.

> **Me:** Can you tell me how I get over a broken heart?

> **Anthony:** Who broke your heart, Bea?

> **Me:** Life, I guess. Does it matter? I just want it to be fixed.

> **Anthony:** As with most broken things, time and attention works wonders. If you're careful with it, it might even heal stronger than it was before.

I stared at the screen for a long moment, my heart tugging in that newly familiar, achy way. Wouldn't that be nice if I could finally move on? I didn't know what that would look like, but I was ready to try. Because this half-life, ignoring festering pain, wasn't the way anymore.

> **Me:** Thanks, Ant. I hope that's true. Good night.

> **Anthony:** Good night, Bea.

I set my phone down and sagged back into the couch, exhausted. My gaze drifted to the package again, and I pulled out the frame. Simple and hammered gold. I slid Lacey's picture inside, a little monument to this weird, wonderful, unexpected place I'd found myself in. To bumblebees on my Benji-bear's head and kids who hadn't let their loss stop them from falling into someone new. To friendship and trying. To change.

I carried it into the kitchen and found the perfect spot to hang it.

I opened the cabinet where I kept my small collection of tools, easily finding what I needed, when the small storage box tucked in the back caught my eye. I hadn't allowed myself to think about its existence in a long, long time, but I'd never been able to bring myself to throw it out.

I slid it out and sank to the floor with it in my lap, the edges of old memories curling around me as I lifted the lid. Inside were crayon rainbows, hand turkeys, and scribbled stick figures with giant hearts and oversized smiles—art projects Maddie and Davis had made for me back when I was more parent than sister.

I'd kept them hidden, as if that would have protected me from the profound pain of losing my siblings. It hadn't made it hurt any less. In fact, not being able to keep even a small piece of them had damaged me more than anything.

I pulled two out: Maddie's rainbow and Davis's turkey. Something shifted inside me. Seeing them actually made me smile. Climbing to my feet, I hung them on the refrigerator. I didn't know if I'd keep them there, but I needed to look at them. To remember.

I carefully hammered a nail into my wall and placed Lacey's portrait right across from them. They looked so out of place in my sleek, modern kitchen, and I loved that. Chaotic. Mismatched. Perfect.

I nodded to myself, turned off the kitchen light, and went to bed. Not healed. Not even close. But I had a feeling I'd rest a little easier tonight.

CHAPTER THIRTY-SIX
Salvatore

ANTARCTICA.

One of seven continents. The coldest place on earth. No native human life. A polar desert. Aside from screaming wind capable of flaying skin off bone, there was no sound. Inland, there were no animals or vegetation. Nothing grew or rotted, so there was no scent.

Save for auroras and stars, for six months of the year, the world turned completely black. Time lost meaning. Days blended into numb monotony.

I'd been in Antarctica for a week. It might as well have been years.

My kids, father, and work kept me tethered. The lone satellite capable of beaming signals down to me.

It was strange feeling so desolate. This was the life I'd been living for years, and I'd been content.

That was before.

Now I knew what it meant to really have Bea, and there was no unknowing.

She had reached out, but only through the app, never to the real me. Even though I felt like I was buried in ice, I was doing my best to give her the space I'd promised. Not going to her in the conference room on Tuesday had nearly broken me. My thumbs had to bleed to keep me away.

But she'd given me *Antarctica*, and I would not go against her wishes until she explicitly gave me the green light.

In the meantime, I'd live with the consequences of my own decisions. Pick apart the choices that got me here. No matter how I'd turned it, I'd come to the same conclusion: I'd fucked up.

Dishonesty didn't come naturally to me, but bending rules—framing the truth to achieve what I believed was right? That I was guilty of.

Bea had called it manipulation. I couldn't argue.

But winning her through lies of omission wasn't any kind of victory. I'd been too fixated on the prize to see that until it was too late.

When she reached out, I would tell her this. That I'd been unequivocally wrong. That I'd learned from my mistakes and would never repeat them. But I had to wait for her to be ready to hear that. I'd already crossed too many boundaries to push this one. If *Antarctica* wasn't safe for her, how would she ever believe *I* was?

A light tap on my arm pulled me from my thoughts. Talon stood beside me, holding a book. It was after dinner. My dad was out on a date. The girls were upstairs in Scarlet's room. It was just the two of us in the living room.

"Excuse me, Uncle Sally."

I cocked my head, giving him my full attention. "What can I help you with, sir?"

He chuckled. Lately, he'd been reading every story he could find that involved butlers. His mind had snagged on that particular curiosity a few months ago and hadn't let go yet. I was slightly worried our library would run out of material before he moved on, but he still had a long list to get through.

He liked it when I pretended to be *his* butler, addressing him formally. He'd roped my father into serving his breakfast on a silver tray and wore white gloves so he could read his books in character.

Tia would have laughed her ass off at her son's latest interest. Then she would have collected herself and researched every way she could support him. Knowing her, she would have found a real-life butler to introduce him to. Now that I had thought of it, I could probably do that...

"What was my mom's middle name?" he asked.

"Antonia. Grandpa passed his name to us both. And your mom gave it to you."

Talon already knew this. But he liked to hear about her. And I didn't mind saying the same thing again and again. Talking about Tia never got old.

"Grandpa must really like his name. He calls me Talon Anthony sometimes."

"It's family tradition. Your mom made him very happy when she gave you that name. If you have children one day, you might pass it on too."

He twisted his mouth to the side. "What about you? Will you name your kid Anthony?"

I rubbed the top of his head. His hair was getting long. I'd have to check my calendar to make sure he had an appointment for a haircut.

"I already have a kid with that name. I don't need another one."

His brow furrowed as he thought that over. "You mean me?"

"Who else could I mean?"

He sank down on the couch beside me, his arms crossed. I twisted to face him, trying to figure out what he was thinking.

He tilted his head back, frowning, then his narrowed eyes darted over me, curiosity and suspicion mingling in his gaze.

"I'm your kid?" he finally asked.

"Yes, you are." My hand slid from his head to rest between his shoulder blades. "You'll always be your mom's, but you're mine now too. She trusted I would do a good job with you. I could never replace her. Your mom was one of a kind. But I learned how to...*be* from her. I remember how much she loved you and your sisters, and now I love all three of you the way your mom showed me. It's not the same, but I hope you know it'll never go away."

My chest was filled with knots, so tight it hurt. Two years wasn't long enough to get over losing my sister. Then again, neither was a lifetime. I loved my parents, but Tia had been the most important and pivotal person in my life. She'd been exceptional. Filled with good and understanding. It still didn't make sense she was gone. My brain could not compute her absence from the world.

But she'd left me with her children. They weren't the same as her, but each of them contained some of the best parts I was privileged to foster every day.

I would never get over losing her. That I had accepted. But parenting her children was the best thing that had ever happened to me. The dichotomy of those feelings sometimes stymied me.

Talon had no such problem.

He shrugged. "Yeah, I know." Then, without missing a beat, he leaned in and asked the important question. "Do you think I should go to the International Butler Academy or the British Butler Institute?"

The change in topic didn't slow me down. I easily shifted back into character.

"I have no opinion, good sir. A butler's duty is to be invisible and indispensable."

He patted my leg, perfectly solemn. "Don't worry, Uncle Sally. You're indispensable to me."

My smile lingered after he'd turned back to his book. It wasn't big or felt deep down, but it had to be enough until she came back.

I was slipping into bed when her text came in, not to me, of course.

Bea: Hey, Ant. Thanks for sending me dinner tonight.

Me: You're welcome, Bea.

Bea: If I mention I'm craving diamonds, should I expect a pile to show up on my doorstep?

Me: As always, I'm at your service. If you would like a pile of diamonds, I would find a way for that to happen.

Bea: We'll stick with dumplings. I'm not much of a diamond girl. I could go for some clarity, though.

Me: If I can provide that, I will.

Bea: How do I decide to trust someone who lied to me?

Me: Do you want to trust them?

Bea: I don't know. I'm still working that out.

Me: If there is a chance you might want that, start with *why* the lie was told and if you believe you would have been given the truth eventually.

This game was maddening, but these were her terms and my one connection to her. Just like with Talon, I took my role seriously, answering her as *Anthony* would, even with my real answers screaming in my skull.

Bea: I don't know if it matters anymore.

I knifed upright, my back against my headboard, heart thundering in my chest.

Me: Would you care to clarify?

Bea: I'm tired, Ant. I don't know why I messaged you. I guess I had a lot on my mind, but I think I need to work it out on my own.

Me: I'm at your service, for whatever you need.

Bea: Sure. I got it.

> **Me:** Is there anything else I can help with?

I stared at the screen for several minutes, hoping against hope for another message, but it never came. She was gone.

CHAPTER
THIRTY-SEVEN
Bea

A MINUTE OR TWO after I got back from walking Benjamin, a frantic knock rattled my front door. I was halfway up the stairs, ready to swap my work clothes for pajamas.

Benjamin let out a woof and trotted to the door. I followed with significantly less enthusiasm.

"Who could that be, Benji-bear? If it's someone trying to convert me to their religion, they're going to be in for it. I'm *not* in the mood for Bible verses today."

He shot me a side-eye before pressing his nose to the door like he could sniff whoever was on the other side. Maybe he could. I'd have to ask *Anthony* if—

Scratch that. Never mind. I'd use a search engine like a normal person.

Peering through the peephole, I let out a breath. Lacey and Scarlet stood on the porch. Of course it was them. It was rare I went more than two days without seeing at least one of the Gallo kids.

"Bea!" Lacey cried when I opened the door. "We're here to invite you to our house."

Scarlet nodded. "Grandpa helped Lacey, Tally, and me cook dinner. If you don't come, you'll scar us for life."

I folded my arms and tried to glare, but it was no use. "I feel like I'm being handled."

Scarlet had no trouble glaring at me. "I bet you would have said no if I hadn't laid it on a little. I learned the art of Italian guilt from Grandpa. He said Grandma had been an expert at it. I'm carrying on her legacy."

"Fine." I sighed dramatically, stepping aside so they could come in while I changed out of my work clothes. "But only because I'm scared of your inherited guilt-wielding powers."

Lacey giggled. "We usually only use our powers for good."

"Usually?" I huffed. "That's not reassuring."

I left them downstairs and ran up to change. Pajamas were off the table, so I settled for a striped off-the-shoulder top and jeans. As I fastened the top button, I paused.

Tore would be there.

It had been two long, confusing weeks since I'd last seen him. Other than my daily texts through the app, I hadn't heard from him. The constant hum of his attention had vanished like someone had flipped a switch, the silence louder than any words he could have said.

He wasn't chasing me anymore.

And maybe that was what I'd wanted. Space. Time to think. I'd told myself as much. But now that I was about to walk into his house with Scarlet and Lacey, my stomach twisted. There weren't many instances I was unsure of myself, but this was one of them.

What if he didn't want to see me?

What if the chasing part was all there had ever been?

No. I wasn't going to do this to myself. Scarlet and Lacey had personally invited me to their house. If Tore was finished with me and uncomfortable with my presence, he'd have to suck it up.

When I got downstairs, Lacey grabbed my hand and tugged me onto the porch. "Come on. You have to see all the food we made. It's gonna be so good, Bea!"

We crossed the street as the light dipped into early evening gold. As soon as we stepped onto their front porch, Talon threw open the door. He was wearing white gloves and holding a silver tray with a plastic wineglass balanced on it.

"Good evening, madam. Would you like a glass of sparkling juice?"

I pressed my hands to my chest and gasped. "How did you know that's exactly what I want, Jeeves?"

Talon dipped into a bow so deep, his glasses nearly slid off his nose. This kid... "I know *everything*, madam. Now, if you'll kindly proceed to the parlor..."

"Parlor?" I echoed, stepping over the threshold with an amused glance at Scarlet and Lacey. They were trying—and failing—not to giggle at their brother.

The moment I entered, I stopped cold. How had they known?

"Surprise!" three voices shouted in unison.

I blinked back tears as I surveyed what they had done. A "Happy Birthday, Bea" banner stretched crookedly along the wall, secured with mounds of blue painter's tape. Flanking the banner were pink, blue, and gold balloons. Streamers were twisted around light fixtures, and more balloons were scattered around the floor.

Tore must have hated this. Chaos in his perfectly orderly home.

This was my first time actually stepping foot inside, and it was stunning. Polished wood floors, thick cream rugs, and immaculate pale-beige walls were the backdrop to his colorful, vibrant art collection. Everything was new and beautiful, and...I couldn't breathe. That was all there was to it. My lungs were smushed from the crushing emotion of all the balloons and loveliness that had been heaved upon me without a second of warning.

"You guys..." I whispered. "What—?"

Lacey threw her arms wide. "Do you love it, or do you *love* it?"

"I—I love it." My voice cracked as I looked down at the plastic wineglass in my hand. "Oh my lizards."

Tony came out from the kitchen in a "Kiss the Cook" apron, wearing a huge, smug grin.

"*Buon compleanno*, Marilyn," he said warmly. Taking me by the shoulders, he kissed both my cheeks.

Talon slid between us, holding his empty tray by his side. "It's Bea, Grandpa."

"How did you know it's my birthday?" I rasped.

Lacey jumped in. "Me! Your birthday's in June, and mine's in August, remember?"

My nose tingled as I nodded. "Yes, darling girl. I remember very well. I just can't believe *you* do."

She grabbed my hand, squeezing it tight. "That's the day we became neighbors and friends. You don't forget something like that."

"No. Definitely not."

Just when I thought things couldn't get worse—or better—Tore appeared at the top of the stairs. He descended slowly, taking in the scene without any discernible expression. His gaze landed on me, staying only briefly before sweeping by.

"Uncle Sally, come here," Lacey cried. "Come meet Bea."

He approached, stopping beside his niece. For her, he smiled softly. "We've met, Lace. You know that."

Her forehead scrunched. "Oh yeah. At the hospital."

I didn't know why I'd opened my mouth, but I couldn't hold back. "Actually, we met before that too." Tore went perfectly still, but I continued. "I've been catering Nox's weekly meetings. I just never realized your Uncle Sally was *the* Tore Gallo who protects all the computers in the whole world."

"Not the *whole* world," he refuted automatically.

Tony and the kids glared at him for keeping that information to himself, and I felt a flicker of triumph. It didn't last long, but it was enough to get me through the moment.

Scarlet hooked her arm through mine. "Come on, Bea. We decorated the dining room too."

Lacey crowded my other side, her fingers wrapping around mine. "And we made you a surprise."

"Another surprise?" My eyes bugged out. "I don't know if I can take it."

She giggled. "You can. You're gonna love it."

She was right. I did love it.

The tablescape was a gaudy masterpiece. I couldn't begin to guess where the kids had gotten the ruffly lace tablecloth and scads of massive, fake diamonds they'd scattered between gold vases filled with tropical flowers. They'd turned my chair into a throne, with balloons tied to the back and velvet material woven through the slats.

I was even handed a crown, which I happily put on my head once I confirmed everyone else had one too.

Even Tore.

Watching him let Lacey settle a tiny silver crown on his head hurt for reasons I couldn't quite put into words. Honestly, though, I'd been jabbed in the heart so many times tonight, what was one more?

During dinner, Tony remarked, "I bet you've never had a birthday celebration like this, huh?"

I shook my head, smiling. "I can honestly say I haven't."

"What did you do for your last birthday?" Scarlet asked.

I picked up my glass, bringing it to my lips. "Nothing, really."

That made Lacey gasp. "*What*? Why not? Didn't your friends throw you a party?"

"They would have, if they knew when my birthday was." Shira had asked me more than once, but I'd told her I was eternal—I didn't age. She hadn't appreciated that answer. "I don't really do birthdays."

I could almost hear Ben scoffing. "*Like you don't do kids? Come on, Buzz. Everyone's subject to the ravages of time and cute children.*"

"Why not?" Lacey cried. "Birthdays are amazing. You get to be a princess if you want to! Everyone's nice to you 'cause they have to be. You can have cake *and* ice cream. It's the closest to magic you can get without having special powers."

"I'm so happy birthdays have always been like that for you, darling." I put my glass down and dabbed my mouth with my napkin. "When I was little, my mom was busy. She didn't have time to make things magic for me, and we didn't have extra money for cake and presents. So I've just never been into celebrating."

I kept my explanation as gentle and sanitized as I could. Tony's deep frown said he understood more than I'd let on, and I glanced at Tore. He was staring into the distance, fidgeting with his ring, stone-faced. Disinterested.

"That sucks," Lacey declared. "Our mom always made our birthdays a big deal."

Scarlet nodded. "She made everything a big deal. We didn't have to wait until our birthdays to celebrate, you know? We had dance parties just for finishing a really good book."

"Mommy took me to the library whenever I wanted," Talon added.

Lacey cupped her hands around her mouth. "That's a party for Tally."

He scrunched his nose. "I don't like cake, but I do like ice cream. And books. I love books."

"I do too," I agreed. "I wish I'd known your mom. She sounds like my kind of lady. Do you think she would have approved of this party?"

All the kids agreed their mother would have loved my party, and that made me happy. I didn't have a burning need to celebrate my birthday, but it warmed me to the bone to be the excuse for them to channel her. They got to practice what she'd taught them, keeping her alive and close to them.

That was why I'd show up to all the celebrations they threw.

If I had to, I would sit through Tore's indifference. Eventually, it wouldn't feel like this. One day, I wouldn't mind how easily he'd accepted we were over.

With time, I'd forget we were ever a thing.

With time, the ache would fade, and he'd become a story I used to tell.

Chapter Thirty-eight

Salvatore

I stood, my hands braced on the counter, staring down at the cutting board I'd already wiped three times, yet still had crumbs. Scarlet had left a streak of marinara near the faucet. Talon's silver tray sat abandoned on the counter. The kind of chaos that didn't bother me as much as it normally would have.

I had other things on my mind.

Everyone was in the living room, the kids shrieking with laughter as my father showed Scarlet some old dance moves of his. Bea's voice threaded through it all, blending so well, it was like she'd always been there.

I was supposed to stay away.

I'd promised her that.

We were still deep in Antarctica with no signs of leaving. Her boundary had been clear, and I'd done my level best to abide by it.

Then she walked through the door.

The sight of her in my home would've been enough to undo me, but it hadn't stopped there. When the kids had put the plastic crown on her head, her eyes had filled with tears. She'd played along when

Talon had switched into butler mode. And her damn shirt had kept slipping off her shoulder like gravity was conspiring against me.

I gripped the edge of the counter harder, jaw clenched tight.

I wanted her. Not only for me, but for her too. The need to pull her into my arms when she'd casually mentioned never celebrating her birthday had been so overwhelming, I'd nearly had to leave the table. If it were up to me, she'd never have to question whether someone would remember her birthday. She'd come to expect it. We'd celebrate the hell out of her, making up for a lifetime of neglect.

But she didn't want that. Not from me.

We were in *Antarctica*.

So I kept my mouth shut and my eyes off her, fighting every instinct I possessed in order to give her what she'd asked for.

"Oh. I didn't know you were in here."

My head shot up at the sound of her voice. "I was cleaning up. Did you need something?"

Beatrice Novak fidgeting, one foot balanced on top of the other, chewing on her bottom lip, looking unsure and off-balance. It was so foreign, I had to do a double take to make sure it was really her.

Then I forced my eyes off her, for both our sakes.

"A few paper towels. Tally spilled his water."

I ripped a sheet off the roll and offered it to her, making sure our hands didn't touch. "There you go."

She sucked in a breath, like she was preparing to leap into something or make a run for it. I couldn't tell which.

I glanced at her, and she finally spoke.

"You stopped chasing me."

Her words were barely more than a whisper, but they struck me in the gut like a sledgehammer. I couldn't form a response. I was winded, and my mind had been wiped clean of intelligible thought.

She nodded, like she'd come to a conclusion. "It's fine. At least I know. Thanks for having me over tonight. This was...well, it was the best. Good night, Tore."

I watched her walk away. Listened to her say goodbye to the children. Imagined them embracing her with all their might.

Through it all, I didn't say a word. Didn't move. Just stood there, grasping the roll of paper towels, replaying what she'd said.

You stopped chasing me.

The floor tilted beneath me. I'd gotten it wrong. All of it very, very wrong.

"She's gone."

I turned, finding my dad standing in the doorway, arms crossed over his chest, looking more pissed than I'd ever seen him.

"She's the one you were seeing."

"She is," I confirmed.

"I know. I'm not stupid." He chuckled mirthlessly. "You might be, though, if you let her leave."

I didn't answer. I couldn't exactly argue with that.

My dad shook his head. "I swear to god, Sal, if you don't go after her, I will."

That got my attention. My head snapped up, eyes narrowing.

"I don't think so," I growled.

He shrugged. "Then go get your woman. If you don't, I guarantee someone else will come along and claim her. They don't make women like that these days, you know."

I stared at him for two long breaths.

Then I bolted.

Out the back door, down the steps, barefoot on cold concrete. I had no plan except to get to her, explain I had never stopped chasing her and never would.

She was on her porch, bending to pick up the keys she'd dropped.

"Bea!" I yelled as I ran across the street.

She didn't turn.

"Beatrice!"

That stopped her.

She turned slowly, eyes wide under her bright porch light. She looked startled. Wrecked. So beautiful, my mind had trouble computing she was real and not some AI configuration.

I ran up her porch steps, stopping in front of her. Her keys rattled in her shaking hands. Finally giving in to my instincts, I grabbed them, holding them steady between mine.

"You said I stopped chasing you. I see why you thought that."

She swallowed hard but said nothing.

"I thought it was what you wanted. Space. Silence. *Antarctica*." My voice broke around the word I hated most in the world. Fuck Antarctica.

"Tore—"

"I want you. Still. Always. If you need time, I'll give it to you. But don't mistake my silence for indifference. Don't ever think I gave up on you."

Her breath caught. "You wouldn't look at me."

I shook my head. "I *couldn't*."

"Why not?"

I brought her hands to my chest, over my thundering heart. "Feel that? That's all the time when I'm with you. When I can't touch you, it physically hurts."

Her tongue darted out, wetting her bottom lip. "I safe worded you."

"You did."

"And all this time, you were honoring *Antarctica*."

I nodded. "Yes."

She squeezed her eyes shut. "I should have known. I didn't even think—" Her eyes were wet when they opened and found mine. "I'm sorry, Salvatore. I made a mistake. What's the opposite of Antarctica?"

"Death Valley."

Her lips twitched into a half-smile. "Of course you'd know that." She took a shaky breath. "Okay then. Death Valley."

Then she was moving, straight into me. Hands fisting in my shirt, face buried in my chest like it was the only place she could catch her breath. I wrapped my arms around her so tightly I thought I might never let go.

"I didn't know how to ask you to come back."

"You don't have to ask," I murmured against her hair. "And I was never leaving."

CHAPTER THIRTY-NINE
Bea

I TUGGED TORE INTO the house with me, tossing my keys and purse on the floor, blindly kicking off my shoes. Benjamin took one look at us and chose to run back upstairs, away from the dramatic humans.

Tore chased me. Without shoes on. Oh my...

I was so stupid thinking he'd given up. All this time, he'd been waiting for me to lift our safe word. I should have known. That was how he thought. Rules were unbendable. And he'd respected mine—to his detriment.

And mine, dammit.

I think I might love this man.

Shit.

Our lips collided and bodies melded. There were things that needed to be said, and that would happen, but not now. I couldn't go another second without *this*.

Tore cradled my face carefully—a stark contrast to the way he was ravaging me with his mouth. Violent lashes of his tongue against mine. Sharp, desperate nips of my lips. Our teeth clashed, and our moans tangled and warred. I felt the tremors in his fingers as they slid into my hair and fisted it gently to tilt my head back so he could kiss me deeper, harder.

We stumbled toward the couch, wrapped in each other. I fumbled with the buttons on his shirt, ripping at them when I grew impatient. Some popped and some plinked on the ground, but Tore didn't seem to notice or care.

Finally open, I pushed his shirt off his shoulders, not giving a damn where it landed. Then I pulled my mouth from his so I could tear my own shirt off. He reached around me, swiftly divesting my bra.

I was a candle, and he was the flame. His long, lean torso was a steady wall for me to melt into, skin on skin. It was a relief to touch so much of him.

I kicked off my jeans, and he yanked off his pants. Our knees knocked into each other as we tugged off each other's underwear and laughed and kissed and fell together, lucky the couch had caught us on the way down.

He landed first, guiding me on top of him. I straddled his legs, our lips breaking just long enough for air, our eyes locked in this wild, breathless moment.

"Touch me," I whispered, slipping his glasses off his face. "Please, Tore."

Leaning back, he cupped my breasts, watching himself hold them in his wide palms. His thumbs brushed over my pebbled nipples, sending a shiver along my spine.

"Like this?" he asked.

"Yes. That's so good." I put my hands over his. "Here." Then I lowered his hands to my hips. "And here."

His eyes flicked to mine as he dragged his hands down to my thighs. "How about here?"

I dropped my forehead to his. "Everywhere, Tore. Please, baby."

I ground against him, needing friction, needing everything about him. He hissed, tightening his grip, then shifted under me, pressing against the heat between my thighs. I gasped.

"I missed you," I choked out. "I was so—Tore, I—"

"I know." His voice broke. "Beatrice, I know. I missed you too. Every second."

He slid his hand between us, cupping my sex. I nodded frantically, giving my permission, already rocking into his touch as he found my clit and circled it with maddening precision. His other hand gripped my hip, then lower, fingers exploring, spreading me open like he needed to know every part of me—reclaim me after too many days apart.

A line had been crossed the moment he'd set foot in my house tonight. The other times, he'd toed it, but it was so far in the distance now, it might as well have never existed.

"I love the way you feel, beautiful." He dug his fingers into the flesh of my ass. "So soft. I can't get enough of your skin."

Moaning, I rocked on his fingers and clutched his shoulders. Muscles rippled beneath his smooth skin. Controlled power barely contained within his sleek exterior. My fingers curled, anchoring myself to him as heat mounted in my belly.

God, this man knew exactly where to touch me and just how to do it.

"Right there." It was coming, rolling over me. So close, like electricity in the air, crackling along my skin. "Tore, that's so perfect. Right there."

His mouth trailed over my collarbone and throat, sucking the delicate skin between his lips. Biting, licking, devouring as I crumbled, shaking, vibrating. I threw my head back, crying out my pleasure, and his lips latched onto my throat, absorbing the sounds he'd coaxed from me.

I kissed him as I came on his fingers, no less desperate for him than I'd been before. The way he pulled me down on his erection, there was no doubt he was riding the same wave.

I snapped my hips, wedging his thick length just right between my slick lips. Almost where I wanted him, but still so very far away.

"Tore." I breathed into his mouth. "I need it."

"Say the words." He tapped one finger on my entrance, teasing, tormenting. "I need them from you."

Another snap, and we both groaned. "Inside me."

"Yes."

His teeth clamped down on the bend of my neck, racking me with full-body trembles. My insides clenched around nothing, searching for him. A whine tore from my throat at the hollowness I desperately needed him to fill.

As I took his length in my hand and pushed up on my knees, he wrapped his fingers around my wrist, stopping me before I could lower myself.

"Bea, I don't have a condom." He grimaced as his tip brushed against my soaked opening. "Christ, I'm sorry."

I shook my head, holding myself back from fighting against his grip. It was good one of us was being careful since I would have thrown caution to the wind. "I've been tested, and I have an IUD. You?"

"Tested, yeah." He exhaled a heavy breath, his hold on me quaking. "Are you sure?"

I licked my parched lips. "Are you mine?"

He didn't hesitate for even a second. "Unequivocally."

"And do you have any more secrets you're keeping from me?"

Again, no hesitation. "I own this house."

I huffed a laugh. "Of course you do. Anything else?"

Everything he'd done was so wild and crazy, how could I not laugh and accept this man had no limits when it came to me?

"You know everything."

"Then I'm yours too."

His hand fell away as I sank down on him, not stopping until my ass hit his thighs and I was filled to the hilt.

Groaning, he slid his palms along my ass, taking hold of me. "There you are." He pressed me down on him, somehow tunneling even deeper. "Right where you should be."

I cupped his throat and slid my nose along his. "I need to go hard, baby. Are you into that?"

His hips bucked with surprising force, making me gasp. "Give it to me, Beatrice."

Keeping one hand braced around the base of his neck, the other on his chest, fingers splaying across the hard ridges of his muscles, I lifted and dropped onto him again, harder. Tore's head fell back against the couch, eyelids lowering to half-mast, lips parted in awe.

I did it again. And again. The sharp slap of skin meeting skin filled the room, filthy and desperate and perfect.

"Oh, fuck—yes," he gasped, gripping my hips, guiding me, meeting every brutal thrust with one of his own, screwing into me just as hard from below.

"You feel so good inside me," I moaned, digging my nails into his chest. "So perfect, Salvatore. I missed you so much, I can't do that again."

His hands clenched as he watched me, unblinking fascination raw in his expression. My body rippled as I bounced on him, and he didn't miss any of it. He wasn't just watching my breasts as they grazed up and down his chest. His gaze traveled over me—my belly as it moved and folded with every shift, my vibrating hips, my thick thighs spread over his lean ones. Inside me, I felt his desire growing impossibly thick and hard.

"You undo me, beautiful," he gritted out. "I can't believe you're mine."

Tipping my face down, I ghosted my lips over his. "And you're mine." My hold on his throat tightened just a little bit. "My very good boy."

His answering groan was a crack of thunder in a clear blue sky, echoing off the walls of my heart, sending shivers through my body.

"Only yours," he agreed. "Fuck me, Beatrice."

I snapped my hips harder, chasing the edge. *Giving it to him.* Just like he'd asked—just like *we* needed. He filled me completely, over and over, the thick drag hitting all the right places, making me dizzy.

A needy mewl broke free. I *had* him yet...

I was still desperate for him.

I leaned forward and kissed him, open-mouthed and messy, our tongues tangling as I continued riding him with abandon. His hands slid up my back then to my ass again, pulling me down hard every time I lifted off him.

"I can't get close enough," I cried in frustration. We couldn't get any closer than we were. I didn't understand this yearning in my gut, but I couldn't shake it.

"You're here. I'm here." He wrapped his arms around me so tight I could finally take a full breath. "I'm here. I've got you."

"I want you," I whined, kissing along his jaw. "Let me have you."

"You do. Completely," he vowed.

"Salvatore." I licked the divot in his chin. "Show me. Show me how I have you."

His grip turned bruising, his hips driving up harder now, meeting me thrust for thrust, a frenzy of motion that stole my breath. Through it, he murmured reassurances. Telling me he was sorry, he missed me, he wasn't going anywhere, he was mine. Calling me beautiful, sexy, unbelievable. Promising me devotion and honesty. Safety and trust.

And he kept fucking me with savage pumps of his hips that made stars bloom behind my eyes.

Perfect.

Sweat slicked our bodies, every breath a shared ragged gasp. He buried his face between my breasts, groaning my name again and again. My orgasm coiled, tight and blinding, building with every brutal grind, every desperate thrust.

"Come with me," I begged, holding his face, staring into those dark, beautiful eyes. "Fill me up, Salvatore. I want to be dripping with you all night."

He nodded frantically, breath catching. "I'll give you what you need, beautiful. I have no choice."

I let go. My head fell back as I cried out my pleasure, my inner walls pulsing and clamping. Tore's answering groan was pained as he held me through it, bracing my back as I thrashed and writhed. And when I thought it was over, he flung me onto my back, yanked my legs to his hips, and pummeled me.

Unrelenting.

Frenzied.

He fucked me into the couch like a madman on a mission to destroy me and stared into my eyes with soft, loving devotion, tipping me straight over the edge again. I was falling blindly, grappling for something, anything to hold on to, but I wasn't alone for long. Tore planted himself at the end of me and buried his face in my throat, shaking in my arms as he coated me with fiery heat.

We clung to each other as we came down, the aftermath as intense as the storm. Tore lay on me, my breasts cushioning his head, his arms tunneled around me. I stroked his hair, my movement languid and wrung out.

Whatever happened from here, I would never doubt this man wanted me. Just like I couldn't deny my desire for him. Even now, bones liquid and a deliciously aching core, I would have started all over again if he'd said the word.

This was surely a little bit of madness.

But maybe *a lot* of everything good too.

"You're mine," I whispered, mostly to myself.

He lifted his head from my chest, his gaze hazy but locked steadily on mine.

"I am, Beatrice," he promised. "I'm yours."

CHAPTER FORTY
Salvatore

Eventually, we both put our clothing back on. I mourned every inch of Bea's skin as she covered it, but it was necessary. If we didn't, there was a danger we'd start all over again and never say the things that needed to be said.

Bea was the first to break the silence. And she did it with blunt honesty.

"I still don't want children."

I slipped my glasses back on, her face returning to me in sharp clarity. "Okay."

"But I love your kids." Her nose crinkled. "Children aren't my thing in general, but those three...well, they've sort of forced themselves into my heart."

I chuckled, though I wasn't sure which direction we were headed. "They have that way about them."

She took my hands in hers, her gaze level on mine. "You have to understand, I will never give birth. That isn't negotiable. I will love your kids—I mean, I already do—but I can't give you babies. This is a hard limit."

I shook my head. "I have three kids. It's already an embarrassment of riches. How could I possibly want more?"

She huffed, as though my easy agreement frustrated her. "Are you saying you don't have the urge to spread your seed far and wide?"

I barked a laugh. "No. I can say I have never had that urge. Is that...a thing other men feel?"

"For my mom's husband, certainly." She dragged in a long breath. "I've done the whole sleepless nights, diaper changes, teething, fevers, feeling like I'll never be alone again. I know, without a doubt, I don't want that."

"Okay."

Her brows shot up. "That's it? You don't have any questions?"

"No. If you'd told me you *did* want a baby, I'd have to put serious thought into it and how it would impact my kids. Telling me you don't? That's easy." I brought her hand to my mouth, rubbing my lips along her soft knuckles. "We spoke about this when we first met. I understand where you're coming from. It's a nonissue."

Her shoulders curled forward as the fight left her. "I'm still scared."

"I've given you a lot of reasons to doubt me. Not purposely, but that doesn't make it better."

I let go of her hand to cradle her face. I'd kissed most of her makeup off. All that was left were dark smudges of mascara beneath her deep-blue eyes, and she'd never looked lovelier.

"It doesn't," she agreed.

"I'm sorry for that." I touched my lips to her forehead. "I'm sorry, blue. In my head, I had a list of steps that had to happen before I told you about the kids and wouldn't allow myself to deviate from it. That you would feel betrayed had never entered my mind. Not until after the fact. I see how shortsighted that was, and yes, manipulative.

At the time, though, I'd been too focused on keeping you to see beyond that."

She leaned into me, her breath feathering against my skin as she sighed. "You think differently than I do. I know that, and I love the way your mind works. But lying, even of omission, has to be off the table. You can't keep things from me, big or small. I won't feel safe with you if I'm always worried about what you're hiding."

"I know what it is to have you and lose you." I closed my eyes, dropping my forehead to hers. "I will not jeopardize this ever again. The last two weeks have been brutal. A lifetime without you is unacceptable."

"A lifetime?" she breathed.

"I don't make moves without thoroughly thinking them through. I see a future with you, Beatrice. I think we fit. Not just you and me, but all of us. If you allow it, I would like to open my life to you so you can see for yourself there's an empty spot shaped just like you."

Her palms slid up my chest and shoulders, stopping at the sides of my neck. "If we don't work out, I'll lose more than just you. I've already lost my siblings, Salvatore. I don't know if—"

"We'll work out."

"You can't be sure."

"I can." I pulled back to meet her gaze. "Do you know the first time I drove by you, it was purely by chance? You were crossing the street, and we were stopped at a red light. I was trapped in a thick fog of grief, but I *saw* you. Two bike messengers crashed into each other while waving at you, and you stopped to help them. I rolled down my window to hear them apologizing to *you* even though you were perfectly fine. Do you remember that?"

Her cheeks flushed, and she tucked her hair behind her ear. "Well, I...things like that happen a lot. My mother always told me I was a magnet for the strange and unusual. Things tend to...erupt around me."

My shoulders shook as I laughed. Of course that was her answer. I'd been called strange plenty of times in my life, so why wouldn't she have drawn me in?

"Bea..." I shook my head, chuckling. This woman was a pure delight. "It doesn't matter if you remember. I do. That day, the fog lifted for the first time since Tia had died. I went home, finished the app I'd been tinkering with in my downtime for ages, then sent it to you because I couldn't not."

"And you followed me."

My ears burned. "Sometimes. I tried to resist, but I got hooked on seeing you, even if from afar. And every time I did, the fog stayed gone longer and longer."

She traced the shell of my ear, a soft smile curling her lips. "I'm glad I could do that for you."

"I'm glad I didn't scare you."

"Never. I was never afraid of you. That might mean I'm a little unhinged, but that's okay. We can be unhinged together."

"You think I'm unhinged?"

Her brows rose, wrinkling her forehead. "I don't think designing an entire app to keep in touch with me, buying my dream house, and following me in your limo is exactly normal." Her smile kissed mine. "Luckily, I find normal boring as hell. You picked the right girl to get obsessed with."

I caught her mouth, kissing her hard and deep. I wasn't sure if I'd picked her or she'd lured me in like a siren, but here I was, devoted, with no plans of ever giving her up.

"It might've started as an obsession." I slid my fingers through the side of her hair. "But as I got to know you, I fell in love with you too."

"You love me?" she squeaked.

"I do. That's how I know we'll work. I've never loved another woman, and I don't have it in me to do it again. You're it for me, Bea. In order for this to end, you'll have to be the one to leave me, and I intend to keep you so happy, you'll never want to."

Her lips parted as she stared at me. "It's far too soon to make those kinds of declarations."

"It's been two years."

"But"—she licked her lips—"can we rewind, just a little? I'm still catching up with us being back together, and you're talking about lifetimes."

"I'm done. No more talk about loving you until I take my last breath."

"Tore!" She shoved me away, giggling. "Stop it. I need more time."

"All right. I'm not so set in my ways I can't compromise. We'll spend the weekend as boyfriend and girlfriend, *then* we'll discuss our future."

She mimed strangling me. "I take back all the 'good boys' I gave you. You're a bad, bad man."

I caught her and buried my face in her neck, my teeth scraping her skin. "Nope. That isn't going to happen. I'm *your* good boy. Say it."

My teeth dug into her flesh, making her scream and writhe. "No, I won't do it!" Between screams, she giggled and slapped at my arms banded around her. "You're so bad, Salvatore Gallo. The absolute worst."

"I'll show you my worst."

I bit a path along her shoulder then licked every spot I'd marked. She squirmed and laughed, doing a piss-poor job of fighting me off her. My cock plumped up as her body flailed against mine. Rolling her onto her back, I rocked against her damp panties, and she arched and bucked, drawing me against her heat.

"Sal," she breathed.

"Bea," I answered, reaching between us to tug her panties to the side. "Say it or I'm going to fuck you right now."

Her lips rolled over her teeth, and she shook her head. Her legs parted just a little more.

"You're in for it," I growled, yanking my underwear down. "I'll show you how bad I am."

I plunged into her in one hard thrust.

Right where I belonged.

❧

The last thing I wanted to do was stumble home at midnight, but Bea understood I couldn't spend the night without some preplanning. And since I'd left my phone at home, I couldn't exactly ask my father to stay in the main house with the kids.

As far as I was concerned, tonight would be the first and last time I fucked Bea and left her after. We'd have to be careful for a while around the kids, but leaving her sated and alone in her bed had gone against every fiber of my being.

My father was waiting for me in the living room, a smug grin sliding across his face when he laid eyes on me.

"I see you got the girl," he remarked.

"I did." I stuffed my hands in my pockets, off-kilter. We'd had the birds and the bees talk when I was an adolescent, and he'd been fairly hands-off with me since. That might've been due to how deeply private I kept my sex and dating life...and the several years of drought I'd had recently. "Thank you for staying. I appreciate it."

He rose to his feet, stretching his back. "It's no trouble, champ. I figured you might be gone for the night. A gentleman doesn't leave his lady after—"

I held up my hand. "I know. I don't like it either, believe me. But I didn't tell the kids I wouldn't be here tonight, and I would hate for one of them to wake up looking for me and find my bed empty."

A flash of pain crossed his face before he schooled it. "You're right to think of that. Tia did a good job picking you to be their parent. But you don't have to sacrifice yourself for them. Remember that."

"I know, and I have no plans of doing that. Tonight will be the last time I leave her."

He nodded, drawing in a deep breath. "She's a very good woman. I haven't gotten to see the two of you interacting much, but from what I know of you both, I like the idea." He kept nodding, slower now. "Yeah, I like it a lot. You'll have a nice balance."

"Thanks," I muttered, unsure what else to say except I agreed with him.

He walked by me, headed toward his attached apartment. As he passed, he squeezed my shoulder. "Happy for you, Sal. Glad you chased her."

"Me too, Dad."

I would never stop.

CHAPTER
FORTY-ONE
Bea

Tore had me on my knees, my face pressed to the mattress, gripping my hips as he drove into me, shoving me toward the headboard with every thrust. Grunting, I braced a hand against it and pushed back, screwing my backside into his pelvis, taking him even deeper.

"Yes," I cried. "Baby, yes. It's so good."

My thighs were shaking and sore, and my core ached from all the attention he'd given me, but I could take it. I *wanted* to.

This wasn't the first time he'd fucked me tonight. Not the second either. After dozing off in a sweaty tangle of limbs, he'd woken me with his tongue, and it hadn't taken long until he was inside me again.

Since the night he chased me across the street a month ago, he hadn't stopped. Most evenings, I had dinner with him and his family and usually hung out with them after too. And once everyone retreated to their own rooms for the night, I was in Tore's bed, taking him then falling asleep with him.

I always snuck out at the crack of dawn, though. I wasn't ready for everyone to know I was sleeping over.

Tore didn't like it, but he indulged me. He'd had two years to prepare for what he wanted us to be. I was catching up quickly, but I wasn't quite there. It wasn't his fault life had taught me to be cautious. And we both agreed we had to be careful with the kids.

He was getting me there, though. Every time I watched him with his kids. Each night we fell asleep together. How he looked at me. The way he spoke to me. Every little thing he did pulled me closer.

He dragged a finger along the valley of my ass and tapped my hole. "I want this."

I looked over my shoulder. The sight of him—rippling muscles glistening with sweat, hungry eyes focused on my ass like he was seconds from taking a bite out of it—made my insides clench around him.

"If you keep being such a good boy, I'll let you have it," I panted.

His gaze lifted to find mine. "You're going to let me have you here?"

"Can you be good?" I teased, breathless.

"Anything to win my prize, beautiful."

I shot him a punch-drunk grin. "We'll see about that."

He reached around me, rolling my clit with the pad of his finger. "I'm going to start by making you come. Are you going to do that for me?"

I nodded into the mattress. "Oh yeah. I definitely will."

With Tore, it was easy. He touched me just right, and I ignited, shaking, clawing at the sheets, begging for relief.

And he gave it to me.

I came until my legs tried to give out, but Tore wouldn't allow it. Gathering me in his arms, he shuffled us forward, my front plastered to the headboard, my back to his chest. His mouth was beside my ear, huffing raggedly as he slammed into me in hard, frantic thrusts while holding me tenderly, kissing my cheek and temple, stroking my hips, whispering love.

He pulsed inside me, coming hard and hot, and we fell, hitting the mattress together, Tore wrapped around my back, one hand on my stomach, the other holding my breast. Those had become his spots.

I liked that he had places on my body he claimed as his own. I'd silently done the same. His glowing ears, the deep line that ran through the center of his palm, the lock of hair that fell on his forehead when he was over me. Those pieces were mine. All mine.

I twisted my neck to blink at him. "We should really sleep this time. It has to be late."

He swiped his phone from the nightstand and held it in front of me so we could both see. "Only midnight. Not too late."

As he was showing me the screen, a text from Sam popped up.

Sam: ?????

I huffed a laugh. "Sam's a man of many words."

"Yeah." Tore tossed his phone and nuzzled my hair. "He's texted me a few times tonight. It's nothing urgent, and I'm off the clock."

"I bet he loves that."

"He won't be pleased, but I don't care." His fingers trailed along my stomach, lulling me into a boneless heap. "I'm with my girl-friend. He can't have access to me right now."

I smiled, my eyes fluttering closed. "Gotta have that work-life balance, baby."

"Damn right." He kissed my hair. "I'll sort Sam out tomorrow. For now, I'm going to fall asleep with my girlfriend and try not to get pissed off when she sneaks out in the morning."

"Wow, she sounds amazing," I teased. "I'm sure she has valid reasons for the sneaking."

"She is, and she thinks she does." He kissed my hair. "Go to sleep, Beatrice."

"Bossy," I whispered.

"Only when you let me be."

I fell asleep with a smile on my lips, warmth at my back, and my heart filled with optimism.

Monday night, I had dinner with my girls. As wrapped up as I was in Tore and the Gallo family, it was important not to forget the rest of my life.

Clara shared details about her quickly approaching wedding. She'd refused the male stripper I'd offered to hire for her bachelorette, but she hadn't denied the Elvis impersonator I had up my sleeve. Of course, I hadn't mentioned him, but what she didn't know wouldn't hurt her.

Shira had started wedding planning now too. She and Roman were low-key, so they were keeping it small, but Shira blushed with excitement and gushed what she wanted her wedding dress to look like. Even though her engagement hadn't been roses and fireworks, she was excited to be married to her man.

And I told them all about Tore and the kids. Shira had met everyone but Tore, but she and Clara were both eager to get to know the new people in my life.

It was still unbelievable I'd gone from happily, staunchly single to fully immersed in an entire family, but here I was. And it felt right.

Nothing and no one would ever replace what I'd lost, but that was okay. They didn't have to. I could miss my siblings down to my bones and love Scarlet, Lace, and Tally to the same depths. One did not negate the other.

It was scary and wild and out of my control, so I had chosen to give in, let go, and enjoy the ride.

When I got home, I sent a message to Tore.

Me: Hey. I'm home. Dinner was fun. Everyone wants to meet you soon.

Tore: Come over.

Me: Did you not read the part about my friends wanting to meet you?

Tore: I did. We can talk about it when you come over.

Me: I'm beat and already in my pjs. Benji-bear and I are going to turn in early. I'll see you in about twelve hours, Salvatore.

Tore: Come over in your pajamas. You can bring Benjamin with you.

Me: Babe, I'm staying home tonight. I wish you'd drop it and ask about my dinner instead.

Tore: If you were in front of me, I would.

Me: Okay. Well…we're not getting any-where. I'll see you at Nox tomorrow. Good night.

Tore: We'll talk tomorrow then. Good night, Beatrice.

I couldn't say I wasn't a little salty he hadn't been able to get it up to ask me about my night, but told myself sometimes things got lost in translation through text. And it wasn't like I didn't want to spend the night with him. I definitely did. But I was tired, and I had to wake up early to do some client prep work. This once, it was easier to sleep in my own bed.

Plus…well, I didn't love him commanding my presence, but since I was pretty certain we were just miscommunicating, I wasn't wor-ried.

We'd squash this tomorrow.

⁂

I was taking out a batch of muffins when my phone chimed, alerting me to an incoming email through my website. Dropping the pan on top of the stove, I shook off my oven mitt to check if it was urgent.

The sender was Paul at Nox Cyber.

Huh.

Frowning, I clicked on his message.

From: pauldelaney@noxcyber.com

To: bea@grazingbydaisyandbea.com

Bea,

Sorry to send this so last minute, but we no longer need your services at Nox. Since we're beyond the cancellation window, we will be paying you today's fee. Please remove Nox from your calendar going forward.

Thank you for your time, and again, I apologize for the late notice.

Best,

Paul Delaney

What the shit?

What the actual shit?

Blood rushed in my ears as I reread Paul's message. I didn't know what to think. Never in a million years had I imagined Nox would cancel my services. That job accounted for a nice bit of my weekly income, and now...nothing.

It was so last minute, what could have happened between last night and this morning?

I sucked in a breath. Surely not...

Had I misread Tore that badly last night? Had he been so angry with me for not coming over, he'd had Paul fire me?

My stomach flipped, the scent of my freshly baked cranberry muffins suddenly nauseating.

Dropping my phone, I braced my hands on the counter, heart pounding hard enough to shake the breath from my lungs.

No. No, Tore wouldn't do that. Not over me not coming over. Would he?

I thought of how terse his final text had been, but that was just Tore. He wasn't exactly flowery with his words, but...

Had I miscalculated?

Had he really been so unhappy with me, he'd felt the need to deliver this swift blow to me and my income?

I almost gaslit myself out of that thought, but it wasn't like this was the first time he'd bypassed me to make a decision about my work, my *life*, without stopping to ask me what I wanted. Tore, the man I was starting to *trust*, had gone around me and hadn't even had the decency to tell me himself.

I was blindsided. Gutted. Pissed off to high heavens.

I swiped at my cheeks angrily and yanked off my apron, tossing it onto the counter, so very done.

His delivery might have been shit, but it had gotten the job done. Message received, loud and clear.

CHAPTER FORTY-TWO
Salvatore

I CHECKED MY WATCH for the third time, then pulled out my phone to confirm I hadn't somehow misread the hour.

I hadn't.

Frowning, I left the conference room, first checking the hallway, then walking to my office. *Empty.* As I'd expected.

I hurried back to the conference room. It was still just as empty.

Where the hell was Bea?

I'd last spoken to her only twelve hours ago, and she had explicitly mentioned we'd see each other this morning. If she'd intended to cancel, she would have told me. *Surely* she would have.

I pulled out my phone again, checking for a text. A missed call. Anything.

Nothing.

Me: Where are you, Beatrice? Are you okay?

I stared at the screen, waiting for her reply, but it never came. Standing here, doing nothing, wasn't right. I felt like I was missing something. Something I should have seen but didn't.

"Paul," I called out, moving toward his desk.

He looked up, his brows lifting. "I've got the slides prepared. Is there anything else you need me to do before the meeting?"

"Where's Bea?"

His mouth opened then closed. He looked around his meticulously organized desk like she might be hiding behind a spreadsheet. Then his brows knit in confusion. "She's not in the conference room?"

"If she were, I wouldn't be at your desk asking you where she is," I replied tightly.

He frowned. "I haven't heard anything from her today. It's strange she isn't here. She's always on time. Let me give her a call—"

"No." I held up my hand. "No need. I'll do that. Please let the team know I'll be missing the meeting today. When it's over, send me a report of what was discussed."

He shot to his feet. "You're missing the meeting?"

I didn't answer. I was already striding toward the elevator.

Paul would handle my absence just fine, and I'd explain later, once I understood exactly what was going on.

Sam stepped out of my office as I passed by. "Hey, Tore. Where's the fire?"

I tried to sidestep him, but he blocked me. "I have to go."

"The meeting is starting in ten. Where do you need to go that can't wait?"

He was already pissed at me for ignoring his texts over the weekend in favor of spending time with Bea. What was one more drop in the overloaded bucket?

Without a word of explanation, I pushed right by him.

Something was very wrong, and I refused to waste another minute before finding out what it was and making it right.

A large man in a Denver Mountain Lions rugby shirt opened Bea's front door, grinning. "Hey. What's up?"

He leaned casually against the frame, looking perfectly at home. When I didn't answer, his brows lifted in amusement.

"Cat got your tongue, bro? You sure you're in the right place?"

"I'm in the right place. Are *you*?" I countered, peering past him into the house.

He looked over his shoulder. "Hey, Buzz. There's a guy on your porch wearing a suit and glasses. Looks like he sat on a tack and it's lodged *way* up there. Sound familiar?"

Turning back to me, he added, "No offense."

I spun the ring on my finger, struggling for composure. "Who are you?"

He held out his hand. "Ben Wells. You must be Tore."

Of course. If I'd been thinking clearly, I would have known who he was right away. There weren't many six-and-a-half-foot-tall, curly-haired, rugby-playing men around, but there were two on this block—the Wells twins.

I shook his hand. "Is Bea okay?"

"Nah." He folded his arms again. "Gotta say, firing her was pretty damn low."

"Firing her? What are you talking about?"

From inside, Bea called out, "Did you say something?"

He turned sideways and yelled, "Yeah, Buzz. Your man's here, looking confused as hell and like he's about to pummel me for standing in his way. Should I let him in?"

A moment later, Bea appeared beside Ben. Her face was pale, eyes rimmed red, and her catering shirt had been misbuttoned.

"What are you doing here?" she asked. "You're missing your meeting."

"Why didn't you show up today? Are you sick?" I bit out more harshly than intended. I felt like I was losing my mind. Like everyone knew what was going on and no one would clue me in.

Ben chuckled. "Oh dear. I fear there's been some kinda miscommunication." He gestured between us. "I'm gonna see my ass to the other room while you two lovebirds work this out."

I focused on Bea. "What's going on?"

Her mouth was a tight line. "I got Paul's email this morning. Ben's helping me get ready for my next gig. I don't really have time—"

I grabbed her arm. "What email? I just spoke with Paul. He had no idea why you weren't at Nox."

Her eyes went wide. "He emailed me, canceling all our upcoming bookings, including today."

"What the hell?" I muttered. "Are you sure it came from him? He appeared just as confused by your absence as I was."

"I—" Her lashes brushed her flushed cheeks as she blinked rapidly. "Tore, I thought you told him to send that email. I thought you were mad at me for last night. The way we left things..." She rubbed her forehead. "I'm really confused."

"Beatrice, no. No, no, no." I stepped into her house and wrapped my arms around her. "No, beautiful. I'm not mad. There's no reason for me to be mad. Until you didn't show up this morning, I would have said I'm the happiest I've ever been—the farthest thing from mad."

All the fight left her in an instant, and she sagged into me, her forehead pressing against my chest. I tightened my arms, holding her close, one hand at her nape, the other stroking her spine.

I buried my nose in her hair, breathing in her goodness. Fresh vanilla with a hint of cranberry. Probably from the muffins she always brought with her to Nox.

"I can't believe I thought you fired me," she whispered. "I thought...I feel really stupid for believing that email was anything other than a mistake."

"You're not stupid. Not even close," I said gently.

With my knuckle under her chin, I tilted her face up and pressed a firm kiss to her forehead. "Let me see it."

She slipped her phone from her apron and handed it to me.

Ben's voice piped up from somewhere down the hall. "I told her to take a chill pill and actually talk to you, but *nooo*. She had to go full emo."

Bea rolled her eyes and laughed, but I didn't miss the way it quivered. "Shut up, Ben."

"I'm just saying," he called back. "It's all right to admit I was right."

I scrolled through her inbox until I found it.

Sent at 6:14 a.m. The sender address looked legit, but I tapped it to confirm, and it only took a second to realize something was off. My mouth tightened.

"Paul didn't send this. This is a spoof. The email address *looks* right, but it's not. I'm going to trace the IP. Someone did this on purpose."

Bea's brows pinched together. "Why would anyone...?"

"I don't know. But I'm going to find out." I gave her the phone back and tucked a strand of hair behind her ear. "I promise."

"This is crazy. I don't get it."

"I don't either." I exhaled, the possibilities sliding around my mind like chess pieces. "I've never experienced anything like this, but in my position, there's always the possibility of gaining unwanted attention. I fear that may be what happened here. Someone tried to go through you to get to me."

Her jaw jutted. "Fuck them then."

I kissed her crinkled nose, her cheek, the arch of her brow. "No one will get between us if we talk to one another."

She puffed up her cheeks and blew out a breath. "Yeah, I screwed up. I don't know why I assumed the worst—"

"I do. I let my disappointment over not seeing you last night get in the way of being a good boyfriend. You wanted to talk to me, and I wouldn't listen." I held her waist with both hands, rubbing slowly back and forth. "I left this door open, and whoever sent this email stepped right in."

She huffed and tucked her face into my throat. "You were a little bit of a dick last night."

"I know." I pressed my cheek to the side of her head. "I had this idea you'd come over after your dinner and tell me all about it. When that didn't happen, I wasn't able to roll with it. I'd fully intended to admit I was a tool when you came to Nox this morning."

"You can admit it now."

My mouth twitched, and relief lightened my gut. "I was a tool."

Her giggle lightened it even more. "Yes. And I was a fuckwit for believing you'd get Paul to fire me. You're obsessed with me."

"That, I am. And Paul's obsessed with your muffins. He'd fire *me* before sending you an email like that."

"That's a very good point." She pulled in a deep breath, her hands fisting the fabric of my jacket. "Are we okay?"

"We glitched, Beatrice. You've now experienced me at my worst—"

Her brows winged in the center. "*That* was your worst?"

"With you, yes. I will never yell at you. I won't abandon you. I won't blame you for anything that isn't your fault. But sometimes, it may take me time to adjust when things don't happen how I've worked them out in my head." I took her chin between my fingers. "When that happens, please tell me I'm being a tool. I'll snap out of it."

I would have to learn to pause. When my plans deviated, I would have to remind myself not to assume the worst and react. Bea deserved that. So did my kids. And I did too.

"Sal," she squeaked. I liked her calling me that. Hearing her say the name I'd been called most of my life was like coming home. "Sal, I love you."

And that was even better.

"Thank you." I cupped her face, tracing every one of her features with new eyes—eyes loved by Beatrice Novak. "Thank you very much for falling in love with me."

That earned me another feathery laugh. "I wish I hadn't said it when I have a million things to get done within the next thirty minutes. I would really like to discuss this more."

"Oh, we'll discuss it more." I pressed my thickening cock into her soft stomach. "You'll stay over tonight."

"Yes. I'll be in your bed."

Behind us, Ben cleared his throat. "Sorry, kids, but I'm still on the premises."

Bea groaned, blindly waving him away. "Go to the kitchen. I'll be right there."

"I'll help you too," I said.

I trusted her implicitly, but there was not a chance I would be letting another man help her when I was perfectly capable. Besides, leaving her now, after what we'd just shared, held no appeal.

She blinked at me. "But your meeting—"

"Rescheduled. Or ruined. Doesn't matter. You do."

She sighed and gave my jacket a shake. "Lizards, do I love you."

"Is that a yes? You'll accept my help?"

"Yes." She pushed up on her toes and kissed my chin. "But I'd like you to say you love me. For future reference, that's an always thing."

I shut my eyes against my own stupidity. "Yes. I do love you. Very much. I was so distracted by you saying it, I forgot to reciprocate."

She laughed. "I know you love me. I just wanted to hear it."

Opening my eyes, I pinned her with my gaze. "I love you, Bea. I don't write poetry or paint, but I'll continue to program apps to make your life easier."

"That's much more useful than love letters." She threaded her fingers through mine. "Come with me. I'm going to put your muscles to good use."

Ben stepped out of the kitchen, flexing his tree trunk biceps as he crossed his arms. "Are my muscles being usurped? I don't know how to feel about this, Buzz."

Bea flicked his elbow. "You feel great about it. And I do too. I'm not meant for manual labor. The more strong men I have to do my bidding, the better."

Ben poked his finger at me. "This is all fine and good. I don't mind my value being measured by how much I can carry, but if you start calling her Buzz too, I'm filing a formal complaint."

Bea snorted. "You don't have an HR department."

"I *am* HR," he said, thumping his chest. "I'll let today's incidents slide if you give me your muffin recipe."

Bea shot him a dirty look as she went to work on packing up the food for her next gig. "Keep dreaming, Wells."

I leaned against the counter beside her. "Don't worry, beautiful. I've got the encryption keys."

Ben raised a brow. "You encrypted a *muffin recipe*? Wow. Nerd love is both terrifying and adorable."

Bea smiled up at me. "Isn't it?"

"Nothing terrifying about the way I love you."

Then I pressed a kiss to her lips with Ben Wells gagging as background noise.

CHAPTER FORTY-THREE
Salvatore

BEN AND I STOOD on the sidewalk, watching Bea drive away. When she was out of sight, he clapped me on the shoulder.

"What's your plan for the day?"

"Finding out who sent Bea that email."

The amiable smile slid off his face. "You're going to handle that?"

"I am."

His chin dropped as he leveled me with a penetrating stare. "I mean, are you going to *handle* that? Because whoever decided to send it messed with my friend's head. When I walked into her house, she was standing in the middle of her living room, staring at a wall like she wasn't even there. It was fucked, man."

Anger simmered beneath my skin, but I kept it contained. "It won't happen again."

"Good." He nodded a few times, his head bouncing. "I'm glad you turned out to be a real one, Tore. Bea's a real one too. She might act tough, but she's one of the most authentic people I've ever met. I'm sure you know that."

"I do." And I found I didn't mind this man seeing it too. I'd assumed I'd be jealous of their friendship, but having witnessed it with my own two eyes, I wasn't. Bea deserved people in her corner. "And you can call me Sal. Tore's for people who don't really know me."

"All right, all right." He bumped me with his shoulder. "Glad to finally meet you, Sal. Bea told me you're into art."

"I am." And I was pleased to hear she'd shared positive things about me.

"I'm getting into it myself. I discovered a couple galleries nearby and got to know the dealers. Maybe, sometime, you might want to go together?"

My brow dropped. "You and me?" This wasn't the direction I'd seen our conversation going. And though the offer wasn't unattractive, I didn't understand why he'd want to do that with me.

"Yeah." He grinned. "I'm in the market for a new friend, especially one into art. What do you say?"

Oh. What *did* I say?

"I don't have many friends," I blurted, immediately regretting it. Christ, I was thirty-two years old. When would I stop being awkward as hell?

"Yeah, same," Ben agreed. "I mean, I've got my teammates, but I already spend too much time with them. And my brothers are my brothers. Shira and Bea are cool, but sometimes, I just want to hang with another guy, look at art, and maybe grab a bite. If you're in, I'm in."

"I...uh—" I spun my ring, thinking it over for a beat. "I'd like that too. I'm in."

I returned to Nox and went straight to my office, determined to find answers.

Leaning forward, elbows on the desk, fingers moving across the keyboard in practiced, silent bursts, I sliced through layers of code and server logs. The email hadn't come from Paul's account. I already knew that. SPF failed. DKIM failed. The headers were dirty. The timestamps were inconsistent. It had been a clumsy attempt at spoofing and came from someone on the inside.

I didn't allow my fury to stop me. That would come later. For now, I remained detached, analytical, solving a puzzle, even if, in the back of my mind, I was almost certain I knew the answer.

The VPN used to mask the originating IP was consumer level and sloppy. Embarrassingly so. I recognized one of the relay nodes from Nox's remote access network.

The firewall logs showed the access point. The timestamps matched. Only one set of credentials had been used in that window.

Sam's.

This wasn't definitive proof. There was a possibility someone else had gotten to his machine and his ID had been spoofed as well. I opened a secondary terminal and ran a fingerprint match, checking for typing cadence, syntax rhythm, script call patterns—behavior everyone had that made them easy to digitally identify.

When the result came through, I stared at it with a stone lodged in my throat. The probability the email had been written by Sam was 97.2 percent.

Still, I kept digging. Before I went to him with this, I had to be sure I hadn't left a single stone unturned. Opening the repository archive, I clicked on a folder no one touched. It contained mail-spoofing emulators we'd built years ago for defensive training to simulate threats.

There it was. The script that had been authored by me. Sam had been the last to modify it...two days ago.

Holy hell.

He'd done it. He'd actually done it.

I sat back in my chair, the wind knocked out of me. I'd built that script to keep us safe, and he'd used it to...what? Hurt me? Hurt Bea? To what fucking end?

My fingers curled against the armrests. I stared at the screen, waiting for something inside me to catch up, but all I felt was confusion.

I didn't move. Didn't speak. Didn't even breathe too loud. I thought and thought, but I could not find the answer. I couldn't even begin to fathom why Sam would have done this.

I'd have to get the answers straight from the source.

I found him in his office, hunched over his desk as if nothing was out of the ordinary. He was flipping through a stack of notes I knew he didn't need. Sam always liked the look of being busy more than actually *being* busy.

"Sam."

He looked up, blinked, then smiled like I was asking about a bug fix.

"Hey," he said, relaxed. "You made it back. The team was in a legit tizzy you missed the meeting."

"We need to talk."

His smile faltered. Just a twitch, but I caught it. His fingers tapped once on the rim of his cup before he leaned back in his chair and studied me like I was the one behaving irrationally.

"What about?"

I stared at him, not moving. "It took me less than ten minutes to trace the spoofed email sent to Bea back to your machine. Do you have anything to say about that?"

He sighed, like this was inconvenient. Like I was being unreasonable for needing an explanation.

"I knew you'd figure it out." He opened his hands on his desk. "Look, I was pissed you were ignoring my calls all weekend to spend time with her. She's been distracting you. Ever since she showed up, you've been off. You missed the investor call—"

"We're not going public."

"You don't seem to get it. This is our moment, Tore. And you're...what? Letting some blue-haired waitress pull you off course?"

I didn't flinch, but something inside me knotted, sharp and hot.

"You forged an email firing her. You used my code. My tools."

"I absolutely did not fire her," he clipped. "I made a snap decision when I was angry, thinking if I put some space between you two, you'd be able to breathe and think rationally. You weren't thinking, Tore. It appears you still aren't."

I stepped forward. He leaned back.

"You had to know I'd trace it back to you."

"I figured you'd gain enough clarity once you were away from her it wouldn't matter who really sent it."

"You were wrong."

"I see that now, and I apologize for acting before thinking," he said, voice calm, placating. "You've always been the levelheaded one. That's what makes you brilliant. That's why Nox works. But this woman is...chaos. She's changing you, distracting you. You can't afford that."

"She's not the problem," I said firmly. It was becoming very clear exactly who the problem was.

"Sure. Maybe she isn't." He shrugged. "Honestly, I'm surprised it's lasted this long. You must be paying her better than I did the first time."

"What?" I snapped. "What the hell are you talking about?"

His brows rose. "Oh. She didn't tell you? Why do you think a girl like her agreed to go out with you in the first place?" He tipped forward again, elbows on his desk. "Money. You liked her, so I offered her cash to give you some extra attention, and she'd been all too happy to take it."

I did not know how to process this new information. If I should believe him. Who I should be angry at. What to do about it. How to react.

All I said was, "We're done, Sam."

I turned and walked out of his office, hearing him call after me—something like, "Don't be mad," or maybe "Come on, Tore."

But I didn't stop. Didn't look back.

Returning to my office, I locked the door and began making calls.

CHAPTER

FORTY-FOUR

Bea

THERE WERE AT LEAST two bobby pins in my bra. Possibly three. I could feel them.

"Hold still," Scarlet muttered behind me, her tone flat with the infinite weariness of a teenager forced into manual labor even though this had been entirely her idea. "You move one more time, Bea, I swear I'm shaving your head."

"I signed up to be your practice dummy for victory rolls, not a buzz cut," I reminded her.

"Well, I might change my mind. Grandpa Tony says it's a woman's prerogative."

I snorted. "If that's the case, I'm going to change my mind about being your mannequin."

As usual, the kids had waylaid me when I'd gotten home from work, dragging Benjamin and me across the street. After running his little legs off in the yard, Benji-bear passed out on the bed the Gallo kids had bought for him, and I'd been roped into getting my hair done.

Not that it had taken much convincing. I was beginning to regret my decision, though, as Scarlet drove yet another bobby pin into my skull.

"Be nice, Scar," Lacey piped up from the arm of the couch where she was taking her official job as bobby-pin passer very seriously. "You're gonna be so pretty, Bea. Like one of Grandpa's movie stars."

I already had one curl pinned lopsided over my forehead and what might've been a section of hair twisted into a misshapen blob on the left. I hadn't seen a mirror, but the look on Tony's face when he'd passed through the living room had said more than enough.

Talon didn't want anything to do with our makeshift hair salon. He sat on the floor by Benjamin, reading quietly over his snores. "*And then Reginald adjusted the silverware placement exactly one point five inches from the edge of the table,*" he said, pushing up his glasses like a tiny professor. "*Because, as everyone knows, precision is a sign of respect.*"

Frank Sinatra crooned from the kitchen, and Tony hummed along as he stirred something rich and garlicky, his "Kiss the Cook" apron tied snug around his waist.

Altogether, it was kind of absurd, but it was also perfect.

Then the front door opened, and a moment later, Salvatore walked into the living room and froze, like his system couldn't process what he was seeing. His gaze swept over us all. I probably looked like a madwoman, Scarlet behind me, jerking my head to and fro. Lacey, bubbling with boundless energy. Talon, reading to a snoring Benji. Tony, belting "Fly Me to the Moon" into a wooden spoon.

He didn't say anything.

Just stared.

Unblinking. Nostrils flaring. Taking it all in.

His eyes locked on mine, and it took two heartbeats for them to soften. His mouth began to twitch, and a laugh traveled from my belly like it had wings and flew out of me.

"Hey," I said.

He bowed his head, full-on grinning now. "What a sight to come home to."

"Not half-bad, right?"

"No." He looked over his kids, my dog, me. "No, there's nothing bad about any of this."

⚜

Salvatore kicked his father out of the chair beside mine at the table and took it for himself. When everyone was seated around us, he threaded our fingers together and put our joined hands on the table.

My heart stopped.

His forefinger stroked the space between my knuckles, giving me a kick start.

I looked at him and whispered, "We're doing this now?"

"Yes." He brushed my chin with the pads of his fingers. "I love you. You're part of this family. The sooner they know how much a part you are, the better."

"Okay." My heart jumped and jittered, doing a wild, excited, terrified dance. "I love you too."

He smiled. "I know."

Lacey, sitting directly across from us, was the first to notice. Her big brown eyes grew impossibly wide as she gasped, her hands flying to her cheeks.

"Oh my goodness. Uncle Sally and Bea!" She shoved Scarlet's shoulder. "Look at them! Oh my goodness."

Scarlet brushed her off then looked at us with narrowed eyes. When she saw our joined hands, her gaze lifted to mine. "What? Really?" I couldn't quite get a bead on what she was thinking. Her poker face was just as refined as her uncle's.

I nodded and leaned into Salvatore. "Yes. Really."

Lacey squealed like she'd just been given her very own unicorn. "Oh my goodness, oh my goodness. Are you boyfriend and girl-friend?" She bounced in her chair, absolutely vibrating. "Do you kiss? Like, really kiss? With your mouths?"

Salvatore coughed. I choked on a laugh.

"Lacey," Scarlet nudged her sister with her elbow. "That's way too much information. And really gross."

"It's not gross. Boyfriends and girlfriends kiss," Lacey shot back. "They kiss and hold hands and go on dates and maybe get married in a big wedding where I get to wear a sparkly dress and throw rose petals!"

Scarlet rolled her eyes. "I guess I can get on board with the whole boyfriend-girlfriend thing, but I'm *not* being a flower girl. I'm way too old for that."

"No one will have to throw anything," Salvatore said mildly, his voice tinged with amusement. "Unless Bea wants to make that part of the contract."

"There's a contract?" Talon asked, looking up from his plate. "Does Bea get paid to be your girlfriend?"

Salvatore blinked. When he didn't answer, I took over. "No, Tally. It's a volunteer position."

"Then what do you get?" Talon tilted his head.

Salvatore looked at me. Just looked. Like he had the same question.

"I get him," I replied, tightening my fingers around his. "That's all I need."

Talon considered that, turning to his uncle. "And what do *you* get?"

Salvatore contemplated this as he wrapped his other hand around mine, trapping me firmly. He didn't need to, though. I wasn't going anywhere. I liked it here, with him—with all of them—far too much to want to leave.

"I get someone who brings laughter to my house," he said softly. "Who makes everything warmer. Who accepts me for who I am. Who loves you guys—and me."

My throat tightened.

Talon nodded and said matter-of-factly, "That's true. Bea does love all of us."

Throughout her siblings' barrage of questions, Scarlet stayed quiet, taking it all in, watching us warily, like she wasn't sure what to make of this news.

"You okay, Scar?" I asked gently.

She shrugged, eyes darting to her lap. "Yeah, I'm all right. You guys are cute and all. I guess...just...don't screw it up. It would really suck if that happened and we couldn't see you anymore."

"I'm not going anywhere, darling. No matter what," I promised.

She met my eyes then gave the smallest nod. "Good."

❦

I didn't miss the way Salvatore had been watching me all evening.

He always did, so that wasn't new, but it was his pensiveness that struck me. Something was on his mind. Probably the email. Up until we closed his bedroom door, we hadn't had a moment alone to discuss it.

He sat on the side of the bed and reached for me. "Come here. I need to talk to you about something and want you close."

"'Kay."

I perched on his thigh, and he circled his arms around me, tugging me into his chest. He didn't say anything as he dragged his nose along my neck and into my hair, breathing me in.

"I didn't know we were telling them about us," I murmured.

"They took it well," he replied.

"Yes. For the most part. Scarlet's wary."

"She's lost a lot. Her being the oldest, she felt it the most." He stroked my stomach and slid his hand beneath my shirt, cupping my breast. "She won't lose you."

"You sound sure."

"I am. I want you to be sure as well. That's what I would like to talk to you about."

With his free hand, he reached into the nightstand and pulled out a slim folder, handing it to me.

I tilted my head. "What is this?"

"It's the deed to your house. I've signed it over to you."

My mouth went dry. "What?"

"The house is yours now, Beatrice. Immediately after I bought it, I had these papers prepared. It was *always* meant to be yours."

My heart thudded. I would have asked if he was serious, but this was Salvatore. He didn't joke about things like this. "Why now?"

"Because we're together. This is serious for me."

"For me too," I agreed.

"Good." He tugged my bra down to pop my breast free and stroked my nipple. "Then I hope this makes sense to you. I do not want you beholden to me for any other reason than you love me. No strings or conditions."

I gasped, both from the rush of his fingers on me and the quiet force behind his words.

"Sal..." I placed my hand over his, stilling his touch though I craved more of it. "I don't feel beholden to you. I never have."

His eyes searched mine. "Good. But I have to be sure. It's yours to do with what you want—keep, sell, rent it out, or turn it into your workspace. Whatever you want."

Tears burned behind my eyes, stupid and fast.

"It's yours, Bea, but I need you to know I want you here, living with me and the kids, full time. It's too soon now—not for me, of course."

I laughed wetly. "Of course."

"But I don't want it to be someday," he continued. "Soon. Our family has been through a lot of changes. Too many, really. But we're in a good place, and I'm certain you would fit in like you've always been here. When you're ready, and the kids are ready, I want you living here."

I blinked, my breath catching in my throat as I looked down at the folder again then back to him.

"That would be pretty amazing." I blinked hard. "Not yet, Sal, but I love that you want that."

He dipped his head to rub his cheek against the swell of my breast, and I threaded my fingers through his hair, cradling him against me.

"Can you see it?" he murmured. "Can you see yourself with us?"

I could. It was crazy because I didn't do ki—all right, I wasn't even buying that anymore. But I'd been convinced of it for so long, it was almost impossible to wrap my head around the one-eighty my life had taken.

I'd done more than wrap my head around it, though. I'd fully embraced these people. They were chaotic, unusual, a little strange. It was no wonder we'd been drawn to each other. They were my kind of people.

My people.

"The thing is," I started, my voice low, "that house was my dream. You know that, right? It's the nicest place I've ever lived that was mine."

He stilled. Listening, waiting, his face over my heart and arms around my waist.

"But dreams change," I whispered, cupping his cheek and tracing the sharp edge with my thumb. "Lately, mine's been looking less like black bricks and everything on this side of the street."

He sighed into my flesh, and his arms tightened around me.

"Thank you for giving me my house. It's a huge, generous gift. I'm not sure I quite believe it. But it's *you*, so I do, because that's who you are. It's why I love you. You've given me so much I never knew I wanted, Salvatore."

He lifted his head, his eyes intent on mine. "Because I know you."

"You do," I whispered. "When the kids are ready, I'll move in here with you guys."

He exhaled like I'd knocked the air out of him.

Then he kissed me like I'd given it back.

Chapter Forty-Five
Salvatore

I WAS IN NO rush and no mood to go hard. With her taste on my lips and her under me, warm and so soft, all I wanted was to sink into her and stay there forever.

Our hands were entwined above her head, legs tangled, bodies joined, ebbing and flowing, lapping at each other's shores.

I dipped my head to tug her nipple in my mouth, sucking gently. Her hips rose, and I became more firm, pulling her higher.

She gasped, breath hitching like she was surprised by how good I made her feel. In a way, I understood her reaction. Nothing could ever compare to this. Nothing could even touch what I shared with Bea. And each time we were together only built on the time before as we discovered hidden corners, intimate secrets, our bodies' tells.

I released her nipple with a light pop, then curled my tongue around the beaded point before moving to the other, my hips never losing their rhythm, that unhurried glide that kept us both on the edge of too much and not enough.

Her fingers tightened around mine where I held them pinned above her, and I could feel the tremor in her arms, the quiver in her thighs. She was beautiful, always, but this way was one of my favorites. Trembling and open, so warm and soft, welcoming me easily into her, showing me just how mine she was with every rise of her hips to meet mine.

Her blue hair fanned out in rolling waves on my white sheets, the contrast almost too perfect to be real. Like it should have been art on my wall, not something I could look at and touch and muss and change and move.

"What are you thinking?" she breathed.

"That you're art, but better because you're real."

"Sal..." Her lashes fluttered, but her eyes stayed open, holding mine like she could see every piece of me, even the parts I wasn't aware of and the ones I had kept locked away. The strangeness she coveted like a treasure. The quirks and imperfections I hated that she not only accepted but loved. She saw everything, and she still looked at me like I was the best discovery she had ever made.

Her lips were swollen from our kisses and a little parted, like she was waiting for more. So I gave it to her.

Lifting my head, I kissed the curve of her jaw, the corner of her mouth, the spot just beneath her ear that always made her breath stutter.

"I never knew a person could feel like home, but you do," I murmured. She was my discovery too. Knowing her, loving her, I'd uncovered feelings and the desire for *more*. More life, more adventure, more everything.

She turned her face, caught my mouth with hers, and kissed me like she was starving for it— sweet and a little desperate. I kissed her back the same way, our bodies pressed close, hips rocking in the same rhythm we'd fallen into from the start. The end wasn't the point. Our joining was.

Steady and slow, we slid against each other. She whispered sweet, filthy words, telling me she loved me, that she'd never felt this way, that the college rumors were true, but that wasn't even in the top ten things she loved about me, that she couldn't get enough of my glowing ears and I was the hottest genius she'd ever seen.

They were the kind of compliments only Beatrice could give. I tucked them away for later, when I could process and maybe laugh and roll around in them like a wild dog.

For now, all I could see and hear and feel was her. Her breath, glazed eyes, creamy breasts bouncing with every thrust, smoky voice in my ear, her hands on me, heart thudding with mine.

Her legs curled around my waist, and I shifted deeper, groaning low as her body clenched around me.

"I've got you," I whispered against her lips as her back arched and she moaned my name. "I've always got you."

She broke apart beneath me in a rolling wave—a gradual build that overtook her, breath catching in her throat, eyes wide and shining, her mouth shaping my name in a soundless cry. Her body trembled, pulling me deeper, holding me there as her release washed through her. And I followed.

I always followed her.

My rhythm faltered. Stuttered. Burying myself as deep as I could go, arms braced, forehead pressed to hers, I let go. Emptying everything into her—every thought, every doubt, every jagged piece I'd never known how to fix. I let her have all of me, and she took it like she always did. Like I was exactly who she wanted and nothing less.

My chest tightened. Not from exertion but the pressure of something bigger. A kind of fullness I didn't have the words for.

My body was limp and sated, but my mind was still trying to catch up. Still reeling from this woman capable of undoing me and putting me back together with a single smile or by wrapping me in her soft embrace.

She stroked my face with the back of her fingers and gave me a hazy, languid smile. "What's going on in your big, beautiful mind now, Salvatore?" she whispered.

"You know me." My voice cracked on the words, and I didn't try to hide it.

"Well…yeah. And you know me. Probably better than anyone."

"I do." I squeezed my eyes shut. "You like me."

"Yeah," she breathed. "Always have."

"From the start?"

"Mmhmm."

She pulled my mouth to hers and kissed me gently, our bodies still joined, still warm, still tangled. The world could burn outside those walls, and I wouldn't move.

There was more we had to say, questions I had to ask, but it could wait a while. What had felt imperative to understand when I'd walked through my door this evening no longer seemed vital.

However we'd started, whatever reason Bea had had to give me her attention, this was real. That, I did not doubt. Not even for a second.

Eventually, our breaths slowed, and the rhythm of our hearts settled into something calm and steady. I eased onto my side, carefully bringing her with me. She curled against me, her cheek cradled on my arm, one leg slotted between mine. I smoothed my hand down her back, tracing lazy circles as her fingers toyed with the ends of my hair.

I liked her like this. Sleepy and soft, her lips curving in the way they always did after she came hard and felt safe. It was even better knowing she wasn't going to sneak out at the crack of dawn. The ticking clock was gone. I had her to myself all night.

"You're staring," she mumbled, cracking an eyelid to peek at me.

"I am. I like your face."

That earned me a drowsy smile. "That's good, since it's the only face I have."

I laughed under my breath and kissed the top of her head, letting the quiet blanket us for a while. As I lay here with her in my arms, it was too peaceful to hurry to end it.

But I couldn't let go of the edge I'd been riding all day. The question that had gnawed at me, even with her in my arms, knowing she was mine and I was hers. I had to ask, get rid of it and be done.

"I've got something to ask you." I brushed her hair back from her face. "It's not a big deal to me. I just need to know."

She pushed up on her elbow, a line carving between her eyebrows. "That sounds serious."

I exhaled slowly then dove in headfirst. "Sam told me something today I would like you to clear up if you can. He said he'd paid you to give me attention when we first met. Is that true?"

Bea didn't move. Not away from me or closer. She froze above me, except the line between her brows that deepened into a bottomless crevice.

I reached for her face, cupping it carefully. "I believe what we have now is real. You know that, right? I'm not asking because I doubt you. I'm asking because I want the truth from you. Always."

"You're joking, right?"

"No." I frowned. "Why would you think I'm joking?"

Her mouth fell into an *O*. "Because you *know* this, Tore. I texted you everything the last day we were together, and you replied. You. Replied! Said it was okay. How could you forget that?"

I stared back at her, stunned.

I had no earthly idea what she was talking about.

CHAPTER FORTY-SIX
Bea

I JUMPED OUT OF bed and pulled on my pajama shorts and top. This absolutely wasn't the kind of conversation one had while naked.

When I turned back around, Salvatore had put on a pair of shorts and was sitting with his back to the headboard, a perplexed look on his face.

"Beatrice, I need you to explain what you mean. When did I reply?"

I held up a hand. "Hold on. I'll show you."

I had a bad habit of never deleting text threads, even those with people I never planned to speak to again. I still had the few Tore and I had exchanged when we'd first met.

Bringing up our thread, I scrolled to the beginning, stopping on the screenshot I'd sent to him after he'd left me in his hotel room.

"Here." I handed him my phone. "It had taken me a few hours to work up the nerve to tell you. I thought you'd never speak to me again once you found out, but I hadn't been able to keep it from you. I'd thought...I'd thought we were starting something real, and I didn't want this hanging over us."

He studied the screen, his brow furrowed. I pointed to the reply he'd sent.

"See? You said you understood and appreciated my honesty. You *know* about the money, Sal. You know I returned what I could. If I could go back and never accept it in the first place, I would. It was stupid, and I was desperate, but it was a mistake. I only took it because I already thought you were so, so cute and wanted to flirt with you anyway. But I already told you that, so I don't understand why you're bringing it up now." My throat suddenly grew tight, and my eyes began to burn. "Tonight was so perfect. I mean, I thought it was. Maybe you didn't. Maybe you're regretting telling the kids about us. If that's the case, we can slow down—"

His hand shot out, gripping the side of my neck. "I didn't send this text."

My mouth came to a screeching halt. "What do you mean? You see it right here with your own eyes. You definitely sent that text."

"No. I didn't see this." His thumb hovered over the time stamp on his reply. "This says it was sent at 5:17 p.m. My sister was being taken off life support at that time. I don't know where my phone even was, but I wasn't reading or sending texts."

"What?" I exhaled every ounce of my righteous indignation. "Then who—?"

He let go of me to grab his phone and tapped on our messages, scrolling back to the beginning. Buried deep under my confusion, I was pleased he'd kept our text chain like I had.

He turned the screen to me. "I haven't deleted anything, but I don't have a text from you. Or a screenshot. And you can see I never replied."

I didn't have to look very close to see he was right. The texts I'd sent and received weren't there.

I lifted my eyes to his. "What's going on, baby?"

He shook his head. "Sam was the one who told me about the money."

"It was five hundred dollars. Back then, that meant a lot to me."

His nostrils flared as he released a breath. "I know, beautiful. I understand why you took it. I'm not angry at you. I love that you tried to tell me. You're everything I always knew you were, and this only confirms it. I'm furious, though."

"At Sam?" I guessed.

"Yes. He shouldn't have put you in that position," he gritted out.

I was pissed at Sam too, but for an entirely different reason.

My immediate need, however, was to eliminate the distance between Salvatore and me. I crawled across the mattress and up his body. His hands slid to my hips, helping me straddle his legs. I cupped his neck, and he held my waist, our chests flush.

"I noticed you, Sal. That first night, you blushed, and I thought you were so adorable. You came back the next night, and I was secretly hoping it was because you thought I was adorable too."

"Not adorable. Stunning and mean."

I grinned. "Yeah. You like me mean." I rubbed my nose against his. "Sam approached me, asking me to give you extra attention. And I accepted because, well, I needed the money. If you'd been any other customer, though, I would have told him to get fucked. I took it because it was you, and I wanted to flirt with you anyway. The money was a very nice bonus."

His grip on me tightened, the tips of his fingers digging into the give of my flesh. "He never should have put you in that position."

"No, it wasn't fair to either of us. But you need to know, that third night you came back? Even if he'd never given me a dime, I would have sat with you when you'd asked. And I would have said yes to a date because I was so fucking smitten with you."

His head cocked. "Smitten?"

I laughed. "Tony's wearing off on me, I guess. It's a good word. I was—and am—totally into you. I hadn't expected it, but it happened, and I went with it. I'm sorry this makes how we started messy, but for me, it was real and true."

"It doesn't matter to me." He touched his lips to mine. "Even when Sam told me what he'd done, I didn't doubt you. I wanted to understand exactly what happened, but the bottom line is, there's nothing anyone could tell me about you that would make me doubt you."

"That's because no one knows me the way you do."

"That's right. Some of that knowledge I stole."

I reared back, frowning. "Did you hack my hard drive?"

He chuckled. "No. I resisted. I mean *Anthony*. Through him, I peered into your life without your permission."

"Oh." My frown lifted. "Well, I always had a feeling *someone* was behind him. If I'd known it was you, I probably would have started sexting."

"*What*?" A laugh shook his shoulders, and he buried his face in my throat. "Christ, Beatrice. I never know what you're going to say."

"I'm keeping you on your toes, baby."

He smiled against my skin. "That you are."

I let him hold on to his happy for another minute then sighed. "We need to talk about Sam. Why did he bring up the money now? What do you think his intentions were?"

He sobered, leaning his head back on the headboard. "I know his intentions: to drive a wedge between us so I would focus on Nox exclusively."

My stomach dropped. "He's been trying to get you away from me?"

"He's been trying to control where I put my energy since we met, and I've let him. It's how we worked back then, and the dynamic remained...well, until Tia died. After that, I had to make some huge changes he didn't like but had to accept."

Sam could really fuck right off. If I saw him again, I would tell him that.

He shook his head. "He's been subtle about it, but he never stopped pushing me in the direction he wants me to go."

I rested my hands on his chest, feeling his steady heartbeat. "Sal...what else has he steered you toward?"

He didn't answer right away. His eyes were unfocused, distant, like he was riffling through mental files, looking for patterns. When he spoke again, his voice was quiet, almost too calm.

"Sam had my phone two years ago. He had to have replied to you then deleted those texts. There's no other possibility." His jaw worked as he mulled over his next words. "The email you got this morning...I dug through our servers and discovered it'd come from Sam. He sent it to you."

My jaw hung open. "Holy hell. The man has lost the entire plot, hasn't he? What did he think would come from doing that?"

"Steering me. Always steering me." Exhaling, he banged his head against the wood behind him. "He wanted you to give me attention two years ago so I'd agree to sign the DoD contract. He'd been right. It'd been the logical next step, and I'd been digging my feet in."

I shook my head. "It doesn't matter if he was right. He went about it the wrong way."

"Yes," he agreed. "But he's always been this way. Not just with me. With everyone. He is single-minded and thinks he's always right. Often, he is, but—"

"He doesn't get to move you like a chess piece. What he did today was beyond the pale. It's one thing to spring surprise investors on you at a dinner meeting. It's shitty, but it's business. But for him to meddle in your personal life—in *my* personal life? No, Sal. I don't accept that. It's not okay. And next time he gets pissy, the outcome could be far worse."

"Beautiful," he said, taking my face in his warm hands, "it isn't okay, and there will not be a next time."

I searched his face. Something in his expression cracked open a spot in my chest I didn't know could ache like this. It wasn't only anger. Grief was in the mix, darkening his gaze.

His oldest friend had absolutely gutted him.

I slid my hands up his arms and cupped the back of his neck. "I know you're handling it. I'm sure you're three steps ahead."

"I am." His voice was firm but not defensive. He never tried to prove his competence to me; he simply stated facts. "I met with my lawyers this afternoon."

"I'm glad you have a team." I shifted, lowering my forehead to his. "I'm on your team too."

He sucked in a ragged breath. "I don't know how to process this," he admitted. "On the one hand, I'm so angry, I don't know how I'll look at him tomorrow. On the other, I can't believe it's come to this. We built Nox together. We once shared a vision for the future. More than that, we were friends. At least, I thought we were."

My fingers slipped into his hair. "You were. I'm sure you were. People change. They get greedy, and some drop their masks, showing you what a piece of shit they are."

"Yeah. I know about masks." His jaw clenched. "It won't be immediate. He still has board influence, so I can't be reckless with this."

"Have you ever been reckless a day in your life? You've got this, baby. And if you feel like you don't, I'll be here to remind you you do."

His arms came around me fully, crushing me to his chest. "I didn't want to believe he'd cross the line like this."

"I know."

"But he did."

"Yes." I nodded against him. "I'm sorry. So, *so* sorry."

Silence stretched between us as his breathing evened out. The gears in his brain were still turning, probably plotting how he'd handle what was coming, rehearsing the things he'd say, how he'd act, preparing himself so there were no more surprises.

When he spoke, his voice was low. "My lawyers are working on a draft to restructure the voting rights. I'm consolidating—cutting off anything he can use to apply pressure. It'll take a few weeks, but once it's done, he's out."

He shuddered. As if it physically pained him. Even though I didn't understand exactly what he meant, I knew it would be a huge deal when it happened, and I would be here. If he needed to lean, I'd hold him up.

"You have to do it. It's not just about protecting yourself." I touched his chest. "You're protecting the whole company. The kids. Me."

His eyes met mine. "Always you."

I smiled, slow and sure. "I'm going to back you so hard, Salvatore Gallo. No one touches my man and walks away clean."

He gave a broken laugh and rested his forehead against mine again. "If you weren't on my side, I'd be terrified."

"You like me mean, though, right?"

"I do." He kissed me, long and deep, until we were both out of breath. "My beautiful, mean love."

"Yeah..." Then I thought of something that made me giggle.

He raised a brow. "What's so funny?"

"Nothing, really. It's just...Paul's going to be so pissed."

After a beat, he laughed. "Oh yes. Paul will not appreciate being impersonated."

"No, he won't." I snickered. "He'll have to wear one of his very serious vests to show everyone he means business."

"He does own a large collection of vests, doesn't he?"

"Right? So many vests," I agreed through giggles.

Laughing with me, he tucked me into his arms. We stayed like that for a long time, and when we finally fell asleep, it was wrapped in each other.

No matter what waited for us tomorrow, we had this—laughter and love and arms that didn't let go.

That was a whole lot.

CHAPTER FORTY-SEVEN

Bea

THINGS WENT BACK TO normal-ish. There was a simmering tension in the background. A cold war at Nox Salvatore tried not to bring home, but it was impossible not to see the way the dawning of the end of his decade-long friendship was affecting him.

I took care of him the best I could, listened when he wanted to talk, but there was only so much I could do, especially when Sam was still walking around Nox like he'd done nothing wrong.

I'd been to Nox twice since Sam had sent the fake email. Both times, I'd made sure to seek him out so he could see my face and acknowledge he had not won. I didn't say a word, but I didn't have to. My presence said it all.

As always, Sam could fuck right off.

As soon as Salvatore's lawyers drew up airtight language Sam couldn't wiggle out of, he'd be out of here. To me, it was taking far too long for that to happen, but I'd never gone to law school, so who was I to judge?

I bustled into the Nox conference room, my arms full. Salvatore jumped up from his seat to help me, but I shook my head.

"I have everything perfectly balanced. If you move anything, it will all come tumbling down."

He frowned. "Your system seems to rely too heavily on gravity cooperating with you."

"No way. I am an expert stacker—a skill honed by years of waitressing. You can't just walk off the street and expect to carry five plates without breaking a sweat."

He crowded behind me as I carefully set everything down. As soon as the last bag left my hand, he took me by the shoulder and spun me around. His mouth was on mine before I could catch my breath, but my body was so attuned to his, I instantly melted and kissed him back.

We were being highly inappropriate, considering we were in his workplace—and technically mine—but he was the boss. Who was going to tell him he wasn't allowed to kiss his girlfriend in his own conference room?

A throat cleared behind us. "Excuse me?"

Salvatore's grip on my waist tightened. Slowly, unhappily, he lifted his head. Paul was standing in the doorway, shifting uncomfortably as he looked anywhere but at us.

"Oh, hey, Paul," I chirped, refusing to be embarrassed even though we'd totally been making out in plain view of the open doorway.

It wasn't the first time.

"Hello, Bea." He cleared his throat again. "Sorry, Tore, but there's something I need to speak to you about, and I don't believe it should wait. It's about Sam."

Salvatore jerked against me. The movement was subtle, but being so close, I felt it.

Paul gave a quick glance in my direction. "I can come back—"

"No," Salvatore finally said. "It's fine. Say it now."

Paul's throat bobbed as he swallowed hard. "Right. Uh…well…this is something I wasn't sure I should bring to you, but I've thought about it for a few days, and it's…not sitting right with me. I don't know if you're aware, but most of the office managers in the tech world have something of an information-sharing network. I have a friend at Astrillex—"

Salvatore stiffened, the fingers on my waist flexing. I peered up at him, unsure where Paul was going with this, or why Salvatore had reacted that way. He turned his head to look down at me.

"Astrillex is a tech firm in LA. We were acquaintances when we lived out there, and—" Salvatore's lips rolled over his teeth as he measured his words. "They're loud and flashy and like to brag about their culture while acquiring smaller companies and gutting every original founder in sight. I was not a fan, but Sam was friendly with them."

Paul nodded. "Right. That's exactly right. They're a pack of vultures." Grimacing, Paul yanked his vest zipper up to his throat. "Anyway, my friend Jenna called me last week for a reference on a former intern. Normal, casual talk, you know. Then she mentioned she had seen Sam last week when he'd gone to their office. She hadn't thought anything of it, except she overheard him telling their CEO he'd be able to bring over samples of our threat-mapping framework to show how it could be improved. Called it a 'case study.'"

I wish I understood what Paul was saying, but even as a layperson, it didn't sound good.

Salvatore's fingers dug into my side, just shy of pain. I put my hand over his and threaded our fingers, giving him something else to grasp.

Paul hesitated before adding, "She asked if that was normal for Nox. Obviously, it's not."

"No, it's not," Salvatore ground out.

Paul's face turned ashen. "I'm sorry, but that's not all."

"Christ," Salvatore muttered. "What else has he done?"

Paul took a breath and pulled out his phone. "Last month, someone inadvertently added me to a private Slack channel. Honestly, I didn't think much of it, but one day, I was curious and scrolled. Nothing really caught my attention. Just a few mid-level devs discussing current projects, then Sam joined, and it turned into something else."

He turned the screen toward us, and Salvatore's name was in bold at the top of a message. Most of what I read went way over my head, but a few things jumped out. Someone had said, *'I've noticed he can get stuck in loops and delay approvals for weeks.'* And Sam had replied, *'We need someone who can move fast, adapt, see the bigger picture.'*

Paul's voice was quiet. "Sam started this conversation, framing it as company growth. I read between the lines, and...I think he's trying to get the devs on board to replace you."

Salvatore still didn't move.

"I apologize if I'm overstepping," Paul said, sliding his phone back into his pocket. "But I thought you should see it before things go further. I didn't want to assume anything. I just—"

"Thank you, Paul," Salvatore said, his voice tight, restrained. "I appreciate you coming to me. You did the right thing."

"Of course." Paul yanked his zipper down to his chest. "Is there anything else I can do?"

Salvatore glanced at me then at the table covered in my catering supplies. "Would it ruin your day if I canceled the meeting?" he asked.

"Do what you need to do," I replied.

He nodded then looked at Paul. "Team meeting is canceled. We'll reschedule for later in the week. Bea will put out snacks in the break room before she leaves. Please let everyone know."

"You've got it, boss." Paul hesitated at the door. "For what it's worth, the Slack channel represents a very small portion of your developers. I keep my finger on the pulse here and an ear out for what people are saying. As a whole, most people feel they're part of something revolutionary at Nox and that you're taking us in the right direction."

"Thank you," Salvatore replied blandly.

Paul nodded once and backed out of the room.

Silence fell like a heavy blanket.

I waited, and not just because I didn't know what to say. I was giving Salvatore time to process and get a handle on what Paul had just told him. He had to be overloaded, and I wasn't going to add to that weight.

He stood perfectly still for a few heartbeats then pulled his hand from mine and walked over to the table where I should have been setting up my spread. Bracing his hands on the edge of the table, he bowed his head and exhaled a breath that sounded like it'd scraped his lungs raw.

I gave him another minute.

When he didn't speak, I crossed the room, curling my arms around his middle and resting my cheek against his back. His muscles vibrated with tension, but little by little, some of it eased.

"Tell me," I whispered, stroking up and down his torso in a slow-motion rhythm.

"He went to Astrillex and pitched to them like he was a free agent." His hand covered mine, warm and solid. "He offered to show them a glimpse of our internal threat-mapping models. Bea, this is proprietary work we have spent years refining. It's work we've never published or shared."

I felt his pain more than I understood the specifics, but I knew enough to know in Salvatore's world, trust was everything. It had to be, with how sensitive the data they protected was. And Sam had stomped all over that trust like it was nothing.

Fuck right off, Sam.

"He's never made wanting more a secret. More control, more credit, more visibility. Over the years, I've handed him pieces of what I built because I thought...I thought we were a team and always would be."

He straightened and turned toward me. When his eyes met mine, I saw it. The same mix of anger and grief he'd been carrying the past few weeks. But now, it was slashed with an ugly streak of betrayal.

"I've known for a while he wasn't going to stay if I didn't agree to take Nox public. But this...he wasn't just trying to leave," he said quietly. "He tried to take people with him. He has been planting seeds of dissent among the developers. And I missed it, Beatrice. I did not see what was happening right in front of me. Until very recently, I never questioned his motives. Not when he second-guessed my decisions, not when he contradicted me in front of the board, not when he continued to make connections with companies we should have had nothing to do with."

He dragged a hand through his hair. "I feel like an idiot."

"You're not an idiot." I pressed my palm to his chest. "There's nothing stupid about believing your oldest friend will have your back. That's how most people work. Sam's the idiot for trashing your loyalty."

His throat worked, but no sound came out. I rested my head against him and held him tight.

"It's not just about the company," he murmured. "It's the language he was using to describe me. He took my inherent traits and turned them against me. And I think...he's always done that."

I pulled back just enough to look up at him.

"He'd say things like, *'You know you're not good with people, let me handle the communication.'* Or tell me I fixated too much on the details so he'd make the final call. The truth is, I'm good at what I do *because* I fixate. Details are vital in my line of work."

He blinked hard. "But...I let him. I let him convince me I couldn't run this on my own because my mind works differently than most—that he was the reason we were taken seriously. Without him, I'd stall or get lost in the weeds or become...unmanageable."

"Sal..."

Sam could really, truly fuck right off. Like, right now. Expediently.

He looked down at me, his expression hollow. "The worst part is, I didn't even notice it until recently. His little nudges were so insidious, deliberately steering me into doubting myself. I handed over pieces of my authority, thinking it was my idea."

My stomach twisted. If Sam had ever been a true friend to Salvatore—which I really fucking doubted—he wasn't anything close to one anymore. I was no psychiatrist, but I was pretty sure Sam was an actual sociopath.

"I hate him, Sal." I knocked my forehead against his chest. "You are so damn perfect and loved. I've seen the way your employees look at you. They practically bow. Sam has to see that. No one admires him the way they do you. That has to eat at him. And it must kill him having to ride your coattails because he isn't smart enough to come up with his own ideas. He probably stays awake at night, all alone in his bed, thinking about your beautiful family and gorgeous girlfriend who's totally bananas for you."

Worked up, I kept on rolling. "Sam is a manipulator. In the brief interactions we've had, I've gotten to see how he works, and it's ugly. He found you when you were insecure and tried to mold you into his little robot as if you weren't a fully formed human already. He changed your *name*, Salvatore. He tried to rewrite you." I tugged on his shirt. "That's insane. This man never wanted the world to see you. He wanted them to see a version he thought he could control."

He nodded heavily. "You're right. He caught me when I was low. When I wanted to believe someone understood me without judgment. It took a long time for me to see how much I was shaving off to make him comfortable."

My heart cracked wide open. Salvatore Gallo was as perfect as any human being could be. To think his closest friend had him convinced there was something about him that needed to change made me sick.

"Don't waste another second on that man." I slid my hands up to his jaw and held his face. "You are Nox. This is your brainchild.

You built it into what it is. Sam made you doubt your voice, but I've heard it. It's the clearest, strongest voice I know."

His eyes closed, and a tremor passed through him.

"I see you," I said so fiercely his eyes shot open.

"All of you. Salvatore. Tore. However you want to be known, whatever name you carry, I see *you*. I'm not going anywhere. I will stand with you, whatever you decide to do. If you need to rebuild from scratch, I'll be here with you."

He lowered his head on top of mine, heaving a breath that came from his soul.

"I wish I could have found you sooner," he murmured.

"We found each other when it was time." I pressed my cheek over his thudding heart. "I love you."

"I believe that. And I love you very much, Beatrice."

"Yeah, you do." I tipped my face back. "Now, what are we going to do about Sam? I'd really like to tell him to fuck right off."

He huffed a short laugh. "I appreciate the sentiment, but I'll handle it. My lawyers already have the clauses drafted. I was trying to give him a chance to walk away clean, but that's over now."

"Good," I whispered. "He's not just a liability to Nox, he's a traitor, and I want him out of your life."

He nodded, resolute. "He will be. Starting today."

I didn't doubt he would make it happen. Not for one second.

Chapter Forty-eight
Salvatore

Perched on the counter beside my sink, Lacey swung her legs as she watched me knot my tie.

She sighed. "You look so handsome."

I found her gaze in the mirror. "Not so different from my everyday look, is it?"

Her mouth twisted. "Well, this suit is black, and so is your tie. You never wear black to work."

"True. Very observant." I gave the tie one last tug and turned to my girl. "Clara and Jake's wedding is black tie optional. I can't wear my work suits, and this one is more formal."

"I wish I could go to the wedding too." She perked up. "I bet Bea's dress is going to be so pretty. Can I help you pick her up from her house so I can see how pretty she looks? Please, Uncle Sally?"

Lacey was far too skilled at convincing me to do what she wanted. To be fair, all it normally took was a little pout, batting her lashes, and asking nicely.

I smoothed my hand over her silky hair. "Yes. Why don't we all pick her up? Then you can bring Benjamin here for the night."

Her eyes lit up. "We're going to have a sleepover with him again?"

"Yes, and Bea and I are going to have a sleepover at a hotel. Do you think you can take care of him all night while we're away?"

She nodded. "Oh yes. Definitely." Then she went still, her gaze darting over me. "You'll be back in the morning, right?"

"I will. We might want to sleep in, so let's say we'll be back by eleven."

The brief worry fled her in an instant. "That sounds good. I probably won't sleep in, though."

I didn't doubt that, but for tonight, that would be my father's responsibility. The wedding couldn't have come at a better time. Bea and I needed this after the last couple weeks of putting out fires nonstop.

I'd asked Sam to leave Nox as soon as I'd discovered how duplicitous he'd truly been. He argued. Oh, had he argued. But now that my eyes had been opened, his tactics no longer worked on me. I would not be manipulated by our shared past, nor could he convince me I needed him to succeed, though he tried.

His access to our servers had been immediately revoked, and he'd been escorted from the building. He went quietly that day, but not the next.

Then the calls started. To other tech firms. To every contact he still had. He even tried to go to the press but backed off fairly quickly. I suspected his own lawyers had gotten to him before he could go too far.

Unfortunately for Sam, the whisper network worked fast in the tech world. Sure, there were always firms that were like hungry dogs and would do anything to make a buck, but in the security sector, being incorruptible was vitally important.

And Sam had proven he wasn't.

He hadn't just burned bridges, he'd salted the earth behind him.

I hadn't expected the aftermath of Sam leaving to be so...*quiet*. At first, that silence felt like relief. The absence of his voice in meetings. No more subtle redirects. No more gentle but consistent second-guessing. Just a return to clarity and control.

Sam had built relationships I hadn't cared to maintain—partners I'd tolerated for the sake of his diplomacy, teams he'd handpicked with loyalty to him, not Nox. When he'd left, some followed, while others lingered, waiting to see if I would stumble.

I stayed steady. Each day, I hit the limit of my bandwidth, sealing cracks in the foundation I hadn't seen until Sam left. My meetings with the developers from the Slack channel Paul had shown me had been insightful. Some were pompous jackasses, but others made good points.

It wasn't the logistical fallout that often kept me awake in the hours between midnight and dawn, though. It was *him*. Well...who he'd once been to me—who I'd thought he was.

For a long time, Sam had been the buffer between me and a world often too loud, bright, big. He knew how to read my silences, how to speak in rooms I preferred not to. It wasn't until he was gone I'd realized how much of a crutch he'd been for me. I'd let it happen because it had been easier for him to carry the weight I didn't want.

And through it all, Bea had been my rock.

She'd quietly shown up for me, over and over. Noticing when my shoulders were tight, coaxing me into taking breaks I wouldn't give myself, curling up next to me in bed while I stayed up all night reviewing code or rewriting infrastructure after a team lead had left.

She hadn't tried to fix things for me. Hadn't told me to look on the bright side.

She was simply there. Unfailingly.

Some nights, she sat with me in my home office, watching movies on her tablet just to keep me company. Other days, she'd stop in at Nox to deliver me lunch and ask me to stop working for five minutes to make out with her.

That was my personal favorite form of support.

I'd briefly worried I was now using her as my crutch, but once I'd mentally sorted the differences between my relationships with Sam and Bea, I immediately concluded there was no comparison. Bea was my partner. She didn't speak *for* me—she made me want to speak for myself.

"Uncle Sally," Lacey piped up, regaining my attention, "are you thinking about boring stuff again?"

I smiled softly. "No. Not boring. Important."

She raised a skeptical brow. "You look like you're being CEO-y in your brain."

I laughed. "Well, I'm done being CEO-y for today. It's time to pick up our girl."

Lacey clapped her hands. "Yes! Let's go see Bea's dress!"

⚘

Bea was on her porch, waiting for us when we crossed the street. She laughed when she saw picking her up had turned into a group project.

"All the Gallos are here," she called. "To what do I owe this honor?"

"We're here to pick you up," Lacey sang out.

"We aren't," Talon argued. "Only Uncle Sally's picking her up."

"She knows, Tal," Scarlet said, putting her arm around her brother's shoulders. "Lacey's just being silly."

Lacey tugged at my hand, pulling me through Bea's gate. Bea met us at the bottom of her porch steps, her eyes dancing over everyone before landing on me. Then they lit up like a full moon, big and bright.

"Hello, handsome."

I stopped moving, the smoke of her voice fogging my brain. My father had no such trouble.

He went straight up to her, brushed a kiss over her cheek, and crooned, "Marilyn in orange. What a sight." Then he turned and beckoned me over. "The two of you are a dapper pair. Stand side by side so I can snap a picture."

Scarlet gave my back a shove, finally getting me moving. The second I was within Bea's vicinity, her warm vanilla scent drew me in. I slid my arm around her waist, the raw silk material of her dress bumpy along my palms.

"Hello, beautiful blue," I murmured. "Sorry for the delay. You stunned me."

She pressed her hands to my lapels and smiled. "You're here now. That's all that matters."

"Oh my goodness!" Lacey stood to our side, her hands clutched beneath her chin. "You're a princess, Bea. An orange blossom princess. I love it so much."

Bea reached out, pulling her into our embrace. "Thank you, darling. I'm going to tell everyone I run into tonight I'm an orange blossom princess."

Lacey crinkled her nose the way Bea always did. "Are you kidding me? They're gonna look at you and know it!"

"Where's Benjamin?" Talon asked.

My father patted his shoulder. "How about giving the lady a compliment?"

Talon managed to tear his eyes from Bea's front door, giving her a brief once-over. "She always looks nice, Grandpa."

"True," he agreed. "But that's why you gotta be consistent with your compliments. I've never known a lady who gets tired of hearing how nice she looks."

Talon squinted at Bea. "Your hair is very swirly. I like that a lot."

"Thanks so much, Tally." Bea patted her hair, which was, indeed, swirly. "I appreciate you noticing. It took me a long time to get it right. And Benji-bear's inside. You're welcome to go see—"

Talon was at the door before Bea finished, going to see his dog.

I kissed her temple. "I like your swirls too. And everything else about you."

She tipped her face back, her moon-lit eyes sweeping over me. "I like everything about you too." Then she whispered, "I can't wait to spend the evening with you."

My father clapped his hands. "Not so fast. I said I wanted pictures, and I mean it. Lace, you gotta scoot. I want pics of the lovebirds."

Lacey groaned, peeling herself away from Bea with a dramatic sigh. "I want some with me in them too, Grandpa."

"You'll get your turn," he promised, already lifting his phone. "All right, you two. Smile like you like each other."

Bea leaned into me, her smile warm against my cheek. I let myself relax, wrapping my arm fully around her waist, hand splayed across the silk at her hip.

"Now, one where you look at each other," Tony coached. "Tender. Like you're in a black-and-white flick."

Bea's eyes twinkled. "Are you a director now, Tony?"

"Damn straight I am," he said. "It's a grandpa's right."

I looked at Bea, and just like that, the rest of the world blurred. My father might have taken a thousand pictures, but all I saw was her.

"Ohhh, that one's cute," Scarlet said. "Send that to me. I'm posting it."

"You will not," I said instinctively.

"Too late. It's already in my camera roll," she quipped.

"I don't mind," Bea replied. "Just tag me in it."

"Let's get one with everyone," my dad ordered.

Lacey scurried to Bea's other side. "All the Gallos and the orange blossom princess!"

"Wait for me and Benjamin," Talon called. Benjamin barked once then happily squirmed into the group as everyone bunched around us.

My father stood in front, holding his phone out so we all fit into the shot. "Three...two...one—say 'wedding cake'!"

"Wedding cake!" we all shouted.

"Perfect," Tony said. "Now, off with you two. You've got a party to get to, and we've got a movie night to start."

Scarlet nudged Talon. "Tell them to have fun."

He blinked. "Why do I need to tell them? They're going to a party. Parties are fun. If they don't have fun, that's their problem."

Bea laughed and slipped her arm through mine. "Tally has a very valid point."

We headed for my car as my father called after us, "Don't forget to dance, Sal!"

I looked at Bea as I opened the passenger door for her. "Are we going to dance, Beatrice?"

She slid inside with a teasing smile. "Only if you promise to hold me close."

My chest tightened in that good, magic and shiny way she had a habit of causing, and I closed the door carefully behind her.

"There's no other way I want to hold you, beautiful."

Oh yes.

Tonight, I'd hold her close.

Tomorrow too.

Always.

Chapter Forty-nine

Bea

I didn't do tears. Crying wasn't my thing.

But lizards, did I ruin my makeup watching Clara marry the love of her life. That I caught Salvatore eyeing me like he was seconds from springing up from his seat and gathering me in his arms every time I glanced out at the rows of guests didn't help.

I'd always thought weddings weren't really my thing either, but I could see myself having a sweet little ceremony, as long as the man standing across from me was him.

It was probably time I stopped making blanket statements about what I didn't do. I'd been proven wrong too often recently. But these people kept cropping up and surprising me, making me fall in love and want more. For myself, out of life, for the future. And they made it safe for me to reach out and grab it.

Clara and Jake were married at sunset, in a penthouse loft with views of the Rockies. Shira and I stood by Clara, and Jake had his brother Jeremy and Clara's brother Luca beside him.

Clara glowed, not in the cliché bridal way, but in a way that told everyone how ecstatic she was to be taking this step with Jake. And he looked at her—standing there in her long yellow sheath dress, her thick hair falling in waves around her face, the little bouquet clutched in her hands—like she was the sun itself. During the ceremony, she laughed easily, leaning into Jake, who kept pulling at his tie like he might undo it just to feel her skin on his.

After the kiss where Jake dipped Clara like they were in one of Tony's movies, Shira and I followed the newlyweds down the aisle. Roman was waiting for Sira, sweeping her off her feet the moment she was within reach. And to the side, slightly away from everyone else, I found my Sal.

My feet were on the ground, but it didn't quite feel like it as I made my way to him. Twinkle lights strung overhead glowed and cast soft halos over his dark hair. His eyes were on me, always on me, as warm as the golden sunset.

For one suspended second, he looked like a memory I hadn't lived yet. As I stepped toward him, the world narrowed. Through streaks of rose and gold and fading blue, it was only him. My Sal.

When I finally got to him, he slipped his hand around my waist, drawing me close.

"Did I do a good job?" I murmured, brushing my lips against his.

"I've been to very few weddings, but I've never seen a more beautiful bridesmaid."

I huffed a little laugh. "You're supposed to be looking at the bride."

"Clara's lovely. I like her yellow dress. But I couldn't take my eyes off you." He trailed a finger along my cheek. "You're stunning when you cry, but please try not to do it often. I don't like it."

"Those were happy tears, baby. I saw you watching me. I could tell you couldn't stand it."

From nowhere, Clara's daughter, Nellie, streaked by. Less than a second later, Ben followed, his arms snapping like an alligator. She giggled and squealed as he chased her around servers carrying trays of champagne and guests in their finest dresses and suits, threatening to chomp her to bits.

When Clara noticed, she laughed and shook her head. Jake scowled, but not for long. His bride captured his attention, and the imminent threat of broken glass was forgotten.

"We're going to an art gallery this week," Salvatore said.

I turned back to him. "You and Ben?"

He nodded. "Yes. He mentioned it the day we met. I assumed he was just making small talk, but today, he told me he was, and I quote, 'miffed' I hadn't gotten his number from you. So, he locked me into a plan."

My chest filled like a helium balloon, tight and airy at the same time.

"We both know how you feel about plans." I slid my hands up his arms. "Ben is a good guy. I love the idea of you two becoming friends."

It didn't need to be said, Ben would be a much better friend than Sam ever was. Ben Wells wouldn't try to change him or compete with him. He was the kind of guy who went with anyone's flow. I didn't know if they'd be best friends, but if that came to pass, it would be wonderful for them both.

Salvatore dropped his forehead to mine. "I don't think I would mind that."

After that, we were swept up in the spinning lights, bursts of laughter, champagne bubbles, and tiny sparks of joy during the reception. Clara and Jake did their bride and groom thing, drifting from table to table, hand in hand, greeting family and friends, never letting go of one another.

They were perfect.

Shira and Roman were too. Roman was more than a foot taller, but he curled himself around her as they danced. It was their first real night out since they'd had Jonah, and they looked like they were enjoying every second of it.

I ached watching my friends with their loves. My girls were taken care of. Adored the ways they deserved. Clara had her strong, steady Jake, who was the best girl dad any man had ever been. And Shira had her Roman, who worshipped the ground she walked on and worked hard to make her believe she was the most beautiful, kind, lovely woman on the planet. Because she was.

They were happy and cared for.

And so was I.

The music shifted from celebratory into something slower, and I leaned into Salvatore, slipping my arms around his middle. He splayed his warm hand on the center of my back, his thumb stroking over the bare skin between my shoulders.

"I can't promise I'll be any good at this."

"You admit there's something you might not be good at?" I teased.

"Bea—"

"Sal." Taking his hand, I led him to the edge of the dance floor, away from the twirling couples filling the middle. "All you have to do is hold me. We'll just sway."

He slid his arms around me, a little stiff at first, until I guided one of his hands to the small of my back and curled my fingers into the hair at his nape. His other hand held mine, warm and firm. He was sure about this. Salvatore knew exactly how to hold me.

I pushed up on my toes, my lips grazing his ear. "Now we move."

"Here we go," he mouthed.

He led me in slow circles, barely rocking. His chest rose and fell against mine, tension easing out of him with each rotation.

His forehead pressed to my temple. "This is nice."

I smiled. "You're good at this."

"I'm good at holding you."

"I'm easy when it comes to you. That's all I need."

We didn't speak after that. Didn't need to. We just moved together, locked in our own little orbit while the reception spun around us. I closed my eyes and tucked my face into the crook of his neck, breathing him in.

We swayed, holding each other close. Once again, the world narrowed until it was just us—our bodies pressed together, surrounded by the scent of flowers, champagne, and cake.

"You're smiling," I murmured.

"You can't even see me."

"I feel it. And I like it."

His smiles had been few and far between lately. He'd been buried under the rubble of his decimated friendship and all the work Sam's departure had left behind. Even still, he'd given those scant smiles and rare laughter to me and the kids.

And I was always greedy for more. More of Sal's laughter. More carefree moments. His dry humor...well, everything about him.

He angled his face close to mine. "I like when you're happy."

This man...he didn't get it. He couldn't possibly understand how much I loved him, how badly he wrecked me.

The lights flickered above us, like shooting stars in a man-made sky, and I melted into him completely. Tonight, there was no more stress. No more fires to put out. No more Sam or Nox. No more anything but us.

"I'm very happy," I finally replied.

"Good." He moved his hand up and down my back, matching the smoky rhythm of the song. "I'm finally seeing the light, Beatrice. We'll have more nights like this and fewer of you falling asleep while I work next to you."

"I'll be patient for as long as it takes."

"Because you love me."

"Yeah." I tipped my head back so he could see my smile. "And you love me. Like, a lot."

"More than a lot," he agreed.

"Say it."

He smiled. "I love you, beautiful blue."

Later, when the music came to a stop and our feet were all danced out, Salvatore and I returned to his car. We were driven through the city and down sleepy streets lined by houses with dark, yawning windows.

Salvatore frowned when he finally pulled his mouth from mine and glanced outside. "Igor's taken a wrong turn. We're nowhere near the hotel."

"No, this is right." I bit down on my lip, my pulse skipping a beat. "I canceled the hotel. We're staying in a house tonight."

A line carved between his brows. "A house?"

"Yep." I tugged on his crooked tie. "A house with lots and lots of places to hide."

It took him only a beat before he got it.

"Beatrice," he growled.

"Salvatore," I husked as the car pulled to a stop in front of an imposing house, a singular light illuminating the porch. I'd arranged for the door to be unlocked so there'd be nothing stopping us when we arrived.

I put my hand on the door, my heart thudding in my chest. "What do you think about playing a game with me?"

"Are you going to run?" The edge of danger in his voice sent a shiver down my spine.

"Yes." I pushed open the door and put one foot on the pavement.

"Are you going to hide?"

I swung the other foot out, poised like a spring. "I am."

His mouth ghosted over my ear. "Then, to the chase, Beatrice. To the chase."

I ran, and he followed—just like he always did.

EPILOGUE
Bea

One Year Later

Salvatore couldn't sit still. It wasn't often he got overly excited, but when he did, he turned into a big kid. He was restless and twitchy, practically bouncing in his seat.

I watched him, chin resting in my hand, biting back a smile as my heart did a merry dance. "Will you be pressing your face against the glass next?"

He didn't even blink. "I might," he said, completely serious, his eyes shining behind his glasses.

We were flying over the Southern Ocean, but Salvatore might as well have been in heaven. After a few days in Chile, we were headed to Australia for the second leg of our honeymoon. And while I didn't doubt this man was over the moon excited to be married to me, this flight was the thing he'd been looking forward to almost as much.

I loved being able to experience this with him. Salvatore Gallo had stacks of money, a beautiful family, a brain so big it would always amaze me, and a hugely successful business. Yet he was still capable of feeling awed over something like this. A flight few people ever took over a place so remote, it was practically untouched. We were the only souls for miles and miles and miles.

I turned to the window, trying to see it through his eyes. The sky outside was so dark, it didn't feel real—endless and velvet and quiet. Below us, only the ocean and clouds. And somewhere out there, far past the horizon, was Antarctica.

"It's the loneliest flight in the world," he added, a little breathless. "Did you know that?"

"You've mentioned it," I said, trying not to laugh. "Once or twice."

He grinned, and it lit me up from the inside out. There was a time when that smile had been rare. Now, it was mine, and he gave it to me freely, without restraint. When we woke up in the morning, when I was standing next to him, brushing my teeth, talking to the kids, dancing with Tony, walking around...he watched me, smiling as he did.

Three months after Clara and Jake's wedding, I'd moved across the street. Sal had been as patient as he was capable of being, only reminding me he wanted me officially living with him once a week. Though he hadn't pressed more than that, allowing me to make the decision.

In the end, it had been easy. One morning, I'd dreaded going back to my place to get dressed. And Benjamin had been pissed I was, yet again, dragging him away from his kids. So we'd stayed. Sal had hired movers that same day. By that night, all my clothes had been hanging in his closet, my makeup in his cabinets, and my shoes on the rack between Scar's and Tally's.

I'd kept my little black house, though. I loved it too much to let it go. It had become my catering office and test kitchen. And on the occasion we had visitors, it doubled as our guesthouse.

Scar was still my assistant, and the only teenager I'd ever met who could make onions cry when she chopped them. Now that she'd gotten comfortable in her role, she played moody playlists, rolled her eyes on schedule, and acted like she was doing me a favor by working with me. And...okay, she was, but I also really loved having one-on-one time with her.

I wasn't her mother. She'd had a beautiful, loving one, and I could never take her place. I didn't want to. But we were more than friends. This, I figured, was what family was supposed to be.

The Gallos had folded me in like I'd always been one of them. No one asked what I could do for them. They didn't expect me to prove my worth or earn my place. They just...loved me. Exactly as I was.

I loved them the same way. Lacey for her constant pep and creativity, Tally's endless curiosity, Tony's warmth and acceptance, Scar's artistic talent and sass, and Sal...my Sal. Just everything about him.

It was a few months after Sam left Nox that he'd turned to me with a frown.

"You don't call me Tore."

"I—" I opened my mouth to argue, but quickly shut it. He was right. "I don't think you're Tore—that's who he tried to make you. Does it bother you? I'll call you what you want to be called."

He cocked his head, contemplating. "No. I like you calling me Sal. That's what my family has always called me."

My heart flipped and flitted, preening with delight to be part of that category. "I'm glad you like it, baby. It feels right."

"I like when you call me baby too." He took my hand in his, dragging his finger along my knuckles. "There's something else you could call me."

"Yeah? What's that?"

His mouth trembled, and his ears glowed as he dragged his eyes up to meet mine. "How does husband sound?"

"It sounds good, if that's what you are going to be. My husband." I didn't torture or tease him. Not over this. "Are you asking me to marry you?"

"Yes." He pressed his thumb to my ring finger. "I have a ring tucked away for you, but the timing felt right now. Will you still agree to marry me, even if I'm doing it all wrong?"

"Yeah, Salvatore. I'd love to be your wife."

The ring, as it turned out, was a vintage emerald on a platinum band, and the most beautiful thing I'd ever seen. It hadn't made me want to marry him more than I already had, but it was another reminder of how deeply this man saw me. If I had an unlimited budget, I'd have picked the exact ring and worn it happily the rest of my life.

When I'd reached my quota of watching Salvatore—I only allowed myself ten minutes at a time to keep from becoming creepy—I pulled out my phone to check for messages and smiled.

Tally had texted new photos of Benjamin. His latest special interest was photography. After reading everything he could about it, he dove headfirst. Sal, as always, had gone all in with him, buying a camera and letting him learn by doing. Benjamin was his favorite subject, but we'd all modeled for him at this point.

I tapped a reply.

> **Me:** Gorgeous, Talon. I love the way you played with shadows in this one. Tell me about it, would you? By the way, Uncle Sally and I are currently over the Southern Ocean. Cool, huh?

I could almost see him gearing up his reply. It would be long and detailed. I looked forward to reading it. The way he thought and expressed himself was as unique and lovely as his uncle's. My husband.

Sighing, I opened my email and froze.

Right at the top was a new one from Maddie Kleinsmith. My little sister.

Holy shit.

A warm hand wrapped around mine, then Sal leaned into me, peering at my face. "You're tense."

Swallowing, I nodded. "Maddie emailed me."

He paused. "Your sister?"

"Yeah," I rasped, my eyes darting over the first words from my sister in more than a decade. "She just graduated, and she wondered if I ever—"

A sob lodged in my throat, too big to move past. Salvatore cupped my cheek, turning my face toward him. His thumb swept along my cheek before he dipped down to touch his lips to mine.

I offered him my phone, and his brow furrowed as he read the rest of the email. When he got to the bottom, he looked up, a spark of moonlight shining in the depths of his dark gaze.

"She wonders if you ever think about her, because she thinks about you often and hopes you're okay." He put my phone down and curled his fingers around the side of my neck. "She would like to see you, Beatrice."

I nodded, my nose twitching and eyes burning. "She's eighteen."

"She can make her own decisions now, and she sought you out." His eyes locked on mine for a long moment. "We'll go back. As soon as we land, I'll make arrangements so—"

"No, baby." I slid my nose along his, my eyes fluttering closed. "I love you so much for wanting to give that to me, but no. You are important to me, and I want this time with you. It's enough to know she wants to see me. When we get back—"

"It will happen." He kissed me again, so soft it took my breath away. "I love you too, and I would give you anything. Don't you know that?"

"I do." I almost laughed at the colossal understatement that was. Even when I hadn't been his, he had handed me the world.

Now that I belonged to him just as much as he belonged to me? Well, the world had only been his starting point. He'd given me the entire universe—a family, security, passion, *him*. I had never questioned his devotion to me, and I was certain I never would.

Curling into his side, I let the dark sky and quiet hum of the plane hold us. They called this the loneliest flight in the world, but I had never felt less alone.

I had Salvatore. I had the kids—*our* kids. I had my little black house, my crazy dog, and wonderful, beautiful friends.

And maybe, just maybe, I'd have my sister too.

This wasn't the life I'd planned. It wasn't what I'd thought I'd wanted.

But it was mine. I chose this.

I chose *them*.

My strange, unusual, *perfect* life.

AFTERWORD

My daughter is my favorite assistant to bring along to signings. Before I began writing this book, we went to Apollycon, which takes place just outside Washington DC. My booth faced a wall of windows, giving us a perfect view of planes taking off and landing at Reagan National Airport. My daughter was thrilled. She kept her flight radar app open on her phone so she could identify each plane we saw—and there were a lot.

I don't have a huge interest in planes myself, but I loved seeing how happy she was watching them. That weekend inspired me.

I already knew who Sal would be, but spending that time with her helped me build out part of his character—and Bea's. Sal loves planes, and he would have been just as mesmerized by that view as my daughter was. And Bea loves him enough to delight in his excitement, just like I delighted in hers.

In the end, isn't that what we all want? Someone who cares for us, sees who we really are, and cherishes our quirks and passions.

So, thank you, Maya, for being unabashedly you. I hope you never, ever change.

I must also thank my sensitivity reader, Hannah G, my editor, Monica, and my proofreader, Rose. I couldn't have released this book with you three!

I have to give a special shout out to Michelle Lancaster, the cover photographer. Not only did she take a gorgeous picture, but she added the glasses for me and they look amazing. You thought they were real, right? They're not! Can you believe it? Don't tell anyone. It's our little secret.

Thank you to my readers for loving this world. This is the last book in this series, but we're not leaving Denver yet. After all, there are still three more single Wells brothers, aren't there?

Stay tuned :)

About Julia

Julia Wolf is a bestselling contemporary romance author. She writes bad boys with big hearts and strong, independent heroines. Julia enjoys reading romance just as much as she loves writing it. Whether reading or writing, she likes the emotions to run high and the heat to be scorching.

Julia lives in Maryland with her three crazy, beautiful kids and her patient husband who she's slowly converting to a romance reader, one book at a time.

Visit my website:
juliawolfwrites.com